Boy

ALSO BY NICOLE GALLAND

Master of the Revels

On the Same Page

The Rise and Fall of D.O.D.O.
(with Neal Stephenson)

Stepdog

Godiva

I, Iago

Revenge of the Rose

The Fool's Tale

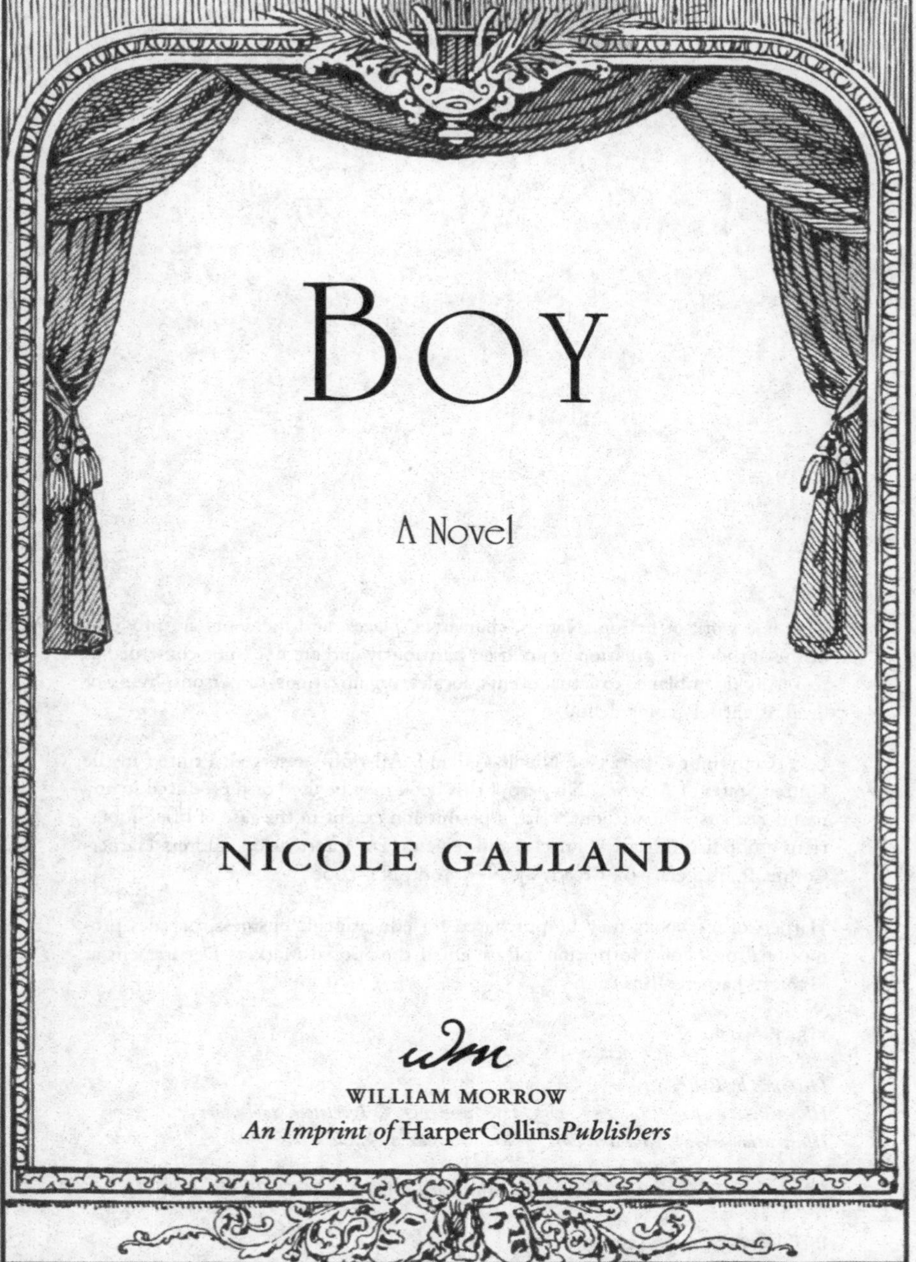

Boy

A Novel

NICOLE GALLAND

WILLIAM MORROW
An Imprint of HarperCollins*Publishers*

This is a work of fiction. Names, characters, places, and incidents are products of the author's imagination or are used fictitiously and are not to be construed as real. Any resemblance to actual events, locales, organizations, or persons, living or dead, is entirely coincidental.

HarperCollins books may be purchased for educational, business, or sales promotional use. For information, please email the Special Markets Department at SPsales@harpercollins.com.

FIRST EDITION

Designed by Emily Snyder
Illustration on pages 24, 157, 185, 198, and 215 © Igor/stock.adobe.com
Illustration on title page and part openers © lynea/stock.adobe.com

Library of Congress Cataloging-in-Publication Data has been applied for.

ISBN 978-0-06-334285-9

$PrintCode

To the memory of my oldest friend, Janice Haynes

Epigraph TK

—EPIGRAPH ATTRIBUTION TK

Boy

Act I

August 21

When the rest of the city had puddles, Southwark had bogs. Some said Southwark was itself a bog: the parish was the unwholesome hindquarters of London, south of the Thames and out of the city fathers' moral purview. Under the lenient eye of the bishop of Winchester, every manner of English low life, and high life, was at hand. Afternoons and evenings, visitors crowded the streets. Women of all social classes thronged with their men into the clutch of buildings called the Paris Gardens, to place bets on the survival of either tethered bears or the half-starved dogs attacking them. No matter if the dogs or the bear got the worst of it, everyone enjoyed the bloody mauling, and someone's wallet was always plumper for it. Bachelors, and those feigning to be bachelors, repaired to the seedy rooms above the bearbaiting, where women wearing practiced smiles and too much perfume efficiently satisfied all carnal cravings. Visitors less inclined toward violence or sex crowded the many stuffy, underlit taverns or alehouses, vying with each other at dice or cards. They stunk up the air smoking the New World weed, tobacco; everyone drank too much and sang songs they'd learned from ballad sheets glued to the tawny plaster walls: chanteys and work songs and drinking songs, sometimes accompanied by whatever lute or virginal was resident. Under cover of the boasting, brawling, and laughter, some fled to avoid their gambling debt or tavern bill, some puked or pissed into the dusky corners. Mostly men, but women too. Everyone was welcome to sin in this seamy underbelly of Her Majesty's great city.

On this side of the Thames, compared to such debauched diversions, theatre was the pinnacle of culture. Every afternoon but Sunday, the round open-air playhouses—the Rose and the larger, newer Globe—welcomed thousands eager to be transported to another time, another place, to put aside their own petty problems and marvel at the struggles of warriors, magicians, doomed lovers, runaways, tyrants, Jews, Moors, orphans, fairy queens, sprites. Playwrights' names were passing familiar to the masses: Kyd, Jonson, Shakespeare, Chapman, Babbage, Lyly, Marlowe (may he rest in peace). The performers were better known and loved. Two hundred thousand people could identify their favorite players sooner than they could the Lord Mayor of London, or their local constable, or even their own distant kin. Edward Alleyn, Will Kempe, Robert Armin, all were idolized. But at this moment, the most acclaimed players were to be found at the Globe Playhouse: Richard Burbage, playing all the heroes, and young Alexander Cooke, playing all the heroines.

This morning, they and all their cohort had endured a rainy rehearsal of a new Ben Jonson play. This was followed by a drizzly speed-through of Will Shakespeare's ever-popular *Midsummer Night's Dream*, which they would perform that afternoon. The clouds had thinned during the final scene. Now the air was steamy and smelled of horse manure.

And of course the ground was boggy, because this was Southwark.

The Globe Playhouse managers had laid down wide planks leading to the gates, that audiences might enter without wrecking their shoes and galoshes. Even so, playgoing was a sodden affair under the clearing skies. Those with the means to pay for a seat would be well enough off, but the thousand-odd groundlings in canvas and lockram who could afford only a penny-ticket would be standing soggy and unsheltered in the big round yard for the whole two hours.

Around the back of the Globe, where the players themselves entered, was an expanse of paving stones canted to drain well. Here Sander

Cooke sat perched on a stool. The other players were crammed into the backstage tiring-house, where it was humid and odorous; Sander always took the hit of being called soft for wanting to escape outside. The flowing green satin skirts of his queenly gown were gathered and piled onto his lap as he frowned at his lips in the little scratched glass. His face, plucked to keep wispy hairs at bay for this last precious season of his apprenticeship, was in shadow. He kept his back to the hazy sun so the white ceruse blanching his face wouldn't melt. Although small for the role, he was playing Titania, queen of the Fairies, not a mortal but a fantastical creature. Marjorie, the dresser, would be out soon to paint heathen decorations across his marvelous bone structure.

He knew he had marvelous bone structure. He had been told this so many times, the angles of his cheek and brow and chin had been so often commented upon, sketched, and serenaded, that his awareness of them was no more prideful than awareness that he had black hair or ice-blue eyes.

Pen, the messenger, a world-weary seven-year-old, came rushing around the curve of the Playhouse. Sander beckoned him with a tip of his head, not looking away from the glass. The boy, reaching him, held out a wooden chit, an inch around. Painted on it was a tiny triton: the sign of the Seafarer Tavern, an arrowshot east toward London Bridge. The Seafarer was in the most congested spot in Southwark, the first stop for southbound traffic off the bridge, the last before heading north back over to London.

"From Mistress Locke," Pen explained, naïve and somber. "The pretty one."

"I know which Mistress Locke," said Sander.

"She would walk with you after the show if you're at liberty." Pen said this with awed envy. Sander rarely met with her anymore. Emilia Locke had a marvelously agile tongue, but she was unkind to her servants.

In truth, his appreciation for her tongue often defeated his lofty intention to forswear her company.

Pen offered another chit, showing a lion painted in gilt: Baron Putney. He and his lady had obscene inclinations. "And this, from a proper lord with a proper lady, they said you'd know them by this. They said come for a late supper." That was code for "orgy."

"I would I were a Catholic," Sander muttered. "All those saints. Such lively curses."

"You don't mean that." Pen frowned.

Sander glanced at him and nodded. "You're right," he said. "I don't. In truth, I would I were a heathen. They have the better curses."

"Why do you want to curse? These are rich people who mean to feed you."

"Oh, lad," said Sander with a tired smile. "They mean to feast upon me." Body and soul, he added to himself. The body had no objections, but sometimes the soul . . . He chucked Pen's shoulder. "Aren't you our Indian prince today? You'd best get in costume."

"May I say yes to them?" Pen asked, shifting his weight. "I shan't get my ha'penny till I return with a reply."

Sander considered. *Midsummer Night's Dream* would be over by half-four, and he'd be out of his gown and face paint by five bells. Mistress Locke, at the Seafarer, would entertain him for at least an hour, maybe two; allowing time to get to Baron Putney's left no time to spend with Joan. Frequently she was here before the show, but today she was off on one of her philosophical pursuits.

HALF AN HOUR earlier, and a mile north under the same clearing skies, Joan Buckler—tresses braided, unremarkable face kept blank, brown work-apron neat—had climbed six steps from the puddled streets of Monkwell Square to a wooden door painted to resemble marble. The panels were ornamented with relief carvings of skulls, bone saws, razors, fleams, skeletons, vials, and at the top, painted in red and gold, the arms of the Worshipful Company of Barber-Surgeons. A gryphon above, chained lynxes in the middle, and at the bottom the motto *De Præscientia Deus*: through the foreknowledge of God. She supposed God had foreknowledge of her intentions, and hoped he would excuse her.

She ferreted herself into the slow current of men in black robes, then pressed leftward toward a pale-haired man. Staying just out of his peripheral vision, she leaned toward him to suggest casual intimacy should someone glance their way. This always worked. Presumed by the door-minder to be the helpmeet of whoever's elbow she was at, she would be waved inside. Once in the darkened anatomical theatre, she could find a corner and listen, rapt, as suturing was described, and gangrene, and amputation. Hugh Platt had lectured recently on using niter for embalming; a few years back, there had been a fresh human corpse—a young woman who'd died of ague—and she'd watched a surgeon dissect it. It was thrilling. Fascinating. The smell was awful but she'd thought to bring a large sprig of rosemary from the garden, and crushed it against her nostrils to keep the stench out. She was riveted: What was more elemental to existence than the workings of the human body? It confused her that none of her kith or kin took such an interest. The next day, arriving early to the playhouse—before the Globe was built, when the Chamberlain's Men were up in Shoreditch—she'd made Sander stand without his shirt on, and with a piece of charcoal she'd sketched all his viscera upon his torso. "Now when you soliloquize about your liver or your spleen, you'll know where they are," she'd said.

"In faith, I've no real need to know that." He'd laughed. "But keep drawing, it tickles."

It would be inconceivable to do such a thing now.

Anyhow today brought something different. The Barber-Surgeons were granted four cadavers a year by the Crown, for demonstrations, but today was a skeleton, the remains of somebody whose broken leg had been set wrong.

"Not you," said the door-minder as Joan neared the entrance.

She gestured in a submissive fashion to the pale-haired man, implying *I'm with him*. The minder shook his head and stepped in front of them both. "A moment, sir," he said politely to the man, who glanced around without marking her. "I remember you," the minder scolded Joan. "The past two lectures. Each time with a different master, but neither of them knowing you when I asked after. I won't have you trying to sell your wares in this establishment."

Joan stared at him. After a moment she repeated, "Wares."

He clicked his tongue. "You know what I speak of."

She didn't at first, then laughed. "You think I'm a bawdy woman," she said incredulously. "You think any bawd with wit would go to a lecture in the Barber-Surgeons Hall, in search of traffic?"

"Pardon, sir, do you know this girl?" the door-keep asked the man.

"This woman," corrected Joan, although that was arguable.

The black-robed man, keen-featured, glanced over his shoulder. His eye ran over her indifferently. "No," he said, sounding bored.

"We'll keep it that way, sir," said the officer, then turned back to Joan and pointed over the heads of the crowd, and down the puddly street. "There lies your way, girl. You're a discredit to your family and you're asking for a cuff on the head the next time."

"GOOD DAY TO you," said Joan.

Sander looked up, surprised. And pleased. "I was just this moment thinking of you. Assumed you were off eviscerating corpses."

She grimaced, squinting into the sun and tugging her long plait. "They wouldn't let me in. I want Marjorie to cut this off—"

"Stop," he said, sharp enough that she did stop. "To hell with the surgeons. You've plenty of others to learn from. Wouldn't you rather deliver babies than chop up corpses anyhow? The midwives don't mind that you're a girl."

"They don't chop them up," she said with tired impatience. "And babies are miracles who come out fine on their own most of the time. I'm interested in things that are not miracles."

"Well, I'm sorry for you but glad for myself," said Sander. "You can hold my glass steady." He nodded to where he had set it down on the extra stool.

"Please," said Pen, growing antsier. "What shall I tell them?"

Joan noticed the chits and pressed her lips together with a mocking hum. "Two in one evening?" she said. "Work or play?"

"It's not work, it's supper," Pen explained in a serious tone to Joan.

"Of course it is," she said, just as serious.

Sander looked at the little discs in his hand. "Give Mistress Locke my regrets," he said, pressing the mermaid back into Pen's grimy palm. "Tell the baron to expect me but that I won't stay late. And mind you clean your hands before you put your costume on, Pen, or you'll make more work for the laundress. If you want to be apprenticed, you must show everyone what?"

"That I'm considerate and responsible."

"Good man," said Sander. "Go about it, then."

Pen raced off the way he'd come.

Sander glanced back up at Joan. "I'm sorry you were barred. But also glad you're here so I may put my lips on right. Wait, though, let's move into the shadow."

"I like sitting in the sun well enough, now it's out," she said, taking the mirror and settling onto the extra stool.

"But the sun will brown your face."

". . . And?"

"And then nobody will fancy you."

"None are like to fancy me anyhow," Joan said breezily. She held up the glass for him.

He picked up the stick of vermillion. "You know we've reached that age. You must be thinking of who'll fancy you." He began to paint his lips again.

"I haven't your grace or beauty, Sander, only an eager mind, and no man fancies that. So it's no man for me, and I thank God for it. Every wife I know is bored and boring." She smacked his shoulder with her free hand, chuckling, and this jostled the mirror.

"Joan. Hold the glass steady or I'll toss you out on your arse and you'll have to admire me from a distance, as the masses do."

"Should I have been admiring you? I didn't know that bit. Here I go, then: ah, Sander, look at the lovely shape of your lips, there."

"I'm copying yours," he said. "Hold the glass up by your head, that I can see yours and mine together."

She did not raise the mirror. "Copying mine?"

"When I've the opportunity to copy from nature, I take it, and you've good lips. Raise the glass, please."

She laughed. "Oh, I doubt that."

"Joan," he said sharply, and looked at her the spooky way the cat did sometimes. "I know the shape of your lips well enough."

"I'm glad they're useful to someone, then," she said, and puckered them.

A pause. A grimace. "Raise the glass, please."

She did, shifting it so the sunlight bounced off the mirror into his eyes, making him wince. "Be careful or the sun will brown your face and then nobody will fancy you," she said.

He tossed down the vermillion and grabbed her wrist.

For as long as Joan could remember, his hand had been slighter than hers, but suddenly—very suddenly, only this moment—his was larger. Not large, but larger. She stared at his fingers, trying to remember when, over nineteen years of neighborly friendship starting in the crib, she'd last paid attention to the shape of his hands. She glanced at his face and saw that he, too, was staring at his grip on her. He ran his thumb across the inside of her wrist, and she felt a strange jolt beneath her skin. "Your bones are so delicate," he said quietly, as if surprised.

"Those are tendons," she said, steadying herself with lecturing. "Not bones."

He released her with a huff of annoyance. "Joan—"

"You're the reason I know that," she insisted. "I learned about tendons because of *you*, Sander. Remember? Portia? *The Merchant of Venice*? 'A pound of flesh, to be by him cut off nearest the merchant's heart.' You began my interest in the Barber-Surgeons."

Sander picked up the vermillion again and smirked. "That's not me, Joan, that's Master Shakespeare. Stop talking, I need to look at your lips."

"But didn't you want to know where there'd be a pound of flesh closest to the heart?"

"*Merchant of Venice* is not in truth a play about surgical procedures. It's about—"

"It's about the quality of mercy, I know, I know," said Joan. "But you truly weren't interested at all?"

"I find it to be more about comeuppance. Anyhow I was mostly interested in learning my lines, we did that one in such a rush. No more talking."

In silence, Sander glanced between Joan's lips and his own in the mirror. Joan had no concern for womanliness, nor was she delicate, but her lips were perfect. They had, from early years, fascinated him the way a portrait or a sculpture might. The lower lip full, narrowing toward the corners of her mouth; the arch of the upper lip sculptured like a recurve bow. Had they been lovers, if their mutual regard had evolved in that direction, he would want to stroke those lips all the time, waggle the tips of his fingers between them, as Mistress Locke and Lady Putney (and sometimes Baron Putney), and others, hoped he would to theirs. But he could not imagine Joan ever asking him to touch her face.

"Your lips are fine," said Joan impatiently, restless and distracted although she was not sure why.

He wanted to think about how delicate her wrist had felt, but that confused him because it made him want both to mention it and to avoid mention of it, to keep her near so he could look at her and to make her go away so he could think about looking at her, and anyhow he could not do any of that when he had to finish getting into costume. "Will you tell Marjorie I'm ready for her?" he said, making a curt gesture that meant it was time for Joan to stand up.

"Marjorie doesn't paint your face until after you've played Hippolyta in the opening scene," said Joan. She winked at him. "I pay attention, see?"

"Rick Robinson's Hippolyta today," he said. This irked him, but he preferred that to the agitation her presence was suddenly causing him. "Today I'm only Titania."

Her eyes widened and she drew in a breath. "Oh, Sander! They're training up your replacements!" A teasing grin, as if speaking to a toddler: "The end of your apprenticeship is finally in sight. Are you pleased?"

His face hardened. She sobered.

"You're not pleased."

"I cannot have this conversation now," he said.

"I'm sorry to have said it," she said. "I didn't . . . but, no, sorry, I cannot understand you. What apprentice doesn't want his freedom? To be a man and free to—"

"I *will not* have this conversation now. To hell with your lips." Again, he gestured her to stand.

"All right," she said in an appeasing tone, rising to her feet. "I'll go. I'll be watching with the groundlings. Try to be more interesting than the skeleton I thought I'd be ogling today."

"Farewell," said Sander.

"Enjoy supper with your handsome baron," she said in a knowing tone, and was gone.

Sander counted to three, then stood up from his stool, walked to the Globe Playhouse's outer wall, and kicked it once but furiously.

He wanted to punch it, but could not risk Titania having bloodied knuckles.

August 22

THE FOLLOWING AFTERNOON WAS WARM and wonderfully dry. The dryer the air, the less the stink and the less the smoke. And it was sunny, a good day for gardens. Joan had finished her share of the spinning and the shopping—a rope of onions, some lengths of sausage, Thames salmon straight from the fishwife's pannier—and her duties in her father's shop. She headed north toward her favorite garden plot in all of London.

Joan's father fashioned buckles and pins. This meant he was friendly with all the haberdashers and tailors of London. Since the time Joan could walk, she'd tagged along on his professional calls and had met, among others, one James Cole of Lime Street, a portly Flemish gentlemen of middle years.

In his ledgers Master Cole was a wealthy silk merchant, but in his soul he was a natural philosopher, collector of oddities, and above all, a botanist. As was his neighbor, the venerable and ancient Hugh Morgan, Her Majesty's chief apothecary. Cole and Morgan had been charmed by toddler-Joan's precocity, and had nicknamed her La Pucelle, the maiden, after Joan of Arc. So charmed, they had invited her to visit their adjacent gardens whenever she pleased. As soon as she was old enough to navigate the city on her own, she'd memorized the route from Southwark across London Bridge, weaving adeptly through the crowds of affluent shoppers seeking hats and perfumed gloves, the water bearers with their conical back-packs, cattle on their way to Smithfield, carts with vegetables or fabrics or tobacco, teeming shops and traitors' heads rotting on pikes, to return to the quiet gardens of Lime Street. Master Cole, from Antwerp, and Master Morgan (born in Wales), were amenable to any friend making their way in. Their gardens were her Eden. Master Cole's was a quarter acre of exotic imports and his own horticultural experiments; Master Morgan's was twice the size, similar in affect.

Before she was eight, Joan could identify every herb and flower in both gardens and list their uses, even exotic specimens like Peruvian nasturtiums and Chinese daylilies. By the time she was nine, she knew how to render leaves, stems, flowers, roots, buds, and berries into medicines or poultices. At ten, she was not only helping with the mechanics of grafting plants, she understood the premise well enough that Master Cole had charged her with determining the next grafting experiment for his small orchard outside the city. It was the only time she'd ever ridden in a carriage, and the memory still thrilled her: the jolting speed, the savory odor of the leather seats, the landscape rolling by so rapidly, and all of it so high off the ground. The estate was rolling fields and woods and livestock: sheep and goats and horses, and the cleanest, fattest hens she'd ever seen. The orchard alone was twice the size of his entire London property. Two holes were already dug and soaked, in anticipation of her experiment.

She had declared they should graft the root of a Reine Claude plum with the trunk of a Perdrigon plum, for the former could handle poor soil conditions and the latter yielded a sweeter fruit. Cole and Morgan applauded her; two specimens were grafted and planted; and five years later, a well-pleased Master Cole had presented Joan with the first ripe La Pucelle Plum. It was delicious. He repeated the graft, planting a quarter acre of his rural orchard with Les Pucelles; these had just begun to fruit this growing season. Over the years, Joan had helped graft other kinds of fruit trees, and had been Master Morgan's assistant developing cultivars of medicinal perennials. He was tall, and ancient, with brittle knees and hips; this gave Joan an excuse to get her hands in the soil.

Cole and Morgan knew Joan had an interest in surgery, but they considered this a distraction. It was clear to both she was a natural philosopher and, more specifically, an experimental botanist like themselves. To make sure she could continue her endeavors as an adult, both kept an eye out for some young bachelor-botanist she might marry, someone intelligent enough to deserve her, but not so wellborn to think she did not deserve him. They had mentioned this to her three years ago, when she was sixteen, and even though they'd assured her it was years away, she'd looked so mortified, they'd chuckled and promised to say nothing of it again.

But they continued to look. They knew her worth.

Both men's garden gates were bolted at night, but in daylight hours she had leave to walk in unannounced. Today, as she closed Master Cole's gate behind her, she saw from across the plot him and Master Morgan's silver-haired figure, in a doublet weighed down with decorative buttons. There was a third man she did not recognize. The stranger's dress was understated, dark blues with no points or decorations, as if he did not wish to draw attention to himself. He was handsome and dark-complexioned like Master Castellanos, the Greek who fashioned instruments for measuring the stars. Joan marveled that anyone in sooty London could earn a living doing anything dependent on the sight of stars.

The three men stood in the central patch of garden that received the most daylight. Here is where Master Cole had planted saffron crocuses, and also his newest import: thin-skinned "love apples" from the New World. They grew on fragile little shrubs, not so hardy as a rosebush.

"Ah yes, *tomatl*," the stranger was saying as she approached, with a casual gesture to the love apples. "Very ancient, long in use in the Americas. I believe Hugh Platt has some in his Martin's Lane gardens."

"And not poisonous?" queried Master Morgan.

"I assure you, no," said the stranger.

"Quite the opposite, I've heard," said Master Cole with a smirk, and raised his forearm with a clenched fist.

"Not as potent as the humble plum," said the stranger. His accent was lovely, Joan thought—a low, comfortable growl. He said something she could not make out except the phrase *La Pucelle plum*. Then she could hear the rest: "But I am curious about these saffron crocuses of yours. They can grow in this clime?"

All three stared toward the ground, and in their concentration they did not notice Joan, even once she was standing between Cole and Morgan.

"Those'll be blooming soon," she said of the autumn crocuses, and all three looked up, startled.

"Ah, La Pucelle!" said Master Morgan. He smiled, but the affectionate crinkles around his eyes and mouth looked strained. She wondered why.

"Master Morgan, Master Cole, God ye good day." She curtseyed, and smiled at the stranger. He had beautiful dark eyes that stayed on her as he bowed. "Forgive my intrusion."

"This is Joan," said Master Morgan, in his contralto lilt. "She is a student of natural philosophy and botany, and we have the fortune of being her mentors. Joan, this is Cristóforos Pantazis. He has journeyed from Greece, along the Mediterranean coast and up through Spain and France, with different seeds and roots to share with us."

"It is my pleasure, young lady," said Pantazis. "We were just discussing La Pucelle Plum, and I understand you are La Pucelle."

She had just been wondering about Things Greek, and here was a native she could speak with. "I'm so glad I am here to meet you, sir," said Joan, dipping into an informal curtsey, "and so honored to join this conversation."

The men exchanged glances. Master Morgan flushed an obvious pink and studied the crocuses again. Master Morgan—with whom she discussed medicines that cleansed the bowels, that caused puking, that eased the passing of gas—that same Master Morgan now looked like a Puritan who'd been caught flirting with his sister. Odd.

"We are," said Master Cole slowly, his English honed with the precision of a Flemish childhood, "having a business discussion. It is not the best day for our usual conversations."

"Of course," said Joan, hiding her disappointment. The stranger had such a nice face, she wanted an excuse to keep looking at him, especially since he would be able to answer her question about Greece, but never mind. "Since I've come all this way, and it's such a good day for the garden, shall I weed the potato bed? I imagine we should harvest the new cultivar soon."

The three men exchanged glances. "We must examine the potato bed," said Master Morgan, almost apologetically.

"We might take the conversation inside," Pantazis suggested. "That is more discreet anyhow."

"Good," said Master Cole quietly, "if we discuss approaching Essex on this matter."

"I was thinking Hugh Platt—" began Pantazis, but was interrupted:

"The Earl of Essex?" Master Morgan said, startled. "Goodness, James, this hardly seems his sort of enterprise. He is not known for playing the long game."

"He's about to lose the monopoly on malmsey tariffs," said Master Cole. "He might become interested in other enterprises"—he tipped his head toward Joan and whispered—"that are not for all ears."

"Don't worry, I won't eavesdrop," said Joan. "I'm not interested in business, and I've nobody to sell your secrets to. It's a beautiful day out, you get some fresh air while you can, it's rarely this nice in London."

"Joan," said Master Cole. She could almost feel his mind scrambling to find words, to tell her . . . what?

Saffron crocuses. Love apples. Potatoes. Plums.

All amatory.

Aha.

Love apples and potatoes were new and exotic, but even Joan knew from street gossip that dried plums in syrup were offered by the bowlful in brothels. The understated Master Cole, when not dazzling the neighborhood with his range of interests, collections, and wisdom, was also a shrewd businessman. Suddenly the plum-tree orchard took on a tawdry mercantile hue. But the men could not discuss that in front of her. Heaven forfend. The Barber-Surgeons excluded her because they thought she was a whore; her friends were excluding her because they knew she wasn't one.

She gave them a knowing smirk. "Be aware, sirs. I know what you speak of," she said slowly and clearly. "You are doing a terrible job of hiding from me the nature of your business conversation. I commend you for your attempted discretion, but I confess disappointment that you see me as a female first and a fellow naturalist second."

"Joan," said Master Cole again, in a placating voice. Morgan looked as if he were mentally composing a more articulate apology, but not having completed it, he said nothing.

"I'll let myself out," she said, and gave them the sunniest smile she could force onto her lips.

Not one of them said a word or raised a hand to stop her. The silent eleven strides back to the gate was the longest walk she had ever taken.

SHE REACHED THE Globe just after *As You Like It* finished. From the lane, she could see some of the audience heading for John Heminges's alehouse, the Happy Sow, a stone's throw from the Playhouse on the same marshy plot of ground. One of her sources of income, when she wasn't in her parents' shop or with Dorothy the midwife on Morgan's Lane, was helping at the Sow. It was always open just before and just after a performance, and she tended to be around then anyhow, for her daily hello to Sander. Heminges was a shareholder in the Chamberlain's Men, and he had hired a young couple, Hal and Molly, to run the alehouse, with their lodgings above it. Molly was with child and nearing her time.

Heminges was the shareholder to whom Sander was apprenticed, which meant Sander was expected to assist at the alehouse too. He'd deftly evaded such ordinary obligations by offering to train the younger apprentices in singing and dancing. This saved the company money while endearing him to all the younger boys. Sander could endear himself to anyone.

The crowd mustering at the alehouse door was bigger than the alehouse itself, and everyone was chattering at a pitch suggesting gossip. This meant one of two things: the baby had come, or Sander Cooke was gracing the masses with a post-performance entertainment.

She changed course toward the Sow. It was a plain, solid little building, half-timbered, the wattle and daub painted pale blue. The young boy-player, Kit, at fifteen already burlier than Sander ever would be, was standing in the doorway and letting only certain people enter, relishing his power to decide who was worthy.

She was seasoned at angling her way through a crowd, and had barely slowed her pace to reach the door. Kit recognized her and gestured her in while continuing to shake his head at nearly everyone else. Inside, in the funk of pipe smoke and the haze of lantern light, a few dozen strangers from the audience were standing or seated, some with cups or bowls or tankards, others still empty-handed. As always, the mix of classes meant an omnium-gatherum of accents, attitudes, ruffs and collars, scents and smells. Civet and iris blended with horse sweat and lanolin. Modest farthingales brushed against fustian breeches. Wadmol sleeves bumped silk ones without insult. Molly and Hal were absent. John Heminges, rumpled and fatherly, wearing his own linen shirt and doublet but still in his garish costume breeches, was feverishly filling cups for waiting patrons.

Meanwhile Sander, willowy and graceful, was standing on a knee-height table built for just this purpose: he was singing. The top of his head nearly brushed the low ceiling. He was in his own street clothes—blue doublet, breeches, hose—and had removed his Rosalind wig. But his face was still painted, white skin, red lips, blue veins, dark pink cheeks, brilliant eyes outlined in black. As Joan entered, he was drawing out the final, filthy line of "Watkin's Ale" and then switched to "It Was a Lover and His Lass," cuing the delighted audience to join him in the chorus:

When birds do sing,
Hey ding a ding a ding,
Hey ding a ding a ding,
Sweet lovers love the spring.

She watched him, her irritation from the Lime Street awkwardness fading. He was magnetic, and all eyes were staring at his beaming face. They were carousing with Alexander Cooke! This was a moment they would boast of to their neighbors.

Joan angled her way through to the counter. "Here to help," she offered Heminges, who gave her a grateful look. She pulled a wooden tray out from between two kegs and began to load it with cups of ale. "Who's paid?" she asked, shouting into his ear over the ding-a-ding-a-dinging.

"Sander's admirer bought a round for the house," Heminges shouted back into her ear, his thick whiskers tickling her cheek. He gestured to a corner. She looked.

There sat a gentleman of middle age, with a neat beard and broad forehead. He sported a sizable ruff over his clothes of ermine-trimmed black velvet, a fringed velvet cloak, and a tall rimmed black hat. The man's expression was a blend of pleasure and appraisal: it mattered to him that all of these people were enjoying his generosity. She recognized him although she could not place his name. A few years earlier, when Sander was all-boy, still far from man, this same gentleman had been so enthralled with his ethereal beauty that Heminges had to take him aside to explain that the apprentice boys were not "available." Sander, amused, had described all this to Joan. The gentleman had protested with tremendous indignation that his regard was platonic. But he'd remained an admirer: whenever he came to the Globe, it was when Sander had a leading role, and afterward he tended to do something extravagant—buy drinks for the company, toss flowers at the stage from the lords' box, any kind of public declaration that he was Sander's greatest adorer, no expenses spared.

"Must be nice to be wealthy," she said as the applause grew louder; Sander segued into a different song that was both slower and more suggestive; a Dowland piece, Joan thought.

"Francis Bacon is not wealthy," said Heminges with a rough laugh, handing her two more cups. "It's mad of him to spend money like this, especially when the money's borrowed."

Joan nodded, recognizing both name and reputation. "Fascination can be a corruptive force," she said, glancing up at Sander. He had added steps to his performance, a pavane embellished with waggling hips and buttocks. She couldn't see his face from here, but judging by the timbre of his voice, he was grinning manically. Everyone looking up at him appeared lovestruck.

"*To see*," Sander sang, seducing the crowd. "*To hear, to touch, to kiss, to die with thee again, in sweetest sympathy*—"

"Die in my arms! Mine!" shouted half a dozen thrilled female voices. Joan saw him gesturing toward someone, and wondered if he'd just arranged a tryst with a wink. The young woman he'd been reaching toward clearly seemed to think so. Joan wondered, briefly, what it must feel like to exchange such looks with Sander. The thought made her feel peculiar and she shrugged it off, focusing on finding patrons still awaiting cups.

When everyone had a drink in hand, Sander bowed, then curtsied, then bowed, then curtsied, then turned the bow-and-curtsey into its own choreography, which he repeated until it got applause, and then slid off the table as the alehouse cheered.

As if he had not just been the center of attention, he presented himself to Heminges. "How may I help?" he asked, slightly breathless. "Hello, Joan," he said as an afterthought, patting her cap.

"Master Bacon," said Heminges. "He looks as if he'd like a word with you."

Sander glanced over his shoulder. Francis Bacon was sitting up a little straighter, eyebrows pitched, staring meaningfully at him. "I believe," said Sander, "I'm about to be invited to supper."

"Sander," said Joan, grabbing his arm. "I've a question for him."

He put a quick, shushing finger to her lips. "Not here. But if he's taking me to supper, then there will be plenty of learned men to ask. I'll return straight." He hailed Bacon and began to walk toward him, the crowd parting reverently. Two young women, bareheaded, pink-cheeked, in matching yellow silk, were daring each other to touch his shoulder, but they were too overcome with giggles to reach out in time. Joan scouted the room for unattended cups and bowls and took the tray around to collect them.

When she returned, the tray stacked, Sander was behind the bar again. He nudged her with his elbow. "I'm to join Master Bacon at Lord Sheldon's. What's your question? I'll supply you an answer by tomorrow."

Heminges gestured them to shift so he could exit from behind the bar. They settled in the nearest corner. Some eyes were still on Sander, but most drinkers began to take more of an interest in their ale and exchanging gossip: the ambassador from Barbary had been seen flirting with one of Her Majesty's attendants; John Dowland's new book of songs was either far inferior or far superior to his last one; the cook at Essex House quit after the earl hurled a roast goose across the dining table.

"What's the question?" Sander repeated.

"Did humans ever climb Mount Olympus? And if they did, what did they find there, and if they didn't find the Greek gods living there, why did they keep believing the gods lived there?"

Sander's gaze grew vague; he cocked his finger, and Joan repeated the question. He gestured again. She said it again.

"Did humans ever climb Olympus?" Sander echoed carefully. "And if so, what did they find there, and if they didn't find Greek gods living there, why did they keep believing the gods lived there?" He glanced at her. "That right?"

"Perfect," she said. "Thank you. I met an actual Greek today and thought I'd get to ask him, but I lost the chance." She considered telling him about her embarrassed botanists and their sex-foods. Even a few weeks ago, that would have led to the two of them falling against each other in hilarity. But the way he'd grabbed her wrist the day before, somehow it now felt awkward to mention, even playfully.

Heminges approached, holding out two pewter cups. "There you be," he said. "Thanks for the help, Joan. We'd not have survived the crush without it." He offered Sander an indulgent smile. "And you, my lucky apprentice," he said, handing him a filled cup, "you have tomorrow entirely off."

Sander was surprised. "Do I? We've a show I'm not in?"

"Oh, we're doing *Midsummer's*," said Heminges, "but Kit will cover for you. He was fine as Hippolyta, time to see if he can do both Hippolyta and Titania. So you've a free day. In truth we need an errand run up at the Revels Office, but I won't task you with it, since we both know you'd weasel out of it anyhow." Sander's smile had slid off his face so fast Joan expected it to make a crashing sound on the floor. Heminges did not notice; he patted Sander's shoulder in a *no-need-to-thank-me* way and headed back to the bar.

"Hey," she said, nudging Sander's boot with her own. "It's for Kit's training. It's not a reflection on your worth. Obviously," she added, gesturing to the crowd.

"They're replacing me," he said, his voice hollow.

"Of course they're replacing you," said Joan. "That's how it works. They still need boy-players and you're no longer a boy."

"But . . . they're *replacing* me," he said, sounding almost nauseated. "They're replacing *me*."

"Just as you replaced Nick Tooley, or Bobby Gough," she said. "Nick's still around. This is not death. It is a far more pleasing transition, and you've known it was coming from the day you arrived. I remember years at a time when you were thrilled that your apprenticeship started earlier than most so it would end earlier than most, because you couldn't *wait* to be finished—"

"Joan," he said, so soft she almost couldn't hear him. "What'll I do? This is all I have. It's all I know. I don't know how to be a man."

Joan raised her hand in a soft fist and began to uncurl her fingers, then paused. Their childhood sign language, used in public when they needed privacy, had just two gestures: a hand with fingers either furling, or unfurling. The meanings were contextual, intuitive. The closing hand meant every variation of "me, not you": *I'll handle this* or *you do nothing* or *stop it* or *don't*; the opening hand was just the opposite: *your turn*, or *you decide* or—as now—*I know you can do this*. But she realized this moment required more than just a gesture. "What's the difference between a man and what you are?" She smeared the face paint off his temple with her thumb. "Besides the decoration, I mean."

Sander's expression had bled into a thousand-mile stare. "I've no idea," he whispered. "And truth, for you alone: that makes my stomach churn. I know I must aspire to it, but it's as if aspiring to be a stranger."

She could think of nothing useful to reply with. So she opted for distraction, and cuffed his shoulder, winking at him. "I'll dock my hair," she said, "Then I'll show you how it's done."

THE GENTLEMEN DINING at Lord Sheldon's table wore jewel-toned velvets over silk sleeves attached with gold points. Sander knew them all by sight and reputation, but none to speak with, except for Master Bacon to his immediate right, dressed in ebony and silver. Sir Edmund Brooke, the new Master of Markenfield, made eyes at Sander from the moment they were introduced, and did not stop. He was lean and handsome, with a dry, sardonic wit; eventually Sander acknowledged the interest with a quick, encouraging smile. John Heminges no longer expected him home much before dawn, on nights like these.

The conversation, over oysters, had left him cold. He had no feeling for cosmology or mathematics, and yet every man at table expected him to have a studied opinion on such matters, for all of them were vying to impress, specifically, Sander Cooke. Sander was used to such attention; it was regular enough that he noticed the absence of it more than its presence, and graciousness was easy when he understood the conversation.

But pretending to know geometry was tiresome. The most engaging aspect of the evening (besides exchanging the odd flirtatious look with Sir Edmund) was watching Francis Bacon. His searching hazel eyes and quick gestures showed an unrelenting vigor, as if every exchange of ideas left him unsatisfied and wanting more debate.

Sander was relieved when, over the boiled beef, talk turned to political gossip. That was useful for learning who was in or out of favor; he could pass that intelligence along to Heminges, who would use it to plan their tours. For all his shirking of mundane apprentice tasks, Sander knew the company's survival strategies. They could not, for instance, accept a request to perform at Essex House, because the earl was under house arrest for bursting into Her Majesty's bedroom while Her Majesty was undressed.

After Walter Raleigh had been disparaged and Hugh Platt chortled at for his preoccupation with feeding the poor, discussion shifted to East India. Then to trade routes. Then to ancient history. Finally, he had an opportunity for the sole thing he cared about tonight.

"Ancient history contains a puzzle I sometimes muse upon," he said.

Eyes turned to him. He received the stares with an ingrained casual grace, head raised, shoulders relaxed, voice resonant.

"We are all-ears," said Sir Edmund from across the table. The other guests assented, exchanging gracious looks. Sander already knew that each man wished to be the first to respond to whatever he was about to say.

"Did the ancient Greeks ever climb Mount Olympus?" he asked the table. "If so, what did they find there? And once they found no gods living there, why did they continue to believe that gods lived there?"

Jaws all around the table had twitched to open, but Francis Bacon spoke first. "A fascinating subject, Sander," he said and glanced at the company, his eyes commanding them to stand down. "At some point, certainly, men began to climb—we know this because there was an altar to Zeus on the summit," he went on, leaning his spare frame forward. "There are even descriptions in classical texts commenting on how thin the air was, requiring those who ascended to carry sponges moistened with vinegar to breathe through. Which of course must make us wonder: How did they determine that vinegar was the correct solution for this task?"

Sander felt disappointed that it was such a simple answer. He'd wanted something anecdotal to deliver to Joan. The servers cleared the beef dishes and a moment later brought roasted venison from the carver's table. The scent of oranges and almonds wafted with it.

"May I rephrase my query, sir?" He waited, bright eyes attentive, for the approving gesture from Bacon.

Bacon smiled. "I cannot imagine ever refusing a request from Sander Cooke." He turned his head to the side, as if to put his ear closer to Sander's voice, and raised his eyes toward the ceiling while listening.

"Prior to the building of that altar, how likely is it that men would have climbed the mountain, let us say, casually? And then, the rest of my question remains: once they were up there and saw that it was an inhospitable cold place with thin air, why did they continue to believe it was the home of the gods?"

Bacon had been nodding throughout his rephrasing. "I have thoughts on this," he said.

"I would hear them, sir."

"First, throughout most of antiquity, most men would not have climbed Olympus, because they believed it would be *hýbris* to do so."

"*Hýbris*," said Sander, as if savoring the word. "*Hýbris*."

"Yes." Returning his eyes to the table at large, Bacon said, "I presume we all know the word means 'presumption,' or 'arrogance,' or 'vanity.'" To Sander: "In Greek mythology, the gods punished Bellerophon for his *hýbris* when he attempted to fly his winged horse, Pegasus, to the top of Mount Olympus."

"Bellerophon," said Sander, nodding. "Pegasus, the winged horse. Interesting."

"Believing this myth, most Greeks would not have presumed to climb," Bacon continued. "That is to say—and this is the heart of the matter—their behavior was determined by beliefs they had been raised to unthinkingly accept."

"Their behavior was determined by beliefs?" echoed Sander, as if this was the most riveting information he had ever heard.

"Well, yes," said Bacon, his weight shifting, almost as if he were a young boy transported with excitement by his own thoughts. "Although if we are honest, we all do the same. Which is regrettable. However, there is also another answer, which is the beginning of a more interesting conversation. At some point, some intrepid souls *did* climb Olympus. They did, in fact, reach the highest peak, which we know because they built an altar there. Even though they plainly saw that no gods dwelled there."

"Yes, yes, let's speak of that," said Sander. "For my chief question is: Why would they keep calling Olympus the home of the gods, after they saw with their own eyes that they were mistaken?"

"Yes, the answer is especially instructive, my friend," Bacon said, the darting eyes settling on Sander. "The beliefs they had been taught caused them to invent an explanation that supported those beliefs."

"An explanation that supported those beliefs," said Sander. "But what explanation would be supportive of those beliefs? Do you think?"

A few of the diners began to open their mouths again, but Bacon shot them a look, and they relented. Servers cleared the venison, and the yeoman of the cellar brought fresh silver cups of French wine, before clearing the ones already there to a copper tub under the cupboard.

Bacon's eyes uplifted again. "Perhaps they told themselves that the gods simply could not be seen by mortals. Or that Zeus threw a deceptive veil over everything."

"Interesting," said Sander. "Gods could not be seen by mortals, or Zeus was throwing a deceptive veil over everything. Tell me more." By now he saw men exchanging bemused glances and hoped nobody would question his verbatim repetitions.

"Whatever it was," Bacon continued, "they never said, as they ought to have said, *Here is new knowledge that contradicts what we already believe, so let's reconsider our previous beliefs*. Instead, they said, *We already know what is true, so let us interpret what we see now in accordance with that which we already know is true.*"

"In accordance with that which we already know is true," said Sander in a thoughtful voice.

"But that is faulty thinking, Sander," said Bacon, leaning forward again, as if to trap Sander's gaze in his own. "Interpreting new information according to prejudicial thinking is no way to learn, but 'tis how most of human history has stumbled along for centuries. That is why I would teach a new approach to research and interpretation, and am devoted to the mission of educating men about it. I am advocating a method I call inductive logic. It is a way to look at new knowledge without the bias of old beliefs."

Of the eight other men at the table, five found some quiet way to express impatience to each other. This included handsome Sir Edmund, who shot Sander a rueful grin. Bacon ignored them all and bent his attention confidingly toward Sander.

"As a talented and well-read man of drama, you will sure appreciate that in the golden age of the Greeks, Euripides addressed this very issue in his play about Bellerophon."

"Ah, Euripides's play about Bellerophon," said Sander, who had never heard of Euripides. "Of course, but pray remind of me of the passage."

"One character says to another, 'I believe there are no gods, but never fashion an opinion based on my beliefs—think for yourself.'"

"I would like to play that role," said Sander. Affecting a heightened stance and voice, he declaimed, "Never fashion an opinion based on *my* beliefs." He glanced around the table, and wagged his finger at several of the men. "Think. For. Your. Self."

There was a spatter of applause. Each of the men he'd singled out smiled. Sir Edmund's smile was so attractively intimate that Sander casually decided he'd go home with him if asked. Then he returned his attention to what really mattered:

"In sum, then," said Bacon rapidly, patting Sander's hand, "howsoever the Greeks treated Mount Olympus, they were never thinking for themselves, but only taking as a given the beliefs they had been told to have. This is a failing that we, in this modern day, are also guilty of, and we must overcome it through the felicitous discipline of inductive logic."

"That sounds like a fascinating and important aim," said Sander, patting Bacon's hand in turn. "I assume you are writing essays on the matter."

Bacon tipped his head. "I am putting notes together. But essays only reach those with the money to buy them and the leisure to read them. All of society must shrug off outdated thinking—the uneducated masses more than anyone. I would there were a way to instruct the common man on this."

Sander took his hand and held it. "Sir," he said, "I heartily echo your desire." He signaled for another cup of wine.

August 24

Never fashion an opinion based on *my* beliefs—think for *yourself*," concluded Sander.

It was two days later. The haze of coal smoke hung leaden and heavy; neither of them cast a shadow on the flagstones as they sat head-to-head on the low wooden stools.

Joan had been staring at the ground, listening as he'd recited Bacon's answer. "I want to learn more about his inductive logic," she said now. "I'm the common man he should be reaching."

"I agree. But there are so many barriers, especially—"

"Especially my sex," said Joan. "Girlhood is a nuisance."

"Oh, I disagree," said Sander in a sweet falsetto, with an exaggerated simper as he smoothed his Rosalind skirts across his lap. "I would stay a girl forever and ever and *ever*. Although"—his lowered his voice—"I met a handsome knight at supper who *rather* liked me as a boy."

"Well, you are the fairest girl I know." She laughed into his shoulder. "And the fairest boy." She grabbed him in a huge hug, ducking her head to avoid his painted face.

Sander wrapped his arms around her and squeezed. He noticed, again, how he was somehow suddenly larger than her, at least in parts.

Their limbs were equally slender, but his feet were now too large to fit her boots, as they once had.

"Remember when you could wear my galoshes," Joan said.

"You witch, I just had that thought."

"I wager those would still fit me," she said into his shoulder. "But not the doublet. Remember the doublet, from my cousin? The yellow velvet with the matching feathered hat all covered in buttons, that we took turns lacing each other into and pretending to be pirates." She laughed. "You might still look lovely but it would never fit me aright, now I have these mammaries."

Sander released his grip and stared down at her. "These what?"

With a pert expression she gestured to her chest. "Awkward protuberances found in those who reproduce viviparously."

She was pointing and so he looked. Either a heartbeat or an hour later, she snapped her fingers right at his nose and he looked up sharply.

"You and your big . . . words," said Sander, not intending the hesitation to be comical, but Joan laughed. The laugh sounded a little strained.

"They're just bodies, Sander." Her dismissiveness had an odd edge to it. "Mere lumps of flesh that our souls walk around in."

"That our souls *live* in," he corrected. "And so the quality of those lumps determines the quality of our entire lives."

"That's nothing you need to worry about," said Joan. "My lumps of flesh impede all my ambitions, but your lump will always serve you well—"

"Stop that, now you're doing it on purpose," said Sander. Joan seemed confused—then, wide-eyed, she flushed so red he realized he was mistaken. There were only two of them and yet they seemed to be having three different conversations at once. He shoved the mirror at her and she took it on reflex.

"Hold this up, that I may copy your mouth."

She held up the mirror. He felt relief at the excuse for silence as he dabbed the vermillion onto his lips.

When he'd finished, he set the little brush on the ground beside him, and held out his hand for the glass. She dropped it onto his palm.

He kept his hand there, staring at it, wanting her to determine what happened next.

"Well," she said. "Father needs me at the shop. If you've any assignations tonight, I hope they enjoy your protuberance." She stood up and gave him a chaste kiss on the top of his head. Before he could think of a retort, she had disappeared around the curve of the Globe.

Sander set down the mirror, then gathered his skirts as he stood up. He walked to the wall of the Playhouse and kicked it, once, ferociously.

"You've done that before," said a familiar voice. He spun round to see William Shakespeare giving him a knowing look.

PLAYING ROSALIND WAS a joy. Always. She was the largest female role ever penned for the English stage, and Shakespeare had written her specifically to show off the bedazzling, unnerving charms of Alexander Cooke. First disguising herself as a boy, that boy—like Sander—pretended to be a girl, and even without wigs or skirts enthralled everyone she-he-she met. After Joan first saw *As You Like It*, she'd told him, "If ever your head were going to grow too big, this role would cause it. But you seem to have retained your humility," and he had responded, "Just toward you." Only Richard Burbage and Robert Armin—the company's leading man and comic wit—were likewise offered custom-written roles.

The applause was always thunderous, thousands of hands and thousands of stomping feet, voices—often wafting the stink of beer and garlic at them—*huzzahing* themselves hoarse. The company accepted the adoration graciously and then retreated to the fetid tiring house to change. All four boys performed in *As You Like It*, and it took them longer than the men to return to their normal appearance, because of painted faces, bodices, and the most complicated of the wigs. Sander took the longest because he helped the others with their costumes before attending to his own.

When he stepped out into the cool late-afternoon haze, onto the paving stones behind the Playhouse, the crowds were gone, but Heminges was waiting for him. He put a finger to his lips, a gesture Sander mirrored with a questioning look. Heminges pointed off to one side and Sander followed with his eyes.

Thirty paces away on the muddy lane stood two figures who did not belong on a muddy lane. One was Francis Bacon, in his excellent silks and velvets. The other was a woman in even more extravagant dress. Her gown was a pale orange, almost white, stretched over a broad farthingale and covered in onyx buttons, which also graced the edges of her cloak. The raised hood of the cloak kept her face in deliberate shadow, but passersby—there was always some score of audience who drifted back here hoping to see the players in real life—gawked at her anyhow. Liveried servants in red and yellow with chevroned badges stood at a distance pretending not to listen to the conversation. A breeze, too feeble to clear the skies, was yet enough to muffle any voices. Then Bacon raised his, and Sander heard this much:

"My most esteemed lady, again, I swear I have done all that may be done. You know me, so I beg you, judge me by efforts, not their outcome. I cannot sway Her Majesty's mind toward your brother. Your ladyship has greater sway over Her Majesty than I do."

Her words could not be heard but the tone carried: the lady disagreed.

"I am flattered that you credit me with such influence but I assure you, I am unworthy of that credit," said Bacon. "Do you not think I'd have prevented his lordship's confinement to begin with? He made me what I am, my lady, I would do anything in my power for him, but that power is limited."

Sander's mouth gathered itself into a surprised O. He understood enough to put the pieces together: "he" was the unruly, wildly popular Robert Devereux, Earl of Essex, longtime patron of performers, poets, and Francis Bacon. "Essex's sister?" he whispered.

"Penelope Rich, yes."

"But she never comes here. She always sees our shows at court."

"If I had to hazard a guess, I'd say she wanted to confront him away from prying eyes," said Heminges. "She sat in the lords' box, veiled, and he was in the upper gallery. One of the lads taking money at the gate says after the crowd disbursed, she followed him back here. I saw her approach him and truly he seemed unprepared. I warrant he was tarrying to speak with you, not her."

Sander tried not to stare, but Lady Penelope Rich, née Devereux, was more exotic to him than a live unicorn would have been. "I have never seen her cross before," he marveled.

"You've only ever seen her at court. She's desperate on her brother's behalf. The royal court is gruesome, lad. Keep out of it."

The cloaked figure signaled to her entourage and strode out of sight around the curve of the Globe.

"Look away," said Heminges, and they both pivoted. "And now we chat until he approaches and we pretend we never saw that."

"Saw what?" said Sander. Heminges nodded his approval.

When Bacon approached, they appeared believably surprised.

As usual, Bacon's light, quick voice gushed with praise; as usual, Sander responded graciously, bowing, then playfully curtseying, then bowing again; as usual, Heminges stood close to Bacon to remind Bacon not to stand too close to Sander.

"My dear young friend," said Bacon, clasping and unclasping his hands without seeming aware of it, "I confess I've come for more purpose than to praise your skill as a comedian. I was so struck yestereve by the originality of your question about Mount Olympus, that I have come in person to commend you for it—"

"—I am honored, sir—"

"—and to make an offer," Bacon pressed on, shoulders raised with friendly urgency. "I was just thinking that if you've the appetite for more such conversations, especially regarding the development of my inductive logic, there are many opportunities in my circle of acquaintances. I can't promise how felicitous any such opportunity would prove to be, but I would be honored for you to be my guest at any suppers I am summoned to."

"Oh," said Sander, surprised. He glanced at Heminges for guidance.

John Heminges knew it was Joan with the appetite for such discussions. "I'll let you respond out of my hearing, lad," he said, then lowering his voice: "But I'd counsel you, tell the gentleman." He touched the rim of his hat and headed toward the Happy Sow.

"Tell me what?" Bacon asked.

Not once in all his years of apprenticeship had Heminges steered him wrong. Sander would chance it. "My closest friend from childhood has the mind of a philosopher, but no access to much learning," he said. "Throughout our youth, I have made myself an agent of this friend. That is to say, I ask learned men questions that are not my own, and memorize the answers, and deliver them to my friend. I have in years past even asked such questions of you."

Understanding dawned on Bacon's face. "The repetition. To memorize the phrases."

"Yes, sir. I don't always understand the words, but I'm a lightning-quick study, that's all."

"How intriguing," said Bacon, his eyes rising heavenward as he considered this. He looked a shade disappointed that Sander Cooke was not his would-be acolyte.

Sander sucked the inside of his cheek a moment and nearly fidgeted. Strange how this moment made him more nervous than any entrance he could remember onto the Playhouse stage. "I think Master Heminges encouraged me to tell you this in order to follow it with a request."

"I am listening."

Why was it so difficult to make eye contact? It would be rude to speak to Francis Bacon without looking at him, even if the great man himself spent half the time talking to the ceiling. He steeled himself and forced his gaze to settle upon the gentleman's left eyebrow. "Is it possible that I might attend these gatherings you speak of, in the company of my friend?"

Bacon looked enthusiastic, hands fidgeting, but then frowned. "I dine with officers and statesmen, or Her Majesty's appointees, or extremely wealthy merchants. Ordinary citizens do not belong at such tables, I fear, as much as I would like to educate them."

"I'm an ordinary citizen and you welcome me."

Bacon gave him an appraising smile. "You are Alexander Cooke, the most adored young man in London. Your friend has not your reputation. I'm sorry to give you such an answer, but we will do no favors to anyone, subjecting either side to company so alien to them."

Sander had expected this, and had a response: "Then might my friend attend me as a servant? Simply stand in attendance on the conversation without participating in it?"

Bacon blinked. Frowned. The hazel eyes studied him. "Would he be willing to debase himself so?"

Sander barely repressed a nervous laugh. "I believe it, sir, yes."

"You find the prospect amusing?"

"I believe *he* will find it amusing." One pronoun, and now he was deceiving the great Francis Bacon. For Joan's sake. Which made him more eager to accomplish this.

Bacon mulled it over. "So the proposition, as I understand it," he said, eyes drifting upward again, "is that you will do me the honor of accompanying me at such gatherings, and I will ensure that your friend may attend, as your boy."

"That does seem to be the proposition," said Sander, in a tone much smoother than his thoughts. "Does it please you?"

Bacon tipped his head, his face softening. "I would be eager to enlighten an unschooled pupil's mind. Those without formal training in how to think are often the ones whose minds soonest grasp news ways of thinking. Such knowledge, distributed among all levels of society, will improve society. So I find the proposition agreeable." He smiled at Sander. "In some ways, even more agreeable than if you were the would-be philosopher. A true innocent, being shown the light—there is something satisfying to it. I'll send a message tomorrow to confirm. Shall my boy find you here?"

"Indeed, or anyhow with Master Heminges's people," said Sander, trying to maintain his offhanded mien. "As it suits you." With a winning wink, "As you like it, so to speak."

"Indeed. And again, a wonderful performance today," said Bacon. "Shakespeare has been fortunate beyond all reason that you have been an apprentice in the Chamberlain's Men during these productive years of his. I cannot conceive how they will ever replace you."

Sander glued the offhanded expression to his face. "I thank you, but I'm sure there are boys enough in London."

"There is only one Sander Cooke," said Bacon, in a wistful tone.

"As there is only one Francis Bacon," said Sander smoothly. "And as there is only one Jack Buckler."

There was, in fact, no Jack Buckler. Yet.

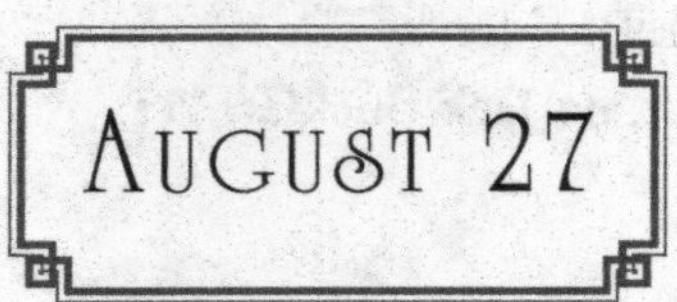

August 27

Joan knew a wig-broker on Silver Street, but Sander insisted they go to Gresham's Royal Exchange instead: the merchants and artisans of London's sprawling emporium were known for their discretion. It was a massive place, an entire city block with dozens of ground-floor stalls and shops opening onto a huge and busy courtyard. Two wigmakers sold their goods here, each busy enough not to remember a young couple with a peculiar request. Such was Sander's reasoning.

"Provided we pay them," said Joan as they walked squinting into the afternoon light, elbow to elbow through the loose crowd of shoppers and merchants. "But I've no money spare, and you've nothing save your fame."

"You'd be surprised what my fame can purchase," he said, nudging her as they moved through the bustle.

"I wouldn't be surprised at all," Joan retorted. "But 'tisn't your fame that purchases a thing. Your fame merely makes the rest of you a desirable commodity."

"I think you're saying I whore myself," said Sander, drily amused. He raised the corner of his blue apprentice cloak to his chin and batted his lashes at her.

"Can men whore themselves?"

"I've no idea, so I'd best make the most of whoring while I'm still not one," lisped Sander in a singsong tone.

"Hey! Rosalind! *Love is merely a madness*!" It was a young man's voice, amused but admiring; Sander put the right sort of smile on his face to acknowledge the attention.

He turned his head away, so that he had further to turn his gaze, which gave the gesture a coy coquettishness. "*Sell while you can*," he quoted back. "*You are not for all markets*." As the youth and his friends laughed at having scored such a real-life interaction, Sander leaned in and whispered to Joan, "To your left, there's the one we want, where that fop has just exited."

They entered through the open door of a shop, some ten feet wide, and the echoing murmurs of the huge brick courtyard dropped away. Their shadows preceded them onto the broad floorboards. A counter ran the width of the room, delineating the area to await a shave or a wig-fitting, but the shop was empty of customers now. A well-dressed older man, middling height and not unhandsome, sporting an elegant periwig, stood behind the counter. On the shelves of the back wall, high up out of reach and dimly seen in the lamplight, were a dozen wigs on wooden bulbs: long, short, curled, white, black, ginger. Mostly ginger. Red hair had been craved by every sycophantic courtier in London since Elizabeth took the throne more than forty years ago.

I'll handle this, Sander signed to Joan, closing his hand into a loose fist. "Good day to you," he chirped, and removed his felt hat by the rim. The man nodded without interest toward their silhouetted forms. Sander tapped Joan's shoulder to nudge her farther inside, out of the sun and toward the lamplight.

The moment they were no longer backlit, the wigmaker's expression changed. Either he recognized the boy-player, or simply found him beautiful.

Sander tugged at Joan's linen cap. She batted his hand away while reaching for the brim, and as she pulled it off, her thick plait tumbled down her back, falling past her waist, sleek and pale. Sander scooped his arm around the braid, and presented the length of it. "We've some hairs to sell you," he announced.

The man's eyes widened, perhaps at the thickness of it. "There are hair-brokers a-plenty," he said tentatively, as if he had chanced upon a marvelous bird and didn't want to startle it to flight.

"And then there is *you*," said Sander, in an approving tone.

The man considered him for a long moment. Sander beamed back.

"This is irregular," the wigmaker finally said.

"Excellent, for so are we. Shear it right off," said Sander, and made a slicing motion at Joan's shoulder. She smiled nervously. "It will take any kind of dye well, being practically colorless itself."

The man shrugged. "Hugh Platt's new dyes will work on any hue. What matters is the health of the hairs."

"Shall I unbind it, sir?" Joan asked, taking the braid out of Sander's hands and fidgeting with the end of it, like a painter testing a new brush.

"No need," said the wigmaker. "Let me see it."

Sander nudged her shoulder with his own again, and she stepped up to the counter, offering the wigmaker the plait. He held it so close to the lamp she was afraid he might singe it as he trotted seasoned fingers over the strands. "'Tis healthy enough," he said in a neutral tone.

"I have my mother to thank for that," she said. "But I will take credit for keeping it clean."

He held it up, followed the sweep of it to the nape of her neck, considering the length. "What do you imagine is the worth of it?"

Sander cleared his throat. "In truth, we wish to sell you the plait only to buy some of it back again. That should influence the fee it brings."

The man frowned at him.

"We require a thing made of this very hair," said Sander. "Merely some of it as a braid to fasten under a cap, so that none will know it's been cut."

The wigmaker frowned more deeply. "This is an unusual request," he said.

"Indeed, 'tis an unusual situation," said Sander. He had such an earnest innocence to his tone that Joan steeled her expression against whatever falsehood he was about to utter. "I am an apprentice with the Chamberlain's Men, that used to perform in Shoreditch but now are resident at the Globe in Southwark—"

"I thought you looked familiar," said the man. "I believe you've worn some wigs I've made, that came to you secondhand."

"Indeed, that's why we've chosen you now," said Sander. "Of all the wigs I have donned over the years, the ones with your mark are always the best made, and the most comfortable. I am always grateful when our donors have the good sense to have been your customers."

The man smiled, pleased to accept the flattery.

"Tragically," Sander continued, "there was a mishap in the tiring house yestereve, and my Rosalind wig was ruined."

"I see."

"I know not how familiar you are with *As You Like It*, but Rosalind first appears in the Duke's court and then flees to the forest disguised as a young man. In the court, she wears a simple plait to signify that she is the unloved niece. I wear it only for a few scenes. But 'tis important to have the right wig, so Joan here has offered to provide me with an emergency replacement."

Joan pursed her lips to keep from cackling. The wigmaker was incredulous. "You're giving up your plait so the lad may wear it for one act?" he asked her.

"I'll return it her, of course," said Sander. "And then she can do whatever she likes with it. But meanwhile, just as Rosalind must counterfeit to have cut off her hair, Joan must counterfeit to have *not* cut off her hair, so we need a plait that I may use on the stage and she may use at home."

Joan could barely prevent herself from gawking at him. If the same absurdity were coming from her mouth, the wigmaker would already have shooed her from the shop for a liar. There was a glamour around Sander, as potent as a witch's spell. For years now she had watched this glamour grow, brighten, expand; other than the Chamberlain's Men, she was the only one who saw right through it.

The man was studying Joan, not Sander. He cocked a finger at her, and they leaned toward each other over the counter. "Lass," he said, "do you understand the sacrifice you're making, just to help the lad out?" She nodded. "And you're willing?" She nodded again. "Not to be needling in where I haven't been invited, but is it possible you're besotted and not thinking straight?"

"Besotted?" Sander interrupted, sounding insulted. "Sir, this is my *sister*."

The man took a step back and held up his hands in an appeal. "No impudence intended." He glanced between them. "Now of course I see the family resemblance, how foolish of me not to have noticed at once." This was a lie, of course: Joan was hazel-eyed, with a soft face, almost a walking embodiment of bland; Sander's hair was black and his eyes crystalline blue; his chiseled cheekbones paralleled his jawline. They could have been different species. "I meant no offense," the wigmaker repeated.

"None taken," said Sander. "It must have been the sunlight blinding you." Joan, not trusting herself to speak, nodded and made a vague gesture to imply agreement.

The wigmaker glanced at Sander with more interest now. Sander flashed him a pleased and knowing smile. It reminded Joan of her father's face once he was confident that he would land a fish he'd hooked.

"I apologize for presuming the young woman was your sweetheart," said the wigmaker.

"It's a common mistake," said Sander. "And often serves my purpose, to let people believe I am spoken for."

That smile, thought Joan. She knew how this would go now.

The wigmaker, having taken a moment to lock eyes with Sander, turned now to Joan,, as if indulging her. "How is it, to have such a famed brother?" he asked.

"Oh," said Joan, sounding intrigued, "is Sander famous? I wasn't aware."

The wigmaker laughed; Sander threw his arms around her and clenched her hard. "That's why you're my favorite sister," he said, chucking her on the shoulder as he released her. "You keep me humble."

"I doubt that's possible, beloved brother," said Joan. And then, making use of the only political gossip she was familiar with: "You might as well say Lady Rich keeps her brother Essex well-behaved." The wigmaker laughed again.

Then there was a brief moment of perfect silence among the three of them.

"Step outside for a moment, sister mine," said Sander. "I'll discuss payment, you needn't concern yourself with that."

"Should he not cut my plait off first?" she asked. It was a stalling tactic. She felt strange about leaving but told herself there was no reason for it. The wigmaker had a pleasant-enough manner, and Sander would not be doing this if he did not want to. Sander never did anything he did not want to.

"First we'll discuss the terms, then we'll cut the tresses," said Sander. He took her by the shoulders, turned her around, and walked her toward the buzz of voices and movement outside the door. He repeated the subtle gesture of closing his hand: *I know what I'm doing here.* "Buy some bread for supper," he said, nudging her toward the hazy glare.

"I've no money," she objected, turning back to him.

"Here, then," he said with a long-suffering-older-brother sigh. From the purse on his belt, he fished out a few cents. She held her hand out flat and he slapped the pennies onto her palm. "White bread if possible. With butter."

"This isn't enough for a white loaf."

"Smile at the baker and it might be."

She rolled her eyes. "God's wounds, Sander, you've no notion what it is to not be Sander Cooke."

He pinched her cheek. "Come back soon," he said, and pivoted her back toward the door. "But not too soon."

"Ha," she said, not laughing, and left.

Sander closed the door and remained with his back to the wigmaker, for just the right length of a pause. Then he pivoted, slowly, with a certain smile on his face. He returned to the counter and gazed at the older man.

The wigmaker shook his head, looking regretful. "Ah, lad, John Heminges is a friend of mine, and I know better than to touch his apprentice. I saw what he did to that furrier back when—"

"Back when I was twelve," said Sander. "I'm still his apprentice but I've reached my majority and he's long since given up guarding my orifices."

The wigmaker snorted with surprise, pinking a little. They regarded each other for a moment.

"She's not your sister."

"As good as."

"Too plain to be your sister." It was a statement, not a question, and Sander felt his jaw twitch.

"Too lacking in vanity, you mean," he corrected, his voice tight.

The wigmaker nodded, more to himself than to Sander. "Here's a proposal," he said. "I'll take her plait and then return half to you in a simple braid fastened to the underside of a cap. I can do that right quick, it's simple. I'll keep the rest for my own stock, and we'll call it an even exchange. You owe me nothing."

Sander blinked in surprise. "Truly?" he asked, incredulous.

"You're not used to that, are you?" the man said. "Having your favor declined?"

"Oh, is that it?" Sander retorted, archly. "Bragging rights? You wish to be the one to say, *Sander Cooke offered himself to me, but I couldn't be bothered*. That's more original than *I had Sander Cooke*, I suppose. I respect that."

The man shook his head, giving him a knowing look. "That's not it, lad."

"What, then?" Sander said impatiently.

"I'm the one to say: Sander Cooke should save himself for the one he loves."

Sander stared at him, expecting to blush but feeling himself instead grow pale. Suddenly he had a headache.

August 28

Sander pinched a servant's costume from the Playhouse stash the day after their visit to the wigmaker. He handed the bundle of moth-eaten canvas and frieze in a drawstring bag to Joan, who hid it under her mother's cloak on a peg. That evening, she borrowed four yards of linen bandage from Dorothy the midwife and added them to the bag. For four interminable days, she went about her ordinary life without ever glancing toward the cloak. She spent her hours tidying the shop and itemizing decorative trims, collecting monies due from customers, spinning, cleaning the chicken coop, cooking pottage, checking her mother's questionable bookkeeping, forming loaves of cheat bread and bringing them to the French baker on the corner, with the double-*B* Buckler mark on it.

Then one foggy morning, as she shoved open the shop doors, a torn strip of parchment fluttered to the mossy ground from where it had been wedged between boards. On it were sketched a pair of five-pointed stars in black, with a smudged square of red below them. A rough sketch of the Bacon coat of arms. Joan grinned so broadly she felt the tendons in her neck jut out.

She went at once back upstairs for the bandages; went out to the privy; removed her bodice and shift. She began to wrap the linen tight around her chest, flattening her breasts. The binding was no worse than lacing her bodice—more comfortable in fact, with no boning down her front. But once she had put her clothes back on, she was disoriented by the pressure being in all the wrong places. She'd thought it would remind her of years past when she and Sander stole her cousin Andrew's doublet and she'd stormed around the block, snickering like a pirate, and giddy with freedom. Now she felt wedged into someone else's body. Somebody more centered but less mobile. She liked the sensation, but it felt naughty to admit it.

Her parents were absentminded in general, and most especially toward her. They failed to notice her flattened front all day as she performed her back-of-shop chores and spinning and mending, often crossing paths with them. In the late afternoon, when the air had warmed and the sky had cleared, she slipped upstairs to collect the drawstring bag, and went back out to the privy to put on her disguise.

It took longer than she had anticipated. Nothing was alien—she'd seen every article of her father's wardrobe in the laundry—but to don it without guidance was a clumsy matter. The first thing off was her cap with its attached braid, which she had worn awake and asleep since the moment she'd received it.

Transformation achieved, she shoved her own clothes into the drawstring bag and stepped out of the privy. She waddled awkwardly toward the kitchen, then changed tack, circling the garden plot a few times to adjust to her new stride. She was not sure how wide apart her feet should track, to accommodate the oddness of breeches fabric brushing against itself between her thighs. She lacked Sander's grace, and now more than ever.

When she stopped feeling ridiculous, she walked inside, through the kitchen and the shop's storeroom, through the shop in full view of her father, and out the front door, calling to him as if it were an ordinary afternoon. He never looked up. She had anticipated that.

But when she greeted Sander in the slanting amber light outside the Hawthorn Tavern, he gave her a look worthy of her efforts.

"Good lord," he said softly. "Your height's the only thing familiar."

"The redistribution of weight and mass," she said, glancing down at her body. "Very disorienting. I tell my own limbs what to do, and then seem to be watching somebody else's limbs attempting it. I'm not sure if I'm even blinking as I normally would."

He stepped back to appraise her, and the sweep of his gaze paused at her chest. She felt her shoulders hunch protectively, on reflex. To cover the awkward moment, she wanted to make a jibe about missing protuberances, but nothing came to mind.

"So I'm believable?" she asked instead.

Instead of answering, Sander said in a distracted voice, "I never noticed what a slender neck you have."

"Is that good? Bad?" She fidgeted with her collar, clapped a protective hand over the nape, suddenly chilled. "Should I have a wider ruff?"

"Your neck is unremarkable," he said, "except to me in this moment, but I'll recover."

"That's good. Don't miss your supper on account of swooning over my neck."

"It's nothing to fret about, I meant." He shifted his weight, and she noticed he was holding a wooden flask. "I like the shorter hair around your face, your eyes seem larger for it. And"—here he pushed his voice down below his natural speaking range, so that he was growling more than talking—"being known for elegant girlish calves myself, may I say: nice turn of the ankle, Buckler." He chucked her on the shoulder.

And he ogled her flattened chest again but tried to hide it.

She should have insisted they meet an hour earlier, to get used to all this before having to counterfeit in front of other people.

"Watch yourself, sirrah, I'll damage anyone who says I'm girlish," she grunted, holding up her fists and jutting out her lower lip.

He laughed, the carefree cackling from their childhood, a sound she had not heard in months. If nothing else went well tonight, the moment made all the effort worthwhile. As the laughter naturally faded, lamplight licked his right cheekbone, making him look sculptured and gaunt. "Is my servant Jack ready?"

"You must give me a moment to prepare. Counterfeiting is as natural as breathing for you, you're been trained to it. Your livelihood depends on how well you personate the other sex."

"Thank the gods your livelihood does not."

She tensed. "Am I not a passable boy?"

He brought his lips to her ear. "Not enough protuberance," he whispered.

"Oh, shut your mouth." She made a brief grunting sound, choking down nervous laughter.

"You'll be fine." He stayed close, speaking softly. "Now to the rules. Don't gawk. Avoid eye contact. Call me master and beg my pardon if you require my attention, but make no conversation with me. Or anyone. Your precociousness will not be tolerated here as you are used to. Bacon has agreed you may be in the room—"

"That's wonderful."

"Sh, listen." He closed one hand around her elbow and tugged. The proximity calmed her, never mind that a moment earlier his staring at her chest had done the opposite. "You are only allowed to remain on the pretext that I require a special brew prescribed by the apothecary, in lieu of ordinary wine. You're to hold the bottle and keep my cup filled." He handed her the wooden flask. "Just ale, in truth, but seasoned with rosemary so it smells medicinal."

"Clever."

"Master Bacon's scheme."

"Shall I anticipate refilling it, or wait for you to signal me?"

"Anticipate. As if we had a seasoned master-servant relationship."

"And otherwise I stay mute and listen."

He nodded.

"If for some reason I must need speak privately with you—"

"Do not need that, Joan."

"My name is Jack. What if it's urgent?"

"If you truly must, then approach and whisper at my ear, as we're doing now, and we'll pretend it's to do with the drink. We'll say . . . it encourages cold, damp humors, to slow my masculine evolution."

"Wonderful how you're never possessed by that fear," she said, too gently to be a tease.

"Have you a better conceit?" he demanded.

"No, master, pardon." She buried her face against his sleeve and made a squeaking sound, bouncing on the balls of her feet.

"*Joan*." He pulled away.

She released him, took a slow breath, demonstrating calm. "Pardon, master. I have now purged myself of excess excitability. I shall be quiet for the rest of the night."

"Women who claim a single squeal means they'll be quiet for the rest of—"

"No need to finish that statement," Joan said crisply.

THE HAWTHORN TAVERN pretended toward the rustical. It was lit by large horn-lanterns and whatever light the hearth threw. A resident lute in one corner could be played by any customer who had the skill, but out of tradition, they would be shouted down if the songs weren't to do with country life. Joan had been here as a child, and remembered to look for the row of stags' heads mounted high along one wall and baskets full of stale lavender in every corner. The support beams were rough-hewn, the walls painted with images of partridge hunts.

Bacon had hired a private room upstairs to host a supper that he almost certainly could not afford. The man was so chronically in debt, there were tavern songs about him. Joan knew one. Not from Sander, but from her father, who'd used it to illustrate the difference between being in debt and being poor. Francis Bacon's empty purse was self-imposed. His longtime patron, the Earl of Essex, gifted him secondhand velvets and silks, and yet still Bacon carried the largest haberdashery debt in all the Inns of Court.

As they headed for the stairwell, she recited to herself the list of men Sander had told her to expect. The one familiar name was Thomas Babbage, a jack-of-all-trades cherished by both the Revels Office and all the playing companies for his knack rigging theatrical effects. He bore the reputation of an inventive problem-solver, speaking rarely but always to the purpose.

The other guests were merely names to her: Richard Carew and George Gavell. All Sander had told her was that they were both "rigorous, original thinkers."

"So you don't know what they do," she'd said.

"I wasn't listening," he'd replied breezily. "They're for your benefit, not mine."

This had silenced her, the sharp awareness of how much was being done for her. Sander Cooke was used to such favors. Joan Buckler was not.

They went up the narrow wooden steps, nearly steep as a ladder, lit by a single sputtering lantern at the top. After ascending through a dense strip of tobacco funk, suddenly upstairs the air was cleaner. The landing at the top faced two open doorways. Lamplight and men's voices spilled out of the nearer one. Sander glanced a final time over his shoulder and grinned at Joan. He raised a closed hand and unfurled his fingers: *You can do this*.

They stepped into the room, which was bright for having but one small window. The walls were whitewashed plaster, and the furniture all a pale timber. Sycamore or ash, Joan guessed. A motley collection of candles and wall lamps made it cheery.

There were four men seated already, at a table set for five. At the head was Francis Bacon. His clothing was elegant, all black velvet and silver trim; his expression was both savvy and aggrieved, as if he were in mid-argument with one of the other diners.

The man to Bacon's left wore a colorful brocaded doublet bedecked with glass buttons; this was, she guessed, Babbage of the theatrical tricks. The two on the other side, sharing a long bench, were in muted black; probably not Puritans, but educated gentility who had more important things to mind than their wardrobes. Unlike Bacon, none of them exuded an air of argument.

As Sander entered, all of them stood, and Bacon came around the table to greet him, his demeanor softening. "God save you, sir," said Sander. The two mirrored each other as if beginning a dance: a doffing of caps, bending of knees, bowing of heads. Joan studied the great man as they did this: he was slight of build but otherwise looked like any gentleman she'd seen, except that over his aristocratic paleness he was ruddy-cheeked. She liked this in him; it made him less a statue than the others, and more human.

Sander acknowledged the greetings of the other diners, and graciously accepted their praise for his Adriana in *Comedy of Errors*. Francis Bacon approached Joan. For the first time, she was Jack being looked at by a stranger. She felt herself blush and was riveted by the cold fierceness of his eyes. The expression was so witheringly shrewd she was certain at once that he'd already seen through her disguise.

But the calculating gaze stayed focused on her face, without straying to the rest of her. She thought she saw a flash of disappointment that Sander's friend was not so beautiful as Sander. Finally, he offered her a private smile that felt both challenging and conspiring.

"So you," he said, soft and quick, "are Jack."

She passed! Jack officially existed. The muscles in her cheeks tightened as she suppressed a grin.

"Indeed, sir," she murmured, in the deepest voice she could.

"I like your mind, Jack, the little I've glimpsed of it." It was a whisper, delivered with brisk, unadorned frankness.

"I am in awe of yours, sir," she replied, and looked down to keep herself from blushing.

"I've chosen you, accept that without niceties. And these other men will add to your store of knowledge without even knowing." He turned farther into the room and continued in a normal speaking voice. "Keep yourself by the door, boy. Your master will sit there." He gestured to the foot of the table as he returned to his own place at the head of it.

Sander and the other diners had exchanged courtesies already; now Sander sank gracefully onto the cushioned stool. A small man with a badge of Bacon's crest brought around a ewer and pitcher for everyone to wash their hands.

"Wine?" asked Babbage, offering.

"Thank you, no," said Sander. "I've brought my own physic for tonight. Jack, lad, fill my cup." He held it up without a glance at Joan. She was about to walk in front of a room of men who thought her one of them.

From door to table was just two steps. Joan felt Bacon's eyes on her but the others found a servant beneath notice. She was both relieved and irritated by this. She poured, and the scent of rosemary tinged the air.

Sander drank a mouthful, made a face. "Tasty, but astringent," he announced, since they were watching him. Nobody asked him what condition it was for, but Joan felt their curiosity and wondered if rosemary-infused ale would now seep into supper parties across Cheapside. She stepped back to the doorway, flask in hand, eyes averted. And she waited.

SHE WAITED A long time. An hour at least. After grace came pottage, bread, then roasted conger eel, paraded past her in succession by the cook's boy. She stood unmoving, feet planted farther apart than felt natural to her, occasionally bending one knee or the other against fatigue. Sander, strangely, seemed to have forgotten his prepared lines, and conversation fell to the other guests; Joan found them dull. Her enthralled vigilance waned and she turned her ear to the sounds below, but with the door closed she could make out no conversation from downstairs.

Babbage expressed regret that Hugh Platt was not here, Platt's *Jewel House* being full of interesting examples of experiments and science that would make him welcome at the table; Bacon sniffed that "the brewer's son" (Platt) was in mourning for his father, who had left him more money than a commoner would ever make good use of.

George Gavell, who was revealed to be a surgeon turned rector, abruptly changed the subject, positing the immoral implications of acting training for boys. Bacon objected, shifting on his cushion, pointing out that Sander Cooke had turned out well; Sander rebuffed Gavell in greater detail, citing the skills and social qualities that apprentice players were exposed to: the importance of obedience, discipline, and diligence; the ability to read, to speak well, to move with decorum; familiarity with social etiquette.

"You've lost the argument, George," Bacon said. "Anyhow, we have more urgent matters to discuss." This was aimed at Sander, but before he could speak, Babbage asked everyone's opinion of Ben Jonson's latest masque, and at that point Joan began to think about her upcoming week. She would have free time enough to go to Dorothy the midwife on Morgan's Lane, and also Master Castellanos, the astronomical-instrument maker, whose shop was on the Strand . . . and perhaps even Master Cole and Master Morgan, whom she had not visited since the beautiful Greek man had come about the plum trees. She had never gone so long a stretch without stopping by their gardens, even in winter. They might still feel awkward, and so it would be up to her to somehow make things comfortable among them all. How best to do that? Show up with a question. Ask them to teach her something. Something other than how to make bawdy money from a little girl's botanical experiments . . .

The cook's boy entered again to add roast pigeon to the table, and Joan was startled back to attention at a fortunate moment. "I am interested in hearing more about this inductive logic you mentioned when you and I dined last, Master Bacon," Sander was finally saying.

"And here we go," muttered Gavell with long-suffering amusement.

"I would ensure I understand the fundamental premise," continued Sander. "Is it correct one must begin the study of one's subject with no assumptions or beliefs about it whatsoever?"

Bacon shoulders rose and fell with his breath. "That is a simplistic description," he replied, "and there is more to it that might make for interesting conversation another time. But in essence, yes." Joan kept her eyes lowered but could feel his attention brush over her. "We must always observe things without bias or pre-existing beliefs to understand them. And further, we must experiment with the aim of discovering what we don't yet know, rather than seeking to validate what we think we already know. In fact, one specific element that defines inductive logic is that we must plan and carry out an experiment"—and here she heard him poke the table fiercely for several words, as his chair creaked—"with the aim of *disproving* what we believe we know. And then only if we *cannot* disprove it, may we continue to hold our old beliefs about it, or embrace new ones we've just tested. This requires casting off old superstitions, and assumptions, and theologies—"

"Not all theologies, of course," said the rector. Joan raised her eyes enough to watch the conversation. Bacon had a fire-flickering energy compared to the stolidness of the other men.

"Absolutely all theologies," he retorted. "I am a devout Anglican, but I do not believe nature operates according to the whim of God. There are rules—formed perhaps by God or perhaps by the nature of Nature herself, but they exist and they are valid. We should learn them. They will improve us. Removing the conditioning of religion, or habit, or hearsay, or tradition, and seeing what is truly there, instead of what we have been *told* to see, or *wish* to see. This is difficult. But important."

"It's more than difficult," said the rector. "'Tis impossible, since some reality is greater than mere mortals can grasp. We must take the word of—"

"No, George," Bacon interrupted. He glanced around the room and made direct eye contact with Joan, smiling fleetingly—it left her breathless—then looked back at the rector. "We are no longer in the age of the crusader. We are able to consider Nature independent of God." Directing his attention back to Sander: "I am still developing the practical nuances of this approach, but we must hold ourselves rigorously accountable to how we assess knowledge, for the betterment of mankind."

Sander bowed his head as if in tribute. "Thank you for elucidating, Master Bacon."

"Indeed, yes, thank you," said barrel-chested, laconic Richard Carew, next to Rector Gavell. "'Tis so important, and yet so challenging, to study information and make sense of it without assuming you already know something. Something that is at best an untested, but familiar, presumption."

"Precisely," said Bacon. "Richard, grace us with some examples of this from your own work. 'Tis important for people to see practical applications, lest they dismiss it as mere rhetoric, and I find your projects most felicitous." As he spoke, more food was being brought in: meat pies. Pork, she thought, with clove. She should have eaten before coming here.

"I'm sorry to say I have examples only of the need, and not the fulfillment," Carew began. He turned from Bacon to Sander. "I've just completed a topographical survey of Cornwall. There are different beliefs regarding the origin of the region's name. Some say it is geographical, that it is from *Cornu Walliae*, the Horn of Wales. Others attribute it to an early settler of the region, whose name is now lost. There is no way to prove which belief is accurate, and so each local denizen bases his beliefs on the fact that his grandfather told him it was so. For me even to question their perceptions is an insult to their elders."

The statement had been delivered to the boy-player, and Joan could read him even from behind. People always wanted indications that they'd interested Sander Cooke. She saw the tension in his shoulders; saw, as nobody else saw, how his foot fidgeted. She knew these signs meant he felt trapped, and years of instinct overtook her. Before Carew could continue, she stepped forward and leaned in, murmured, "Pardon, master."

Every man in the room frowned at her.

"Pardon, sirs," she said, remembering to bow instead of curtsy.

"Yes, Jack," Sander said, nodded his head apologetically toward Bacon, and then to the diners in general. Bacon looked concerned; the others, almost disgusted. "Excuse me, gentlemen." He rose. At once, each man was halfway to his feet, as if Sander were a lady about to depart. Bacon gave Joan a questioning look; she lowered her gaze.

Indulgent and effeminate, Sander smiled and gestured them to stay where they were, waving languidly. All of them chortled. "Out on the landing, Jack," Sander said, and nodded toward the door. He smiled and blew one kiss over his shoulder as he stepped through the door. Joan pulled it closed behind him.

"Thanks," she whispered, relieved to be in darkness. The warm, unhurried sounds of tipplers and diners rose up from below.

The coquettish look slid off Sander's face. "The man means well enough, but . . ." He rolled his eyes.

"Master Carew. I noticed."

He gave her a pained smile. "Thanks you for rescuing me. But Bacon said you were not to interrupt."

"But I've a follow-up question anyhow—"

"Of course you do—"

"—and I know he'll want to address it. For clarity. Ask, is't possible that our forefathers acquired knowledge in this same manner—by inductive reasoning, by empirical study—and some of that early knowledge was correct? Which would explain why ancient knowledge is, in fact, sometimes—"

"Slow down," said Sander. "Line by line. Is't possible that what? And truly, Joan, you mustn't do this again. You saw how rude they all found it."

"Sorry," Joan said. "I thought I was here to learn."

"He is only expecting you to listen, for tonight. I know it's hard for you but—"

"If I speak again, you've leave to paste my mouth shut."

"If you speak again, the other guests will beat me to it."

". . . THEREFORE, ISN'T IT the case that we need not re-examine *all* knowledge?" Sander asked this directly of Bacon, who'd raised his eyes toward the ceiling, listening. "I mean things such as how to brew beer, or graft plants, or navigate the oceans. Surely there are items about which we may say, well that's known now, let's not worry ourselves over it. Must each generation question everything from scratch?"

"Of course not," said Bacon. "That would be exhausting and pointless. Certain things, once understood, do not require chronic re-investigation."

"Such as the fraud of transubstantiation," offered the rector.

"George, we are discussing natural philosophy, not theology," said Bacon, brisk. "But Sander, the scope of your question is limited to the mechanics of human enterprise, rather than the laws of Nature."

"Forgive my ignorance, sir, I do not follow."

"For example, we have known for millennia how to sail, and for decades how to circumnavigate the globe. Just as the work of shipwrights has improved with time, the tools of navigation have, and will continue to, as well. The improvements will depend upon continued study of the ocean, which my method will facilitate."

"Hugh Platt has already improved upon a number of processes by experimentation," Babbage said. "Distilling water and spirits, making cider, preserving things in sugar—"

"How happy for the brewer's son to contribute to housewifery that way," said Bacon with casual dismissiveness. "I speak of greater matters. And I believe that the improvements matter less than the initial discovery, for the initial discovery was something new that *changed* humanity. This is what I would have people understand: the marriage of tested logic and original thinking will free our future from our past."

"I heartily concur," said Carew.

Bacon nodded. "I am glad to hear that, Richard. Sander, here is another concern: there are many things yet to discover in Nature, but we cannot chase down all possible knowledge. There is too much of it. Therefore, the correct ideas to pursue are the ones that could improve mankind. Random experiments, undertaken just for the sake of seeing what will happen . . . such things are a waste of time and resources."

Joan affected a sneeze. Bacon's gaze shot in her direction, and then straight toward Sander. Sander picked up his cup and held it out behind himself without looking. "Attend me, boy," he said.

"Is your boy sick?" asked Gavell.

"Now, if he were," said Bacon, pouncing at the chance, "do you believe you are at risk of contagion, or do you believe illness has other sources, such as cold weather, or God's will? *These* are the sorts of questions inductive logic responds to, with useful consequences."

"Quickly now," Sander said with a gesture, since Joan had hesitated to walk while Bacon spoke.

Joan brought him the bottle. He avoided her gaze, but as she refilled his cup, he turned his head to expose his ear to her. Bacon raised his glass. "Is this not an excellent wine?" he asked. "Let us have another round." The others turned toward him and away from Sander, and Joan began an urgent whisper.

"Ambrosia," said Babbage. "Especially to the Earl of Essex, whose fortune is now dependent on its tariff."

"An indelicate comment, sir," said Richard Carew, and as Joan plunged ahead with her whispered query, bits of the table talk slashed through her attention: references to the Star Chamber, Twickenham, Penelope Rich. Eyes began to drift back toward their end of the table, and Bacon shot them an impatient look. Joan whispered faster. She knew she was displeasing Bacon—she didn't care about the rest of them—but the question felt urgent and he was so enthusiastically discussing his new method, she knew he'd want to address the topic.

"Richard," said Bacon. "Tell us what your next adventure in topography might be."

"I'm considering the southeast," said Carew, with a disgruntled glance at Joan. He began a narrative on the ridges of Kent, as the server re-entered with a tray of cheese.

"Pardon, Master Carew," said Sander, somehow listening to him as well as to Joan. "I had the privilege of encountering the Cliffs of Dover, October last, when the Chamberlain's Men were touring. I would enjoy hearing your thoughts about them"—Carew opened his mouth to comply but Sander raised one graceful finger and continued—"after we finish the previous conversation, which my servant rudely interrupted." He glared at Joan, who bowed apologetically and stepped back. "My dear Master Bacon, if I may—"

"Please," said Bacon tersely.

"To return to the heart of my query, by what means may we determine what knowledge needs be reconsidered, and what doesn't? Must we question our established knowledge of herbal remedies, for instance? Shall we forever attempt to improve the baking of bread, or brewing of beer?"

Joan bit the inside of her cheek to hide frustration that he'd botched her question. That wasn't what she'd asked; she'd asked about the intersection of inductive reasoning and established knowledge.

Bacon looked at Sander, at Joan, again at Sander. He pursed his lips, shook his head slightly; the question as asked was unworthy of the disruption it had caused. Joan agreed. "There are those, such as Hugh Platt, who wish to improve how beer is brewed, or discover new healing properties of plants," said Bacon, eyes darting about the room. "Let them. I commend them. But that is not a question about the *method by which* knowledge is attained. I am nonplussed you would ask such a question in this context."

"Thank you," said Sander. "Forgive my silliness. I am quite happy to cede my position of inquisitor for the evening and allow others to steer the conversation." Joan, who was still looking at her shoes, understood this was aimed at her and wondered how to repeat the question accurately anyhow. "Perhaps," Sander was continuing, "Master Carew will now tell us what he knows about the Cliffs of Dover."

"Oh yes! It is true that they are white," Carew began, with basso cheerfulness. "I assumed that was a poetic liberty and that they would be woolen-hued, or perhaps dun, but they are indeed white. As a dove is white. As snow is white. I believe this is due to—"

How exasperating it would be for herself and Bacon both, if the rest of the evening was about geography. "Pardon, master, your brew," she said quietly, stepping toward Sander.

He waved her away without looking at her, then signed, by slapping his fingers closed against his palm: *Stop*. "Back, boy. I require nothing more from you this evening."

"Pardon, master," Joan insisted, "the apothecary bade me—"

"Impudent servant," said Bacon.

She stepped back as if slapped.

All the men at the table, save Sander, were staring at her as if she were a misbehaving dog. She felt her face pulsate with embarrassment. "My deepest apologies, sir. I am only following orders."

For the first time all evening, Bacon seemed planted in his chair, self-contained, aware of himself as the head of the table. "You have overstepped yourself. Leave your master's flask on the table beside him and remove yourself to the landing."

Joan was too mortified to move.

"Now," said Bacon.

"You must excuse my—" Sander said.

Bacon interrupted. "He lacks the manners enough to remain in the room with us. It was a mistake to allow you in here, boy, and it won't happen again."

The silence that followed was so loud, Joan thought she'd gone deaf. She feared blood would spurt from the pores of her cheeks.

Nobody said anything, but their eyes contained courtrooms.

Sander kept his back to her, unreadable, unmoving.

She forced her heavy feet to walk to the table and set down the wooden flask. "Pardon, sirs," she whispered. She backed up to the door, then pivoted and stepped out onto the shadowed landing.

After an agonizing moment the voices within began to speak again, at first in low and tentative tones. Grasping the banister hard for balance, she nearly tumbled down the stairs, wobbled to the tavern door. Outside, just around the corner from where Sander had admired her an hour earlier, she spat up bile and then gagged on her humiliated tears.

September 3

"What the devil was all that about?" Richard Burbage growled, grabbing Sander's shoulder in the crowded backstage area. Burbage was a lion of a man; he could have lifted Sander over his head if he'd had the room.

"Take it outside," suggested Augustine Phillips through the din, shrugging himself out of his merchant costume.

Burbage, in linen shirt and breeches, doublet half-laced, shook Sander hard enough that all of him juddered beneath his costume-shift. "You were vicious out there. This is a comedy. I'm the comic villain but you were the one oozing petulance. What's the matter with you, boy?"

"It's not a comedy," said Sander surly, jerking his shoulder away from Burbage's hold. He reached up to unpin his wig.

"I assure you, it is," said Burbage. "Ask our esteemed playwright if you don't believe me."

"It shouldn't be a comedy," muttered Sander, and closed his eyes to focus on finding all the pins. "Especially if you're the lead. You're hopeless at comedy."

Instant silence. Sander opened his eyes to a swath of empty space around Burbage and himself. The others had stepped back to the walls to keep a distance. The onstage magic between these two became a rough brotherly regard off the stage, but it was always Burbage taking Sander down a notch; Sander, the model apprentice, never disrespected anyone.

Burbage's face was a marvel: for a moment he seemed about to burst into flames of rage. But then, abruptly, he shrugged and started laughing.

"You're mad," he said, slapping Sander's shoulder. "I thought you were being an ass, but 'twas plain madness for you to say that to me. Heminges, your boy's possessed, fetch a doctor to bleed it out of him." He brushed past Sander, threw open the door, and stepped outside into the cloudy afternoon, reaching for his laces.

Sander removed his wig and handed it to Pen, then pulled off the shift.

"God ye good den," came Burbage's voice outside the door, with a chuckle. "Are you here for the beloved brat? If you'd like your money refunded, take it up with Heminges, I'm sure this is his fault somehow." An inaudible response, then Burbage opened the door a crack and called inside, "Sander! Get your glowering little self out here."

Sander cursed under his breath and grabbed his shirt.

"Not your finest work today, Alexander," Francis Bacon said from without, in the tone of a tutor. Burbage roared with harsh laughter. "I need a drink," he declared, and headed toward the Happy Sow under a shadowy sky.

Sander, hastily dressed and face still painted, stepped through the heavy door, then pushed it closed. Bacon was in black silk and hazel-green ruff, and gave him an expectant look. "Hello, Master Bacon," said Sander, his face and voice as neutral as he could manage. "I apologize for my abrupt departure last night."

"You were appallingly rude," Bacon said, voice hardening. His fringed cloak swayed as he shifted his weight from foot to foot. "Almost as bad as your ill-bred friend. The two of you."

"I cannot excuse his behavior, but I can account for it, and mine," Sander said, staying neutral. "Jack was distressed, and I felt the need to calm him down."

"And that outweighed taking polite leave of some of the greatest minds in London?"

"The greatest minds in London are made of tougher stuff than my poor ignorant friend."

The briefest pause. Bacon glanced at him with the expression of a wronged lover considering forgiveness. "That's accurate, anyhow," he said. "And by what method did you calm him down?"

Sander grimaced. "He was gone by the time I followed him out, nor was he at his own home when I sought him there. I do not know where he is, and I am to blame for all of this."

"You are to blame for some of it. The fellow is responsible for his own actions."

"I should not have asked you, and once you so generously said yes, I should not have agreed to your scheme," Sander interrupted, wanting this conversation to be over so he could rub his face paint off. "All the responsibility of making it work fell on him, and he was unprepared, which was not his fault."

"And so he misbehaved," said Bacon.

"Yes," Sander said.

"As did you."

"Yes. For which I have already apologized, so I hope you will now excuse me." He reached for the door latch, but Bacon held up a hand to stop him.

"We have not finished this conversation," he said.

Sander scratched his temple where one final hairpin remained. He pulled it out. "Very well," he said, eyes averted. He still had to oversee the other boys' costumes, plus it was his day to sweep and tidy the tiring house. "Pray finish, sir."

"I agree that you were responsible for some of last night's embarrassment," said Bacon crisply. He signaled his servant, whom Sander hadn't noticed. "Your friend was responsible for more than you were. But the greatest fault is mine."

Sander looked up, surprised.

"Yes," said Bacon. "It is to my shame that I presumed your friend would be at ease in social engagements, as you are. 'Twas folly to set up the scheme of a supper, which only created obstacles to the actual purpose of our being in the same room together."

Sander had had this same thought during his sleepless night, but never expected to hear it from the man himself. "I appreciate your saying it, sir. I'll pass along your statement to Jack, once I find him, in hopes it will mitigate his shame."

"No, you won't. I shall tell him myself," said Bacon.

Sander blinked.

"If the boy and I both wish me to instruct him, then I should instruct him. Not create a scenario that prevents me from instructing him," Bacon said.

Sander blinked again.

"When I summon you, bring him to my chambers in Gray's Inn."

". . . Truly?"

"But he must dress better," said Bacon. "His shabby servant's togs last night looked borrowed from your Playhouse stash."

Sander allowed a sheepish shrug.

"He requires a uniform fit for appearing at the Inns of Court," Bacon said. He held out his left hand and offered Sander the coins he had been fussing with. "My tailor is expecting him. Send word when he is better dressed."

September 7

It had been a week of comedies, to entertain the thousands of visitors the Southwark Fair attracted. *Much Ado About Nothing. A Comedy of Errors. The Taming of the Shrew. As You Like It*, which especially pleased Sander; the role of Rosalind, the girl disguised as a boy-who-pretends-to-be-a-girl, had catapulted him from popularity to outright fame. More than that: he loved her. Loved that she was playful but not shallow, fierce but never brutal, and equally at ease in skirts or breeches. If God would grant him a single wish, it might be to play Rosalind forever.

Now it was an overcast Tuesday afternoon. The company had paused rehearsal for cheat bread and chicken pottage, redolent with cloves and mace. Then the trestles were cleared away and napkins and spoons collected, and the prompter opened the playbook to begin running lines for that afternoon's performance: Ben Jonson's *Every Man out of His Humour*. The clouds showed signs of clearing, but Sander knew better than to trust that. He sat cross-legged at the lip of the stage and gazed out at the huge intimacy of a thousand empty seats. The streets outside were overstuffed with fairgoers, but inside here was still. Empty, the Globe was a safe harbor, almost sacred.

Full, of course, it was sacred in a different way, for he became a demigod.

"Lad," said Heminges in his ear. Sander glanced over and recognized the consoling expression.

"Kit's replacing me in *Every Man*," he guessed archly, before Heminges could say it. Within a year, the boy would be playing all his roles. Even lovely Rosalind.

Heminges offered him a wan but well-intentioned smile. "You hate Jonson's plays, anyhow. And you especially hate that role. Consider yourself liberated. You needn't oversee the boys, or clean up after. Your time's your own for the rest of the day. Unless you'd make yourself useful by taking a message up to Tilney at the Revels Office—"

Sander was staring at him hard enough to make Heminges stop. "Oh no, I'd best spend the afternoon securing my own future."

"Your future can remain within these walls, Sander," Heminges said. "You know that. We all wish for that, lad. Obviously."

"Sir, we have had this conversation—"

"And we shall have it again, as often as it takes to stick between your ears. Half the boys don't even stay the term of their apprenticeship, and not a one has ever enthralled audiences as you—"

"And yet, sir, that means nothing," Sander interrupted. "Not one shareholder in the company began as an apprentice. Professionally, my apprenticeship is meaningless."

"But not your talent or your training, lad. Plus you've a comprehensive understanding of managing a company. The Master of the Revels likes you more than he likes Shakespeare or Burbage, and he's the one who makes us at court. You're excellent with the younger boys and train them better than any of us can. You're a benefit to the company, even if you are truant at half your other chores."

"Maybe more than half," Sander admitted.

"Definitely more than half," Heminges said, chuckling. "But yours is a rare talent. We've trained you and cherished—"

"You've trained me well, to do something only done by your apprentices."

"Your talent is exceptional. You'll always have a home with us."

"Will I?" Sander shot back. "What roles will I be given, when Burbage plays all the heroes and Robby Armin gets all the laughs, and new boys will take all my parts?"

Heminges looked at him, as stern as such a kind man could be. "We won't make you a stagehand, Sander. But there's more to being a shareholder than performing. And you were apprenticed to me through the Grocers Guild," he added, grabbing for Sander's arm when Sander pulled away. "Sander, if I can balance acting, managing this company, and brokering coal sales, you can—"

"I've no head for commerce, you've seen me humiliate myself trying," the boy complained. "Please be honest, sir. I know how to earn and keep the trust and admiration of others, and I'd become a man of business if I'd any aptitude, but you know I haven't. Theatre is the only thing I've ever had a head for, and suddenly my livelihood depends upon how many scripts happen to require an elegant countertenor. Look at me," he said, wresting from Heminges his slender outstretched arm, waving tapering fingers at his master. "I haven't waxed masculine in any way with age. I am no stouter nor brawnier except in comparison to Joan, perhaps. I must needs pluck a bit of down off my chin, but this body is as delicate as any woman's, and always will be."

"John Sincklo's thinner that you," said Heminges.

Sander rolled his eyes. "John Sincklo's thinner than his skeleton. Anyhow he's got other income—he owns a bakery with his brother, no? If I've no other livelihood, how will I even earn enough for bread?"

"You could start your own bakery," Heminges said, half jesting.

Sander did not jest back. "With what capital or expertise? I can't even follow instructions for bookkeeping. I still have nightmares from your trying to teach me mathematical problems. *There is a cat at the foot of a tree the length of three hundred feet. This it goes up each day seventeen feet and descends each night twelve feet. How long till it reaches the top?* Or, *Three merchants have formed a company—*"

"Yes, lad, I know them."

"But I don't! Lord help me, I can recite them to the syllable, drunk or asleep, but still cannot make my brain work to solve them. Joan had to explain the one about the merchants, and I forgot what she said minutes later. 'Tisn't laziness or lack of industry, sir, 'tis genuine ineptitude. I'd be a failure as a businessman. How may I even contemplate marriage or children when I won't know if I can keep a roof over my head from season to season?" demanded Sander. "As well-mannered and charming as I am, if I've naught but my training, why would you tell me not to use it?"

Heminges's stare hardened with understanding. "You want to be a courtier," he said, despairingly. "Or a hanger-on. If you choose to become some baron's resident pet, you will never be allowed marriage or children anyhow."

"Perhaps that's how it should be, then. Perhaps I'm not man enough for such responsibilities."

"I didn't mean that. I meant, once you're a sycophant, you won't be courted and indulged by anyone, as you now are. You will be under an obligation to whoever clothes and feeds you. I know you, it won't sit well."

Sander sneered. "You speak as if my only option is to hire myself out by the hour."

"That's not true," said Heminges. "You've other paths. Remember Robin Dodge? Lived up to his name and became a cutpurse. Until he was caught and hanged. Or Josias Brown, that's now the company tailor—"

"I know who Josias Brown is," Sander interrupted. "I listen to him go on about playing Zenocrate every time I need a hem lowered. I'm glad for him he had the aptitude for tailoring. I don't, so I hope it will not sound too petulant if I say: Lord save me from such a life."

"The Lord might not, but the Chamberlain's Men will," said Heminges. "Do you think we would put so much into training and educating you, and then disown you? You're pawky enough to replace me as company manager, and Phillips already keeps the books. Still, if running errands for the men who feed and clothe you is beneath your dignity, then you've the rest of the day free to scout for better prospects."

"Can you fault me if I do?" demanded Sander. With his fingers he caressed the air, showing off their length and gracefulness. "I am a delight to the eye and the ear. Charming and winsome. An attentive listener. I dance, and sing, and play sundry musical instruments. I can speak at length on some few topics—not so many as Joan—and what I speak about is of interest to lords and ladies. I bring with me a whiff of celebrity. 'Tis the sole capital I have—I've no money or jewels or land or brawn, and no other marketable competencies. So please do not begrudge my investing in my future with the qualities I do have."

"Remarkable how a boy with barely a penny to his name is so eager to sell himself into England's most fickle market," sniffed Heminges. He rose with obvious annoyance and walked back into the tiring house.

SANDER ROAMED ABOUT dampened Southwark for an hour, cheek by jowl with the hordes of country folk visiting for the fair. He was wasting the time until Joan might be expected at the Playhouse. The clouds had not completely cleared, but he could feel the shadows shifting, and the occasional liberated ray of sun would slap the choppy surface of the Thames. He ignored the usual glances of people staring at him; he knew they were trying to recall why they recognized those eyes, that gait. Inevitably one would place it, and he'd use a careful smile to acknowledge a gasp or cry of delight, before disappearing into the crowd.

To occupy his mind, he fidgeted with his mental roster of the courtiers and noblewomen who already fancied him enough to perhaps want to keep him underfoot. It was a private obsession that began the first time Kit had replaced him in a small role.

He assessed all possible patrons in descending order according to their wealth and influence at court. His instinct was always to top the list with Robert Devereaux, Earl of Essex. Essex had been Elizabeth's youthful favorite until he'd returned prematurely and defeated from a military stint in Ireland, which led to his being put under house arrest most of the past year.

. . . So Essex no longer belonged at the top of the list.

. . . Although his fate was improving. He was still banned from court, but this past week he'd been permitted to travel around the country. And he was receiving loads of visitors: nobles of all standing, captains, cavaliers, and even Puritans. Sander could not imagine what the earl would speak of with Puritans, who hated the arts as reliably as Essex patronized them. Sander shuffled him down to third on the list, just below Robert Cecil and that attorney general fellow Coke.

But neither Cecil nor Coke seemed to be the patronage-offering sort, and he knew Francis Bacon disliked Coke. Upsetting Bacon imperiled Joan's tutelage. And Bacon had a long history with Essex. Essex went back to the top of the list, although with reservations.

He wanted a quiet ale at the Swan with Two Necks, but no spot in Southwark was quiet this week, so he returned to the back door of the Playhouse, even though he had no need to be there, in case Joan came at her usual time. She had been rapturous since he'd taken her to Bacon's tailor, and he liked to see her joyful. He settled on his usual low stool outside the tiring-house door. The air was cooling toward autumn, but even under clouds, the ground had a lovely damp warmth from months of lengthy days.

Two boys came racing each other around the curve of the building. One was Pen, the company's message-boy, in linen and wool; the other was older and unfamiliar to Sander, and dressed in black and green satin. They pulled up to an abrupt, clumsy stop in front of him, elbowing each other and trying to stifle their giggling as they bowed.

"Boys in silk should not giggle," said Sander to the older one. "Pen, I'll hear your message first."

The smaller boy held out a little painted disc, cornflower blue with a crescent moon. Sander was pleased to see it.

"And what is Lady Melcombe's message?" he asked.

"She invites you to come to her after supper," said Pen.

"Report to her that I'll come at the usual hour," he said. "And now you, in silks."

The older boy bowed. "The Earl of Essex requests the pleasure of your presence at your soonest convenience. He would make use of your recitational talents and will pay you for them."

Sander barely hid his astonishment. Perhaps being scratched from the Ben Jonson play was the happiest misfortune of his week.

"I'll come at once," he said.

Act II

September 7

The Bucklers' small house was on New Rents near St. Saviour, a brisk five-minute walk past the Globe. This put them close to London Bridge, whose wealthy merchants were some of the best clients of Joan's father. Joan had finished her chores early today. She'd churned the butter while her parents were still at morning prayers; before mid-day, the week's laundry hung on the line. She liked this time of year. The air was dryer as it cooled, but not yet so cool that coal smoke was at peak pestilence in London skies.

Her usual rounds took longer than usual; getting anywhere during the week of Southwark Fair meant losing hours of one's life to queues and crowds. She took requests from mercers and tailors for buckles and clasps; returning, she gave these orders to her father. Then she snuck out to the privy, transformed herself—with less struggle than before—into Jack Buckler, and strode out again, right past her distracted parents.

It still felt peculiar to walk like this, sans skirt or braid, her shins exposed. She watched the casual swagger of the boys leaving their choir practice at St. Saviour and tried to imitate it—feet stomping, arms swinging, chest broad, taking up all the space the women and girls avoided taking. She hadn't got it quite right yet. That made her too nervous to risk a wherry, lest the boatman see through her disguise. Better to take the time to cross the bridge.

London Bridge might take fewer than five minutes to cross at midnight, but dawn to dusk it was such a rowdy, jostling, over-trafficked hazard that common wisdom said to anticipate an hour. And during Southwark Fair, it might take two.

Beyond the rotting heads of executed prisoners on spikes, the scores of shops—butchers, jewelers, haberdashers, grocers, knife sharpeners, tinkers, portrait painters, bakers—summoned thousands. Add to this the suppliers for all these, as well as the innumerable pushcarts, livestock, and residents, and then the added traffic of people who were using the bridge as all bridges are intended, to cross a river. Eyes, ears, and nose, the senses were assaulted.

But it was anonymous. She could run these rapids faster than most in a skirt. The breeches did not hinder her, and by the time she had jostled her way to the northern shore, she could walk without thinking how to do it.

The Barber-Surgeons Hall was nestled against the city wall, way up by Cripplegate near the glassmaking plant. There were different routes to jog north and west from here to there; today she chose the larger, crowded roads, to continue to protect herself with anonymity. New Fish Street to Gracechurch to Lombard, Cornhill to Cheapside to Wood to Silver.

As she neared the Barber-Surgeons Hall, she slowed to join the small throng of entering men. Her heart thudded harder as she curbed her pace: this was it, the ultimate test of how mannish she could be. There were a few women, perhaps five in a crowd of two hundred. They were all on the arms of a husband or a father, and noticing this made her both jealous and defiant. She spread her shoulders wider, claimed more space without asking permission. It felt absurd, yet thrilling.

Her glance fell on a familiar face, but she couldn't place him or recall his identity: a swarthy man, in well-made but understated clothes. He was talking to the physician who treated the Chamberlain's Men, and she navigated through the crowd, head bowed, toward them.

"—in comparison to Athens," the man was saying with an unusual accent. Joan realized with a start that it was Cristóforos Pantazis, the Greek from Master Cole's garden.

But Pantazis was a botanist, not a physician, so she might be wrong. She stared, trying to recall details of his appearance from their brief encounter. As if feeling her eyes on him, he looked in her direction. Yes, it was him, with those beautiful dark eyes. He gave her a questioning look—do I know you?—and she twisted away before he could realize the boy he saw was the girl he'd met a few weeks earlier.

Immediately she found herself staring into another familiar face, five paces distant with a stream of dark-robed men between them. She recognized this face at once: the green-eyed matriarch of Southwark apothecaries, Eleanor Duckworth. She was dressed in her signature russet, with silver lace woven into her coif and silver buttons down her doublet. Eleanor was the companion of Dorothy Tibbet, the midwife whom Joan assisted. Joan smiled on reflex.

Eleanor looked confused, and then recognizing Joan, she gaped. Her mouth moved to form Joan's name, but she stopped herself and gestured instead. Begrudging the detour, Joan wove her way through the flow of Barber-Surgeons to her.

"God ye good day," she said, remembering to bow like a boy. "How remarkable to encounter you all the way up here."

"I assure you, it's not," said Eleanor, with superior dryness. "I came looking for you."

"What, here? Half an hour's walk from Southwark?"

"Of course here. You always come here when they have a lecture." Eleanor gestured at Joan's clothes. "Clever disguise. I warrant in these threads you'd get in. But I've an urgent request to make on Dorothy's behalf." She did not sound urgent. Eleanor Duckworth carried herself with the self-assurance of someone unaccustomed to needing to point out the importance of her presence.

Joan already knew she would say yes, even if she didn't want to. Eleanor had the gravitas that made it impossible to say no. Next time there was a lecture, she'd keep her gaze straight ahead and allow for no distractions. "What is it, then?"

"Dorie's got a man in, very ill, she's tried everything I have in stock for hours now but nothing helps. I must prepare some caricostin, and that will take all my attention. But Goodwife Stott has a baby coming."

"Busy day."

"You're the only one who knows both my shop and also Dorothy's practice."

Joan was shocked. "You'd have me deliver a baby? That's unlawful, I'm not—"

"She'll tend them both, the ailing man and the mother in labor, but she needs assistance, and I must return my attention to compounding."

"You found a free hour to come fetch me."

"My niece is minding the shop, but she's too young to do anything else, and she doesn't know you, so I couldn't send her to find you. It was worth losing an hour of my time to win an afternoon of yours. May I point out," she added, "you will get your hands more satisfyingly dirty with us than you would in that airless lecture hall."

Joan glanced over her shoulder at the crowded entryway. There would be other lectures. And it was best not to risk exposure by proximity to Pantazis.

"That's true." She sighed.

"Good," said Eleanor, as if congratulating Joan for responding correctly. She added, "Dorothy would not like to hear me say this, but I should warn you, it's likely we will lose the gentleman."

"I hope you're wrong for his sake, but I'd have been viewing a corpse inside the hall anyhow, so I'm prepared."

Eleanor gave her an approving look that bordered on affection. "If Dorie and I could have a daughter," she said, "we would want her to be you."

SANDER HAD BEEN in Essex House at least half a dozen times with the Chamberlain's Men. He'd paid little attention to the grandeur of the house itself, his focus always on helping with props and then getting into costume.

It had been simple enough to get here, with Essex's own boy. The earl's sleek boat across the Thames, cushioned and canopied, brought him to a private wharf. There was a slope up to the foot of the Essex gardens and orchards, filled with beehives and knot gardens and fruit trees and what he assumed were rosebushes. Then a promenade garden between the orchards and the house, with a bowling green to one side of it and a tennis court to the other. The outbuildings around the edges of it were attractive enough—sheds, a dovecote, a chapel, a kennel. But huge Essex House itself was unattractive, with no decoration visible from anywhere. From any approach, it was unimaginative in its design, and stingy in its embellishments. The many wings and ells had simple gabled roofs, and plain windows of unremarkable size. Sander found it all an ill fit. He remembered Robert Devereux as gallant almost to the point of foppery—complicated, charming, and well decorated. His house was not. But then, he hadn't built it, just inherited it.

At the wicket gate he declared himself, and was admitted by a liveried fellow about his age, who stared at Sander while trying not to stare, while Sander pretended not to notice.

"I will take you to his lordship," he said, and led him into a minor palace redolent with rose and civet oil.

ROBERT DEVEREUX, 2ND Earl of Essex, was a handsome, dark-haired man in the prime of life. Today he was wearing an ivory doublet over an ivory shirt, with ivory breeches and ivory stockings, each article glowing with the declaration that here was a man far removed from any kind of dirt or labor. It was, Sander thought, an interesting choice of habiliment for a military hero who'd failed his latest campaign.

The earl sat in the best chair in his receiving room. It was nearly a throne, with a hooded back, carpeted cushion, and fringe on the seat. Red linsey-woolsey drapes backed it, with borders of gold leaf. The wainscoted walls were painted red with gold leaf decorations, which caught the flickering light of the candlebranches. Rush mats on the floor softened the sound and added a hint of rosemary to the fusty room.

The woman sitting near Essex could have been his twin, save that her hair was dyed and curled to resemble the queen's. This was Lady Penelope Rich, the earl's jasmine-scented sister, whom Sander had last seen scolding Francis Bacon behind the Globe Playhouse. She was wearing the same pale-orange gown as the other day, but with black sleeves laced onto it. Sander felt dull and underdressed in his blue apprentice's doublet.

Lady Rich had always been as enthralling to Sander as Sander was to most of London. She was the most scandalous noblewoman in England, somehow remaining in the queen's graces while flaunting every social convention that defined womanhood or political self-preservation. Famously the wife of Lord Rich and mother to his seven children, she was also famously the mistress of Baron Mountjoy and mother to an ever-growing clutch of his offspring too. The soldier-poet Philip Sidney had penned adoring poems about her in her youth. John Dowland had composed a galliard in her honor that Sander had danced to on the stage. She was old enough to be his mother, and still the most beautiful woman he'd ever set eyes on. She knew everyone worth knowing in all of England and half of Scotland.

If anyone could connect him to a patron, Penelope Rich could.

He'd have had no access to her on his own. How wonderful that young Kit had replaced him in that Ben Jonson play this afternoon.

Sander doffed his felted cap, placed one lithe turned-out leg ahead of him and bent the other into a deep bow, first to the brother and then the sister.

"My Lord and my lady, I am honored to have been summoned here," he said, trying to steer his mind away from the acute awareness that if he could somehow be taken under Penelope Rich's wing, his problems became solvable.

The pair studied him a moment. He was used to this; it always took people a beat to adjust to seeing that familiar face without its cosmetic embellishments.

"Even prettier without a wig," declared Lady Rich. Sander deliberately blushed.

"That's not why he's here, Penny," said the Earl in a dismissive tone. To Sander: "I have summoned you to read a letter aloud. You do read, I assume?"

"It would be hard for him to memorize so many lines without reading," said Penelope, beaming at Sander as if he'd done something to please her. Which made him want to do something to please her.

"We do have such players, milady," he said. "They memorize their lines with the help of the prompt-man. But I have the privilege of literacy." Back to the earl: "What letter would your lordship have me read? And wherefore?"

"There has been a correspondence," said Essex, "between myself and a member of Her Majesty's court."

"It's Sir John Stanhope," said Penelope in a rushed, conspiratorial voice to Sander. "In case it takes us a quarter hour to reach that detail."

"I am suspicious," Essex continued loftily, ignoring her, "of the intentions of my correspondent, and I wish to hear his letter as if 'twere out of his own mouth and from his own person. I have seen you imitate certain personages on the stage, so I know you can do this. I take you for a mimic. A discreet one. A youth in your situation is surely invited places where discretion is important."

"Perhaps," said Sander, discreetly.

"I will describe to you the exchange we have been having, so you may understand the context," said Essex. "In fact, I'll read you my own contribution to it."

"Robert," said his sister, in the tone of an affectionate, long-suffering older sibling.

"'Tis only fair," argued Essex, pleased with himself. "He is reciting for us, I shall recite for him." Back to Sander: "Perhaps you have heard, as it seems to be the talk of London, that although I am freed from house arrest, I still may not set foot in court." Sander kept his face blank. Essex gestured dismissively. "You needn't deny it, I know 'tis spoken of. Things have been ungentle between Her Majesty and I, but perhaps you do not know the details."

"Nor should I," said Sander, demure and insincere. "I am in no position to assess the deeds of someone so far above—"

"Enough of that," said Essex. "My actions have been wildly misrepresented by my enemies, most especially that hunchback Robert Cecil. I was in Ireland with orders to subdue the island. But it was not to be subdued with the number of men I had, and Cecil prevented our sainted queen from receiving my letters begging for more troops. And so I did the only reasonable thing: I struck a truce with Tyrone, and came home to inform Her Majesty. But she, having believed the vile lies of Cecil—"

"Robby," said Lady Rich, in a tone that was at once comforting and scolding. "Elide the details and come to the heart of this visit." She gave Sander an apologetic smile.

"Well then," said Essex. "The heart of the matter is that I must convince Her Majesty to allow me near her person. Somebody wrote me with advice on how to do so."

Stanhope, Penelope mouthed to Sander. *It was Stanhope*, and they exchanged knowing smirks.

He had a private jest with Penelope Rich! Thank God Kit had replaced him in that stupid play today.

"I do not know if I should trust the man who wrote me."

"Meaning Stanhope," said Penelope.

"The correspondence began with my having written Her Majesty a note, of which I have kept this copy."

From an ivory table beside his chair, he pinched a paper between thumb and forefinger, and held it up. Essex's reading voice was a prettier tenor than Sander had anticipated, and Essex was clearly enthralled at the sound of it. "Haste, thou paper, to that happy presence of Her Majesty," he began, lamenting. "Whence only I, unhappy I, am banished! Kiss that fair correcting hand, which lays now plasters to my lighter hurts, but applies nothing to my greatest wound. Say you came from shamed, languishing, despairing Essex."

"An excellent and heartfelt note," said Sander. Shakespeare would have winced. "And what was Her Majesty's response?"

"She did not reply. A few days later, I wrote this." He set down that letter and picked up a second. He did not check which paper he was picking up, which meant he had staged and possibly even rehearsed this recitation. That seemed Essex-like.

"Our guest understands the essence of your correspondence," said Penelope.

Essex pouted, but set the page down.

"It was a heartfelt, moving letter, but again, she did not respond," he said. "So I was forced to write to her a third time."

"Which he also does not need to hear," she said, before he could even reach for it.

"I reminded her that my license to tax the import of sweet wines is soon to expire, and she has not confirmed renewing my rights to it. If she does not, then I am undone, for that tariff is my only revenue. Again, I did not hear back from her. But *then*, I received a letter from Sir John Stanhope. I trust you are familiar with him?"

Of course Sander was familiar with Stanhope. Sir John—although an indifferent courtier, holding no particular post yet somehow always near Her Majesty—was easy to remember from his affected style of speech. He rolled his *r*'s like a Scotsman but sounded otherwise quite southern. And he had a fidgety way of rubbing the knuckle of his ring finger with the tip of his thumb.

"I am cerrtainly familiarr with Sirr John," said Sander. He glanced at Essex but also at Penelope. Her mouth at rest had the curve of a sassy smile. He wondered how best to keep her interest, without seeming impudent or presumptuous.

"Excellent," said Essex. "Sir John professes to be a friend of mine, but of course he's a sycophant of Hunchback Cecil, who is now in favor over me. Stanhope kisses my arse only when he feels it will be of use to him, and undermines me when that suits his purposes. So I question if I should trust him now. He could be a cog in some machine of Cecil's."

"And my role in this?" asked Sander.

Essex reached back to the side table and picked up the final paper. He held it out.

"Here is his letter. Read it aloud so that I may hear it as if from him, which will allow me to better assess if he is sincere."

This was a strange request, but Sander had entertained stranger. He took the leaf. It was written in the Italian hand, readily legible, so he began to recite at once without bothering to read it over first.

"*I prresented yourr letterr to Herr Majesty*—pardon?" he interrupted himself, looking up at Essex, who was chortling. Penelope smiled.

"You're excellent," she said. "You sound like him already."

"Doesn't he?" Essex grinned.

"Thank you," said Sander. After a perfectly timed pause, he raised his free hand to begin the thumb-and-finger fidget, which prompted more approving laughter.

"*I prresented yourr letterr to Herr Majesty who, afterr perrusing it once orr twice, dirrected me to answerr you, saying that your grratitude was everr welcome, and seldom came out of season. Morre in commission I had not, but I might note by herr speech to me—afterr she read again the last parrt of yourr letter—that if you continued yourr demonstrrative prrofession to take little comfort in liberrty, rresort of frriends, orr any otherr delight, until you had assurrance of the end of herr displeasurre, then it would hasten the grrant of what you desirre.*"

"He means the wine license," murmured Essex to Penelope, as if she wouldn't know this.

". . . *I hope I have not exceeded my dirrection by deliverring my own obserrvation, which I do with the purrpose of furrtherring that which I wish forrrrrr you.*" He looked up. "That is the end of it, my lord."

"Thank you. Most excellent." Essex and Penelope looked at each other for as long as it took Sander to take a breath and let it out again. Then Penelope nodded her head to one side.

"It is very much like Her Majesty to enjoy flattery and beseeching," she said. "I believe Sir John speaks sincerely and to the point. But as I've advised you, allow me to sound her out, indirectly, through her other ladies, before you write another letter. She does not like to be prodded to action. Which I said before he wrote to you, so really, you have nothing gained by this exercise." Her eyes, dark darts of merriment, moved toward Sander. "Except the pleasure of Alexander Cooke's performance."

"'Tis never an ill thought, to check one's assumptions," said Essex.

"As Francis is ever harping on about."

An open door. "Mean you Francis Bacon, m'lord? I have the privilege of being on friendly terms with him."

Penelope looked pleased. "We are very fond of Francis—"

"No," said Essex, "we *were*—"

"—and of his brother Anthony, who lived under this roof for years. They have done well by us, and we by them, since our salad days. Francis was invaluable to my brother when Robert joined the Privy Council—he never took a position without first seeking Francis's advice. We are as close as family."

"No longer, sister," said Essex. "Francis has a constricted mind, for all the large thoughts in it."

"If you mean he would like to constrict you from political suicide—"

"Anyhow," Essex said, with a dismissive wave at her, "well done, lad, I'll reward for your skill. And we'll have some wine." He picked up a bell on the table and rang it. The servant from outside entered, and Essex leaped up and went to speak with him at the door.

At that moment, from the far side of the room, a clock struck one brief bong to sound the quarter hour, followed by four measures of "Pastime with Good Company," played as if upon a clavichord by an uninspired student. Sander glanced toward the clock.

"Isn't that charming?" said Lady Rich. "Robert's newest toy, purchased while shut up alone in here for weeks, to pass the hours."

"Who is playing, my lady?"

"It's mechanical," she said in a conspiring whisper. "Robert is newfangled. The gears create the music!"

"Fascinating." Sander was not sure what was expected of him now. He tried to imagine the best thing to say to hold her interest in him.

"I saw your Rosalind this summer," she said. "Several times, both at court and at the Globe. And if I did not say so prior, I never cease to marvel at your Rosaline in *Love's Labor's Lost*."

"Thank you, my lady, but of course Will Shakespeare takes credit for the writing—"

"But it's nothing till the players speak the lines. Nobody remembers the writers. You are a delight, and every bit as skilled as Richard Burbage. And I will add, more versatile."

"My lady, thank you," said Sander, dipping his head.

"But may I ask you something?" she said, her tone confiding. "You must be reaching the end of your apprenticeship. Will you remain with the company, or have you other plans? 'Twould be a shame to lose you to some mundane profession." He made sure his smile was satin-smooth as he marveled at her broaching the subject. "I'll be sad enough not to see you in a skirt, but not to see you perform at all would be a grievous disappointment. I'm sure you'd be enthralling, even in breeches. Please tell me you'll stay with the Chamberlain's Men."

"I am not decided yet, my lady," he said breezily. "Boy-players often have disappointing careers as men, as we have had all the mannishness trained out of us." He steeled himself for the usual response: growing manly came easily to any boy who wanted it. Such an easy claim to make by those who had no cause or need to prove it.

Instead, she protested: "But there are older women you might still play!" She gestured, in a lazy circular motion, to herself. "We are worth personating, think you not? I recall your astonishing Constance in *King John*. That speech about her absent child. As a mother, I was transported. There should be more of that. Will Her Majesty not, some day in the future, be depicted? And who will do that? A squeaking boy? Or a beautiful androgyne like yourself? If I managed the Chamberlain's Men, I would keep you in skirts until your dotage."

A clumsy pause as he tried to wrap his mind around this astonishing premise. "Well, I . . . I like that notion well enough, but I lack the agency to change convention. Had God made me to grow burly, I'd be more confident of a future on the stage, but He has seen fit to keep me light. So I suppose I might be in search of a patron. Someone of standing who would appreciate having a cultured entertainer about."

Her eyes upon him always seemed to be laughing, not with cruelty but with playful mischief. Suddenly he felt foolish, and the absurdity of his presumption clear to him: in a city full of well-spoken, cultured men, who would need an effeminate young man of no status or utility lounging about?

"I shall keep an eye out," she said. Gesturing toward the door: "And here's our cellar-man with malmsey to drink." The more she smiled, the more the corners of her eyes crinkled, which somehow made them sparkle more.

THE CLOUDY AFTERNOON was warm enough for the three women to sit outside on a bench together, to escape the smell of blood and vomit and death within. They had sat in silence for long enough to hear St. Thomas's church bells toll a quarter, then a half, of the hour. An endless stream of people passed them heading away from the fair, or home to supper: surgeons from the hospital, clockmaker, brewers, dyers and tile makers and dockhands come from downriver. Dorothy, scandalously, lit her clay pipe and drew in the tobacco smoke on a long, measured breath. Eleanor had poured each of them a silver-handled pot of her strongest ale, scented of cinnamon. Joan drank hers quickly. She was shaken and exhausted.

"You intended to see a corpse today," Eleanor reminded her. Her tone was not unkind, but neither was it comforting.

"Not that one," Joan said. "Not a newborn."

"We cannot alter fate," said Dorothy but sounded melancholy. She was shorter and rounder than Eleanor, a ruddy face and short, thick fingers that often managed to work miracles. "Still, it is hard to believe the God we hear about in church would create such random tragedies. That poor woman. Good her sister was able to help her home."

"At least the gentleman survived," said Eleanor philosophically. "You raised him from the dead, I'd say."

"Just common sense, in the end," said Dorothy. And then to Joan, who had opened her mouth to ask, she said, "Too tired to explain now. Come by tomorrow or the next day."

They sat for some moments in silence, sipping their ale, Dorothy smoking, as the sun continued to slant.

"Take our minds off it, lass. Tell us: What are you about these days, when you're not studying corpses or plants?" asked Dorothy.

"A female Hugh Platt," said Eleanor under her breath, approvingly.

It felt good, for adults to take an interest in her. "I'll tell you if you will keep it confidential," she said.

She told them about Bacon. They were delighted. Dorothy wrapped her in a hug, and even Eleanor squeezed her around the shoulders, radiating self-satisfaction, as if she somehow could take credit.

"Maybe he'll find you a decent husband," Eleanor said. She was opposed to Joan being married off to any ordinary fellow. Back in June, Eleanor had stalked a young tinsmith she'd heard discussing dowries with Joan's father; Joan never learned what Eleanor had said to him, but he never came around again, and she didn't mind.

"Bacon believes I'm a boy—why do you think I'm dressed like this? This is all Sander's doing. I wouldn't even have these clothes on my own, let alone access to Bacon."

"That lad has always been one to do anything for you," said Dorothy. "He worships you. Always has."

The pleasure she felt, hearing that somebody else had noticed this, confused her. She said nothing but felt her cheeks grow pleasantly warm.

"What's Bacon teaching you, then?"

"I'm to learn about a way of looking at the world analytically," she said. "'Tis a philosophy he's forming, that he calls inductive reasoning."

Eleanor and Dorothy exchanged knowing looks. Eleanor's face broadened into a smug smile, and Dorothy guffawed.

"What?" Joan asked.

Eleanor shrugged. "A mutual acquaintance has mentioned this to us," she said. "So we've heard of Bacon's revolutionary idea, to approach things by experiment and observation, rather than traditional beliefs."

"Yes? And? Why are you laughing?"

Eleanor rolled her eyes.

"'Tisn't new, lass," Dorothy said, still chuckling. "Not for myself and all empirics like me. Hugh Platt has been doing the same work for years, but he's not noble-born. He's worked with all manner of folk in London, from botanists to blacksmiths, yet men like Bacon turn their nose up at him. Eleanor both studied with and tutored Platt. Every day, I practice that which Platt performs but Bacon only talks about it. And thus by association, so do you." She slapped her thigh and took another deep draught on her pipe. "You out-Bacon Bacon, lass!"

SANDER WAS KEPT on at Essex House. Penelope Rich asked him to sing; to play the lute; to sing to her lute-playing; then she asked her brother's resident musician to play so that the siblings might dance an esperance with Sander. The three washed hands, said grace, broke bread, shared cheese and wine. Each quarter-hour the clock would strike and play a phrase from a different tune: a Banester antiphon; a William Byrd pavane; something that sounded like that upstart Philip Rosseter.

After an hour, he still did not know if Lady Rich was flirting, assessing, or simply appreciating him. But she offered him, without his asking, what he needed most.

"Have you any particular sort of patron in mind?"

"Intelligent ones," he said. "Who might allow me leniency in the cut of my beard. I am especially drawn to those who study natural philosophy."

The noble siblings exchanged amused glances. "Hence your friendship with Francis," said the earl. "A shame he cannot keep enough funds at hands to hire pretty sycophants like yourself."

"I'm sure we can find some other prospects," Penelope hummed. "Who'd like you just as pretty as you are now."

He left Essex House feeling heady and walked along the Thames toward London Bridge. From the spots between estates where narrow alleys gave access to the river, he caught glimpses of the water, spangled with sunbeams from a break in the clouds. The afternoon clatter was still on, carts and wagons and printers and bricklayers and bakers and laundresses and dogs barely avoiding slamming into one another as he approached the arched pedestrian entrance. The bridge itself was overrun with folk going to or from the Southwark Fair. He walked with his head down, wishing he had Joan's aptitude for slipping through a crowd. Some half-score times, people recognized him well enough to point while elbowing a friend, but the crowd was too loud for anyone to hear his name when it was shouted; he relied on the sheer press of people to keep adorers at a distance. Finally he reached the southern end, continuing to creep toward Maiden Lane and then, at last, the Globe. As he passed the Happy Sow, he saw the door begin to open for the post-performance crowd.

At the same moment, applause came rolling across from the Playhouse. The thunderous applause. He tamped down a nightmarish rush of fear, a bodily belief that he had missed something. The role Kit had replaced him in was not a leading one, but he was still receiving attention that Sander was not.

No matter, Sander reminded himself. It had given him the opportunity to impress Penelope Rich. This was as it should be. His future was brighter because today, that applause from within the curved walls was for someone else.

He stepped into the Sow, took a moment to drink in the warmth as his eyes adjusted. The husband, Hal, was strewing fresh rushes across the wooden floor.

"Good day to you," said Sander, and Hal looked up.

"Sander! Greetings! Will you be entertaining the customers today? They'll have missed you, with young Kit stepping in." He winked as he dusted his hands, finished with the final armful. "I saw a bit of his first scene and the lad's fine, you know, but he hasn't your style."

"Ah well, I'm sure he'll find his way to his own style," said Sander graciously.

Without further comment he began to help prepare the room, pulling benches off tables to settle in the new rushes blanketing the floor. He threw open the shutters of the nearest window, pulled a tray of cups out from behind the counter, and looked around with an air of intended helpfulness.

"Thanks," said Hal. "It's heartening to see even the famous people lending a hand."

"How's the bairn?" asked Sander, remembering why Molly was not here.

Hal grinned. "Oh, she's perfect. Perfect. Almost as perfect as her mum. They're both asleep upstairs, I'd say go up and take a look, but if they wake up, Moll will never forgive me." He laughed. "Anyhow, it's been a good thing to have Joan around, so I'll take any other hand that's here, and thanks to you."

"Joan's not here today?"

"She had some other thing that needed doing. One of those barber lectures, I think. You're a fine stand-in, though," he said cheerfully.

Sander smiled as he began to stack the cups near the cask of ale. These ordinary actions felt exotic to him, as if he were playing at being a regular person. A secure roof, reliable work, an affectionate and dependent family . . . just how most men spent their lives, from emperors to serfs—to actors, even, but not his sort. The normality was unremarkable, and yet he had no idea how to obtain even a semblance of it. The shareholders of the Chamberlain's Men owned houses in their hometowns, but not even Will Shakespeare could afford property in London. So how would Sander Cooke ever expect to?

He pushed this thought away.

Also, Joan had told somebody else, but not him, that she was going to the Barber-Surgeons Hall. He didn't like that.

He put on what Joan called his Society Face, a feint of interest and enjoyment that he could maintain for hours even when miserable or exhausted. He wore this not only with Hal, but also with the scores of playgoers who streamed into the alehouse. For an hour he laughed and sang and danced and flirted.

At the end of the hour, the alehouse had sold double the usual take; at the end of the hour, scores of people had stories to tell their kinfolk about the afternoon they drank with a famed performer.

Sander was just an hour older.

"ENOUGH WINE AND chitchat," she said with a smile, taking the chased-gold goblet out of his hand and placing it on the ivory table beside two of the many beeswax candles lighting the room. "Let's undress. 'Tis late and I've awaited this all afternoon." She shifted on the velvet settle so that he could unlace her.

Sander had first met Lady Sarah Melcombe when he was hired to sing a hymn at her husband's funeral. Two years later, after seeing him play Rosalind, she'd summoned him to the small, ornate receiving room of Melcombe House, patterned paper on the walls, rose-scented rush mats, embroidered cushions everywhere, for drafts, comfort, decoration—and told him, matter-of-fact and friendly, that she would like him to fuck her now and then. Just so she'd be in practice when she found a decent second husband. She was barely older than he was, with a distractingly sumptuous softness to her face and figure. It was whispered that her much-older husband had died in bed from an excess of excitement while making love to her, and this was easy to believe; the rumor resulted in a score of bachelors and widowers lining up to court her. She had refused to marry again until she felt she must, for financial reasons Sander was unclear about.

At that first summons, back in June, she'd assured him she was not besotted with him, but she approved of how well, in his performance, he seemed to understand hearty women like herself. Then she'd climbed on top of him, and minutes later they were naked. Her body was softer and rounder than anyone else who'd wanted him; he liked the novelty. And he was relieved that she did not expect him to perform romantic affection, or anything else. It had been, and still was, the most uncomplicated pleasure in his life.

"Who's after you this week?" he asked, pulling at her laces. The bedchamber was roomy, scented with honey and lavender. He liked it here.

"A baron," she said. "Older even than my husband was, and childless. Very indulgent and pleasant fellow, and our circles overlap. But he would take me away from London—he claims the air is clearer up in Hereford."

"It is," said Sander. "We've toured there. Lovely cathedral, decent taverns."

"Dull, though, I imagine. I said no more chitchat. Kiss me."

"Where?" He pulled the gold-silk lace out of an eyelet and enjoyed the hint of nipple he'd just liberated.

"Everywhere, of course. Whatever you expose." Purring: "I'll return the favor."

He pulled the other end of the lace out of the opposite eyelet. "Do you happen to know Robert Devereux or his sister?"

She laughed. "For Heaven's sake, Sander, that's not wooing. Those conversations are for afterward. Unless you want to fuck one of them as well, and describe it to me while you take me."

"It's not like that," he said. "It can wait." Another eyelet empty, and he leaned down to run his tongue over the nipple. She sighed and lolled her head back, stretching the expanse of pale skin.

"That's better," she said, and reached for the buckle of his girdle. "Let's take this off."

There was a rapping on the heavy door.

Sarah frowned. "I told the servants not to interrupt us." Louder: "What's the emergency, Holman?"

"My lady." The voice from the other side of the door was apologetic and resigned. "There's a pair of messengers who will not leave until they give you their message face-to-face."

She closed her eyes and sighed with annoyance. "Who sent them?"

"Baron Stonehouse." She grimaced in the candlelight as Holman continued: "They have a lute, m'lady."

Sander and Sarah met eyes.

"Hereford?" Sander asked.

She nodded, then covered her face with one hand and pressed her head against his shoulder, her loosened hair cascading over both of them. She was shaking with suppressed laughter.

"Can we invite them in to play for us—"

She slapped his arm playfully and sat up, making a face. "Obviously not, scoundrel." A long sigh, and she was collected; raising her voice, she directed it back toward the door. "Holman, tell them I have retired for the evening."

"M'lady, they have anticipated that and say they have come to sing you to sleep. It's two women, my lady. They bear rose-scented candles and are to report back to their master how you receive them."

She sat up straighter, pursed her lips with more overt impatience now. Sander kissed her shoulder and said, "I'll go."

"There's no way out without your walking past them."

He nodded with his chin to a corner of the room. "Didn't you say there was a servants' stairwell up from the kitchen to this room?"

"No, just a hatch in the floor to hand things up and down from the kitchen. You'd be jumping down about six feet and landing in the larder."

"Not as nice as landing in your lap, but I'll survive it."

She pressed her hand against his upper thigh, and his entire body lurched toward her. "I want you to stay," she whispered, and pouted.

"He wants to marry and support you," Sander made himself say. "Don't jeopardize your future for one evening of pleasure."

"Come back tomorrow."

"You might be betrothed by then."

"Come anyhow. Swear you'll come."

"If there's a sack of flour in the larder to keep me from breaking my head open, you may rely on me to come here." He felt under her skirts and reached up as far as he could, which was stupid, for it only made him harder. "Here, I mean."

She clenched her thighs together to trap his hand, kissed him hard on the lips. "It will be all the sweeter for the delay," she whispered.

Holman coughed from the other side of the door.

"Ten minutes," she called out to him. "And please have Cook move a bag of flour—"

"My lady," said Holman, who had either heard or anticipated this detail, "Perhaps a cushion."

JOAN'S DREAM WERE plagued by thoughts of the newborn. She willed herself awake, shivering and sweating at once, then pushed the covers away and got up from her trundle, slipping past her parents' bedcurtains. Her wool compass cloak was on a peg by the door; she took it, and also the lantern and flint. Then she reached into an open box of household miscellany, and fished about with one hand until she found a small leather bag. Clutching bag and lantern, she went out and down the stairs to the street. The moon was new, and the street was very dark.

First she lit the lamp and hung it from a hook on the corbel. Then she settled herself on the bottom step, the cloak tight around her. From the bag, she drew out of a handful of small sticks, most tin, some lead, some bronze. They were twiglike, and all different lengths—two inches up to half a foot. These were the detritus of her father's work. As a child, she'd stashed them away before he could melt them down to use again.

She untied and opened the bag, drew out four sticks, and arranged them into a rectangle. This was how she and Sander had begun their favorite after-hours childhood game: each would in turn add one stick to a given figure so that slowly it transformed into something else: a diamond evolved into an eagle, a trapezoid became a wizard; a triangle would grow into a church. Doing it alone would be dull, but she hoped the ritual of it would soothe her.

She examined the rectangle. Then added four legs. A tail. A neck.

A shadow fell over the pieces, and Joan looked up startled. "Hey," said Sander, "You've skipped my turn."

She gasped. "What are you doing here?"

He shrugged. "I was returning from somewhere."

"And your route back from somewhere to Heminges's—across the river—happened to take you past my house?"

"I designed it to. I find it comforting to pass this place sometimes."

"I'd think it would be painful," Joan said gently. Sander's parents had gone to France just after he was born, in hopes of setting up a goldsmithing interest there; he'd lived with his grandparents on the floor above Joan's family until he began his apprenticeship. His grandparents had died soon after and his parents never returned.

He shrugged.

"Well." She patted the space beside her. "Come take your turn, then."

He sat, snugged up against her on the step. Considering the image, he added one line where a head should be. She added another, sloping it to give the creature a long, tapering face. He studied the figure again.

"Are you not cold?" Joan asked. She loosened the cloak and offered to share it with him. Sander did not take it, but he slipped one arm under the cloak, across her upper body, and squeezed her shoulder. There was something tender and dizzying about having only his arm under the wool with her. Whoever's bed he was coming from—it was surely someone's bed, this late—had but a fraction of the intimacy with him she did. She wondered why she suddenly felt the need to remind herself of that.

They sat there for a long moment in comfortable silence.

"Whose turn is it?" he asked.

"I've lost track," she said.

"I'm glad you were out here as I was walking by," he said. "It's my favorite thing about today. And it's been a good day."

She smiled. "It's also my favorite thing. Although my day was not good." She rested her head against his shoulder. He rested his chin on her head.

Neither of them spoke for several minutes.

"Well," said Sander. "I must to sleep. It's *Taming of the Shrew* tomorrow. But darling Jack, Master Bacon will summon us to Gray's Inn soon."

She sat up straighter, pleased.

He slipped his arm out of the cloak and, rising, kissed her on the cheek. "Sleep deep and wake rested, my friend, for the world needs you well. Every bit as much as I do."

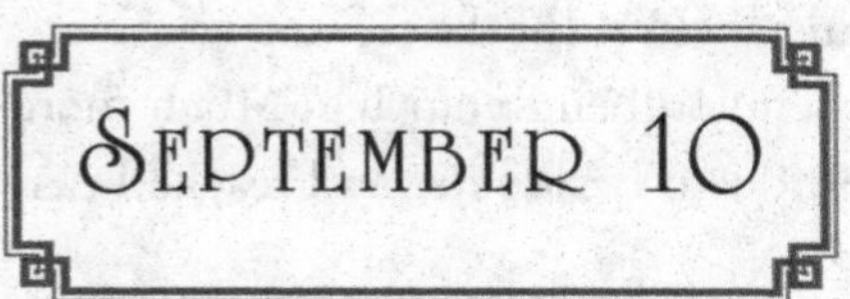

September 10

Disguising herself would never be quick, but these new clothes made it easier. Francis Bacon's tailor had been swift, and excellent. That he was outfitting a young woman to pass as a boy was obvious, but he never commented on it. She intuited he would not tell Bacon, although her jerkin boasted the Bacon badge. The largest mirror she'd ever seen rested against one wall of his shop, between windows that let in floods of light; when she tried on the finished work, she'd been fascinated watching the young man in the glass ape her movements perfectly. It was the first time she had actually seen herself dressed as a boy, and she was pleased how much she liked the fellow in the mirror—her long-lost twin, whose adventures she was eager to join.

Sander was waiting for her at the Blackfriars Stairs. He studied her, not bothering to hide his amusement, as she awkwardly disembarked the boat that had just brought her across the Thames. Even her own shadow distracted her as she shuffled up the broad stone steps.

"Just walk," he advised, grinning, when she was close enough. "Don't try to walk like you've got something between your legs."

"I *have* got something between my legs," she retorted. "All this fabric."

"Well, you're walking as if it were shoved up your arse, so stop that at least."

"How do I pass, otherwise?"

He smirked and clapped her on the shoulder. "Well enough, son. They'll not throw you out of Gray's Inn, anyhow. But a word of wisdom: tie off the garter just below the knee, not above it, so your stocking won't get baggy when you bend your leg. Much more flattering. I'll fix it for you." He knelt down beside her and reached casually for her lower thigh.

Her breath caught and her leg jerked away before he could touch her. "Flattering's of no urgency," she said, trying to ignore whatever that feeling had been.

Sander hadn't noticed. He stood. "Let's to it, then." He clapped his arm around her, pulling her alongside shoulder to shoulder, and gestured up the alley that led from the river. "It's not far from the Revels office."

"I barely know those outskirts of the city, past the Strand," she said.

"It's full of lawyers, but I'll protect you." He winked, squeezed her shoulder tighter. "It's not quite a mile," he said. "Don't fall into a puddle with your new boots."

They went up the slope from Blackfriars, passing workshops where scales were built, and abaci, and virginals. At the Holborn gate they headed away from the heart of the city, the road broadening and congestion easing, houses blossoming with signs of wealth: larger windows, sometimes of stained glass; higher gates with larger yards behind them. At the Holborn Bar, Sander nodded to the guard, and nudged Joan to turn right onto Grays Inn Road. Her eyes widened as the enormity of the compound rose up before them: a long brick wall appointed with white stone. There were windows, so it must be a building, but it went on for an arrowshot up the road. Across from it were open fields and more fine houses. But this hulking entity on their side of the street was intimidating and fascinated her. She'd seen Whitehall Palace across the river many times, and Westminster, but those were grand, tall, public buildings . . . this place, huddled to the northwest of the city, out of the center of anything, seemed to have been set down by some stern demigod as an irreligious cloister.

Sander was watching where her gaze went. "It's a little friendlier once we're inside, especially Coney Court, where his rooms are. He's organizing gardens and walks and such. Maybe you can help him plant some trees."

"I've lost my interest in trees," Joan said. She had not told him about the plums.

"*Branching* out then, are you?" He nudged her ribs.

"Aren't you clever. Stop, though. I'm nervous."

"Jack." Sander stopped, pivoted her by the shoulders to face him. "You are a handsome young man—not too handsome, no worries—"

"That's reassuring."

"You are smart and capable and he knows that, despite what happened at the Hawthorn. You're being summoned. He wants you here as much as you want to be here. All will be well."

She reached up to enfold his hands, resting on her shoulders, in her own. "Thank you," she said.

Sander's lips twitched with amusement, and hers with nerves. She looked away first, toward the entrance; he gripped her shoulders tighter, and when she returned her gaze to him, he'd sobered. His eyes ranged over her. He nodded, and released her. "Then here we go." He headed toward the gate, with the casual grace of someone used to being granted entry wherever he went.

THE REINTRODUCTIONS HAD been concluded, and the niceties and the apologies exchanged. They sat in Bacon's office, large windows letting in clouded light. The room was smaller than she'd expected but still handsomely furnished, everything made of carved and polished oak, or pale soft leather, or silk. Embroidered cushions pressed against windows to keep out drafts. Rush mats covered the floor. Diagrams hung on the paneled walls. Piled onto the desk, and stacked on shelves around the room, were composition books.

She and Sander sat on a bench across the desk from Francis Bacon, who was undistracted by his surroundings. Joan could not imagine ever growing used to such a room. She watched Sander's eyes glance about the place, with cool appreciation but nothing near her awe.

She saw a flash of almost childish adoration on Bacon's face when he first gazed at Sander. "Now then," he said, collecting himself. "As you will remember from our unfortunate evening at the Hawthorn, my current interest is with inductive logic."

"Yes, sir," said Joan, in her huskiest voice. "I would learn more of it, sir, for my understanding is limited and flawed."

"That is felicitous," said Bacon, "as I desire an untrained mind as whetstone, to sharpen my own thinking." His eyes turned toward the ceiling beams, and his tone shifted into eagerness. "I consider it urgent that such as yourself may better your lives with education of this sort under my tutelage, no matter what your formal schooling. You will learn by proximity to me, and I will learn by adjusting my approach, when your misconstruing shows me that my teaching is unclear."

"I . . . had not expected to be useful to you, sir."

Sander nudged her, pleased for her; she ignored him.

Bacon lowered his eyes to meet hers; even his smile had a fierce energy to it. "But how could you not? A good student is as useful to the teacher as the teacher to the student. Sadly, they do not think so at Cambridge and Oxford, where the students learn nothing but to believe what they're taught. But the true use of learning is to breed soundness of judgment, which requires the willingness to question. For all the hungry minds in this city, you are a rare find for my purposes." Joan, too thrilled to speak, ignored a second happy elbow-nudge from Sander. Bacon hurried on: "I have pressing obligations to Her Majesty's court. Today we've only time for a brief exercise to see how you grasp the fundamentals of induction. I do not require you to excel, this is simply for me to assess your current understanding."

"Whatever you ask, I will strive to fulfill."

"Excellent. Use my system, as you understand it, to demonstrate how the planets and the sun revolve around Earth."

Joan blinked in surprise. "Do they? I have of late been speaking to

Master Castellanos, do you know him? A maker of astronomical instruments, with his shop on the Strand? He says otherwise."

Bacon frowned. "Is he a mathematician?"

Joan brightened. "Indeed, he is an ardent student of the work of John Dee. Many a winter evening he has wasted, attempting to teach me formulas that I cannot begin to fathom. Hugh Platt is a friend of his, they often discuss mechanical devices."

Bacon closed his lips into an expression that was not quite a grimace, but not quite anything else. "How much tutelage have you received from him in mathematics? I may have to undo the damage."

Taken aback, Joan said, "Little enough. I have no aptitude for it. But you sound disapproving, sir; I'd have thought such things would be a worthy pursuit to you."

"That's true, lad, but 'tis no simple matter to separate the wheat from the chaff. We must cast aside *all* pre-existing beliefs about whatever we are contemplating. This extends to a reliance on all formulas, including mathematical. So please, exile from your mind what your mentor has said, and let us begin with an empty slate. Now: What are some simple observational data that suggest the sun, stars, and planets revolve around Earth? Answer me shortly."

Joan could sense Sander beside her trying not to squirm.

"Well," she began. "To begin, I suppose . . . the fact that we watch those objects move across the sky?"

Sander relaxed. That must have been his answer too. How irritating that he'd worried she wouldn't think to say something so obvious.

Bacon nodded. "Yes. We see them move with our own eyes. We see their consistent patterns. Each celestial body moves at its own rate, and on its own path. What?"

Joan had raised her hand. "Excuse my confusion, sir, but . . . is it not mathematical formulas that express those courses? Is it not calculations that allow astronomers to predict eclipses and meteor showers?"

"Insightful questions. Yes, but the formulas involved are grounded in empirical evidence we see with our own eyes. Anything else?"

Joan chewed her lower lip and nodded. She felt Sander shift again beside her and saw him curl his hand closed, signing *Stop*. She barely resisted the urge to slap his arm.

Bacon made a welcoming gesture, shifting in his chair with an impatient air. "Don't be shy, but speak quickly."

"Thank you, sir. Is it not possible that, however much we trust our eyes, we have a limited point of view about what is moving where, in the cosmos? Rather as, when you're on a slow-moving boat in the Thames and alongside you is a stationary boat, it can appear that you're staying still and the other boat is moving. So, what if trusting our eyes is not enough? I believe that's why Master Castellanos says we must use mathematics."

Bacon presented a relaxed open hand toward her as he spoke, as if he meant to offer her new wisdom. "That is an excellent illustration, Jack. Let us look deeper at it. After you've made the error about which boat is moving and which is stationary, how do you eventually learn that you're mistaken?"

"You . . . look around more?"

"Exactly," said Bacon. "You gather more information. You observe over time that you're moving relative to the shore, as well as to the other boat. Yes?"

Joan nodded.

"In other words, your continued observations eventually reveal the truth of your situation. You do not need abstract mathematical formulas to establish whether you are the one in movement. Do you agree?"

"Yes," said Joan.

Bacon smiled fleetingly. "So we are in accord. And although I disagree with the notion of heliocentrism, I like that you are thinking about these things and exposing yourself to different ideas. But the purpose of this brief exercise was not to examine the minutiae of astronomy, so we shall not spend our brief time today on that. I asked about astronomy solely as an exercise in inductive reasoning. That is to say, many discrete observations leading toward a general theory. Do you see how an accretion of individual observations suggest that heavenly bodies revolve around Earth?"

She could almost hear Sander willing her to agree with Bacon.

"I see how they appear to revolve around Earth," she said. "Yes, I do. But just as we don't immediately know which boat in the Thames is moving and which is still . . . is it not possible that mankind has not yet made observations enough, to know with certainty which heavenly body is the center of the universe? Should we not converse with those who have a different perception, to see if either side might benefit from the other's observations?"

"We are talking at cross-purposes, lad. Of course astronomers should compare notes. But today I am only trying to assess your ability to adhere to the logical principles of inductive reasoning."

Joan lowered her eyes and tried to stay calm. Sander was rigid beside her. "I thought I was doing that," she said, "by suggesting that more observations might be called for."

"I'm sure you don't mean to imply that Master Bacon has insufficiently studied the matter," Sander said, sounding nervous. "Most of this is going over my head, but it—"

Bacon softened. "All's well, Sander. Jack, lad, you're correct that further study is always good, and I applaud your suggestion of sharing research. I see you striving to emulate my protocol. It is difficult to do that well, and as you lack the training for it, your efforts are especially notable. I do not fault you for going astray here."

Joan pursed her lips to steady herself. "I do not understand how I'm going astray by suggesting—"

Bacon held up a warning finger. "My boy," he said. "Our time is, and will always be, limited. Your focus here has shifted from the premise of inductive reasoning to the mechanics of astronomy. It is pleasing to me, on principle, that you would continue to poke at the subject. But astronomy unto itself is not what I wish us to poke at."

"I apologize if I have been presumptuous."

Bacon smiled. His fingers pressed against the desktop, as if it could absorb his edgy energy. "Apologies are not required. Unworthy distractions are an inevitable part of study. I too have stumbled and erred, many times. It is a sign of an avid pupil."

She wanted him to keep teaching her, so she said only. "Thank you, sir. I am grateful to hear that."

"This has been satisfying," said Bacon, standing up from his desk. "You have a grasp of inductive principles, and that's what I wished to assess today."

"Thank you, Master Bacon," she said.

"I'll send for you again within the month, I hope much sooner. My intention for our next session is to give you a subject to discuss. Something practical, perhaps to do with agriculture or horology, or some such."

"Jack has studied with many kinds of natural philosophers," said Sander, like a proud parent. "Botanists and apothecaries and geographers and physicians and surgeons."

Bacon looked surprised.

"That's not right, sir, I know no physicians," she said hurriedly. "I sneak into the Barber-Surgeons Hall to watch the lectures, and can follow what they're talking about, that's all."

Sander gestured toward her while giving Bacon an expression that seemed to say, *Isn't Jack clever?*

Bacon looked intrigued. "My theory desires practical applications, so this is most welcome news. I will consider all fields you might know something of, and at our next meeting, you will examine some aspect of what you've studied, using inductive logic. I will point out to you whatever flaws I find in your approach, and take notes on how you correct yourself. How does that sound?"

"Terrifying," Joan said.

Bacon grinned. The expression, on his face, was disorienting. "He's honest, anyhow," he said approvingly to Sander.

"Not always," said Sander in a conspiratorial tone.

"Lad, terror is uncalled for. I will never judge you for what you do not know or grasp. We are both servants to the cause of making my ideas serviceable to anyone, regardless of their schooling. Even mistakes are useful pavers along the path."

"Thank you, sir," said Joan.

"His other practical interests are scientific instruments, mapmaking, herbalism, botany, horology, alchemy—"

"Thank you, Sander," said Joan quickly, before he could add midwifery. "I am gratified that you have noted my amateur inclinations."

She felt Bacon staring at her; she glanced at him to see his eyes were moving between her face and Sander. "You're fortunate to have a friend who so believes in you," he said. "May you keep faith with each other better than I have with some of my erstwhile confederates. That is all for now. Sander, as always, it is a delight to see you. I must have you to supper again soon."

"The company leaves this week for a tour, but upon our return it would, as always, be my honor, Master Bacon," said Sander. He stood. Joan stood. "Let's go, Jack." He bowed, and nudged his knee behind Joan's to make her copy him.

Joan managed to string together several sentences of obsequious gratitude for Bacon, and then followed Sander out of the room.

THEY DIDN'T SPEAK but hustled toward the river in failed hopes of avoiding heavy foot traffic. The queue of people waiting to hail boats across the Thames was already halfway up the slope, ending near the door of the Rowers Tavern. Tradesmen, merchants, luthiers, fishwives, apprentices in apparel identical to Sander's, bakers and laborers covered in brick-dust or paint, a line of humanity murmuring in sundry accents and languages, heading home to Southwark.

The two of them turned into the shaded alley that edged the Rowers and, out of habit, both pivoted so Sander's back was to the street as they faced each other. If he paused in easy view for more than a moment, he would be recognized.

"Let's just walk," Joan said, gesturing downriver to the bridge, blazing in the slanting light. She tried not to sound aggravated.

Sander leaned against the damp alley wall. He stared at her. The alley was full of dozing cats.

"What?" Joan said at last. "He's wrong about the sun circling the earth."

"Joan," said Sander patiently. "Of course he's not wrong. He's Francis Bacon."

"And he's wrong." Their voices reverberated in the narrow stone enclosure. She pursed her lips together and spoke more softly. "I warrant he is a man of genius, of intelligence surpassing anything I can approach. And yet, Francis Bacon's faith in Francis Bacon is the pre-existing belief that keeps him from unbiased thinking. I wish I might point that out to him."

"I don't recommend it. Anyhow, as he said, it doesn't matter, does it? Astronomy. And he's giving you another chance, so all's well."

She scowled. "You're just indulging me, as if I were a willful youngling. As if philosophy had no more merit than what you do in your leisure time. Do you even think I'm clever?"

"Zounds, you're peevish suddenly," Sander said, and straightened, stepping away from the wall. "You know I'm in awe of your mental capacities. You're the most intelligent person I know. With one exception. Who was it? Oh yes: Francis Bacon." He patted her cap; she swatted his hand away in annoyance, but he grabbed her wrist mid-swat and slapped her hand at his own face. "Ouch! Joan! Stop smacking me!"

Joan laughed, a little, despite herself, and Sander released her.

"I regret my peevishness," she said.

"And also regret demeaning my hobbies?"

"Never that," she said archly. "Bedding half of London is a trivial way to spend your precious hours."

"What should I do with my precious hours instead?" he asked. "I fain would spend them in the company of my dearest friend, but alas, all she ever wants to do is learn things."

"I spend less time pursuing knowledge than you spend pursuing bedmates."

"Not true, Joan."

"If I'm wrong, it's merely word-play: you don't have to pursue them because they pursue you."

"So that's why you're peevish," he said. "I'm wasting my life and you disapprove." His crystal-bright eyes bore into hers as if he could read her mind; flustered, she had to look away.

"If you say so."

"Well then," said Sander. "A proposition: I'll spend less time on my dalliances if you'll spend less time on your studies. And then, as when we were young, our spare time may be always together. What say you?"

She felt a swelling warmth under her sternum as she considered this. "I do miss those twilight ramblings," she allowed.

He extended his hand. "So: a pact?"

"No." She crossed her arms. "You're asking me to give up bettering myself, while all you're giving up is lechery."

He crossed his arms in imitation of her. "I amend the proposition, then," he said. "Continue your studies and I'll attend you. Not just at Bacon's—anywhere you wish." He swept his cap off, whirled it in a spiral and returned it to his head. "I shall be your devoted *aide d'études*. What say you?" He tugged at her hand and, freeing it from her crossed arms, held it in both of his.

His smile made Joan feel buoyant. Unnerved by the acuteness of her pleasure, she tried to blunt it. "And how must I reciprocate, to be worthy of your selfless gesture? Come along on your trysts?" she asked ironically.

Sander released her as if she'd stung him. "Lord, no," he said. "None of them is worthy of you. Or even worthy of me, when I'm in your company."

She narrowed her eyes. "So you'll just give up all those pretty lips?"

He studied her a moment, his face unreadable. Then took a breath, as if steadying himself for something unpleasant.

"That's no loss," he said. "Your lips are prettier than anyone's."

She felt herself pink.

"You know that," he continued. "I've told you often enough before."

"In jest."

"No."

"I always laughed."

"You did."

A pause, and then, deliberate and slow, she said it: ". . . this time, I didn't laugh."

"Yes, I noticed that," he said. His gaze shifted to the alleyway.

A strange silence settled between them. They were accustomed to comfortable silences. This was different.

Now what? Joan wondered. If she could twist the moment into a jest, everything would be easy again.

She couldn't think of anything. The season for jests had run its course.

Lowering her gaze from his face, pretending to study all the cats, she tried: "So are you saying that since you're giving up all those, y'know, lips, and mine are nicer anyhow, are you planning to go without lips at all, or do, do you, do you need— for God's sake interrupt me, Sander."

She looked up to discover that he too was pretending to study the cats. "I don't know what to say, Joan." His discomfort matched her own. She did not have many friends her age, but enough to have heard stories and to therefore know how badly this was going.

A sudden insight: "You've never kissed anyone unless they asked you to, or unless they kissed you first."

His determination to keep staring at the cats was impressive. "A point to Joan."

"So you won't kiss me unless I ask you to?"

His fair skin had flushed a riotous pink. "Ha, sounds ridiculous when you—"

"Because it is ridiculous," she said, without malice. "I'm not going to *ask* you, as if it were a *favor*."

"Joan—" He looked pained, and she felt sorry for him.

"I'm not going to ask you," she repeated. "I'd just outright kiss you, I suppose, only I lack your knowledge of how best to do it." Her face was so hot she thought she must be purple.

He was staring down at her. His blush subsided; he went pale.

"I've thought about this," he confessed. "Recently. But it would change the world."

"The world *is* changing," she said. "I'll kiss someone, some day.

When I do, it will change things between us. If it's you I kiss, that bonds us. If it's anyone else, it sunders us. We should consider that."

"That's my Joan, forever sensible."

"Am I wrong?"

"If you were wrong, I'd be teasing you right now, instead of feeling mildly tortured."

Both of them were still a moment longer.

"I can't stand this," Joan announced. "Just do it and get it over with, or I'll have to do it, and we both know I won't do it right."

Sander rested his palms on her cheeks, his fingertips brushing her temples. "Are . . . are we really going to, then?" It was a nervous rhetorical question, sardonic in tone, as if the answer should clearly be no.

"If we don't, then we'll each constantly wonder what's going on in the other's head. That'll ruin our friendship, so we might as well try it and hope that it takes."

He frowned. "And if it doesn't . . . take?"

"Then we'll pray the attempt has not ruined the friendship."

Sander looked warier than she'd ever seen him. "So the friendship's at risk whether we do it or not—"

"Yes," she said, growing exasperated. "So we damn well might as well try it, at least."

He stared at her a moment, hesitant and distressed. Then he brought his face down to meet hers and pressed his mouth against hers.

She was instantly so light-headed she almost fainted. She kissed him back, pressed soft flesh against soft flesh, and moaned. The moan worked on him fast: his arms wrapped hard around her, his body pushed against hers, and one leg moved behind her to lock her into his embrace as he leaned her back against the wall. As she tipped, she grabbed his shoulders, grazed her mouth across his, closed her lips over his lower lip, and ran her tongue along it. His tongue met hers.

Joan pulled her head back a little and smiled at him. "Listen to us," she whispered. "Listen to us groaning. Is that normal? Does it always happen?"

"Please muffle your brain for just this one moment," Sander begged.

"Just kiss me now and pick it apart later. Will you do that?"

"I feel odd all over and I'm dizzy, is there someplace to lie down?"

"This is too fast," said Sander, and took a small step back, loosening his grasp of her.

Joan met his gaze. "How long does it usually take you to end up prone?"

Sander brought his hands to his forehead and pressed his thumbs against his temples. "Zounds, I . . . I am at sea."

"You'll be in the Clink is where you'll be, if anybody sees you," said a gruff voice from farther down the alley. Startled, they pulled away from each other and looked. The tavern owner had come out a side door with a small bucket of something greasy; the cats all leaped up and trotted toward him, mewing. "I won't tattle on ye, but I can't have sodomites loitering. The constable will hold me accountable, and I'm not from here so he's already hard on me." Sander lowered his head and turned away to avoid being recognized. The fellow was hardly looking, anyhow. "Sorry, lads. If you can get yourself to Deptford I hear there's a place there has refuge for your kind."

". . . Thank you, sir," said Joan.

Keeping his face away from the stranger, Sander took Joan by the elbow and started toward the street.

"That's the best proof yet my disguise works!" she said with quiet delight.

"Let's take the bridge," he said, sounding so irritable she felt a shiver of unease.

"Sander—"

He stopped just before the alley opened to the street with its snarl of waiting commuters. Leaning over her he said into her ear, "That was stupid." Joan tensed and looked down, sick with disappointment. "I mean because of how you're dressed, that's all." He squeezed her elbow. "Not any of the rest of it, how can you even wonder? But we must find a way to . . . I mean, there has to be . . . I don't know where to . . ."

An irrational fury flooded her limbs, and then evaporated, leaving bitterness. "How disappointing of me, not to have a private bedchamber to offer you," she said.

"It's not disappointing," said Sander. "But I've never, I mean I've never had to . . . We need privacy. Once we have it, then we can figure out what we want to do with it."

"We know what we want to do with it, Sander."

He was flustered. "I will find privacy. For us. Somehow." Pause. "Remember we used to hide out in your parents' henhouse—"

"*No*," Joan snapped. And then she laughed noisily enough for people waiting in the boat queue to glance over. Sander pivoted toward the tavern wall to avoid being recognized. "Can you imagine," Joan said, her words hiccupped with laughter. "Sander Cooke, cavorter in the finest beds of London, kisses the Buckler girl in her parents' chicken coop. Lord, how the balladeers would croon."

"I would be thrilled to kiss you anywhere," he whispered.

"I don't want to kiss you in the chicken coop," she said, shaking with nerves and giddiness. "For God's sake, this is not a—"

"We have to move," he said, turning and taking her by the elbow. "No time to let eyes linger." He lowered his head and plunged through the queue, nodding in respectful apology to two wigged men in black robes as he pulled Joan between them. She followed without protest, hurrying with him toward Thames Street. "I will find us someplace," he said. "I promise."

"Not the henhouse."

"Not the henhouse. But there's no privacy under your parents' roof nor at Heminges's, with all their children under foot."

"Does this mean," Joan asked they hustled along, "that your romantic life rests on your being so lazy and pampered that you've never noticed how lazy and pampered you were?"

He stopped so abruptly she lurched past him, and he took the chance to bring his mouth to her ear. "Not anymore," he whispered.

"I like that answer," she said.

"Also," he said, beaming down at her in the dusk. "I know where we can go."

September 11

Even for first thing in the morning, Sander could not remember ever feeling so bumbling and tongue-tied. He had to time this request well. He had to ask at home, in private, when Rebecca Heminges and the children were distracted. Or perhaps on the walk to the Playhouse? No, once they arrived, there would be no chance at all. Best to ask at home. Morning? Night? Wait until the right day?

Then he remembered, with piercing displeasure, that the Chamberlain's Men were leaving the city next morning on tour. If he didn't ask Heminges now, he'd be in this state for a fortnight.

"You're deep in thought there, Sander," said Heminges. Sander had been staring into the embers of the coal fire. "And I'll wager it's not contemplation of all the mundane things that bother me."

"Ashes, Sam," said his wife to their oldest son, brushing by them to the front of the house. Ten-year-old Samuel, in half-laced vest, had been reading words aloud to his youngest sister, Kate. He kissed the top of her head and handed her the slate, then went out the back for the ash bin. "You all right, Sander?" Rebecca Heminges asked as she bustled back in the other direction. She set down the baby, John, beside eight-year-old Alice, and reached to stop two-year-old William, who had taken off his nappies and was proudly pissing into the cooking fire. Alice carried John to Thomasina, who was trying to read the Lord's Prayer, and began to help her, in a loud voice, with the words. Thomasina protested in a louder voice that she needed no help.

There could never be privacy in this house, not with six children underfoot, and Rebecca about to burst with a seventh.

"Sir," he began, implausibly awkward. "Master Heminges—"

Heminges laughed. "It's John, lad. Or it will be soon enough, so you might as well practice saying it."

"I've an unusual favor to ask." He stopped, appalled he could not remember the speech he'd written in his mind and memorized during a restless night.

"I'm listening," said Heminges with an avuncular smile.

"It is . . . unorthodox. Before I ask the favor, I beg you to promise me that if you find it an overstep, that you will deny it, without telling any of the other shareholders. I would not have my presumptuousness trumpeted about."

Heminges shrugged agreeably. "You're a good lad, I can't imagine you asking anything I would need to decline."

Sander began to speak, stopped himself, took a breath, let it out. "This." Another breath. "This is not an ordinary." And he ran out of breath to speak. His cheeks were hot. Rebecca Heminges had disappeared into the back room, carrying a clean linen cloth and the fire-dampening William, who was hooting with laughter while shrieking in protest.

"Take your time," said Heminges.

"It has to do with. Joan," he said. The muscles of his mouth were not cooperating with his will.

"I'm fond of Joan," said Heminges.

"So am I," said Sander. His face was so hot. "And she is fond of me and." His eyes were darting about stupidly. His hands, of their own accord, began to gesture haphazardly in front of him, indicating nothing. "And our affection for each other is. Changing."

Heminges face beamed. "I am delighted to hear that, lad. And not at all surprised."

"There is a difficulty. And I had a strange notion of." He had to take a deep breath. "Of a possible solution to the difficulty."

Heminges stared at him a moment, with sudden displeasure. "It's as I feared," he said. "You've been offered everything you want for so long now, you have no idea how to ask for something that you don't already know you'll get." He leaned back on his stool, against the wall near the fire. "Go ahead. Ask."

"It is desirable to have some private time. With her. There is no place. Except I thought perhaps." He glanced at the older man. "I hope this does not seem disrespectful."

"Oh, for the love of God," muttered Heminges. He huffed and got up from the stool, crossing to the wooden cabinet across the room. He opened the smallest drawer on the top and pulled out a large key. "Yes," he said. "After hours. It's all yours. Just stay out of the lords' gallery above the stage. Of course," he said, and tossed the key back into the drawer, "it'll have to wait until we're back from tour."

"How did you know what I would ask?" Sander said in amazement.

"Sander," said Heminges with affectionate exasperation. "I've been expecting this for months." Sander's face went slack. "We all have."

". . . Who is we all?"

"All of us."

"In . . . this house?"

Heminges guffawed. "In the Chamberlain's Men, lad. And yes, Rebecca, of course."

Sander brought his hands to his temples. "What?" He breathed.

"Dick Burbage wagered half a pound that it would take you 'til October to ask me for the key. That's a week away yet, so I've won the bet." He winked. "I'll split my winnings with you, since I've you to thank for it."

"You are not serious."

"Plenty of side bets as well. You always sit outside, so it's easy to have these conversations. Shakespeare thought you'd be at it by now, so he's lost out to Armin."

"Joan must never know this," Sander said. It was the first statement he'd managed without stammering.

Heminges nodded. "Of course not." He grinned. "And since you've three shillings coming to you, buy her something along the way." He turned to the back room. "Rebecca! Sander asked me for the key."

"At last!" came his wife's cheery voice through the curtain. "I'll be right out with his linens."

"What?" said Sander, stupefied.

"No rush, love, remember we leave tomorrow dawn." To Sander: "She wanted you comfortable so she's collected some bedding to take along. And she's already sent our old straw bed, it's rolled up under the props table." He grinned. "It's been there for a least a fortnight. Everyone knows why it's there. They all glance at it each morning to see if it's been used."

"I was not expecting this conversation," said Sander in a strained voice. "I. I. I don't know what to say."

"I've rendered Sander Cook speechless," Heminges hooted. "*And* earned half a pound. Not a bad start to the morning, and I haven't even had my breakfast yet."

September 23

Joan's father declared it was the season for peddling his finer wares throughout the finer neighborhoods of London. She was grateful for this extra labor; it distracted her from Sander's absence and the Globe's shuttered silence while the Chamberlain's Men were touring. And her errands took her near to shops and mentors she cherished: Master Castellanos on the Strand, Flemish instrument makers at Blackfriars, the luthiers of St. Dunstan, the archery suppliers near St. Paul's.

She had not called on her botany mentors, Master Cole and Master Morgan, since the uncomfortable visit with the aphrodisiacs, and she was quietly grateful not to have the leisure to call upon them now. She wondered in passing what happened to the Greek gentleman, Cristóforos Pantazis.

Because it was near home, Joan had found time to stop at Eleanor's apothecary every day, without being sure why she felt drawn to do so. Even though she had no time to visit properly, she would enter the small shop, not four paces wide, breathe in the textured scents of the herbs and poultices and oils, run her eyes over the inventory in clay jars and wooden canisters on the many shelves, wish Eleanor a good day, and scurry out.

On the eighth consecutive day of this ritual, she heard Eleanor call Dorothy into the shop before Joan could duck back out again. Joan pretended not to notice, deliberately busying herself in comparing the aromas of different batches of dried chamomile in their urns. She could hear the older women muttering together but did not catch specific words—until they were quite distinct, almost certainly on purpose.

"I agree there's something to it, but she's not with child," Dorothy said, and then added, with loud approval ". . . *yet*."

Joan snorted and turned in their direction. Her face was hot. The two women studied her, then exchanged glances. "Tansy, then," said Eleanor. "Worm fern, artemisia, rue, thyme. Although I'm short of worm fern, like usual."

"Pepper?" suggested Dorothy.

Eleanor made a face. "That's a barbarous concoction from centuries ago. Wild carrot, though. Except we've none of that either, I fear."

"Do you think I don't recognize that recipe?" Joan demanded.

"Do you think we don't know you came in here wanting it?" Dorothy shot back, eyes mirthful. "Only it's taken you a week, and you still haven't come out and asked."

Joan said nothing. She could feel how red her face was.

"I do hope it's that pretty boy," said Eleanor, as if continuing a breezy bit of gossip.

"We'd have heard about it, were it someone else," said Dorothy. "Joan, dear heart, tell him to consider sheep's intestines from the butcher—"

"I'm sure I'd be the first to put that expectation on him," Joan said.

"So?" asked Dorothy, with a cheerful leer. "It'll be a night of firsts."

"Y'know, though, Dorie," said Eleanor, "young men in the throes of passion—I would not trust them, especially if they've no practice with prophylactics. Safer for her to take care of things herself."

Dorothy sighed. "That's accurate. Wretchedly unfair though."

"What's fair about any element of men and women mating?" asked Eleanor, with bored disdain.

Dorothy slapped her elbow. "Don't say that in front of her," she said. With a glance at Joan: "You'll be fine, dear heart, just tell him to be gentle."

"Tell him that if he isn't, he'll have us to answer to," Eleanor added. She stepped behind the counter, and shooed Joan back into the shoppers' area. "I'll make up your infusion."

"Nothing's happened yet," said Joan.

"But first I need sage, mugwort, and chamomile, love," Dorothy told Eleanor, as if Joan hadn't protested.

"All the chamomile's on the counter," said Joan. "Is it for a fumigation? The jar on the right has the driest herbs."

"Thank you, dear heart," said Dorothy, reaching for it. "I've never met a laywoman who knows so much about floating wombs." She blew Joan a kiss and went back through to her workroom.

FOR SANDER, THE tour was torturous. Adulation was so ordinary; what was waiting back in London was novel, and the only vital thing. As the days cooled and shortened, he received invitations from last tour's dalliances; he wanted nobody but Joan and yet was desperate to distract himself. So there was debauchery most nights. Several bored married women whose husbands were in London. A retired madam in Southampton; a wealthy merchant couple in Exeter; a pretty widow; a goldsmith with strong and agile hands.

He decreed these encounters nothing more than pleasurable exercises for his health, and was able to believe this until he returned to London.

He'd requested to ride pillion behind the messenger who would arrive a day early. After some playful abuse from Richard Burbage, and no little teasing from the company in full about his reasons, he was allowed to go. The ride was rough and dusty—it had been a dry fortnight—but finally he was deposited beside the Globe, where he doused his face clean with the last bit of water in his leather flask. He dried it roughly on his canvas sleeve and looked up, blinking, to see Joan.

He saw her from a distance; she did not see him. She was walking into the Happy Sow, no doubt to help. The slope of her shoulders, the way her woolen skirt swung as she walked, the arc of her hand as she waved when entering the alehouse—these were so beautiful, at once so pure and yet provocative. Immediately, he walked around the corner to be sick into the mud, appalled at what he'd done during his nights away.

He couldn't bring himself to go in and greet her.

INSTEAD, RETREATING BACK to Heminges's, he made ink from ash and vinegar, sharpened a quill, and sent word to Bacon: he was back but might soon go on tour again, and he hoped the great man might have a moment of time in which to tutor Jack. Bacon sent a response by his servant Pierre before sundown. The one hour he had free this week, as it turned out, was tomorrow afternoon. *Come at three*, he wrote.

We will, Sander wrote back. Then he sent the messenger with a note to Joan, asking her to meet him at the Blackfriars steps the next day at half-two.

He barely slept that night.

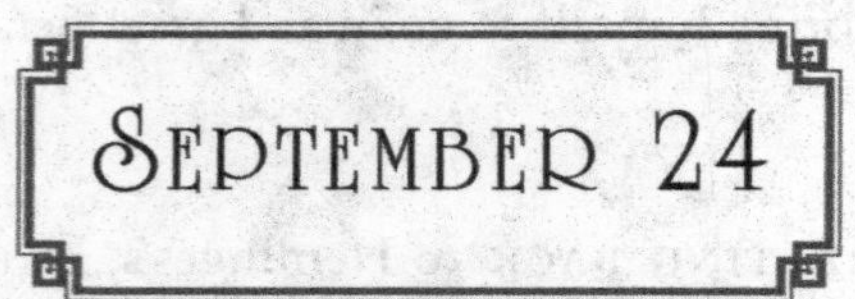

September 24

He had spent all morning fidgeting around the house, trying to help Rebecca Heminges with the children. But he was too distracted to be good for much, imagining how he would kiss Joan at their reunion on the Blackfriars steps. The thought of it thrilled and terrified him, as he had not been thrilled and terrified in years.

The wherry appeared out of the river fog. Joan headed up the steps toward him. Dressed in her boy's togs. He knew they couldn't risk it; there could be no kiss.

She stopped an arm's length from him, her body quivering with nervous anticipation. "Well," she said.

"Well," he said.

"I'm sure you had a good old time on tour."

"I missed you," he blurted. "I thought about you all the time."

She tried to hide her pleased relief, but her cheeks reddened. "Good," she said. "So it wasn't me imagining things."

"God, no, Joan," he said.

She looked at him. "Well, good," she said.

They stood there, achingly close, for heartbeats.

"I suppose we can embrace anyhow, brother mine," Joan declared, and threw herself at him.

"Careful!" he said, bending forward to prevent her pressing herself against his groin. The grip of her arms felt wonderful.

"I'm so glad you're back," she whispered. They stood squeezing each other, Sander's face buried in her cap to avoid being recognized.

THE BOY WHO had escorted them to Bacon's study said an emergency had arisen but that Master Bacon was content to trust them in his study until he could return.

They sat as they had the first time, on the bench across from Bacon's chair. The air between them felt charged, and Joan had to sit on her hands to prevent herself from touching Sander.

"Have you obligations once we're done here, or may I claim your time?" he asked.

"I've waited weeks for you to claim all of me," she said.

He was trembling. She was making Sander tremble. That seemed impossible. Oh—she was trembling too. "I've a place to take you," he said. "A comfortable place."

Her gaze turned toward him without her permission and she smiled shyly. "Where?"

"A place you know well, yet do not know at all." He looked pleased with himself.

Joan thought a moment, then guessed, "Backstage at the Playhouse?"

Sander deflated. "How did you guess that in less time than it took me to think of it?"

"I had the benefit of your giving me an excellent hint. You had to think of it all on your own."

"I want to kiss you desp—"

Francis Bacon, the sleeves of his black robe swinging, rushed into the room and went to his chair without a glance at them. The boy who'd shown them in was tailing him and accepted Bacon's hastily removed hat. With a denuded quill pen and a look of ferocious concentration, the great man scratched out a note on a scrap of vellum, using ink from the finest glass inkwell Joan had ever seen. He shook coarse powder over the document, waited a moment, then blew on it with staccato efficiency, folded it, sealed it, and handed it to the boy. "Tell his lordship I await his response."

The boy nodded, bowed, and was gone.

Bacon closed his eyes, took a deep breath, held it, and then let it out. Then opened his eyes so abruptly that Joan nearly jumped.

"I appreciate your patience," he said, directing this to Sander. "It has been a trying day."

Sander gave him an indulgent look. "If I may somehow lighten the load—"

Bacon smiled briefly, a look of both poignancy and irony. "Some noblemen are impervious even to your charms, Alexander."

"Ah. What's he done now?" asked Sander in a conspiratorial voice.

Bacon glared at him, glanced at Joan, and returned to glaring at Sander.

"You needn't worry, sir, I've no idea of whom you speak," Joan said.

"That's true," said Sander, shaking his head, as if this were a pity. "Jack has such a weak head for courtly matters, I worry he forgets who the queen is."

"I'm not *that* ignorant," Joan objected.

"He's not that ignorant," Sander allowed with a wink, then sobered. "But, sir, I believe I know of whom you speak. His sister called me to perform for them both the other week. They like me well enough."

"Caution," Bacon said, in a low voice. "I know you're clever, Alexander, but that's playing with fire." He took out a kerchief from the purse at his waist and dabbed at his temple with it. A faint floral aroma wafted across the desk. Iris, Joan thought. Very costly.

"What I mean is, they trust me," said Sander.

"They trust no one."

"They trust me," Sander repeated. Bacon gave him a look of worried intrigue. "If you are engaged in business regarding them, consider me your servant. I know you have the best interests of Her Majesty and the realm at heart, and I would be honored to assist your aims."

Bacon considered him through narrowed eyes. "He's just written to Her Majesty again."

"Imploring her to pity him," Sander said, with a confiding smile. "And renew his license on imported wines."

Bacon stared at him. Joan wished she knew enough to understand what this discussion was about. Finally, Bacon nodded. "Yes. She would have done that already if she had any intention of doing it at all. Now, even if she had been considering it, she must refuse him, or it will seem as if he may get whatever he wants by imploring her, and she cannot allow that. So she must refuse him *because* he implored her. I couldn't make him grasp that. How can a man so astute at chess be so inept at strategy in real life?"

"Sir John Stanhope convinced him to implore again, sir."

Bacon blinked. "How came you to know that?"

"As I said, they trust me. If you think of steps you'd like to take, I will assist you."

Bacon pursed his lips. He shook his head, as if shaking away an insect. "Time grows short, and this is not why we've met." He sat up straighter and looked at Joan. "Good afternoon, young man."

"God ye good den, Master Bacon, sir. Thank you for giving me another opportunity. Your patience with me—"

"None of that, lad. You have potential and I am pleased by your earnestness. So." He sat back in his chair. "You shall educate me on a subject, either using inductive reasoning to explain how we can know it's true, or else how we might use inductive reasoning to test its verity. Do you understand the exercise?"

Suddenly Joan was terrified. She would fail at this. He would scoff at her and lose interest, and then Sander would also scoff, to stay in Bacon's good graces, so that Bacon would continue to seek patrons for him. They shared entire worlds she had no entry to, and never would: cabals and social circles Sander was welcomed into because he was the celebrated boy-actor, because he ravished and was ravished by those who granted entry to those circles, because he was ambitious to maintain his elevated status. A month ago she'd have been nervous only for losing the opportunity to study with Francis Bacon but now she feared losing Sander.

"I understand," she said, hoping she sounded calmer than she felt.

The small side door opened and Bacon's man, Pierre, came in with firewood. He placed it log by log into a lidless wooden chest. Bacon took no notice of him.

"The subject is the healing arts. I know something of it, but I would learn more, especially given my own physic is not as hearty as I would like. Educate me." He offered a small reassuring smile. "Choose some medical cure you have witnessed or heard about, and describe to me why it works, or why it is believed to work. Can you do that?"

"Of course, sir," she said, because one must always say yes if Francis Bacon asks about one's capabilities. "I will speak of . . ."

Her mind went blank.

She could not remember anything she'd ever studied. All she could consider was how he would receive her. She could not remember what the inside of the Barber-Surgeons Hall looked like or even where it was; when she turned her inner eye that way all she saw was Bacon's look of anticipation. She could not remember the name of the two older gentlemen on Lime Street who had invited her to create a tree by grafting. She couldn't remember what kind of tree and could barely remember what grafting was. She couldn't remember the name of the mapmaker, or the astronomer, or the couple who made botanical drawings, or anything they'd ever taught her. There was nothing in her universe but Francis Bacon's judgment of her. "Medical," she said to herself. "Medical. Physical health."

Bacon gave her a curious look. "Is there a problem?"

Eleanor and Dorothy. Those names, she could remember. And even so, she could remember nothing other than her most recent visit.

"I have it," she said. "There is a common treatment for problems of the—" She almost groaned at the poor choice of topic, but she truly could not recall anything else. So she soldiered clumsily on. "Problems of female anatomy." Bacon blinked in startlement and his brows pinched together. She pretended not to notice. "The treatment is called fumigation, and it consists of burning a variety of herbs, some near the mouth and some near a woman's, er, nether—"

Bacon sat up in his chair and shifted. "Jack," he said. His eyes flicked to Pierre, still fussily arranging logs. "That is an imprudent subject, more apt for Hugh Platt's housewifely—"

"Master Bacon," Sander interrupted. "If I may argue to the contrary?" He offered Bacon the smile Joan had seen him use a thousand times, the one that always earned a *yes*.

"You may," said Bacon, although grudgingly.

"As we none of us have wives, this topic is impersonal to us. This means Jack's observations are not biased by a prior belief system, as he has no cause nor opportunity to have developed one." He turned to Joan. "Is that an accurate statement, Jack?"

"Perfectly," said Joan approvingly, buoyed by his sideways support. "From someone claiming ineptitude on these topics, that's an astute observation." She turned back to Bacon. "I often assist a noted apothecary and he works with everyone—in fact he is Her Majesty's apothecary—so I find myself exposed to unexpected medical situations."

Bacon raised his brows. "Her Maj . . . Hugh Morgan mentors you?"

"Not formally," she clarified. "But . . . yes."

"Remarkable," murmured Bacon. "You're an intriguing lad. I wish we had the leisure to converse. I am surprised by your topic, but for the purposes of this exercise, you may continue with it."

Joan took a moment to collect her thoughts. "Everyone in London uses the same fumigation technique to treat a condition called floating womb, but different healers have different explanations for why it works. I need not go into any detail about the process itself—"

"Indeed," said Bacon.

"But each practitioner has a different belief about *why* the procedure works. Thus, when it does work, each one says, 'aha, it worked because my belief about why it works is correct.'"

Bacon leaned toward the desk. "Interesting," he said. "And relevant to our studies. An example, please."

"Of course," said Joan, realizing she would survive this. "Classical medicine, including Hippocrates, holds that the womb is its own creature, with its own will, and it will move away from foul odors and toward sweet ones, therefore you must burn something foul and something else sweet and put them in different places, to encourage the womb to move away from the foul and toward the sweet, thereby resettling it within the body. So anyone who adheres to a classical system of the healing arts will inform you that's why fumigation works. But there are other kinds of healers who adhere to the more recent belief system—which they call knowledge, of course, and not belief—that health depends upon the balancing of the humors within the body."

"I'm familiar with that, of course," said Bacon. She heard Pierre sweeping the hearth. Then noises suggesting he was building a fire. "And I confess, it had not occurred to me to question the premise of humors, although of course I should have, as it has never been systemically tested for negative instances or false premises. Well done, lad. Thank you for alerting me to my own blind spot." He gave Joan an approving smile. More astonishing to her, he added, with a wink, "If I'm not vigilant, you might bring me around to heliocentrism. But for now, forward with the humors."

"Well, according to those such practitioners, distresses in the womb means that there is a humor imbalance, and the burning of herbs near the entrance to the womb has a drying effect, which achieves a phlegmatic purge of the womb, thus restoring the patient to balance and therefore to health."

He nodded, mulling. "I confess—to my own surprise—I find this example worth contemplating. Please go on, I'm curious to hear other explanations."

"I've just one more. Herbalists and apothecaries explain the success of fumigation on two things. First, different herbs have intrinsic beneficial effects on different organs. Second, the best way to deliver the potency of herbs directly to the womb is through smoke, as air is the gentlest way to penetrate living tissue." She waited for a nod from Bacon, then concluded, "All of these healers are using the same method, but have different beliefs about why the method works, based on beliefs they already held before they even learned the method."

Bacon held up one finger. "That is not my inductive method, but it is an example of why my method is needed. What I would hear from you now is your own approach to fumigation, and how you might test your own belief."

"Yes, sir," continued Joan, gaining cautious confidence, "were I myself a healer, no matter what sort, I would use this same method. But I would do so not because I believed in humors or herbs or wandering wombs. I would use it because I have seen that nearly every time it is used, it has beneficial results. An accretion of individual instances supports my theory that it will likely nearly always work, regardless of what beliefs anyone might have about it. My understanding is limited to what I witness myself."

Bacon had narrowed his eyes thoughtfully. "That's a beginning, but not enough."

"How might he improve his approach?" Sander asked. She felt his nervous but admiring attention almost as a physical caress. *Go ahead, you'll be fine*, he signed without a glance at her, unfurling his fist into an open hand.

"Is there a way to examine the technicalities of *how* it works?" asked Bacon.

"As it happens, I think I know—from many observations, not from belief—why it works."

Bacon looked intrigued. "What experiment did you contrive to test it?"

"No test or contrivance, sir, just consistent observation. The fumes usually make the women sneeze or cough. When they do so, the fumigation works. When the smoke does not elicit such reactions, it doesn't. The coughing exercises many small muscles in the center of the body, causing them to spasm and then release. That goes a long way toward expelling things from any womb, I assure you."

Joan realized, after the words came out of her mouth, that she had made the fatal error of delivering this with a confiding smile.

Elbow on desk and chin on fist, Bacon looked at her in silence for what felt like hours. A host of thoughts and emotions seemed to parade across his face. She had delivered her logic, given her best proof of understanding. He was trying to decide what to say to her and there was nothing left for her to do but to relax into the waiting, and accept his critique, even if harsh, as graciously as possible. Through the lead-paned window, she could hear law students laughing together in the courtyard, and a horse whinnying somewhere.

"Pierre," called Bacon. "You may leave."

"*Oui*, monsieur," said the servant, and let himself out the smaller door.

Finally, Bacon flicked his gaze from Joan to Sander. She didn't dare turn to check Sander's expression.

"Sander," said Bacon.

"Master Bacon?" Sander said, smiling and leaning forward, performing the action of gracious anticipation.

Bacon pointed a finger at Joan, his stare staying locked on Sander. "Is this person female?"

Sander froze and made a small, pained noise. Joan's stomach clenched so tight she couldn't breathe.

"I require an answer, Alexander," Bacon said. He was calm. Given his usual demeanor, the calm felt menacing.

Sander opened his mouth and seemed about to say something, but then didn't. He closed his mouth. Opened it again. "I suppose," he said, almost comically slowly, thought Joan. "I suppose that is a possibility."

Bacon continued to look at him. His eyes were cold and unblinking, like an adder's. Finally, he nodded. "I am appalled that you deceived me. But I confess my displeasure is somewhat mitigated by her brazenness. And aptitude."

"I apologize for the deception," said Sander, quiet but heartfelt.

"As do I," said Joan. Sander shushed her. Bacon continued to stare at Sander.

"Master Bacon, I was certain you would not agree to this if you knew her sex."

"Correct," said Bacon.

"I believed it was unfair for her to be deprived for that reason, when she has curiosity and intelligence that far outweighs most men I know. I have never met man nor boy of her rough background with such a nimble mind."

"I warrant that," said Bacon. "What is her name?"

"She is capable of conversation," said Sander.

"What is her name?" repeated Bacon.

"Her name is Joan."

"Has she a husband? Parents? Who has allowed this?"

"I am a maiden, Master Bacon," Joan said, her blood beating in her ears.

"Joan," Sander warned. "Don't."

"My parents are indifferent to my activities, so I'm displeasing nobody but you. Sander was doing me a kindness, as we have been friends since childhood."

"Stop talking," hissed Sander, repeatedly making the sign for *Stop* against her leg.

Bacon finally looked at her. "If you are about to tell me I should not fault Sander for this deception, it is presumptuous of you to tell me what to believe."

"Fault him if you will," Joan retorted, "but he was acting out of generosity. I was the one acting out of selfishness. Your wrath should be limited to myself."

"God in Heaven, I've no wrath toward either of you," Bacon said impatiently. "I'm a member of Parliament and the Queen's Counsel. I save my wrath for enemies of the state. You are beneath my irritation. You're naught but a distraction." A brief pause. "You were an intriguing distraction to begin with, and even more so now."

". . . Sir?" she said.

"Women are forbidden within the walls of Gray's Inn. Next time, we shall have to meet outside somewhere."

She blinked in surprise. Beside her, Sander gasped with relief, sat up straighter.

"Master Bacon," he began, but Bacon returned his attention to him angrily.

"You are more at fault than she, Sander. You are a friend. She's just a saucy stranger. She has merely tricked me; you have wronged me."

"I apologize and will endeavor to win back your trust, and I am grateful you will not punish her for my sins," Sander said.

"She might be useful," Bacon said. He returned his attention to Joan. "It is its own experiment, to see how much an unschooled girl might benefit from my teachings. Females make up half the population, so I suppose bettering mankind must include bettering the female."

"That is the spirit in which I approached this too," she said.

"Careful, girl," he said. "Do not congratulate yourself for your dishonesty. But the deception is trifling compared to the rest of my concerns, and it is behind us now." Almost to himself, he said, "For all his concern with the masses, the celebrated Hugh Platt has not taken an ordinary girl under his wing. I have here a unique arrangement." He returned his attention to them. "Before anything else, the three of us must agree to be honest with one another from this moment on." He stood, strode to a shelf across the room, and returned with a large leather-bound Bible. "Will you swear to that?"

Sander slapped his hand on the Bible. "I swear," he said.

"I swear," Joan said, nudging Sander's hand aside.

"And," Sander added, "I will do whatever penance you require to demonstrate I'm still worthy of your good regard."

"I'll hold you to that," said Bacon. He turned to Joan. "It will likely be weeks before I have a moment to continue our work together, but I will send for you through Sander when I can."

"I am speechless with gratitude and humility, Master Bacon," said Joan.

"With language like that, and your cunning at misdirection, you'd make a fair courtier," Bacon said, wry. "Let yourselves out there, I have another meeting." He pointed to the small door that paralleled the one they'd entered, in the opposite corner.

They bowed, thanked him again, and exited. They found themselves on a small wooden landing, dimly up-lit from a window on the floor below. Mirroring each other, they clasped hands and muttered astonished oaths of relief.

"Let's get out of here," whispered Sander.

"God, yes," Joan whispered back. "Before he has a change of heart."

The staircase before them was steep. At the bottom was a long, narrow room with black gowns hung in rows on pegs, and above each, on another peg, a flat black cap. A mirror—nothing so nice as the one at Bacon's tailor's shop—was at the far side. There was a door that allowed them to a yard, and on the far side of the long narrow room was another set of stairs going up. Sander looked around, trying to orient himself.

"That's the law students' dormitory ahead of us, I think," he said. "So these must be their robes for moots." He plucked at one. It was sleeveless. "Yes, these are the students'. Bacon lent us one for *Merchant of Venice* while Josias was seeking a bencher's robe for me in the courtroom scene." He grinned and pointed around the room. "And do you know what this place is?"

". . . Besides the room where the robes live?"

"It's the room I kiss you in." He wrapped his arms around her, squeezed her hard to him, and pressed his mouth against hers. She sagged happily into his arms. It was their second kiss but already the most comfortable, familiar thing in life. She brought her hands to his face, ran her fingers up into his black hair.

Footsteps clattered, echoing, in the dormitory stairwell. They pulled apart, and darted for the door.

THEY DIDN'T SPEAK on their trek back to the river: two young men, one lanky and beautiful in ordinary apprentice blue, one nondescript in fine black tailored wool, rushing homeward side by side. The air could have been quivering between them, there was such tension.

When they reached the boat queue, Sander pulled his cap forward to avoid being recognized. He shivered and shoved his hands under his armpits to try to warm them. It was late September; the days were growing shorter but the temperature had not yet changed, so why was he cold? He glanced at Joan. She'd been staring straight ahead with a pained expression on her face, but felt his look and returned it. Immediately she smiled.

"That was an unhappy face you wore just then," said Sander, to make conversation. It disturbed him to feel awkward with the person he knew best in the world. A few years ago, when women first began to throw themselves at him and his cock led him around London while the rest of him followed in a grateful daze . . . several beautiful ladies had seduced him, each of whom he was sure he was besotted with, each of whom was generous and satisfying—and each of whom he inexplicably wanted nothing to do with immediately afterward. Ever. For no reason he could find, just a visceral need to eject them from his orbit. He was appalled with himself but he could not feign otherwise. There had been but three or four such lovers out of scores of paramours. But it spooked him, that a desire he was so certain of could dissolve in a trice, causing hurt. If that happened with Joan, he would be the loneliest person on earth, and there was no way to know if it would happen until it was too late to prevent it.

"Where are you?" she asked, with a slight frown. "You're not here. With me. Do you not want to be here with me? Tell me if that—"

"Don't be ridiculous," he said. "Of course I'm here."

"Well then answer, please. What do you think? About his knowing?"

"He still values you."

Joan looked away, shaking her head. "He'll treat me differently."

"Don't take this amiss, but he was never attracted to you anyhow."

She glared at him. "I don't mean that. Eros is not at the core of *everyone's* relationships, just maybe yours."

"I don't think—"

"This would be a foolish thing to have an argument about," said Joan. She looked away again, and took another step down the slope as the queue progressed. Behind them were at least another dozen travelers waiting to cross the river.

He was already losing her, without even having had her. He leaned over and whispered, “If I’m being an ass, I apologize. I’m all nerves.”

“I’ve never seen you nervous on your way to an assignation,” she retorted, still looking away.

“This is different,” he said. “Obviously.” When she didn’t speak, he pushed on: “I barely know those others. You are . . . central.” He reached for her hand, but she pulled it away.

“Not in public, not while I’m in breeches,” she hissed. The queue moved forward; there was only one person ahead of them now.

“Do you think this is just another tryst?” he whispered into her ear. “If you have that impression then I’ve done something awful somehow. The very opposite is true.”

He felt her relax against him. He noticed his hands were not so cold now.

THEY CROSSED THE Thames in bobbing silence across a glorious slab of angled amber light. Disembarking at the Winchester stairs, they pushed through the press of tipplers and travelers and strangers, the soft cascades of smells and sounds, accents and animals, toward the Globe. Down Maiden Lane, past the Happy Sow, to the paving stones by the door to the tiring house.

A large padlock held a bolt in place. With a rare clumsiness, Sander fished about in the canvas drawstring purse at his waist for the key. He unlocked it, the mechanism clunking as it released. He pulled open the wide door. “Now then,” he said, and collected himself enough to gesture her in.

Joan had spent countless hours just outside this door, but in seven years she’d never once stepped across the threshold. Sander latched it behind them, then crossed to one of the padlocked stage-entrance doors, unlocked and opened it as well. Out beyond the stage, the Playhouse yard was filled with slanting sunlight. Joan stood in the middle of the curved wooden room that made up the backstage. She felt like an intruder; she could almost hear the absent players objecting to her presence.

A table was snugged up near a wall, under a staircase to the musicians' gallery. It was covered with random-seeming objects: three small boxes wrapped in foils, jewelry, scrolls, a handheld scale. Around the rest of the room were pegs with costumes hanging on them, and on one wall was a sort of cage, locked, with fancier costumes hanging from a rack. The room reeked of stale sweat. "My other home," said Sander, not noticing her awkwardness. He tossed the linens toward Joan, who startled but managed to catch the bundle.

The bed pulled out more easily than he'd expected. Joan unfolded a sheet and laid it down, covering the straw. "Has Sander Cooke ever seen a grander love nest?" she said in a self-mocking tone.

Sander grabbed her around the waist and gripped her hard against him. His skin tingled. "Stop that," he said, nuzzling her temple. "Any place containing Joan Buckler is grander than a palace." He pulled away enough to see her face. "May I undress you?" he asked, strangely shy.

She drew a sharp breath and then smiled. "If that's what happens next."

"I'm not your tutor."

"Yes, you are. But I learn fast."

He reached for her collar and then stopped. "Bacon will never forgive us if we rip the clothes he commissioned for you."

"Then you must be slow and careful," she suggested, batting her eyelids at him.

"I want to be quick and careless."

"Too bad," she whispered, and tapped his nose with her fingertip. Her gentle playfulness dissolved his hesitation, and with his arms still tight around her, he threw them both down onto the bed.

Quickly, expertly, he unlaced her black doublet and trousers; beneath these were a linen shirt and stockings. Joan held her hands up over her head, and he tugged off the shirt, hungry for what awaited . . . but what awaited was her torso bound in linen bandages.

"Deceiving vixen." He chuckled.

"Ay me, my secret's been discovered," said Joan, pantomiming an alarmed gesture. Then: "The end's tucked in just here, by my elbow."

They knelt upright, Sander's arms hooped around Joan as he unbound her, gathering the linen in a clump as he went. When there were two rounds left, he could see every detail of her small breasts clearly through the gauzy fabric.

"Ohhhhh," he said, and forgot how to move.

"What's wrong?" she said. "You don't like what you see?"

He pitched himself at her; she fell back with him on top of her. His mouth found hers, his tongue found hers, his hands pulled at the remaining bandage and shoved it down toward her waist, then both hands clapped themselves onto her breasts and stroked them, thumbs pressing onto nipples. She gasped with surprised pleasure, then moaned, then laughed at herself for moaning, then moaned again, and by now his mouth had left hers and slid down to her neck, her collarbone, her sternum, her left breast, her right breast, then he ran his tongue down her midriff to her naval.

"You taste like fresh rainwater," he said, pulling back a moment, then lowered his mouth to the smooth skin below her belly button. When she gasped again, he said, "Now your stockings come off."

"I can do it quicker," she offered, beginning to sit up, but he reached a hand to push her gently back down without glancing away from her waist.

"No, you can't," he assured her. "Reap the harvest of my experience."

And almost instantly she lay nude upon the sheet.

"Aren't you clever," she whispered, looking up at him, watching him while his eyes roved over every inch of her.

"Just well-trained," he said, and dragged his gaze back up to her face.

"I feel all a-flutter," she said, pleased.

He stroked her cheek. "We've not even started with the fluttering."

He undressed himself, and caught her gaping. "That doesn't look at all as it did when you were seven," she announced, raising up on one elbow and pointing.

"Neither do your breasts," he said.

"It's far more interesting than my breasts. Shall I touch it?" she asked, and then reached out before he could reply.

He cried out and crumbled to the bed beside her. "Slow down." He smiled and nudged her hand away, so that they lay nude, side by side, facing each other.

For a moment, they lay in silence, as he tried to judge a respectful next move. He could scarcely believe they were lying together like this.

Joan looped her leg high over his and jerked his buttocks toward her with the back of her calf. She rocked against him.

"You're trying to kill me." He laughed under his breath.

"Isn't this what's supposed to happen next?" she asked, pushing herself up against him.

"Joan." He breathed. "I've never been with a virgin before, but I know it hurts and I don't want to hurt you."

She stared at him for a moment, confused. "Do you . . . want someone else to take me first?"

He grabbed her to him. "God, no. But we mustn't rush. You must stay intact until—"

"What an inconvenient moment for you to be a Puritan!"

"Trust me, Joan, there's a world of pleasure to be had before we try the act itself." He smiled. "Look, I'll show you."

THEY LAY WITH arms and legs wrapped around each other, dozing and then resting together. "This might be my favorite part," Joan murmured, her nose nestling up against his collarbone. "Which is saying a great deal, because what came before was breath-taking."

Sander's throat tightened. "Yes," he said. "But only now."

"Hm?"

He squeezed her. "This was never the best part, before you. Usually, I seek an easy exit. I want to stay here holding you all night."

"Good," she said drowsily, and kissed his collarbone.

He kissed the top of her head. There was always a certain kind of reassurance that swept over him when an audience applauded him; he thought it took a thousand strangers to give him such security. Now a single person soothed him with a sigh. *This must be what home feels like*, he thought.

Act III

October 12

"What's this about?" Heminges demanded as he entered the steamy tiring house full of half-dressed men. To his left, Augie Phillips (shirt, stockings, breeches) grasped Sander Cooke (linen shift) by the neck; to his right, Dick Burbage (linen shirt and nothing else) glowered like an angry god. Will Shakespeare, between them with hands calmly outstretched, was the only one fully clothed and breathing calmly.

"The brat lunged at me," Burbage said.

"He insulted Joan," Sander snapped, wriggling his shoulders against Phillips's grip.

"It wasn't an insult, sweetheart, it was a question." Burbage.

"It was a question asked in a particular tone," Shakespeare amended, to Heminges. "Sander objected to the tone."

"Sander objected to everything," Sander clarified angrily.

"What'd you say, Dick?" Heminges asked, tired.

"He called her a harlot!" Sander struggled again. Phillips tightened his grip.

"I didn't," said Burbage. Then, to Heminges, reasonably, "We're pleased for him. I simply asked if she's more experienced than we've all presumed."

"He didn't say it nicely!" shouted Sander as Heminges muttered to Burbage: "That was uncalled for."

"He might have laughed it off," said Burbage. "I would have."

Heminges gave him a look. "Would you have laughed it off, were it the first love of your life?"

"Listen to yourself, John, you know she's not the first, the boy's landed in more laps than all of us combined. It's a marvel London isn't littered with his bastards."

"Not fornication," Heminges said. "Love."

Burbage rolled his eyes. But then he grimaced. "I did not mean she's light. I know she isn't. I was simply—understandably—curious."

"'Tis no business of yours," said Sander.

"Now there you're wrong, lad, because this is my property," said Burbage. "John's indulged you by giving you a key, but that's a privilege any of us can revoke. And I will do so, if you're an ass. I mean more of an ass than usual. I've never met an apprentice who shirks their chores as much as you."

"That's not to the point," said Heminges, placating, although it was true.

"You could just take her up against a wall someplace," Burbage continued, ignoring Heminges. "That's what most boys your age do—"

Phillips almost lost his grip as Sander snarled and lunged again, but—

"*Pardonnez-moi*," said a voice from behind Heminges.

The speaker was a wiry youth in a messenger's uniform with a badge of black stars. Sander had last seen him laying down a fire in Grey's Inn.

Sander shoved a triumphant elbow at Phillips. "Let me go," he huffed. "I'm being summoned by Francis Bacon."

JOAN KNEW THE route to curving Lime Street, almost to a pothole. It was a few weeks past the equinox, so Master Cole's garden was not yet being put to bed for winter, but the love apple—*tomatl*, Master Pantazis had called it—looked sapped of strength. A single red sphere lay rotting at its base, gelatinous; she supposed he had left it there to see if its seeds would volunteer to sprout come spring. Likely he had preserved more seeds, though, and would be experimenting with them; the thought of discussing this with him and Master Morgan pleased her but did not soothe her nerves.

The garden was empty of humans, although Grijs, the cat, was stalking around the potato bed. The day was damp, the smoke of coal fires creating a pungent shawl that hung over this part of the city. Southwark had better air this time of year, since the breeze blew the smoke over the river and up this way.

She glanced through the windows, but the house seemed empty. This was the time of day when she usually found the two men in each other's company. She headed for the gate to Hugh Morgan's garden.

This garden was larger, surrounding the Morgan house on three sides. As Her Majesty's Apothecary Extraordinary, Hugh Morgan oversaw the royal herb gardens at Whitehall and Richmond, but he used his own plots for experimenting and for collecting exotic specimens from the Continent and farther off. At least two bushes had been grown from seeds Sir Walter Raleigh had brought back from the New World as a gift. A nettle tree from southern Italy, with its astringent purple berries, was Morgan's great pride here, but she knew that his estate in Battersea, some hour's ride out of the city, boasted a Judas tree, which she had only ever seen sketches of. Despite her anxiousness, it made her happy to review what she knew of each raised bed as she passed by them. But she required the men themselves.

As she approached the side door, she saw them through the windows, seated in carved wooden chairs near the fireplace in Morgan's study: the tall, wiry, arthritic Welshman and the stocky Flemish. They were sitting pitched forward, and through the diamond panes she could see each gesturing in turn, as they vigorously but affectionately debated. Approaching, she could hear their voices. *I've missed this*, she thought, her heart softening. And then told herself, *Courage*, for what she would do next.

"THANK YOU FOR coming on short notice," said Bacon, fidgeting with the long sleeves of his gown.

"I was happy to be summoned," said Sander, doffing his plain flat cap.

"You might not say so once you've heard the purpose." They were in Bacon's office. Outside, the air was raw and the sky the color of dingy linen. These things made the attractive elements of Bacon's office even more attractive. Pierre the servant had donned a leather apron to bring in firewood, and now added a log to the small crackling fire. Sander wished they were sitting closer to the hearth, but this was warmer than the Globe. He wondered what it would be like, to be stretched out beside a fire like that with Joan—

"You offered to help me with Essex," Bacon was saying. Sander blinked away his daydream.

"I did."

Bacon sat leaning forward, elbows on desk, chin resting on fists, an almost wistful pose. "I need help indeed, but this is delicate."

"I am your servant."

"Her Majesty will not soften toward his lordship. He is political poison, but I owe much of my advancement to him, and I would make one final attempt to help him back to her good graces. For the good of the realm, not merely my sense of obligation."

"I would be honored to assist you with such an undertaking," said Sander, not adding the obvious: *It will endear me to him and to his sister*.

Bacon sat up straighter. "I must tell you straight that it requires subterfuge," he said. "For a worthy cause, but still, it is counterfeiting."

"I spend my life counterfeiting," said Sander. "Counterfeiting to be a woman, to be wealthy, to be in love with certain people, or to hate others."

Bacon shook his head. "Your audiences wish to be tricked. They are willing participants in your counterfeiting."

"Do you not think Her Majesty wishes to believe in Essex's reformation?"

"The parallel is imperfect but I applaud the bent of your mind. I will tell you, then," said Bacon, "and explain your brief but vital role in it."

He opened a box beside his desk; out of this he pulled three letters and laid them on top of his desk. They were written on the smoothest paper Sander had ever seen. All three were signed by Robert Devereux, Earl of Essex, and bore the Essex seal. The writing was crisp and black—this was the dearest kind of ink to make, oak galls crushed in wine and mixed with copperas soot.

"Read them," Bacon said, gesturing him closer to the desk.

They were not so self-pitying or overwrought as the one Essex had recited. But the style was Essex. All three were addressed to Bacon's brother Anthony. Sander knew little about Anthony Bacon except that he, like Francis, had been an intimate and beneficiary of Essex's largess for years; Sander thought he lived abroad now, working as a diplomat or spy.

In worshipful prose, Essex lamented to Anthony that losing Her Majesty's regard meant losing all life's meaning and goodness.

Bacon studied Sander with unnerving intensity as Sander reviewed the letters. "I don't understand why he wrote these," Sander said, looking up from the desk. "He's already tried writing directly to Her Majesty, to no effect."

"Perhaps to express the misery he suffers to a sympathetic confidant."

"His sister and his wife were not ears enough for his lamentations?"

A pause. "An excellent point. In which case, if the writing could seem suspect . . . can we be certain he penned these himself?"

Sander shrugged. "'Twould be an odd thing for a third party to invent. I have never seen his lordship's script, but the tone sounds familiar. And that's his seal."

"Tone can be imitated," said Bacon. "Handwriting can be forged."

"Well, the seal, then," said Sander. "I presume your brother knows that seal well enough."

"As does Her Majesty. Which is why, when she stumbles upon these letters, she will know they are his. Even though"—he opened the top drawer of his desk, yanking out of it a small metal object—"they are not." He showed Sander the object. It was a copy of the Essex seal.

"W . . . what?" said Sander, feeling stupid. "Why?"

"Since the letters are not addressed to her, when she encounters them, she will read them trustingly. She will have a chance to hear how truly heartsick he is. Without the intent to manipulate her."

"But he *is* manipulating her."

"No, he's not," said Bacon. "I am. The earl lacks the subtlety and strategy to have plotted such a thing. He wrote a draft and it was insufferable, so I took up the project myself. But he truly is sick at heart. I have written countless letters for him over the years, including to his own kinsmen, and none has ever faulted us. These letters are, despite being forgeries, as authentic as anything he has ever written."

"I see," said Sander, unconvinced but willing to play along if he could somehow reap a benefit. "And what is my role in this?"

"I need these letters to be planted near Her Majesty so that one of her inner circle will encounter them as if by accident. What do you think of that?"

"I think Will Shakespeare would make a marvelous comedy of the premise," said Sander.

Bacon nodded, his complacency undiminished. "Comedy begins in chaos and ends in order, with goodwill restored. That is the intended outcome here as well."

I should have said farce, Sander thought, but kept it to himself.

DESPITE HER UNCERTAINTY, the reunion had been quick and easy, because they all pretended there had never been a sundering. Joan accepted this convenient insincerity; it allowed them to return to a status that was craved by each of them. After a few minutes before the fire debating the most fragrant cultivars of roses, Master Morgan in his apothecary robe suggested they go out to the garden, to show Joan their latest project. Joan held her hands up in polite interruption.

"It gladdens me to see you both," she said, smiling at them in the flickering light, "but in truth I have come here with a purpose. I am usually the listener, but may I speak some few moments without being interrupted?"

The men exchanged looks, as if concerned they might be called out again. But then Master Morgan smiled.

"Of course, Pucelle. Our ears and our attention are all yours."

"Agreed," said Master Cole, nodding.

She wished she had Sander's aptitude for memorizing speeches. "As you may recall from several months ago," she began, "I know what your intentions are regarding my plum trees."

"Joan—" Master Cole began.

"Please let me finish. I am not cross at you. I was cross before, but now I—"

"The profit will be shared with you," Master Cole said.

She stopped, surprised.

"One third of whatever we make will go toward a dowry," said Master Morgan, "but we could not tell you, lass, as we did not want your parents to perceive anything unsavory about the source of the money."

"We are still strategizing how to offer it anonymously," clarified Master Cole.

"I . . . Thank you," she said. "I believe you. And I appreciate that consideration."

"But?" prompted Master Morgan.

"I am grateful to hear that, but I did not come here to complain. I came to tell you I believe you are misguided. About the plums."

"They have been in great demand," said Master Cole. "So I would not say misguided, no."

She pursed her lips and nodded. "Very well, then," she said. "I was going to propose an experiment to see if the plums do, in fact, function as . . . as they are presumed to, or if it is the power of suggestion—men believe they have benefits to fornication, and therefore respond to them as if they did."

Her using the term shattered all delicacy. She watched them exchange glances and could almost hear the unspoken conversation:

Master Morgan, speaking from the heart: *Our little Joan is grown enough to talk of fornication! Now what?*

Master Cole, speaking from the head: *Well, let's talk of it.*

"Is that not a meaningless distinction?" asked Master Cole. "If you begin with the plums and end with the intended effect, does it matter if the activating element is in the fruit or in the mind?"

"From the perspective of scientific inquiry, I should think it matters a great deal," said Joan. Hugh Morgan looked tickled that his friend had been scolded. "But I recognize you are also men of commerce, so I will let that go. And in truth, the rest of my proposal is intended for you as men of commerce."

Again they exchanged glances. "Continue," said Master Cole.

"You know that I am friends with an apothecary and a midwife, who are in business together."

"Women," said Master Cole, as if that meant something more than itself.

"Women who know women's needs," Joan amended. "There are certain herbs that I know they would pay well for, if they could trust them to be potent and reliably available. They have the knowledge of using them, but not the land or resources to grow them. I propose you enter into an agreement with them. I would help you develop the heartiest and most potent cultivars."

She enjoyed how often they were exchanging glances.

"Of what herbs are you thinking?" asked Morgan.

Hugh Morgan had the same expertise as Eleanor; he would know what she was after. "Rue and artemisia," she said, and then continued as if it were an innocuous recitation, "marjoram, parsley, pennyroyal, tansy, marigold, peony, thyme, lavender, wild carrot, and worm fern."

"Worm fern?" said Master Cole. "Is that not the one also known as—"

"As prostitute root, yes," said Master Morgan, his eyes narrowed. "Joan, those are all herbs that prevent conception."

"That's it," said Joan, pleasantly. "If you're helping men to fornicate, 'tis only fair you help the women they're fornicating with to avoid unwanted consequences. The men, and therefore society at large, will benefit from that as well." She looked at them. "What do you say?"

Again, the two of them exchanged freighted expressions.

"Hugh Platt might be interested in such a thing," said Cole to Morgan. "It is not precisely his focus—he's more concerned with poverty and famine—but he pursues the well-being of society through agricultural inquiry. This might appeal to him."

Hugh Morgan was studying Joan and did not answer. Finally he said, sounding almost wistfully paternal, "So you've a paramour at last, then? What's he done, to be worthy of La Pucelle?"

"I MUST NOT be associated with these letters in any way," Bacon was explaining. "So they must follow a tortuous route from myself to Her Majesty to occlude their origin. Happily I have the right person to lay them in Her Majesty's path."

"Who is that?"

"Do you know Bess Blackstone?"

Sander shrugged. "I know the name, but nothing interesting about her except she is the devoted mistress of some count or other."

"Yes. The viscount Clarence. He, like myself, has reasons to be well-disposed toward Essex. Bess has been invited to a supper party at Baron and Lady Hastings this week. I can stir certain pots that would result in your being invited to the same table."

"How can you arrange these things?" Sander asked in mild amazement.

Bacon looked pleased with the admiration, but then shrugged. "If I could not do so, I would be a failure at my work. In this particular case, half my work is done by simply uttering the name of Sander Cooke. I do not know the full guest list for his honor's dinner, but I warrant there will be potential patrons, should you choose to make yourself charming."

"Am I not always charming?" said Sander, with a theatrical bow.

Bacon ignored the flourish. "This would be an opportunity for you to expand your own circle. Lord Hastings himself might be interested in having a resident entertainer. Will you do this?"

"With all my heart," said Sander. The scheme was ridiculous, but potential patrons never were.

October 15

There would be eight at table, he was told when the official invitation arrived at the Globe. Two days later, after the company's first reading of a new Shakespeare script—*Troilus and Cressida*, with himself and Burbage playing opposite each other, as usual—a performance of *Julius Caesar*, and a pleasing hour with Joan, he took a wherry to the Hastings address, near Whitehall Palace. There was a full moon, visible as a bright spot in the murky sky. It was the first night that felt chill enough to know winter was approaching.

He was let into the hall. This was opulent: floors of ochre tiles, plaster walls tinted pale rose with gold-leaf geometric patterns, pearl-hemmed woolen hangings by each door.

A tall, broad-shouldered lute player stood near a brazier, serenading guests as they arrived in their wrought and powdered tiffany and velvet. The musician had a soaring, sweet contralto, which contrasted startingly with his dense beard. Sander moved toward him. He looked about Sander's own age. Sander nodded greeting, smiling, and the singer's eyes widened, in a way that Sander knew meant he was recognized. The singer recovered, and returned his full attention to the piece, something Italian, full of arpeggios. When he finished, Sander said, "Beautiful playing. Lovely voice."

The fellow beamed. "Praise from Sander Cooke," he whispered back. His speaking voice was too light for the mass of him, but the effect was pleasing. "I thank you. I might well die of ecstasy."

"Please don't," said Sander. "Stay alive and continue to delight our ears. Does the baron employ you often?"

"His lordship and his lady keep me," said the singer, almost bashfully. "She is fond of music in the house, and my penmanship is good enough to make me useful to them both in other matters. It lacks the glamour of your life, but I am grateful for it."

Sander glued his Society Face into place to mask his disappointment: so the baron already had an entertainer in residence. Still, if this youth could find standing in a baron's home, then it was not arrogance for Sander Cooke to imagine himself worthy of an earl, or even a duke. "I am grateful to be here to enjoy their fine choice of musician," he said graciously.

"You will not remember me, but we were at St. Paul's together as children. Before John Heminges apprenticed you."

Sander studied the face behind the beard. ". . . Mark," he said. "Mark Hatton? We learned to dance together?"

Again, the young man beamed. "You remember me!" he whispered. "You've given me much to boast of today, Master Cooke."

"Sander, please," he said, chucking him on the green silk sleeve, knowing it would please the fellow. "If you'll excuse me, I must—" and he nodded at the open door to the dining room.

It was an elegant house, but small. The greatest extravagance was a fireplace at each end of the wainscoted dining room, so that the baron and his lady, at either end of the table, would have equally warm backsides. As if to make up for the expense of firewood, the candlelight was sparse. Good. Darkness would make it easier to hand off the forgeries.

To one side, the oaken cupboard glinted with silver and glass. Two couples hovered by the nearer hearth, pale faces up-lit, jewels aglow; a woman who must be Bess Blackstone stood in the shadows in the center of the room. Sander scanned the fireside figures, and saw with a start that the couple in bright velvets were the very handsome Baron Putney and his comely wife, the occasional hosts of small discreet orgies. Sander had seen them fully clothed infrequently; it took him a moment to be certain. He had declined their last two invitations and hoped they would stop asking; sharing a table would be awkward. But he was not here for enjoyment, only to deliver the letters to Bess Blackstone. And scout out patronage.

The other couple was older, dressed in dignified but subdued tones; the lady's doublet and headpiece were studded with pearls, so they had means. As soon as he'd accomplished his errand, he could spend the evening charming them.

He skirted around them toward the figure in the shadows. Other than her coif, which sparkled silver in the firelight, he could barely make her out, it was that shadowy. Good.

"Have I the pleasure of meeting Lady Blackstone?" he murmured, leaning in toward her.

"I'm not a lady," said a mellifluous voice, amused, right in his ear. "But if it's Bess the viscount's mistress you're after, I'm your girl."

"The viscount Clarence is fortunate in love," murmured Sander. "And I would offer you more courtesy, only I would not draw attention to us at this moment." As he spoke he was untying the purse at his belt.

"Agreed, and likewise," she murmured back. Her voice had a resonance like Lady Penelope Rich's, as if it always held a smile. "His lordship and I still talk about your Rosalind. We tell all our friends to see *As You Like It* whenever the company is doing it."

"I am gratified," said Sander. He reached into his drawstring purse. He had rehearsed this move a score of times over the past two days and was confident he could do it undetected. Now he drew out the forged letters, rolled together into a tube an inch thick and a handspan across. "Perhaps you will do me the honor of allowing me to sing to you in the comfort of your own home. I can accompany myself on lute or mandolin." As he said these words he shifted his body to shield the letters from view of those by the fire. He slipped them into Bess's waiting hand.

"I shall encourage his lordship to issue you just such an invitation," she purred. "To know in advance that you would grace us with your presence would mean the world to him. Shall we send to the Globe?"

"That is the surest way to reach me," Sander said. He had kept his ring finger extended in her direction and waited for her to tug it, a signal Bacon had instructed him would mean she had now stashed the letters.

There. He had accomplished it. So quick, so simple, with momentous outcomes. This was a thrill he'd never known before: to be a small invisible cog in the machinery of state, rather than an idol of the superficial theatre world. It gave him a sense of substance, of meaning, as if he had dined on fruit all his life and was now being offered venison.

He could become a spy, an intelligencer. He had just demonstrated that he had the aptitude, and he liked the satisfaction of accomplishing his task. The next time he saw Bacon, he'd ask for his opinion of this notion. Spies, diplomats, and operatives were eternally useful to Her Majesty. Some lord could keep him on the pretense of his being the resident performer—which he would do, of course, and splendidly—but his real worth would rest in something far more important that almost nobody would ever know about. Joan would approve, he knew. What a marvelous solution. In truth, Joan could also work for the state. She could scout for scientific inventions that might attract Her Majesty; if she became an expert on one topic under Bacon's tutelage, she could be the royal agent for projects related to it—glassworks, salt harvesting, anything involving botany. He preened privately for having sorted out their lives so neatly.

Bess Blackstone had sauntered away from him back toward the fire. Sander glanced around the room, his eyes adjusting enough to make out its scale. The sunset glow from the bow windows had faded, but there was enough light to see this was a well-appointed chamber, the wainscot painted with flowers and vines, the drapes embroidered with gold thread that caught the candlelight.

"You insult us, sirrah," said a familiar voice just behind him. He took a long, controlled breath to calm himself, then pivoted toward the speaker.

"Your lordship is mistaken, surely?" he said to Baron Putney with an insipid smile.

"I am not," said the baron. "You twice sent us the message that you are too busy for social engagements, but not only did you find time to attend this dinner, you have just planned an assignation with that whore, right under our noses, days after rebuffing our invitation for a second time."

"I was not—" Sander stopped himself. With nauseating clarity, he saw the whole of his situation illustrated like a map of the cosmos Bacon had on his wall.

He was not of the population to be suspected of court intrigue—and that was to his benefit, but that impression had to be maintained.

He bent his head. "Pardon me, my lord, I understand your ire, and I'm ashamed," he said.

"'Tis insulting enough you would plan a dalliance with that harlot, but to do so in front of my wife is an affrontery that exceeds all scolding. My lady is far fairer, and of better breeding."

"She is, indeed, my lord," he said, head still bowed.

"Our supper next week, which you have declined to attend, will be honored by the presence of a number of nobility and gentry, any of whom might have offered you the patronage I know you're desperate for," the baron continued.

Sander knew a cue when he heard one. "I wonder, my lord," he said, in a groveling voice, "if any action on my part might compel you to forgive my bumbling rudeness."

"To begin with, call off your plans with that toad-faced bawd. I assume we will have the satisfaction of your presence at some point in the future and I will not have you bringing into my home such diseases as her sort carry."

Joan had drilled into him an abhorrence for sloppy logic, so it made him almost nauseated not to point out that Bess Blackstone—famously devoted to her lover—had, for years, been intimate with far fewer people than the viscount or himself.

"Of course I will, how witless of me to have even entertained the notion," he said.

"It was, yes," said the baron.

"Once I have forsworn her, I would mollify you further in whatever manner pleases you."

The baron took Sander's chin and turned it so that the two of them stared eye to eye, inches apart. "Indeed you will," he whispered. Somehow, Sander made himself smile. "And you will begin by arriving an hour early for the dinner invitation that you mistakenly declined."

"It is generous of you to consider renewing your invitation."

"I'm doing more than that," said the baron. "I'm informing you that you will attend, else I'll tell the doxy's viscount that you're poaching his fruit, and mark me, he will castrate you."

Sander performed the sounds and gestures of a young man not wishing to be castrated. "I shall call it off instantly," he said.

"Do so now," instructed the baron. "In my hearing."

They approached Bess Blackstone; Sander was prompted by Putney to speak; Bess responded to news of their canceled assignation as if there had, in fact, been an assignation; further, she communicated her disappointment to Sander and her resentment to Baron Putney, but also made it clear she would—grudgingly—cease to vie for Sander's favors. Sander felt as if he were a bolt of silk being haggled over by two mercers, one of whom was armed.

"One final thing," said Putney. "I saw an exchange of love letters between you. You will throw those into the fire."

Sander's stomach flipped over. Bess Blackstone sighed with annoyance, reached into the embroidered satin purse hanging from her belt, and pulled out a scroll. She handed it, glowering, to the baron.

"What are you doing?" Sander gasped.

"Prithee do not read it," Bess whispered. Her lips, visible from the firelight, resembled Joan's. He craved Joan; he wanted to be who he was in her company, not who he was right now.

"You will not presume to tell me what to do," said Putney. He unrolled the single piece of paper and adjusted his stance until the firelight brightened the page. "*Beautiful witch*," he read aloud. "*You have beguiled me from afar and I must have you.*" He looked up in disgust. "Really, Sander, such blather."

"I found it charming," said Bess Blackstone, in a hurt voice. "You have shamed me enough for one evening and our hosts have not yet even received us. Sander, sweet boy, it was not to be. Blame this bullying lord you seem enthralled to." And she sashayed in her broad skirt, radiating wounded dignity, to the fireplace on the other side of the room.

Sander caught himself gaping and shut his mouth. His regard for this woman, whom he would likely never meet again, expanded as his own self-congratulations shrank to nothing. That she knew to have a decoy letter was marvelous to him—but also, in hindsight, an obvious necessity, and he was a dolt for not being likewise prepared.

It would be a long evening.

And perhaps he should reconsider his plans to be a spy.

THEIR OWN PRIVATE scents mingled with the bare wood and musty fabrics of the tiring house. He still refused to take her virginity, but they had finessed the ways in which they touched each other, so that they climaxed together—a marvelous detail that Sander attributed to Joan's earnest interest in how bodies worked. Every evening she begged him to consummate their intimacy and every evening he refused; every evening she complained of the irony that she, of all people, was the only one he'd ever refused to penetrate; every evening he explained that, unlike any other coupling in his life, there could be no retreating from such a union. "In my heart, it would bind us as surely as marriage vows."

"Well then," Joan would say each evening, which Sander chose to think meant, *Well then, I will not press you*, although each night following, she would ask again.

The evening after Sander's encounter with Putney, after Joan snuggled up against him, and said her usual *Well then*, she added, to clarify, "Well then, I will be your wife. So what's the problem?"

"The problem is I have no home to bring a wife to."

"We mustn't do the deed until you have a *house*? God in Heaven,

Sander, not even William Shakespeare has a *house*!"

"He does in Stratford," Sander said. "But you're missing my point. I can't wed you without being a good husband, and I lack the means for it. I will find the means somehow, but I haven't yet."

Joan sighed a long, noisy, exaggerated sigh. "If you *insist*," she said, and then she laughed.

"Let's say we wed tomorrow. To where do I bring you home tomorrow night? Heminges's fireplace? Your parents' shop? We can't live here, backstage. But." He sat up enough to kiss her forehead. "Please know, all that I do, I do in service to our future. I have lost all appetite for any other lips or arms."

Joan's face lit up. "I hadn't ever thought about that, but it's a lovely thing to hear."

"At a dinner last night I had to sit beside someone I've been familiar with of old, and it turned my stomach."

Joan gave him a disbelieving look. "Don't lay it on too thick there, Alexander Cooke," she said. "I am not jealous and you need not reassure me."

"It's not a reassurance, Joan. It's a discovery."

She raised her head to kiss him from below. "I like when you discover things," she said. She grabbed his hand and pushed it down between her upper thighs. "Here's something in need of your discovery."

"You relentless little strumpet," he said, collapsing on top of her and laughing in frustration.

October 16

In a rare gesture of parental concern, Joan's mother insisted she not leave the house without a warmer cloak. The cloak in question had been used all summer as a display surface for her father's finer wares, and so she first had to unclasp and unpin two dozen items, and then—perhaps this was the real reason for her mother's suggestion—re-pin all of them to her summer cloak. And so she was late to her own appointment.

By the time she reached the apothecary, Master Cole and Master Morgan had found the spot, introduced themselves to Eleanor and Dorothy, and requested the shop be shut up for their private business conversation. The shop, however, had not been shut up; Eleanor and Dorothy would not make themselves unavailable to those who called upon them. Joan found the four of them standing equidistant across the counter from one another, in the small room lined with shelves of herbal preparations. The men seemed to be wilting under Eleanor's regal strictness.

"Apologies, I was detained," Joan said in a rush.

Cole and Morgan greeted her by name as Eleanor announced, without greeting, "Never mind. We've all been discussing how to interest Hugh Platt in this undertaking, so we've made good use of the time."

"Indeed," said an unexpected voice. Joan jerked her gaze toward it. Standing distant from the others, to the degree anyone could be distant in so closed a space, was Cristóforos Pantazis. He was inspecting two different stalks of lavender in the light from the window.

"I believe you've met—" Master Morgan began.

"Yes," said Joan, recovering. "The gentleman from Greece. Are we considering business on an international scale?" she asked Master Cole. "I'd only meant to broker a local arrangement."

"I am local," said Master Pantazis. "I've bought a patent of denization, and purchased some acres north of the city. I would not have them lie fallow."

Joan considered him a moment. "If I may presume to guess, you wished to grow my plum trees there, but the soil will not support them, so you're seeking options. Especially since Master Morgan's land at Battersea is not so well suited for the crops we are discussing, as it's too close to the Thames to drain well."

Master Pantazis smiled in gentle admiration. "Your friends' approbation of you is not misplaced. Also, I know Master Morgan and others such as Hugh Platt are attempting to improve lavender grown in this climate, but I have a small estate in France that is already producing excellent lavender."

"Well, the more, the merrier, I suppose," said Joan, without finishing the thought: *the fewer, the more meat*. She busied herself with an imaginary something on her thumb. It bothered her that she found him handsome; she had from her first glance of him, but it felt wrong to admit it now. But perhaps that was nonsense. And she was pleased that her idea was taking root—was already growing beyond her own dreams for it. "I do think if we are going to make particular infusions available to women who might be dependent on them, we should be rigorous in our approach," she continued. "It does not matter if the plums' potency relies more on belief than on fact, but we cannot be so cavalier about this undertaking."

"Of course these herbs work," said Eleanor, in her most Eleanor of voices, so that Joan felt foolish. "I have been relying on them for years longer than you have even existed. The challenge has always been consistent potency, not the medicinal properties of the herbs themselves."

"It's admirable that you're concerned," said Pantazis to Joan. "But I must agree with Mother Eleanor. Our energies will go into ensuring the potency."

"And meanwhile we should also educate whoever is making use of the herbs," said Joan. "They should know why tansy works, or rue, or marigold. Encourage them to understand—"

"If they wish to," said Dorothy. "I've had women come in not even clear on how they ended up with child, and preferring to remain in darkness. No wonder Mary is believed to be a virgin; half the women in London are just as ignorant."

"That is indelicately said," said Master Morgan, more amused than discomfited.

"My point," said Dorothy, "is that we should make information available to those who want it, but there may be few enough of them. Not everyone is interested in the workings of their own bodies as you suddenly seem to have become, Joan."

Joan blushed. "Perhaps that's because it's never occurred to them there is a benefit to it," she said. "I am fortunate not to have been deprived of learning on account of my sex"—she gestured toward Cole and Morgan, both of whom looked pleased—"and I should like other females to have my good fortune."

"Speaking of fortune, I believe the playhouses are letting out," said Dorothy, in a knowing tone. "And you have fulfilled your mission here, by getting us all in the same room. Well done, my dear. Go enjoy yourself and we old people shall continue scheming."

Abruptly fidgety—because of Pantazis, which again made her upset with herself—Joan ducked her head. "If you're certain I'm not needed—"

"I wager we don't need you as much as he does." Dorothy chuckled. "Come tomorrow and we'll tell you what we have all agreed upon."

"It's someone from the playhouses?" said Master Morgan, sounding dismayed. "Nobody in Southwark is worthy of La Pucelle. Joan, pardon me, I would never say—"

"If you would never say it, then don't say it," counseled Eleanor, in a tone that silenced Master Morgan. "We approve. And we do not easily approve."

"I believe that," said Cole under his breath as Joan darted out of the shop.

THE SCENT OF Joan lingered on him everywhere, long after their farewell kiss. He was let into Baron Putney's dark-paneled entrance hall; a blank-faced liveried page boy carrying a lamp gestured him to follow down a corridor and up a wooden staircase. He wished he could keep the taste of her on his tongue all evening. Everything he did—even everything he would do tonight—was for their future. When he reached Heminges's age (and had retired from his decades-long and profitable position as an Essex man, Essex having been restored to favor through the device of the forged letters), he would sit smoking a clay pipe in front of his fireplace in his home and tell his children (when they were old enough, when they were grown) the lengths he had gone to, to procure a position that would ensure their mother, his wife, access to the most educated minds in the nation. They would be cultured because he was their father, and intelligent because she was their mother. He felt his throat constrict, imagining this, although never before tonight had he contemplated children. But what a waste it would be for Joan to be the end of her line. He would do whatever he had to, to achieve a future full of Joan.

Whatever he had to.

He had followed the page boy without paying attention, since he knew the way well enough.

Whatever chamber the Putneys slept in, they had a separate one for their debauches. He had arrived in it. He wore his apprentice clothes because he knew they liked that. The walls were lined with painted and spangled curtains, and open braziers on each wall had mirrors near them.

The room smelled of musk and ambergris and the fire kept it warm. There was a large couch, with cushions heaped upon it, and—not visible and not often used—leather restraints looped around each leg. He had been so eager, his first time here, to agree to every possible expression of lust that either asked of him. Some part of him had thought, *This cannot be what God made bodies for*, but his own body had disagreed, and disagreed, and disagreed. And they, the Putneys, had been so pleased with their new toy, they had invited friends the second time, and his body continued to respond to things he was sure did not occur outside this room. There had been a brief period when it was his favorite room in London.

Looking at that couch now almost made him sick.

"Alexander," said the lady's voice in his ear. "I'm so pleased you are feeling friendly toward us again."

"How could I not be, m'lady, when you make it so very worth my while?" he said, the recitation nauseating. He was furious at Joan; he might have enjoyed this still, were it not for her changing everything inside of him.

And then he wasn't furious, but heartbroken. She was going back to her quiet, dull home; she had no idea what would transpire here tonight, and he would never speak of it. He'd told her only that he had a supper engagement at which he would meet wealthy patrons who sought a resident entertainer. Now he wondered if that was even true, or just a line Putney had used to get him back here.

Lady Putney, bodice already unlaced, reached for his blue cloak, and pushed it off his shoulder. She reached for his collar, searching for pins to pull out. He knew from experience he was to remain passive and allow her to. The baron sauntered into the room in nothing but his shirt, smiled with wolfish satisfaction, and began to arrange the cushions on the couch.

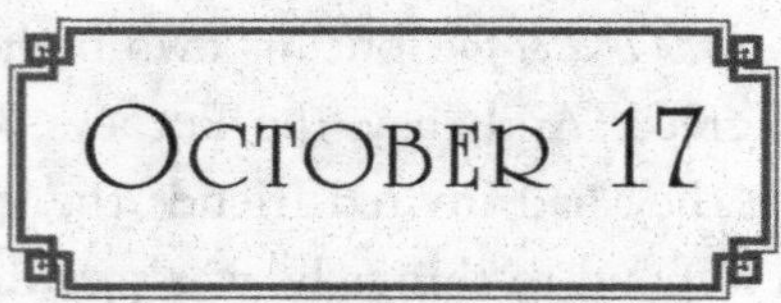

October 17

THE EARL'S MEN, I WOULD call it," said Essex. "*Essex's Men* is too sibilant."

Sander was amazed. "And you are forming this new company . . . when?"

The clock struck a quarter-hour and King Henry's "Pastime with Good Company" played tinnily somewhere.

"As soon as Her Majesty renews my monopoly on wine imports," the earl said. He leaned against the canopied back of his receiving chair, the light from a strategically sited stained glass window bathing him in amber and rose light. "Which, thanks to your invaluable assistance with Francis's letters, should be soon. So I will thank you now, in the humble manner that an impoverished nobleman might"—he gestured to the vermilion silk shirt and breeches that he had offered Sander, which now lay wrapped in linen on a bench. The clothes would never fit him well, but the gifting of one's private clothes was an ageless ritual, and Sander understood the weight of it. Essex had just given Sander pieces of himself to wear—"and will thank you again with patronage as soon as I am able."

"I was honored to be of service to Master Bacon and your lordship," said Sander, bowing his head. "But forming a company from scratch is perhaps a more involved undertaking than you realize, m'lord."

"Not if you're involved, lad," Essex said.

The night before felt like a bad dream; he could not bear to think of what he'd done at Baron Putney's, no matter if it were for Joan's sake; it was without Joan, and that made it abhorrent. And their only guests, when guests arrived, had been interested in him for the same reasons the Putneys were.

Then now, today, to suddenly be offered this most astonishing opportunity, with nothing unsavory about it . . .

"A troupe requires more than just a leading man, my lord," Sander continued, bowing his head. "As honored as I am that you believe I have the reputation to make it possible. It requires a company of players, and a playhouse, and writers—"

"The Earl of Oxford has always wanted to write plays," said Essex breezily.

"Oxford's prose is so heavy-handed it would sink the royal barge," said his sister with a gracious smile, from her own cushioned seat to the earl's left.

"Her Majesty admires you, lad. She'll help me set it up. Once she finds the letters and reads them and forgives me—'tis a month away at most. You see," he continued, directing this to Penelope, "it's all as I said it would be. I knew Francis would come around and see things from my side."

"I'm not sure he's done that, brother," Lady Rich said. "I think he perceives that you have endangered yourself and he is trying to save you."

Essex shrugged. "As long as he's successful, his motivations matter not. So, lad, I prithee, consider it. I mean once your apprenticeship is over, of course, I don't want the Chamberlain's Men coming after me with daggers."

"That's just a few more months, sir. Apprenticeships begin and end on Lady Day."

"Excellent. We shall dedicate all performances to Her Majesty, of course."

"Your lordship does me greater honor than I have words to speak," said Sander. "But not to belabor the point, I cannot act in plays that don't exist. I appreciate, and joyfully accept, your praise of my performances, but your lordship must know that I could not do what I do were there not excellent playwrights penning lines for me."

"Everyone fancies himself a writer, lad, twill be simple enough to find scripts."

Sander paused. "Your lordship, I am partial of course, but the Chamberlain's Men outshine every other company in London because we are the only one with a resident playwright, who is a shareholder in the company."

"Ben Jonson?" asked Essex, looking appalled.

"Brother, don't be ignorant," said Penelope Rich. "He means Will Shakespeare."

"I did not realize Shakespeare was a shareholder. How . . . sophisticated."

"It is. The company is tightly knit. The collective investment of the shareholders, I believe, accounts for the quality of all the work on that stage, including mine. I am eager to say yes to you—this is an honor and an opportunity greater than anything I've ever even thought to pray for—"

"You're welcome," said Essex, pleased with himself.

"—but your lordship, I've had the privilege of living in John Heminges's home for seven years, and he is the company's manager. So I understand all elements of what is needed for such an undertaking to thrive. It takes far more than one performer, no matter his fame or talent."

Essex looked even more pleased with himself. "Well then," he said, "you shall be my lead player *and* my company manager. And compensated accordingly, of course. You have delighted me by saying yes, and we will shall speak of it again, as soon as Her Majesty has restored me to grace. Which shall happen soon now, with greatest thanks to you. Now, come into the dining room. We'll drink your health."

October 18

SANDER ASSUMED THE ONE THING Joan wanted more than Sander Cooke was Francis Bacon.

So he delayed telling her of Bacon's new summons until she was spooned with him between the worn linen sheets, sated but still virginal, facing out an open doorway toward the stage. Sunset was earlier now, and the high walls of the Playhouse cast everything in shadow.

Joan was incredulous.

Sander explained: "He can't risk a female sneaking into Gray's Inn, now that he knows what you are."

"But another supper? He was so dissatisfied with me at the last one," she said.

"You won't behave like that again," said Sander. "His terms are that you're not to speak or draw attention at all, whatsoever. He asked if you were capable of that, and I assured him that you were. Don't make a liar of me."

"I won't. I'm satisfied to simply listen for a change. Who'll be there?" she asked, leaning back against him. "I'd love a hydrologist or geometer. I've not studied either of those disciplines."

"He gave no names, but his aim is some philosophers for you and some patrons for me. He still frowns at my regard for Essex, even though he's the one who—" He stopped himself. "He has his own investment in Essex."

Joan groaned. "All this courtly scheming. You have better things to do with your attention. You were going to join me in my scientific adventures, do you recall?"

"That's because we wanted to spend time together. Do you object to how we're spending it instead?" he asked, nuzzling her nape and cupping a hand around one of her breasts.

She grinned. "No. You were right all along: this is better than philosophy."

"I thank God for that reply."

She twisted around in his arms so that she faced him. "You should thank *me*," she whispered, and walked her fingers down his abdomen.

IT WAS THE Hawthorn—the same tavern, in fact the same room, as that earlier unfortunate supper. Sander exchanged a familiar nod with Bacon's servant, who was playing cards at the bottom of the stairs. The room: the same pale furniture, the same hodgepodge of lamps and candles.

Joan made a brief, unhappy sound when she entered behind him. Sander worried she'd twisted her ankle or lost her balance, but stopped himself from turning to check. Tonight, she was his boy; solicitous behavior from him would seem suspicious.

He took in the assembled faces. Besides Bacon, who winked at him when their eyes met, there were four other men. He recognized the one to Bacon's right: Richard Carew, the sonorous-voiced mapmaker. Carew had been at that first supper here, when Joan behaved so unfortunately; Sander guessed she was embarrassed, which accounted for the strange noise she'd just made. The dark-haired gentleman across from Carew, also in somber clothing, had an intellectual air to him, so must be some kind of philosopher, and therefore invited for Joan's sake. The other two guests had clearly been invited for him, judging by the extraordinary ornateness of their dress and their dawning delight as each recognized Sander Cooke out of costume. They rose to their feet and bowed with much excited self-conscious clumsiness, like a duo of *marrionettes* controlled by drunk puppeteers. His mouth responded with a self-deprecating smile, which only thrilled them more; he could sense Joan, behind him, trying not to laugh.

Introductions were made and hands washed. The man across from Carew was a Greek named Cristóforos Pantazis. The two obsequious guests were knighted gentry, Sir Andrew Someone and Sir Douglas Someone-else. They were nondescript, although their clothes were not, and they were almost interchangeable: brownish hair, hazel eyes, some thirty years of age, of average build, with identical accents that imitated Her Majesty's. They wore similar jewel-encrusted doublets of vermillion with black sleeves attached by gold-tissue points, and ruffs of pink-starched cambric. Each gushed variations of the praises Sander was accustomed to: He was hailed for his natural grace, and elegance, and talent; each declaimed how honored they were to meet a youth of such excellent qualities. He doubted either of them would be of use to him for patronage—certainly not compared to Essex—but he could smile and charm his way through one supper without difficulty, for Joan's sake.

But both knights relentlessly ignored, interrupted, or talked over everyone else to secure Sander Cooke's attention. Soup, bread, roasted halibut, boiled beef, and lots of wine—nothing stopped their mouths long enough for anyone to wrest the conversation from them. He was used to this behavior and had often basked in it, but tonight he felt only acute irritation—mostly at himself, for not predicting it. Worse, both men were consumed with things frivolous and trivial, and almost all of it court gossip, the thing he knew Joan had no patience for. Worse yet, he remained courteous and gracious because he was too conditioned to do otherwise, and so each knight believed that Sander Cooke was enjoying him. And so both knights dug in deeper and spoke much louder, whenever Bacon, Carew, or Pantazis attempted to salvage the conversation with any topic of substance. Bacon was famously dominating in most conversations but he could not wrest so much as a glance from them; they talked over him gaily as if he were not present. Mapmaking, travel, continental philosophy, poetry, even (Pantazi's contribution) preparations for the coming winter as recommended by Hugh Platt (Bacon rolled his eyes at the name); these attempts were all thwarted by the knights' careening giddily back toward speculation of who had caught what disease from whom, or who the real father was of some suspiciously-featured infant, or which simperer was backstabbing which other simperer. Bacon grew exasperated; Carew, bored. Pantazis—once he gave up trying—looked resignedly amused. Especially after the roasted duck, when the conversation turned (despite Bacon's attempts to prevent this) to Robert Devereux, Earl of Essex. The duo spent an entire custard course cackling about the earl's childish antics.

"Do I misunderstand you?" Master Pantazis asked, after listening to half a dozen appalling anecdotes (most of them exaggerated, and delivered with glances toward Sander to see if he was entertained). "You are saying the earl broke into your queen's bedroom? While she was in her nightdress? . . . To, what? Violate her?"

"No, no," said Sir Andrew, "nothing like that, she was surrounded by her women."

Sir Douglas chortled, "The man mounts anything in a skirt, so mayhap he wanted to seduce her into liking him again."

"He does not, erm, pursue *everything* in a skirt," Sir Andrew objected. "He would never make such untoward movements toward Her Majesty."

Sir Douglas laughed. "I'll wager you're wrong about that."

Richard Carew turned on Douglas, stern. "Sir, contain yourself. Rumor's a destructive force."

"Well then," said Sir Douglas, "let us constrain ourselves to evidence. The earl has had at least one bastard son, and at least one revealed affair. Although considering Elizabeth Brydges, who among us would *not* have her, given the opportunity—"

"Do not speak with lechery of one so fair and exalted," scolded Sir Andrew.

"Elizabeth Brydges, *exalted*?" retorted Sir Douglas. "On what grounds would you exalt her?"

"Why, one needs but look at her—"

"Of course, the porcelain skin, the blue veins, the blushing cheeks," said Sir Douglas. "She's a beauty. But does that make her virtuous?"

"Her particular *kind* of beauty suggests purity, yes," said Sir Andrew. "She is fairer than Penelope Rich—and beautiful as Lady Rich is, one cannot call her chaste or loyal."

"But surely you know," said Sander with a tight smile, hoping this would finish the topic, "the fairness is merely paint. The two ladies you refer to have face paints procured from difference sources, so that is the only thing you are commenting on."

Surprised by this turn in the conversation, the knights pivoted in unison to regard him with expectant looks. The sycophancy nauseated him, but he wondered if he could bore them into changing the subject themselves. "When I'm on the stage, my complexion is that same shade of white as Elizabeth Brydges. I happen to know she uses the same Venetian supplier that we do at the Globe. And we use the same blue pencil to sketch in veins."

"Fascinating!" said Sir Andrew. It wasn't.

"So I would ask you," continued Sander, "are you judging her character by her paint or by her *self*?"

Sir Andrew looked baffled. Sander hoped that would end the matter.

But then Pantazis leaned forward and asked, "If I may presume, young man, are you a friend of this lady?" There was something strange about the way he looked at Sander—in his direction, but not quite meeting his eye.

Sander shrugged. "I hardly know her. But we have something in common. For now, I must wonder: Are these gentlemen also judging *my* character by my painted face, or by my real face?" He wished Joan were free to speak; she'd make some cheeky remark that would show subtle approval.

"We're not judging you by your face at all," said Sir Douglas. "That is, 'tis a fair face for portraying women, but it reflects nothing of your excellent character."

"How do you know of my excellent character?" asked Sander. "You esteem me without knowing me, so your esteem comes from what you perceive at a distance. I am a beautiful female, and so you treat me as an admirable male."

"What's admirable is that you *perform the role* of an attractive woman very well," clarified Sir Andrew.

"I must take no credit for that," said Sander. "I was born with this face, and I daub paint onto it. Neither of those things warrants admiration." He could feel the warmth of Joan's approval without a sound or gesture from her. It emboldened him. "If my face was not painted white on the stage, would I still have whatever desirable qualities you attribute to me?"

"Of course, dear boy," said Robert Carew. "Your talent is a thing apart from your beauty."

"I assure you, sir, I am admired for my talent, but I'm *adored* for my beauty." He spoke without arrogance, delivering a fact. "And my beauty is pure artifice."

"I don't—" began Sir Andrew, but Sander held up one delicate hand and kept talking. "Am I as beautiful this moment as I was a few hours ago on the stage? Or am I less beautiful because my face is no longer pale?" He hoped Joan appreciated that, given their disagreements about her always sitting with the sun on her face.

The knights exchanged uncomfortable glances. "You are a man of perfect aspect, regardless of the color of your face," said Sir Andrew, and Douglas nodded and hear-heared him as if he wished he'd thought of this answer himself.

"So you judge no men by their complexions, only women," said Sander, with a tone of finality.

Pantazis smiled at this, and Bacon, noticing, turned to him. "Sir, I am curious how this conversation strikes a stranger to our land."

Pantazis shrugged. Again, he glanced at Sander and yet seemed to be looking through him. "I have not given this much thought. I put my energies into other arenas."

"How admirable," said Bacon. "Such as what?"

"I came to London chiefly as a botanist—"

"Wait, I want to hear his views on beauty," said Sir Douglas.

"Yes! After all, fair complexions are valued by Greeks," said Sir Andrew. "We all know Aphrodite was blond."

Pantazis stared at him for a moment, bemused. "You also know she was a goddess, but I am quite certain you do not revere her godliness, so it is interesting to me that you revere her beauty."

"It is what her beauty represents," said Sir Andrew.

Pantazis shook his head. His expression was patient, nearly paternal, and Sander approved of him for this. It wasn't the interesting evening he'd intended for Joan, but it was evolving into a different kind of interesting; he wished he could read her mind to know if she agreed. "If you wish to hear *my* thoughts on the beauty of *actual* women, you must not look at Aphrodite but rather, at my sisters and my nieces. It is true they crave paleness, but they remain more olive-skinned than all women I have seen in England. Yet I consider them more beautiful than any woman I have encountered here, no matter how pale or refined."

Sir Douglas sat up straighter, and looked displeased. "That is an offense, sir. But I suppose we must excuse you since, as a barbarian heathen, you cannot be expected to know better."

"Sir Douglas," snapped Bacon. "You will not insult my guest."

Sir Douglas waved this away. So did Pantazis. "Sir Douglas, Greece is the cradle of civilization, and my people have been Christian centuries longer than your people. So 'tis *I* who must excuse *your* heathen barbarian ignorance. Which I do." His demeanor remained calm, almost affectionate. Sander envied him the freedom to insult the dolt.

Douglas opened his mouth to retort, but Bacon cleared his throat and drew all eyes to him. "How felicitous, sir, to be reminded the world is larger than our humble island, jewel though it may be." He turned a pedantic stare on the knights. "It is eye-opening for us to be reminded that English conventions of anything—not merely of beauty—are just that: English conventions, and not an objective universal truth."

Sander, pleased, resisted a hopeful backward glance at Joan. This was the language of Bacon the Philosopher, which is what she'd come for.

"Now of course," said Richard Carew, playfully, "if one were Francis

Bacon, in pursuit of truth, one would gather information in search of an objective—"

"Aha! Yes!" said Sir Douglas. "Let us pursue the truth of beauty! Surely this clever Stranger can give us valuable insight on foreign concepts of beauty."

"Not really," said Pantazis.

"Oh, you can, though. Come now!" said Sir Douglas.

Pantazis glanced at Bacon; Bacon, having given up on redeeming the evening, shrugged with annoyance. The Greek shifted his attention, to give Sander a fleeting, conspiratorial grin, which Sander intuited to mean something like, *If this must be the playing field, let's play to win.*

Now it was certain to be a Joan-worthy evening. What other woman could find herself a fly on the wall of such a conversation among men?

"All right then," said Pantazis. "Turkish women paint their eyes with kohl, as our Greek women sometimes do. I believe Chinese women paint their cheeks red. I have heard that the people of the West Indies, men and women alike, cut themselves and have tattoos—"

Sir Douglas made a face. "These populations you cite are heathens, why should we regard them?"

"We were heathens when we invented Aphrodite, and you seem to like her well enough," Pantazis said.

"And we should acknowledge," said Carew, "that our own English ladies paint their cheeks red too. There are berries which make a perfect red for lips and cheeks, from Trinidad—I know this because my wife is desperate for me to find some for her. If a woman of Trinidad put that red on her face, Englishmen would likely not consider her red cheeks beautiful. It's only when an English lady puts that red of Trinidad onto her face that we find it a beautiful red for a face. So, yes, there is hypocrisy at play here."

Sander, starting to enjoy this, said, "You must admit, Sir Douglas, as a nation we are dependent on substances from Asia, or Africa, or the New World, provided by barbaric Strangers, to make our English ladies pretty. Hugh Platt has been experimenting with new cosmetic formulas, but even he relies on imported materials."

He heard Bacon mutter, "Hugh Platt again," under his breath disgustedly.

"Our ladies were embellishing themselves long before the age of discovery," retorted Sir Douglas loftily. "They once were, and still could be, beautiful English ladies without any barbarian assistance."

"Oh yes!" said Sander with mock enthusiasm. "I've been schooled about that as an apprentice player. Should trade with other nations be disturbed, we must know what home-brewed beautifying resources to fall back upon."

"Well there you are," said Sir Douglas to the rest of the table, triumphant.

"Yes, indeed. Let me tell you all about it," pressed Sander, with an exaggerated facade of graciousness. "Let me tell you how English ladies who do not make use of barbarian artifice must burn and pulverize the jawbones of hogs, and mix it with pigeon excrement. And also lead and quicksilver." He beamed. "Beautiful English hogs and beautiful English pigeons for our beautiful English ladies. To make their faces white, to prove they're virtuous. For—let's all admit it—what could better prove a lady's intrinsic superiority than bird shit smeared upon her temples?"

Sir Douglas was red-faced, and the other Englishmen looked taken aback. But Pantazis laughed outright, in an approving tone that made Sander want to hug him.

"Well," said Sir Andrew, huffing. "If that's even accurate, I warrant such a brew was for common-born women. Noble women's toilette would have had nicer ingredients. They're the only ones who should be painting their faces anyhow, as—to return to our original point—that reflects their refinement."

"That's nonsense!" said Sander. "Everything you're saying is nonsense."

"Sander," Bacon growled, but Sander glowered back at him.

"You may throw me out of here if this displeases you, Master Bacon, and I will beg pardon of you later, but this is a conversation about beauty, which is my stock in trade, and I will speak. Sirs," he said, looking at Sir Douglas. "Hear me out. The women you'd demean because they're not pale are the ones growing the English food and making the English medicines and spinning the English flax and wool and providing all the things the pale English ladies require in order to remain pale. You know that I am not a woman, that my pale white face is just a decoration and reveals nothing about who I am. And yet you marvel at me. Any woman in the world can paint her face as easily as I, and you'll likewise think she's a marvel, no matter what she really is."

"Oh no," said Sir Andrew, "you are mistaken. To return *once again* to the heart of the matter: the refinement of a true lady *cannot* be counterfeited."

Sander ignored Bacon's warning glare. "I am living proof that is not true," he said. "I'm a common boy from Southwark and you fall over yourselves to flatter me because I've convinced you I'm a refined lady."

Sir Douglas chuckled. "Wrong! We admire you for your skill at *counterfeiting* to be a refined lady, because we know you aren't one."

"Well then!" retorted Sander, triumphant and righteous, "there are women aplenty at that court who likewise deserve your admiration, because *they* are counterfeiting to be refined ladies, every bit as much as I am."

"That's a gratuitous insult," objected Sir Andrew.

"It's a point of fact," Sander shot back. He hated to say this in front of Joan but she already knew it, and he was confident she would want him to. "I've been summoned to many of their beds, and I've reveled in their need to shed their pretense of refinement." This caused a small ripple, so he pressed on: "Unlike me, they have *genuinely* tricked you. Mostly by applying face paint." He had never felt so gloriously smug before. "Which they got from foreigners."

"An interesting observation," said Pantazis, before anyone else in the room could speak. "I have not had the pleasure of seeing you on the stage, but I myself know women who are not what they appear to be. I find them admirable, both for who they truly are and for how well they pretend to be something else." And he smiled in Sander's direction—but once again, not quite at Sander.

He was smiling at Joan.

Sander stifled his shock, and barely kept himself from whipping around to check her response.

"It is the fate of all women to have to counterfeit," Pantazis continued. His tone was kindly and he continued gazing at Joan—he had, it was now obvious, been looking at Joan all evening. "It is to our shame that we make little room for them in the world of men. That is our loss."

"Is it?" said both knights in the same dismissive tone.

That was enough. Sander stood up because otherwise he would have yelled. He was aching to know what Joan made of all this. She'd spent three hours standing, unmoving and unspeaking listening to these two idiots—had he made up for it? "Apologies, but I've an early rehearsal tomorrow that I forgot about 'til just this moment, and I must leave. Master Bacon, sir, I am always grateful for your generosity." Being well-trained and well-mannered, he went through his flurry of gracious and humble leave-taking, but with the rushed efficiency of somebody trying to excuse themselves before vomiting. Bacon nodded, understanding.

"Come, Jack," Sander said at last, and without glancing at her, gestured for Joan to follow him out of the room.

Outside, he leaned hard against the tavern wall, gulping the smoky evening air. "I'm appalled you had to endure those . . . I cannot even think of words to describe them."

She was already laughing. "Those toads have less brains than earwax," she said. "Sander, you were glorious! A hero to all women, not just me."

He felt a flush of pleasure. Then sobered: "But the Greek. How does he know you?"

Joan stopped laughing, bit her lower lip. "He's a friend of my botanists on Lime Street."

"The tree-grafting gentlemen?"

She nodded. "He met me again—as Joan, of course, not Jack—just the other day. It was good of him not to call me out."

"He never stopped staring at you, though." Sander put his hands on his face and growled. "I'm finished with these games. It's no way for me to find a patron, and if Bacon values you enough, he'll find some other way to mentor you."

"I won't argue," Joan said. Putting a hand on his arm, she suggested, "We'll shake it off together. Have you the Globe key with you?"

He squeezed his hand over hers. "No. 'Tis easy enough to fetch from Heminges. But it will be dark and cold there now."

"I don't mind cold and dark," she said, lowering her voice. "I have you for light and heat."

"Should I be jealous of the Greek?" he asked, realizing that he was, a little.

In the lamplight, mischief seeped onto her face. "If I say yes, will you finally have me?"

"That shouldn't be why it happens, Joan," he said, immediately craving it.

"What *should* be why it happens, then?" she asked.

October 26

On days that were not overcast or smoky, the noon sun—slanting southward with the waning year—lit the Bucklers' shop obliquely through the open door. When it appeared, Joan would bask in the light while she sat at her tasks. Few enough were the hours she spent here lately, and she wished those hours were even fewer. If Sander could secure a livelihood, they could marry. She wondered, half in jest, if her parents would even notice her departure; she seemed to matter to them only when she was of help somehow.

Today she was of help. She was cleaning the stone molds her father used to cast buckles. Later, he would funnel molten bronze into them, without letting her close enough to watch; anything with fire and heat was a man's business. Next on her list of tasks was to separate by size the pearls her mother would fasten to the finish work for ladies' trims.

A shadow crossed her table; she looked up to see a woman, silhouetted, a small bundle cradled in her arms. "Hello, Joan," said a familiar voice. It was Molly, from the Happy Sow. Joan rose and gestured her into the shop, and saw the bundle was the baby.

"How may I help you?" came Buckler's voice from behind the counter. His leather apron was dusted with ash and bronze filings.

Joan had helped out at the Sow more often since the baby arrived. She knew Molly to be a sweet young woman—barely older than herself—but today she looked world-weary, almost besieged.

"Master Buckler?"

"That's myself."

"I'm from the tavern at the Globe, perhaps I've served you a time or two."

He shrugged. "What brings you in?"

She glanced at Joan, then back to him. "My husband is unwell," she said.

"Shall I fetch Eleanor?" Joan asked, moving to the doorway.

"She's already come and gone," Moll said. "And I thank God for her skills and potions. He's out of danger now, but there's months of recovery ahead for him."

"I'm sorry to hear it," said Joan. "Is he in pain? How will you manage?"

"That's why I've come," she said, then turned back to Buckler. "I would hire your daughter to help us, full-time. She's the only one who knows the workings of the building and the business as well as we ourselves do. The Sow brings in plenty of income for Master Heminges, and he says he'll pay whoever you'd need here to replace her."

Joan kept her face neutral. To be in proximity to Sander all day rather than here made her want to squeal with happiness.

"For how long?" asked her father.

"Until New Year's at least, but maybe right through 'til Candlemas," she said. "We'd all be grateful."

He frowned. "They don't perform through the winter at the Playhouse, surely?"

"In and out," she said. "They prefer touring to fine houses and the larger inns, and will sometimes rent an indoor playhouse. But they'll play at the Globe on fine days, and we're open regardless."

"What's this, then?" asked Joan's mother, coming into the room from the back. Molly, shifting her babe from one arm to the other, explained the situation again.

Her parents muttered together a few moments, but Joan could already decipher the substance by the tone: if they were provided with a replacement at no cost to them, they would permit it. She suppressed a cackle of delight.

"My concern is what those sort get up to," said her father. "Both the players and the playgoers. And tavern-goers, to boot. Joan's of that troublesome age where she seems old enough to handle herself but young enough to be taken advantage of. How will you protect her virtue?"

Joan mother's clucked at him and adjusted her woolen coif. "Oh, now, Sander will keep an eye on her, he always has. And she'll still sleep in her own bed here."

Her father considered this. "Well, then, it's just the terms to settle on." Without anyone asking Joan's opinion of the arrangement, they settled on the sum John Heminges would pay the Bucklers for indenturing their daughter. (She was worth more than she'd realized—more than a maidservant, anyhow—and was not sure if she should be flattered or annoyed.)

She followed Molly silently out of the building. From her home to the Globe was the route she knew best in all of Southwark. In the cold sunlight, they trudged up New Rents to the churning river. The riverbank was at its widest in the low tide. It reeked. They passed St. Saviour, St. Mary Overie, Winchester House, the Clink, and when they were finally headed down Dead Man's Place, Joan said, "Your husband isn't ill."

"Correct."

When she offered nothing else, Joan examined her. Molly looked amused now; the appearance of exhaustion was gone.

"Must I guess?" asked Joan. "Eleanor and Dorothy would have come themselves. So I suppose it's Masters Cole and Morgan who are hiring me."

"Whoever those gentlemen are, they're not the ones who've summoned you."

Joan felt a shiver of excited alarm thrum through her. "It's not . . . a Stranger named Pantazis?"

Molly glanced at Joan. "I don't know that name either, but no. It's

Francis Bacon. He's waiting for you at the Sow with Sander. He will explain his need of you better than I can."

TROUBLE WAS OBVIOUS from a distance. They had not even stepped off Maiden Lane onto the Playhouse lot when she heard Sander's voice through an open window in the back of the Sow: "The fault is not mine that your scheme went afoul. I did what you asked of me—more besides, in fact, and I made sacrifices you know nothing of, to cover your tracks, sir."

Leaving Molly to her outdoor tasks, Joan went around to the front door as Bacon's voice within began to argue, but Sander spoke over him: "I put myself in danger so that you might help Essex, and the only benefit to me is that Essex likes me now. Forswear your benefactor in his time of need, if you must, but I will not. I endangered myself, and I will retain the sole advantage I reaped from it, which is his interest in me."

As Joan entered, Bacon's voice rose: "Her Majesty is furious at Essex now—"

"And at you," said Sander, quieting, but smug.

Her eyes adjusted. The two—one in black velvet, the other in blue wool—were standing too far apart for friendly discourse but not far apart enough for shouting. "Now, now, lad," Bacon scolded, just as smug. "I have easy access to Her Majesty, so I have been able to navigate the tempest of her displeasure. Essex has no access—and he likely never will again."

"But that's your fault," Sander said. "You're the one who would have deceived her."

"At his insistence."

"But 'twas your scheme."

"At his insistence," Bacon repeated. "The intent, more than the deed, outrages her. He is out of her favor forever now, do you understand? Don't throw your lot in with him, he is *out of favor*."

Sander shrugged peevishly. "He might yet become one of those lords, of whom there are plenty, who thrive contentedly without dabbling in court intrigues—"

"Now you are being deliberately foolish," said Bacon, his irritation sharpening into anger. "You know he will never be such a one, Sander. The man is possessed by twin demons of light and dark, and both extremes compel him toward Her Majesty, but she will no longer have either of those demons near her person."

"Pardon," said Joan, raising a hand. "I know not why I was summoned here, but it cannot be to witness this."

Bacon started, blinked. "Here you are," he said, the anger leaving his voice. He studied all of her, as if the faded green doublet and skirt were an exotic costume, as if the curve of breast and waist and hip were a language he could not make out. "I am pleased to meet you as your actual self. Jane?"

"Joan," she said. She disliked his comment; she felt no more her actual self now than he had ever seen her. "You may call me Jack if you prefer."

"I'm glad to see you, Jack."

She smiled, mollified. "I am gratified, sir. But why am I here?"

"I wish to employ you. Sander gave me some details of your family situation, which I must confess appalled me. I sent the woman to collect you on a pretense I thought would sit well with them."

"For the record, sir," Sander intervened, "you are terrible at assessing what a good pretense would be."

"Contain yourself a moment, Sander," Bacon said without looking at him. Gesturing to a table, he said, "Sit, I would engage you as my assistant on a project."

Her eyes opened wider than she wanted them to. "Assist you, sir?" she echoed. "Not just be the person whose ignorance you learn from, but assist you? In your research?"

"Yes. It is regarding the tidal behavior of the Thames."

Her delight evaporated. "I . . . know nothing of that, sir."

"Neither do I, yet," he said. "But others do. Sit, sit." She did. He took the stool across from her. "I intend a simple demonstration of my inductive method, by applying it to something about which I know nothing, but other people do, so that the results of my research can be checked against proven facts. Do you see? I am testing the system to demonstrate I can achieve accurate results from it. It must be a simple subject, which regretfully means it will be tiresome."

"If it's tiresome in the name of research, it isn't tiresome," she said.

Bacon smiled. "I congratulate myself for choosing you." He sobered again. "I do have some hesitations about hiring an information-gatherer, as your own biases will determine what information you most notice to gather. But to be honest with myself, I cannot ensure that even I am capable of perfect objectivity, so I am willing to take a chance on you. I had hoped Sander would accompany us, at least when he has leisure."

"Which I said I'll do," insisted Sander, but Bacon talked right over him: "However, we are incapable of resolving a difference that might result in the sundering of our friendship."

Sander cursed under his breath; he curled closed the fingers of one hand, a signal to Joan not to interfere. "Master Bacon. Sir. That is a gross overstatement."

"Sander, I cannot credit you with anything if I cannot credit you with understanding the gravity of your poor judgment. Not even Essex himself has so distressed my feeble constitution."

"I would be grateful," Joan tried again, "if one of you might explain your disagreement in language I can follow."

Sander stepped closer to the table and held his hands out like a storyteller. "Once upon a time, the queen was upset with his lordship, the Earl of Essex!" One arm made a sweeping gesture toward Bacon. "The esteemed Francis Bacon, despite having publicly disowned Essex, sought to help Essex in secret. He forged letters supposedly written by Essex, about how much Essex adored Her Majesty, and then Francis Bacon employed"—gesturing grandly toward himself—"Alexander Cooke, and others, to place these letters where Her Majesty"—a gesture toward an imaginary queen—"would encounter them as if by chance. This was supposed to give the letters a sheen of sincerity that she couldn't trust if the same words were written directly to her by the earl."

"That," said Joan, chuckling, "sounds like a marvelous plot for a comedy by Master Shakespeare."

"Indeed," said Sander. "Her Majesty not only saw through it as a forgery, but somehow pieced together that it was her trusted servant, Francis Bacon, behind it all."

"And barred Francis Bacon from court for a month, and warned him away from any further interaction with Essex," Bacon said in a voice of conclusion.

"I understand," said Joan. "You wish Sander to likewise avoid the earl, and Sander refuses to do so."

"Correct, because Sander has no need to," said Sander, lowering his arms. "The earl's own sister, Penelope Rich, is still Her Majesty's attendant, so clearly Her Majesty is particular about who may or may not associate with Essex. Until the queen herself tells me to forswear Essex, I need not do so, and I won't. I perceive a benefit in staying friendly with him."

"Because you are deluding yourself, as I myself did for years," said Bacon in the tone of an exasperated father. "It will stain your reputation among the very people you wish to charm."

"Pardon, but I must make a request," Joan said. "I wish to work for you"—meaning Bacon—"and fraternize with you"—turning to Sander—"regardless of whatever comes between you. For that to happen, without sending me to Bedlam, I beg you both to refrain from complaining about this Essex matter in my hearing. Please."

She held out her open hand, midway between them. Bacon and Sander glanced at each other. Bacon stepped up to her, took her hand, and shook it. He gave Sander a superior look.

"Fine," Sander said. He reached out for her hand.

FRANCIS BACON HAD no interest in the River Thames. The aim of his project was solely to test his own approach to learning. Joan's duty was to measure things, many times a day, every possible day over the course of the winter. Bacon would then translate her findings into conclusions about the behavior of the river. He would check these conclusions with Her Majesty's Clerk of Rivers, or whoever it was who made their living knowing the ways of the Thames. If his conclusions matched established knowledge, that would be an endorsement of his method. If his conclusions did not match, he would examine them to try to learn why, so that he could adjust his method.

It seemed clear to Joan that this project must be a considerable come-down for him: he had wanted to improve how natural philosophy was taught at Oxford; instead, he was studying muddy water with the unschooled daughter of a Southwark buckle-maker.

The measurements were to do with the amount of silt suspended in a firkin of river water under a variety of specific circumstances: when the tide was low or high; rushing inland, turning, rushing out; when the weather was fair, when it was raining, or windy, or cold; when eel nets were full of eels; when the moon was waxing or waning, when it was new, or crescent, or half, or gibbous, or full. She herself was not to look for patterns, but simply to record precise information.

She was to dress as Jack, which pleased her. A boy working alone along the riverbank was unremarkable, and safer than for a young woman. Bacon had rented a long, low shed on the north side of the river. She brought each heavy bucket to the shed. She set it down to settle, then drained off the water through cheesecloth, and took measurements as well as notes about the texture, color, and consistency of whatever minute flotsam had been caught. It was never only silt. Cradled in the gauzy fabric was anything from dung to offal to fabric scraps to dead haddock to strips of velum to the errant cameo or decorative pin. She was allowed to keep these nicer rarities once she had shown them to him. That was all the wages she got, but through Molly, Bacon paid her father enough to hire a replacement in the shop.

Bacon was right: the work was tedious. And she was doing it alone. He bought her a pair of galoshes, wrapped and oiled to keep out the wet; after a few sodden days, he bought her a gabardine as well. Daily, she would change at the Sow and leave her own things there, cross the

Thames for the hours required, and then, returning, leave her wet things to dry overnight by Molly's hearth.

She learned as she went: the flood tides brought effluent from the jacks of the houses on London Bridge houses; the ebb tide brought offal from the royal slaughterhouse at Whitehall; the phases of the moon changed the intensity of the tidal surge.

The dockside shed was long and narrow, with nothing in it but a table, and windows for light. The days were very short now, which limited her work. The cold was damp and biting, and Sander was not always at the Globe this time of year; as Molly had said, the company sought inside venues when possible. So only sometimes could she warm herself in his arms at the end of her long days.

She began the work wholeheartedly. She enjoyed watching people who made their living on or near the river: the tapsters, the dyers, the fishermen, the ferrymen, the dockworkers; she enjoyed the disguise, the freedom to be someone else; she enjoyed work that differed from what she was condemned to do by birth.

Three weeks in, these pleasures were waning. Her arms were stronger than they had ever been, but her hands had grown so rough, she worried how they felt to Sander's skin when she caressed him. The thrill of helping Francis Bacon to develop a scientific approach to the world—this thrill too had diminished under the day-to-day banality of actions. She dreamed of buckets, sloshing frigid water, spoonfuls of dirty river sand, gloves that never dried. Her muscles ached each morning until they didn't—but then her sleeves were too tight over her arms.

Worst of all, her mind was not engaged. Once she learned the mechanics of the task, there was nothing to the task but physical activity.

One breezy, chilly afternoon, she was examining an odd tin object her bucket had scooped up as the tide was turning. The day was cold but—by London standards—clear, and light through the windows made examination easy. The declining sun hit the surface of the Thames and threw up as much light from below her as above.

The door opened. Recognizing the footfall of Bacon's servant Pierre, she did not look up. But Pierre, having opened the door, stepped back outside.

"Good day," said Bacon. She set the tin object aside and began to rise. But then he went on to say, "I've brought a visitor, whom I happened to meet on the bridge." Cristóforos Pantazis ducked his head to peer inside, and she leaped up.

"Hello," she said, feeling herself blushing to the roots of her hair. She began to curtsey but stopped herself and bowed instead. Like Sander, but without the gracefulness, she thought. Suddenly it bothered her to be unkempt and wearing boy's clothes, and she was bothered with herself for being bothered. "God save you, sir." She knew he was still working with Eleanor and the botanists on the herbs to prevent conception—the Women's Pocket Project, Dorothy called it—but she had not seen him since the supper at Hawthorn Tavern, when she'd worn these same clothes.

Pantazis regarded her, smiling. "And you, my friend."

She blushed worse at the familiarity of the greeting. She couldn't even look at him. "To what do we owe the honor of your appearance?" she managed to ask, hoping the words were coming out in the right order.

"We were discussing you," said Pantazis. "And I wished to express my admiration."

Her blushing somehow intensified, causing pain. She tried to say *I'm speechless*, and found she literally was. Worse, she heard herself release a nervous little laugh that sounded almost mocking.

"You are something," Pantazis said, in his soft voice. "I hope you know that. I approach you through our mutual friend here, because I am unclear who else knows your double identity, and I would not imperil you with unwanted revelation."

Joan gave herself a steadying moment. "Thank you. The women know," she said, "Eleanor and Dorothy. But not Master Cole or Master Morgan."

"I believe they would be gratified to meet this Jack."

Joan shook her head.

"As you wish. It saddens me that women have so few outlets for their intellectual industry."

"I appreciate the sentiment."

"Joan," said Bacon. "Master Pantazis has enlightened me as to your other project."

"The botanical pursuit," Pantazis said. "The Women's Pocket Project. And its cascading impact on both civic health and private industry. I think we should take it to Hugh Platt—"

"You are under-used here," Bacon informed Joan, as if cutting Pantazis off.

"In this fish shed? I would say so," said Pantazis, with dry humor.

Bacon cleared his throat. His eyes drifted toward the ceiling, his hands fidgeting against each other. "I am finding it difficult to take the time, with all my other studies and responsibilities, to translate your notes into meaningful material. I would not have your diligent effort be for nothing, especially given the importance of the work." It seemed to Joan that he was aiming that statement at Pantazis, not herself. "So I propose you interpret your own research."

She heard herself gasp.

"Something is amiss?" asked Bacon.

"On the contrary," she managed to say, "I'm honored. Only . . . where shall I do that work? This room is cold, sir, and the table is too rough to write upon."

"I'll arrange for you to work at the Sow," said Bacon. "We have already taken them into our confidence, and Heminges seems fond of you." With some amusement entering his voice now: "Alexander will approve of that location." That made her blush again.

"May I ask something?" said Pantazis. After a moment Joan realized the question was for her.

"Of course," she said, still flustered.

"The meeting last month at Mother Eleanor's, when there was a reference to your, if I may use the term, paramour. This is Sander? The exercised young actor at the Hawthorn?"

Joan tried to nod but her head would not move; surely Bacon realized by now, but it had never been said. When Sander had first brought her to Bacon, they were only friends.

How very recent and how very long ago that seemed.

"You may admit to it, Jack," said Bacon.

"Yes, then," said Joan, almost voiceless.

"He is a fortunate man," said Pantazis.

"He knows that," said Joan, staring at the table.

"And what mischief is Sander at these days?" asked Bacon, with false offhandedness.

Joan was instantly annoyed enough to forget her embarrassment. "Sir, do we not have an agreement that neither of you speaks to me about anything that might disturb the other?" Bacon made a yielding gesture. "In truth," she continued, "I do not know how he spends his time when he is not with me or with the company, but I've never known such details. He is seeking patronage. He accepts every invitation he receives."

"I apologize if this is indelicate," said Pantazis. "But at that supper, he described himself, without apology, as licentious."

"He was describing what he used to be," said Joan sharply. "That is not what he is now."

A pause.

"Are you certain?" asked Pantazis, so gentle he sounded pitying.

Trying to keep the strain out of her voice, Joan said, "I do not wish to have this conversation, sir, even if your intentions are benign." She turned away from them and picked up a leather cord; with this, she fashioned a piece of cheese cloth over the top of the nearest bucket. "Pardon, my labor awaits me." She tipped the bucket over. Ten gallons of water poured down the back side of the table and splattered on the floorboards, which were set with wide gaps between them near the wall so that the water fell to the mossy bank below. Silt and detritus was retained in the filter of cheesecloth.

"My intentions were indeed benign," said Pantazis. "But I should not have spoken."

"Excuse me, I am in something of a hurry," Joan lied. "Sander is expecting me within the hour and he will be most anxious if I'm detained by a business associate who was speaking ill of him."

Pantazis chuckled. "I see you are capable of taking care of yourself," he said.

"Are you implying Sander is not capable of that?" she demanded, a flash of anger in her voice.

He was startled. "Pardon, I did not intend to stir up such passions. Of any sort," he amended quickly.

Joan set the emptied bucket back upright on the table. "Thank you for your kind words earlier." She wiped her hands clean on her work apron. "It may be said we have an interesting friendship, Master Pantazis."

He nodded, looked relieved. "If that is the worst you have to say of me, then I am gratified," he said. "And to return to my original point, as innocently as I can: he is a fortunate man, and I'm pleased that he knows it."

NOVEMBER 17

THE BUCKLERS' SHOP WAS CLOSED for Accession Day. As suppliers to Her Majesty's yeoman guards, they were expected to observe the anniversary of her coronation with joyful reverence. In contrast, for the Chamberlain's Men, it would be a day of labor and performance, beginning midday and going well into the night.

But Sander's morning was free.

Joan fed the hens, made bread dough, took it to the bakers, then rushed to the Playhouse. The back entrance was already open, the bed draped with sheets and blankets. Neatly stashed in a basket by the door were Sander's cosmetics and mirror glass, which he'd be taking to Whitehall Palace. As she stepped inside, he was already bare from the waist up and fumbling to remove his breeches. Without a word of greeting she hurried to him, pushed his hands away, and did it for him.

There was a sharp chill in here so early. In the afternoons, after hours of cramped habitation by men in heavy costumes, there would be a trace of ambient heat remaining. Not now. Anticipating this, Joan had wrapped a heated brick in a canvas cloth, which she unwrapped and spread over the bed linen before nudging Sander to lie down upon it. Still clothed, she lay on top of him and pulled the coverlet over them

"You think of everything," Sander said with pleased approval as he let the heat of the cloth seep into his back. "Except you forgot to take your own clothes off."

"Too cold," said Joan.

"Roll off me and let's see what I can manage under the blanket."

She had shed her shoes upon entering and the apron came away with a tug. He unlaced her bodice while she untied her stockings; it took shrugging and climbing and pulling and tugging under the heavy wool, until she was in nothing but her long-sleeved shift.

He tugged at the sleeves. "You have worn this to frustrate me."

"All cure lies in your own very capable hands," said Joan. "You have the skills and I, the willingness." She shot one arm out of the warmth of the bed and hovered it over his head. "Cuff."

Sander reached up and closed his fingers around the trim of the sleeve.

"Thank you kindly," she said, in a feathery imitation of the queen's accent, and drew her arm out from the sleeve. "That worked," she said, pleased. "Now the other." Again she raised her hand high, the wrist in reach of Sander; again he grabbed the cuff; again she retracted her arm.

"And now you're encased!" Sander said, rolling on top of her. "You've trapped yourself in your shift and handed yourself over as a gift to me. As a sacrifice."

"Alas, alack." Joan giggled, making a show of wriggling protest. "I live in terror that you will continue to fail to violate me."

"Joan, please." He rested his head on her shoulder. "It's hard enough—"

"Indeed it is," said Joan. "And yet you will not put it to its intended use." She squirmed in his grasp, elbows nudging him for freedom, then reached for the hem of her shift and pulled it up to the level of her ribs, so their nakedness lay pressed together. She reached behind him, lay the flat of her hand on his buttocks, and pushed him closer to her as he moaned with frustrated pleasure.

"Will you at least acknowledge you would not be forcing yourself on me," she said, walking her fingers downward.

"Yes yes yes yes yes, you little siren," he said. "Quite the opposite. It terrifies me that you behave like this while still a virgin. God protect every man in England once you've been fully initiated into the mysteries of sex. I'm preserving your virginity for the public good."

"Like Queen Elizabeth. You see, I do understand politics."

"I wager she's not actually a virgin."

She winked back. "I wager everyone says the same of me. Let's prove them right."

Sander stroked her face. "Nothing will ever be the sa—"

"Shut up, my love," she said. "We've already crossed that bridge. Time to cross this one, and get to the other side at last."

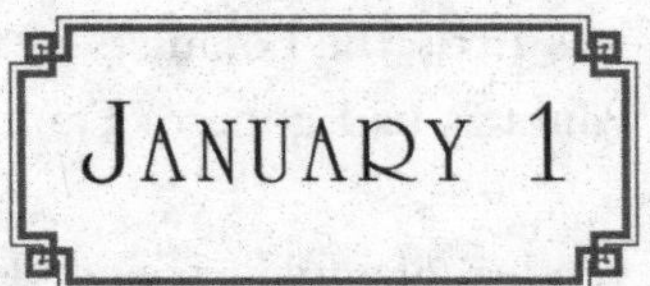

January 1

Joan shifted her weight back against Sander's sleeping form. She savored this, the warmth of his body, his soft breath on the nape of her neck. Above them, the oiled window-cloth glowed softly with sooty morning light. This was the Globe's business office, such as it was, adjacent to the Happy Sow. The straw bed was wedged between the table—weighted with ledgers, quills, and ink-making means—and a large corner chest. It was her first morning waking up in Sander's arms.

That her little life could hold so much contentment amazed her. Every day of these past six weeks had been a gift, from Accession Day through Yuletide. She was entirely Sander's lover, and he—in a darling act of gallantry—had gone to her father before Christmas, to ask his blessing for their betrothal. Buckler, bemused, had given it, without seeming to consider it a serious matter. John Heminges had been pleased but told Sander not to advertise their status while he was still apprenticed.

"Remember, your apprentice oath forbids you to marry."

"I made that oath when I was twelve," retorted Sander. "It also forbade me to fornicate, so I've been violating it for years."

"But, being wise, you will agree with me on this point."

"Grudgingly."

To the outer world, life continued as it had. Her days were busy being Jack and helping Bacon with his Thames project, and although she was heartily tired of hauling buckets, her off-site work grew ever more interesting and analytical. And the Women's Pocket Project was making strides, although there was little the botanists or wisewomen could do in January. Cristóforos Pantazis had gone to France to contemplate his lavender.

Sander—beautiful, tender, playful, patient, daily both more novel and more familiar—was happier than she had ever known him. She took some credit for this but knew there was more to it. On Boxing Day, the Chamberlain's Men had performed *Much Ado About Nothing* before the queen and her honored guest, the Duke of Bavaria; Sander had been singled out for praise as Beatrice. Then on New Year's Eve, Her Majesty had signed into existence the East India Company, and Sander had been hired for the evening to perform at a celebratory dinner, entertaining the Earl of Cumberland and two hundred other wealthy explorers, nobles, and merchants.

It was the first time he'd been summoned to court as a solo performer. He had recited poetry, sung, played the mandolin and lute, shared a cup of metheglin, and danced a galliard with Her (aged but lively) Majesty and then a coranto with her attendants, including Lady Penelope Rich. He'd left Whitehall drunk with excitement, for being applauded while wearing britches.

Now, the next morning, this first dawn of the new year, she felt his arms tighten around her. His face pressed against her neck, and there was a sleepy kiss. A warm hand crept up to her shoulder and tugged, asking her to turn around. She rolled over to face him, draping her thigh over his. He nuzzled her forehead and cupped his hand over one buttock.

"I've never spent a whole night with someone in my arms before," he whispered. "You fell asleep with a smile on your face. I knew I put it there, and I was happy."

"I'm available to fall asleep smiling whenever you'd like to do so again."

"Every night, please." He rolled onto his back, hugged her up against him, grunted with self-deprecation. "Once I've secured a place for us to live."

"It was kind of Master Heminges to offer the office for overnighting. Warmer than the Playhouse."

"And you told your parents what?"

"They think I'm helping Dorothy with a breech birth."

"I'm turning you into a liar. Lying's a sin, I hear."

"You're worth damnation." She kissed him briefly. He kissed her back, less briefly, and then again, and again, until they were lost again in the miracle of each other's flesh.

"You are the one great blessing of my life," he said an hour later, running a finger down the length of her torso. She shivered, naked and uncovered. "You're the only one I'm not performing for."

"Ah, but you like performing," she teased. "And soon you'll get bored with just one partner. You'll dance off to sleep with other people."

"I don't think so."

"Of course not, you're in love, so you're not thinking straight. It won't last."

"I have a better model than you do of a happy marriage. I grew up under John and Rebecca Heminges's roof."

Joan laughed. "I don't want that many children!"

"We'll start small," Sander proposed, as if discussing gardening.

She grinned. "First we need a home. Or a bed, at least."

"I'm making progress on that," Sander said.

"Are you? Tell me!" She rolled onto her side and rested her chin on his shoulder.

"You've forbidden me to give you details."

"Ahhh. So it's Essex."

"He has a plan for—"

She rolled off him, clapped her hands over her ears. "No, no, no. There is no Earl of Essex in my universe."

"For now. That's going to change, soon, and we'll all benefit from it, even Bacon."

"Wonderful," she said. "I'll be sure not to mention that to him." She sat up. "Speaking of Bacon, I'll be late to meet him."

He reached out to press his fingers against her breast, and she made a pleased noise before removing his hand.

"You are very touchable," he informed her.

"I'm sure I'm the most touchable girl in London, but you'll have to touch me later. I'll meet you back here after your show. But I must get dressed now."

"In your boy-clothes? Let me help you," he said.

She laughed, pushing him away. "I'm not falling for that trick. You'd make it take hours."

AFTER MONTHS OF bucketing up Thames water, weeks of collating data and making sense of what she found, Joan had not found much. A few days earlier she'd mixed up ink with materials Bacon sent her for purpose: oak galls, copperas, and wine, and fine mesh to strain it, as well as nice quills, complete with the gift of a Sheffield penknife. She wrote her notes in a clean Italian hand and delivered her report to Gray's Inn. Bacon sent a message back thanking her and announcing he had a new project in mind for her. This delighted her. He was coming to the Sow this morning, and so she'd spread out all her reporting on the table in the corner where she worked, although he already had copies. Awaiting his arrival, by the window, she silently prepared her speech:

> As you see, there are always more particulates in the water when the tide is running than when it's turning, and more manmade detritus with the incoming tide. But we could have intuited these things from common sense, which makes me wonder what your views are about the relationship between common sense and inductive reasoning—

The door snapped open and Francis Bacon's silhouette appeared in it. "Jack," he called into the alehouse. "Come. Now!"

"Shall I gather the—"

"Leave it for later. Come." He held the door open despite the January chill outside.

Joan pushed the papers together into the center of the small table, rose, and went out. He closed the door behind her and with a staccato gesture, pointed east.

"What's the matter, sir?"

"I attended dinner last night at the palace," said Bacon as they began a brisk walk up the graveled road. The stream of people was unending along the major streets: artisans and draftsmen; plasterers and bakers with different kind of dusts on them; laborers and builders (half the city was perennially under construction); butchers in their bloodied leather aprons; robed clerks with ink-stained fingers.

She smiled. "You saw Sander perform?"

"Yes," said Bacon, without pleasure. "He was, as always, talented and charming and beautiful. He also spoke openly with Penelope Rich about something that displeased Her Majesty."

"Do we not have an agreement that neither of you speaks to me—"

"He spoke of his intention to be the leading man in a company of players the Earl of Essex claims he will patronize and fund, despite the earl's having no income for such an enterprise."

"The Earl of Essex is the most popular nobleman in Britain, so people will flock to see his acting company and that is how he'd—"

"The point is, Her Majesty advised Sander not to associate with Essex while Essex is banned from court."

Joan took a moment to consider this.

"Did Her Majesty say the like to Lady Rich?"

"She did not."

"Why not?"

Bacon halted, pulled Joan sharply to the side of the street into the shade of a disreputable-looking tavern. He looked at her through narrowed lids. "It is not for us to question Her Majesty's choices."

"Of course, sir. But based on the information available to you, I'm interested to hear your impressions."

He grimaced. "Given your circumstances, I will indulge you. Her Majesty puts little store in family ties. It is rather that, of everyone in the Essex circle, Penelope alone has nothing to gain from her brother. I believe she is exempt from censure because, needing nothing from him, her loyalty to him will never compromise her loyalty to the Crown. The queen believes that can't be true of anyone who needs something from him. Someone such as Sander." He gave her a pointed look.

"So she did not advise him. She commanded him."

"To sunder himself from Essex? Yes."

"And?" asked Joan, with a sinking feeling, already imagining Sander's reaction. Two messenger boys raced past them, shouting at each other.

"Sander cheerfully assured her that Essex would soon be back in her good graces. For a boy so skilled at reading his audience—especially given his audience in this case—it was a confounding blunder."

This did not match Sander's description of the evening. "He is bedazzled by Lady Rich, so he was just too giddy to think straight."

"The queen scolded his presumptuousness. His apology was more complacent than sincere, but Her Majesty is susceptible to beautiful young men flirting with her, and that seemed to be the end of it—"

"Well, that's good, at—"

"—but only until after he'd left and the fascination of his presence faded. Then she complained to Robert Cecil and Walter Raleigh. And following that, she said to myself and others still at table: *Of course you all must have naught to do with Essex. Or with his confederates.* To which Robert Cecil added—mark me, Jack—*We will notice if you do.*"

Joan did not like his expression and wished she had a reason to look away. "Please tell me why you are informing me of this, sir."

"Cecil is not to be trifled with. He is Her Majesty's right arm, right eye, and right hand. I cannot keep in my employment anyone fraternizing with Essex or his minions."

She felt her mouth contort into an uncomfortable smile. "I cannot conceive that anyone would care one whit that such a common nobody as myself happens to divide their time between you and Sander Cooke."

"Wrong. Robert Cecil has spies everywhere, at Gray's Inn, in Essex's own house, and I'll wager someone at the Globe is in his pay. Given my history with Essex, I'm already compromised at court. Last night was the first time in months I've been allowed in the queen's presence, and her sole argument with me is that she accuses me of continual and incessant speeches in support of Essex. She commands me to demonstrate *less* sympathy toward him than I do now. I know how Cecil's mind works. He will see you as a go-between, as a means for me to circumvent the queen's order to disown Essex, and then I will be suspected of conspiring with him through you and Sander. Especially as I was, in fact, conspiring with him a few months ago, using forged letters in a misguided attempt to save him from himself. And Sander was involved with that—which is my fault, but it makes him more suspect. If Sander will not quit Essex, you must quit Sander, else I must quit you. I pray this is a temporary state of affairs, but 'tis effective at once. Today. What's it to be?"

Joan squinted into the cold sunlight and considered all the ways to answer this. It must have been Penelope Rich's presence that had made Sander such a dolt. Finally she said, "I will talk sense into him."

Bacon gave her a disbelieving look. But then his expression softened. "If anyone can, I suppose it will be you."

"I'll talk to him after his show today."

"When I send word, you will inform me whether he has foresworn Essex or you have foresworn him."

Or I've foresworn you, she thought, but aloud all she said was, "Now shall we go back to the Sow and discuss my work?"

"I HAVEN'T SEEN you naked for at least ten hours," Sander said, ten hours later, reaching for her vest. They were back in the office, a lamp was lit, and playfully he pulled her, kneeling, onto the bed. "Let's remedy that first, and then talk."

She slid his hand away from her laces and held it in both of hers.

"We should talk first, and undress after."

Wanting her, he closed his lips around one of her fingertips and licked it until he felt her lurch toward him. Releasing with a pleased grin, he proposed: "Let's tie them to each other: one article of clothing removed for each sentence uttered. But once we're naked, no more talking."

She gave him a regretful smile. "You might not feel that way when you hear what I must tell you."

"Ah." He examined her face with an impish gleam. "Bacon thinks you must disown me over Essex. Yes?"

She looked down, lips pursed.

He cradled her face between his hands, lifted it to look into her eyes. "Joan, it's not so dire. He's over-worried. Lady Rich gave me the real history while we were dancing."

"That's nothing to do with us, Sander. We've both been given orders. The daughter of a buckle-maker, receiving orders from the Queen's Counsel? I'll not disrespect that."

She looked so fretful, he considered tickling her as a distraction. Better not to. There were women who could be so mollified, but Joan wasn't one of them. He returned to his simple explanation. "Elizabeth has no heir and everyone is jockeying to have their man endorsed as the next monarch. Essex supports King James of Scotland."

"That means nothing to me," Joan protested, but he took her hands and brought them close to him, rubbing his fingers over her knuckles.

"Listen. It's a triangle. Robert Cecil's father executed James's mother, Mary Queen of Scots. So Cecil fears that if James become king, James will cast him out of court—while giving Essex freedom to take revenge on Cecil for poisoning the queen against him. To save his own skin, and for no other reason, Cecil has been plotting to discredit Essex. Essex begged Bacon to intervene, but Bacon is either too cowardly or powerless."

Joan looked appalled. "Sander, that's nonsense. Bacon *did* try to help him, with those ridiculous forged letters. You *assisted* him, so you *know* it's nonsense to claim Bacon has done nothing. Anyhow—" She gritted her teeth and growled in annoyance. "Why must I even listen to this?"

"You don't," said Sander, squeezing her against him. "Our life is none of Bacon's business."

"He disagrees."

Sander shrugged off a niggling exasperation. Joan had no head for intrigue, he reminded himself, and recalled his own anxiety his first few times at court. In a reassuring tone, he said, "I'm sure he doesn't care. He merely felt, as a loyal subject, that he needed to make a formal statement. Just tell him you've foresworn me, and we'll keep on as we are." He kissed the top of her head and reached for her laces again.

She put her hand over his to stop him. "He said Cecil has spies everywhere, which means he might too, and if he suspects I'm lying to him, that's the end of me and Francis Bacon. After all that you and I have both done to place me in such a remarkable position. I can't risk that. I won't risk it."

He laughed. "Then you'll cast me out of your life to keep slinging river mud?"

She shot him a look that was both insulted and pleading. "If you're certain Essex is about to reclaim the queen's affection, just step back from him until it happens. That way I can honestly tell Bacon you're obedient, and this idiocy becomes irrelevant to us."

Sander let go of her. "What kind of friend to Essex would I be then? It is now, while he's out of favor, that I must cleave to him. And anyhow if I desert him, then I'm back to all that patron-seeking we both detest. I'm sticking to Essex for our future. *Ours*, yours and mine together. You're sticking to Bacon only for yourself, not for us. So"—he mimed removing a halo from over his head, then polishing it with an invisible cloth—"I have the moral high ground." He tapped her nose with self-satisfied affection.

Joan frowned in bewilderment. "You're twisting things all around.

Anyhow, your choices aren't just Essex or some other patron. For the hundredth time: stay with the Chamberlain's Men."

"I can't afford to keep a household if I spend my life playing minor parts," he retorted, replacing the imaginary halo. "Essex is our best hope, even if Bacon doesn't see that yet." A pause. A tentative grin. "Y'know, if it's one piece of clothing per sentence, we should both be nude by now." He reached again for her. She pushed him away, looking down.

"You really have no idea, what it is to not be Sander Cooke," she said, angry. "You do whatever you wish, however you wish, and somehow always get away with it. I cannot."

"Joan." He reached toward her once more.

When she looked up her eyes were wet. Her face was reddening.

He felt a surge of rage toward Francis Bacon, who had no right to put any of this on her. "None of this is worth your anguish," he said and inched closer to her on the bed. He reached his arms out to comfort her, but she pushed him off, got up and moved away, so that the table was between them.

"You are too accustomed to the world wrapping itself around your little finger," she said, tears starting to spill down mottled cheeks. "You're too accustomed to your charm bringing you nearly everything you want. I've never even been to court, but I know your charm is not enough there, so why cannot you see that?"

He realized, feeling tired, that he would not win this argument. "If you think that," he said, defeated, "then Francis Bacon has warped your thinking beyond what I can remedy."

"Or perhaps Penelope Rich has warped yours. Essex is her brother, Sander, do you think she is impartial when she tells you things? *I* should be the naïve one here, not you!"

Sander had a trump card when arguing with lovers. He didn't like to use it, but seeing no choice, he reluctantly played it now. "Then you had better leave me, I suppose." He sighed, and blinked his brilliant eyes at her.

He knew she would resent it, but he also knew that it would work. Nobody ever abandoned Sander Cooke; they adjusted themselves as necessary to keep some kind of tie to him.

Then he saw the disgust on her face, and realized with alarm how badly he'd misjudged.

"Do you suppose I worship you so desperately," she said, quietly furious, "that your only responsibility to me is to look pretty enough for me to give you what you want?"

Like a slap, the wrongness of his statement was mortifyingly obvious to him. He felt sick. He felt so sick he almost laughed with despair, but couldn't. He was frozen.

"Retract what you just said," she demanded, studying his face.

He wanted to retract it, to apologize, but he could not remember how to talk. He felt nauseated, and very, very stupid.

She dropped her gaze to the table, ran her fingertips in agitation over the grain of the oak. "Your arrogance will kill you," she said quietly. "And anyhow, I can't keep pace with these people you are so driven to live among. I need a life that I can wake up in each morning and be comfortable. Have you ever, even for a quarter-hour, considered that?"

She waited for a response. As if trapped in an awful dream, he watched her watching him, watched himself trying to form words, unable to make a sound. His body was nothing but mud and lead, dead to his will. He could do nothing but stare at her in hopeless humiliation.

"God go with you, Sander," she said miserably, then rubbed her face, and opening the door, walked away into the growing dusk.

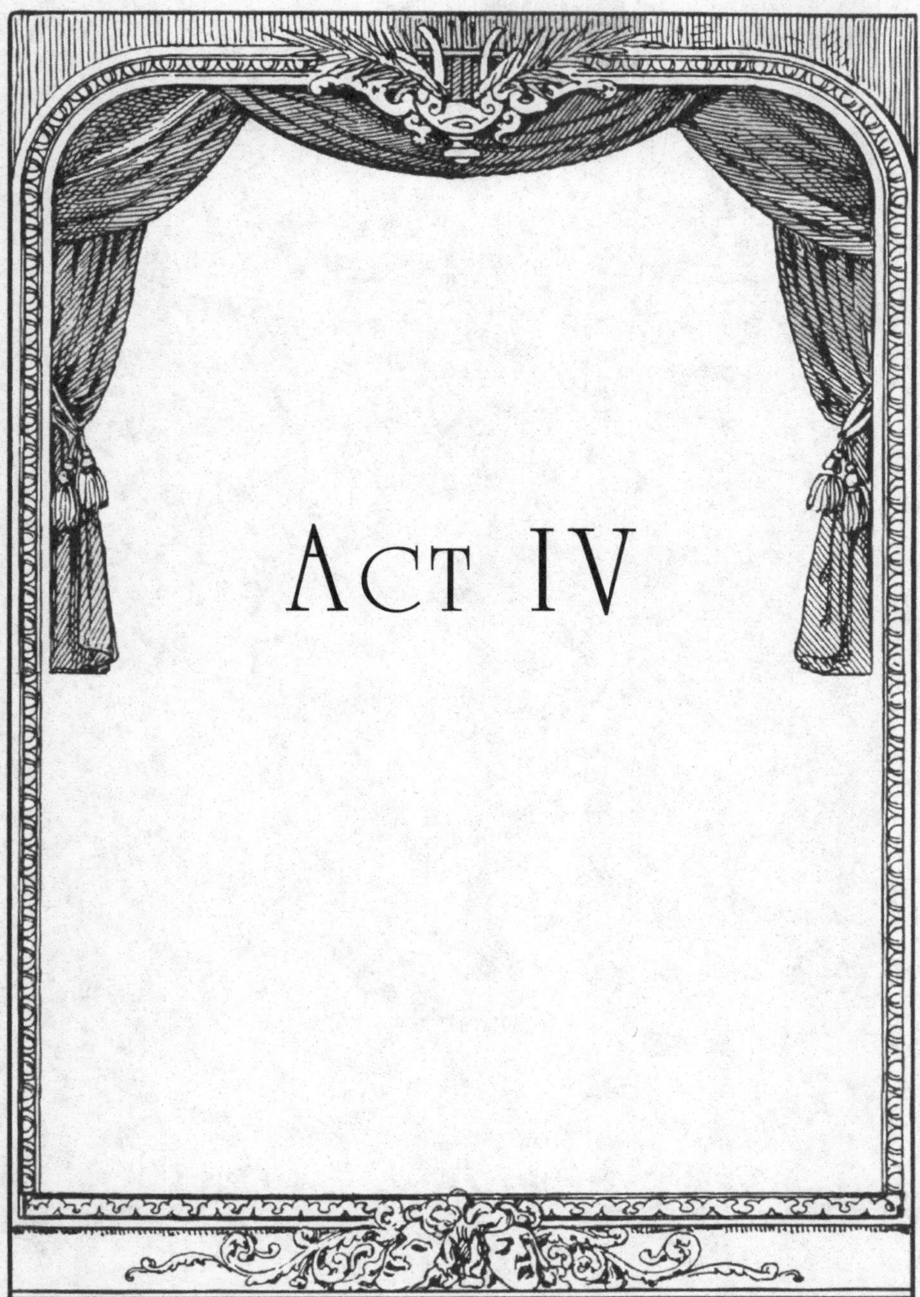

Act IV

January 5

She awoke several mornings in a row, on her own bed, from dreams her body could not tell were dreams. She awoke to the scent of him, the sound of his breathing, the weight of his arm resting over her, but there was no scent, no breath, no weight. Only her parents' gentle snores within the curtained bed. She dragged herself up, put on her layers of linen and wool, wrapped her cloak about her, trudged through cold damp dawns along dirt and gravel to the tavern and helped Molly, waiting for a message from Bacon. Nothing arriving, she would leave before the show finished, back into the cold and damp, to avoid Sander if he came to the Sow.

Four tedious days into this routine, Bacon summoned her. Grateful for a purposeful distraction, she exchanged her clothes for Jack's, and made the trip alone across the Thames and northward. At the gates to Gray's Inn, wearing her jerkin with the Bacon insignia, she was allowed in, and went up to his chambers. She rapped, heard his permission to enter, and opened the door to warmth and elegance and the driest room she'd been in for weeks.

Her feet would not work to move her farther inside. This room was part of Sander's realm, not hers; he had opened it to her and now it hurt her, in some visceral way, to enter it without him.

"And?" Bacon prompted, from his desk, studying her face.

Joan nodded stiffly. "We are sundered."

He visibly relaxed. "Thank you," he said. "I grieve that this was necessary but you have made the right choice for all of us, and I hope it will be temporary." He gestured her to enter.

"But may I say something, sir?" she ventured, and forced herself to step into the room. It felt enormous. Much larger than when Sander was there to steady her within it. "He truly believes that Essex is only trying to protect himself from enemies who are jealous of him."

Bacon sighed wearily. "Everyone is jealous of everyone, and everyone is trying to protect himself. As long as Elizabeth Tudor is on the throne and heirless, this will go on unabated, and exhaust all of us who are striving to keep her government functioning. It is a drain on my time and energy—you have seen this yourself, when you waste days at a time awaiting word from me. Our endeavors mean more to me, but of necessity, my duty's to the Crown. Please, sit down. Since you have made an appropriate choice, I have something to discuss with you."

Joan went to the bench where she and Sander had sat tight together the first time she'd been here.

"Your work on the Thames was exemplary and also, I acknowledge, tedious. Your composition is thorough and intelligent, and the diligent manner of your notes and your procedural consistency are exemplary. It is often said that natural philosophy is a gentleman's game because only gentlemen can be trusted with clear judgment. You are the example that disproves that. I sent your findings to the clerk of river works, and they align with what he already knows as proven facts, so you have helped me to demonstrate the validity of my approach. That was the sole aim of the exercise, and so we are successful. I thank you."

"The thanks is mutual, sir. While I will not disagree about the tedium, it was rewarding to assist you."

"I have an idea for a new project, which I hope will be more deserving of your capability."

She allowed herself a moment to enjoy his tone of voice. What he was not saying, but what he meant was, *I value you specifically*. She felt poignant gratitude toward Sander for first putting her in breeches. "I am happy to hear it, sir," she said. "I have turned my back on the man who would marry me. I welcome the chance to do something worthy of the sacrifice."

"Very well, then," he said, clapping his hands together once, as if to startle old spirits from the room. "To our future undertakings. I have been thinking a great deal about heat and light."

She glanced between the crackling fire and the gloomy skies through the window. "Fitting topics to dwell upon in winter."

"I would collect information about the nature of heat, so that I can begin to say some true things about it."

She considered this. "Heat," she said, "is a less specific topic than the River Thames."

"Indeed. Heat is relevant to every inch of the universe, and makes itself felt in human lives, every moment of the day. It is a topic of tremendous significance that has not received due inquiry. Far more elemental to mankind's existence than those things Hugh Platt concerns himself with—distilling liquids, preserving food. This is much grander than that."

She wondered why he so disliked Hugh Platt; she did not know the man, but every time his name was said, in any context, Bacon bristled. "I presume there are specific aspects of heat you wish to consider first."

He returned to his usual earnestness. "My perception—empirical, but untested—is that heat creates expansive movement. Smoke billows, for example, as does steam."

"Boiling liquids swell and rise," Joan contributed.

"Yes," he said, with an encouraging gesture. "On a hot day, rings grow tight around fingers because the human body swells."

"Wooden doors stick in their jambs—"

"—and then contract enough in winter that we must draw blankets across them to keep the drafts out."

"And yet, sir, ice expands."

"Indeed," Bacon agreed, and the dark hazel eyes returned toward the ceiling as his words tripped out of his mouth almost sooner than he thought them. "So one cannot simply claim that heat means expansion and cold means contraction. The changes wrought by heat and cold are subtler and more complex, and I have in mind a series of small experiments, to be repeated several times under controlled circumstances, that will give me information pertaining to the true nature of heat. Not all of them are fit for you to carry out, as some require the butchering of animals, or greater physical strength than you are like to have, or access to things I cannot give you, such as cannons."

"Goodness," Joan said. She was determined not to show excitement. His wanting her assistance gave her a feeling of power; she did not want to diminish that power by letting him see that she wanted it.

"But most of the experiments can be done by you, independent of me, without drawing unwelcome attention."

"I fain would have some expectation of these experiments."

"Most of them are simple and straightforward and require only a burning glass—are you familiar with that?"

She nodded, mimed the shape of one: "A glass disc that is convex. And the middle part, where it's thickest, concentrates the sun's rays enough to set things on fire."

"I have a number of them and have also procured some thermoscopes, to measure the increase or decrease of heat."

"Those are dear enough, sir," said Joan. She had spent hours of her free time in childhood at the shops of instrument makers along the Strand, watching thermoscope demonstrations with delight.

"Furthering human knowledge requires an investment in the right instruments, Jack." His attention hovered just above her head, and he fell into his rapid speech. "I want to see what happens when a burning glass is used on a source of light or heat other than the sun's rays. You will attempt to heat, or better yet ignite, a piece of cloth, by using the burning glass to focus the rays of the moon, or collect heat from warm objects with no luminous rays at all, such as hot iron or boiling water. Or, another experiment will be to compare how quickly two different burning glasses can ignite an object, if one glass is one handspan from the object, and the other is two handspans distant. Such kinds of experiments. To be performed over and over again, in similar circumstances, until we can be confident of the consistency of results. How does that sound to you?"

"Fascinating," she said, in the mildest tone she could manage. The alternative was to work in her father's shop or at the Happy Sow, so of course it sounded fascinating.

But also, it *was* fascinating.

"There will be other experiments," he said. "Some involving vegetative heat, or the heat of spices, or the heat generated by spirits of wine. My own medical history makes me eager to understand the role of heat in health and healing, but that is further along."

"I am eager to do it, sir. But may I suggest that a series of experiments about heat would be best carried out in a setting with a consistent temperature. The bankside shed I had been working in does not provide that. Nor does the Sow, which is hot when crowded and cold when not."

He gave her an indulgent look. "I have taken that into account. On the Globe Playhouse grounds, there is a small outbuilding near the tavern, which the Chamberlain's Men built to lease, but with no forethought as to who might want it. I am leasing it by the month and will be outfitting it to be your laboratory."

"Oh," said Joan. "I know the little building you mean, sir, but . . . that places me in proximity to Sander, sir."

Bacon gave her a look. "Who?"

Joan considered how to amend her point. "Conveniently, the building you speak of is on the side of the property toward my home. There will be no reason for me to go beyond the, eh, laboratory, and no reason for any of the players to go beyond the tavern. So although the players and I will be near each other, there is no reason for our paths to ever cross."

Bacon nodded. "That is a more useful description of your circumstances. It is no more perverse than at Her Majesty's court, where most of us must navigate around estranged friends or lovers or cousins. You will manage it."

"Of course I will," said Joan, wondering how she would manage it.

"So we are agreed. I will send workmen to fit the space to your needs, and then I shall talk you through each individual experiment. I anticipate within a fortnight, maybe much sooner, it will be taking up most of your day."

"I gratefully accept the position."

"Excellent," said Bacon. "And I have another proposition." He pursed his lips. "This might seem to conflict with what I've just proposed, but I believe they can happen one after the other, or even . . . let me just tell you. Next month, some natural philosophers come to visit from Antwerp. I would introduce you to them, and have you join us at table. But I want you there as Joan, not as Jack."

Her face betrayed her.

"With your permission," he continued, "I would discuss the possibility of your returning to Antwerp with them."

If he'd proposed she swim to Antwerp she could not have been more astonished.

He smiled, watching her face. "We must ascertain the status of women philosophers on the Continent, of course. I was hoping you might go as an apprentice to one of them, or employee, but there is also the possibility of marriage, if temperaments align."

This did nothing to reduce her amazement.

She considered the room, the hearth, the desk, the shelves of composition books. "Why should I want to leave London?" she managed to say at last. "I would be leaving you and all my other mentors."

He shook his head. "Your other mentors are well-intentioned but undeserving of you. They teach you facts, which are useful, but I am trying to teach you how to think *about* facts."

"How can you do that if I'm living in another land, sir?" she asked. "Anyhow I am hardly sharp enough for the average philosopher. I'm more curious than intelligent."

He raised his brows. "To teach you I require only your curiosity. And competence, which you have. As for the method, we would correspond often, and sometimes visit each other. In some ways this is superior to our current arrangement, where you have become a field hand to my ideas.

If you are away from home, then your whole life, every waking moment, can be dedicated to furthering your understanding and education. No more distaff chores or mopping up the alehouse or thankless drudgery in your father's little business. And as you come to understand things, you may share my thoughts with your mentor, or husband, or employee—whatever arrangement pleases—and then, having heard their responses, you may write to me of them, to give me things to think about."

"I am your product, then," she said, "to be exported."

He smiled paternally. "I would not say product," he said. "I see you as my ambassador. Remember, you will benefit from this arrangement."

"How can you be sure that once I'm someone's chattel they will allow me to continue to work with—"

"You needn't marry. Perhaps they'll employ you. Employment would bring income, and you would be free to return to Sander if he comes to his senses. Best to be well away from him, for now, but you need not cut yourself off from a future with him."

Joan sat a moment, lips pursed, staring out the lead-lined windows behind Bacon into the courtyard. "I gave up Sander to work with *you*, sir," she said.

"You would be working with me, just in a different manner. And truly, Jack—Joan—this is but a suggestion. The gentlemen from Antwerp know nothing of it yet. I thought it would please you." He looked awkward. "You might meet them, at least."

She chewed on her lower lip, considering.

"They are not due for a month, anyhow," said Bacon, clumsily.

"Thank you," she said in a strained voice. "I appreciate your looking out for my interests."

There was an awkward silence. Bacon coughed.

"Meanwhile," he said, "let's discuss these heat experiments."

Within moments everything—nearly everything—was set aright between them.

IT WAS A royal barge, but not Her Majesty's own transport. This was more of a royal service barge. Still it was nice to cross the Thames in a boat that size—sixty feet long, nine oarsmen to a side. The full company of the Chamberlain's Men fit onto it, complete with their hand-drawn carts of costumes, props, and sundries.

Sander had been here dozens of times; the adult players, scores. There was always something thrilling about stepping onto royal property and then stepping out of it onto royal steps. No commoner could grow accustomed to that.

Yet Sander, for the first time, felt nothing; just stared down at the murky water, barely noticing the approach to Whitehall Palace.

His moping did not improve. Not as they stepped out of the barge on the western shore. Not as he and the other apprentices, under the direction of the Master of the Revels, unloaded the carts into the lofty hall, where they would be performing in two hours' time. His attention stayed only on his duties, not bothering to look up in wonder at the soaring ceilings; the ornate tapestries; the heavy jewel-encrusted curtains; the stained glass windows of Eden, and unicorns, and arabesque geometry; the enormous doorways and enormous hearths.

Court servants had already prepared the space with heavy upstage hangings to mask entrances and exits. The company had rehearsed this new play on the Globe stage, but the space here was smaller; Sander decided to run through his blocking, to pull his mind out of its gloom. He especially wanted to review the choreography of a ridiculous duel his character was coerced into. All apprentices were trained in fencing, and Sander's natural adeptness meant his challenge in the scene was to appear convincingly clumsy. He began to trot through the movements on his own.

"Richard Burbage!" cried a melodious voice from the far end of the great hall. Sander's eyes—everyone's eyes—shifted toward the speaker.

Penelope Rich, exquisite and rosy, in pale gossamer hues covered with black lace, crossed toward the company. Burbage stepped toward her, doffing his felt hat by the brim and bowing, one knee bent.

"Lady Rich, it is an honor to be recognized by you," he said, loudly, in case anyone hadn't heard her.

Sander paused and watched as she curtseyed, her eyes smiling, her affect buoyant. He tried not to care that she hadn't noticed him yet. "I hear it is to be a comedy, but not a silly one. I am on tenterhooks awaiting the pleasure of your performance, Richard."

Burbage waved in a flattered but dismissive way. "I'm a supporting player tonight," he said. "Will's next role for me is huge, and I must save my stamina for that."

Lady Rich looked expectant and intrigued. "Is that the one everyone has been whispering about? His reworking of Saxo's *Vita Amlethi*?"

Burbage squinted thoughtfully. "He said it was from something . . . French?"

She nodded. "Adapted from the Latin, but of course first it was a folktale. Danish or Icelandic, I suspect."

"Well, Will's never one to pass up stealing a good plot," said Burbage cheerfully.

"But of course everything he writes is tenfold better than whatever he steals from," said Penelope in an admiring voice. "Although the source material itself is excellent—Amleth's father, the king, has been murdered by his brother, and the father's ghost tells Amleth to seek vengeance, yes?"

"He's called Hamlet in Will's version, but that's the one."

"And everyone's dead by the end," Lady Rich concluded with relish. "I do love a good revenge play. I'm eager to discover how he improves this one. Although I'm quite cross if it means less Burbage for the audience tonight."

Burbage gave her a smile almost as charming as the one she was offering him. "Thank you, m'lady, but I wager you'll be pleased with the alternative." He gestured toward Sander.

Sander was trying to ignore a shameful wave of jealousy. Burbage's acknowledgment helped, bringing a flush to his cheeks. As Lady Rich's eyes drifted in his direction he folded forward with his curtsey-bow.

"Alexander!" she gushed, with as much delight as she'd greeted Burbage.

"The brightest star in tonight's firmament," said Burbage magnanimously. He winked at Sander, then headed behind the hangings to change into a duke.

"M'lady." Sander crossed to her and offered a proper bow.

She took his hand to raise him, and then continued to hold it while she studied his face. His eyes would not rise to meet hers.

"Has someone died?" she asked in a whisper. "You look grievous sad, my friend."

His gaze flittered up to meet hers but then fell again. It was petty to discuss his personal heartache. "I wish the queen loved your brother as well as she loves you," he said instead. Which was true.

She leaned toward him and lowered her voice further. "She does, Sander. Keep faith. It will all come out well. Now." She pulled away, beamed at him, and brought her voice back to a normal speaking volume. "Put on your dress, that you may astonish and delight the court."

THE PLAYERS WERE getting into costume behind the heavy curtains at the back of the stage. The younger apprentices could not resist peeking through these, as voices and rustling fabrics filled the hall. Her Majesty's chair was surrounded by a carpet of green fabric strewn with silk flowers. Around it were cushioned stools and benches.

"Pst, Sander! Who's that?" asked the apprentice Kit, pointing out between the curtains.

"Don't do that, Kit," said Sander. "I've told you before."

"But he's got the maddest hat!" Kit argued in a whisper. "It's purple! Only royalty are supposed to wear purple."

Sander joined him grudgingly. He saw the hat Kit meant—a garish headpiece with a huge, swooping white feather—and recognized the man beneath it. "That's blue, not purple," he said. "And the young man wearing it is Lord Darnell." *The first man who ever kissed me*, he thought, but did not say. Intrigued despite himself, he glanced around at the milling audience. There were perhaps forty well-dressed courtiers, mostly ladies. The coifs and caps and ruffs and collars and points and buttons and laces alone—never mind the bodices, jerkins, skirts, gowns, breeches, shoes—demonstrated a collective wealth so far beyond an ordinary Londoner's, Sander could not fathom it. Tonight, he would be the darling of the evening because he was on the stage. But six months from now, how would he ever regain their good regard, when even one such hat would beggar him? He had been intimate with at least a dozen of the courtiers in the room. Most of them had been perfumed. All of them had flattered him. All of them had lovely beds in lovely chambers. After the performance tonight, he knew that each of them would invite him back to those lovely beds. There was no reason not to go, but the thought of touching anyone but Joan made his stomach hurt.

He ought to go with someone anyhow, just to remind himself the world was wide. He studied them, considering, remembering. Edward Brampton's thighs. Lady Beatrice Sharp's breasts and buttocks. Philippa Staunton's everything. He remembered, with some nostalgia but without desire. He would go home alone tonight.

"Hey, you said we weren't to peek, hypocrite," Kit teased. "If it's allowable after all, get out of the way, this is my spot."

"Sorry," Sander said, and went back to his costume.

He kept an ear out as he dressed. His name was on everyone's tongue, in an echoing glimmer of sound from the other side of the curtain: absorbed into fabric, bouncing off stone, over and over again. He heard Heminges, boastfully, and Shakespeare, adoringly, mention him to court officials who came to check on them. He heard Penelope Rich mention him to other nobles in the audience. It was winter. The weather was miserable, the nights were too long, the queen was old and heirless, her golden days behind her. Everyone was hungry to see the incomparable Sander Cooke in this fresh new comedy, *Twelfth Night*, personating Viola, a character written just for him.

Rosalind, in *As You Like It*, was the largest female role Shakespeare had yet written. Viola had fewer lines, but she possessed greater depth, complexity, and nuance, than Rosalind. It required a display of all his acting skills, not only his ability to charm and dazzle. William Shakespeare was acknowledging Sander's breadth of talent. That was not lost on him.

He also knew it was a farewell gift.

THE STORY OPENED with Viola, shipwrecked on a foreign shore, heartbroken because she'd watched her twin brother drown.

Sander was magnificent at heartbreak.

A penniless female in a foreign land, Viola disguised herself as a boy and sought employment with the powerful Duke Orsino, who hired this "boy" to deliver love letters to the Countess Olivia. Although she spurned Orsino's advances, Olivia was smitten with his clever, charming new messenger.

Sander was magnificent at playing all the complicated feelings of being wanted for the wrong reasons by the wrong person, with conscience enough to rue the situation but no agency to repair it.

Then Viola began to fall in love with her new master. Will had written a heart-wrenching but witty scene between the two of them, Orsino giving romantic advice about women to a young man who did not exist, while the young woman who did exist replied in coded riddles, desperate to both reveal and hide her love for him.

Sander was magnificent at tortured adoration.

Viola felt powerless to improve the situation, which only made her more hapless and desperate.

Sander was magnificent at hapless desperation.

At the nadir of her fortunes, Viola-in-breeches was coerced into a farcical, bumbling duel with one of Olivia's suitors.

Sander was magnificent at farcical bumbling.

Her brother's miraculous reappearance reversed Viola's fortune: her true identity and sex were revealed, and a delighted Orsino asked to marry her.

Sander was magnificent at unbridled ecstasy.

IT WAS THE greatest triumph of his life.

Her Majesty, as much on display as the players were, watched with undiminished delight, her ancient eyes sparkling beneath their crepe-like lids. Her huge lace ruff, embellished with seed pearls, framed her face above a sable gown. In those few moments he was behind the curtains, Sander studied her, amazed by the resilience that masqueraded as courtliness. She would be a marvelous character to personate someday. Why was the stage so full of bombastic, prattling older men, but so few women? The queen could wipe the floor with any of her courtiers, and Master Shakespeare had never known another sovereign, yet he had little room for her sort on stage.

After the performance, Her Majesty called Sander to her and graced him with a dry kiss from her thin and ancient lips. Every woman and several men, strangers or friends or former lovers, cooed and clapped and flirted. Of the forty people in the room, twenty-three invited him to sup with them, and it was clear what supping really meant. Even Penelope Rich looked as if she might like to nibble on him.

He'd have given up the role and the adoration in a moment, if that meant he could have Joan back.

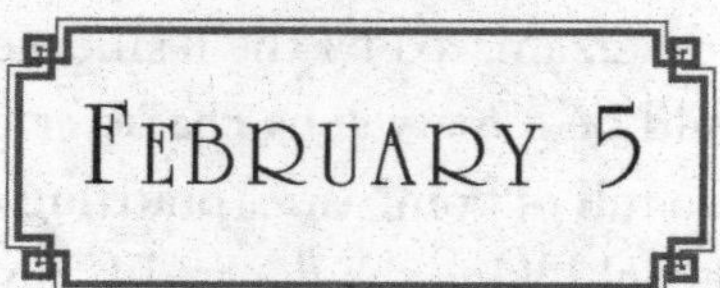

February 5

IT WAS HER THIRD TIME in this same room at the Hawthorn, but her first time seated at the table. She was so accustomed to wearing her boy's togs around Bacon that she felt awkward now in a skirt. Especially since this was her best skirt, saved for churchgoing. Her parents had asked why she was wearing her Sunday clothes on a midweek evening; she'd said a friend was an aspiring portrait painter and needed subjects, so she had volunteered. They accepted this incuriously, and here she was.

She had survived the formal etiquette of being greeted by foreign visitors unaware of her social inferiority. The two Flemish each spoke English and wore black, with topaz and peridots sewn in patterns down the front of their doublets, which struck Joan as an invitation to be robbed at knifepoint. Their needle-laced ruffs and wrist-cuffs seemed old-fashioned, but also elegant. There was, in both men, a dour yet kindly frankness. She was not used to such a thing in well-dressed Englishmen.

Perhaps she would like it very much.

She had received their courtesies with words that Bacon had written for her to memorize; she was now seated across from him. To either side were the two visiting philosophers, cousins from a family of affluent sugar merchants: Basiel and Jakob Zaal. *I can survive this*, she thought. *No need to feel discomfit*. She had walked past Pierre, who stood outside the door as servants should, and his eyes had neither mocked nor condemned. She could survive this.

The pitchers and ewers were brought to the table for handwashing, and for the first time in this room, Joan used them. The door opened behind her. She turned to see who it was.

Cristóforos Pantazis entered.

Joan gasped; Bacon chuckled in response. "We met by chance at Gresham's this afternoon and agreed you might like a familiar face," he said. "Pray come in, Cristóforos, and meet my other guests."

"I've just come back from my concerns in France," Pantazis said with a bow, directly to her, with a private wink. Somehow she kept her wits about her enough to rise and greet him.

Sander's beauty had been present in her life from infancy; she was so accustomed to it that it made no impression on her. Pantazis was the first man she'd ever found handsome for handsome's sake. She yearned to be deemed pretty by him. It was an unfamiliar and excruciating sensation.

But also, she was pleased to see him. And she flushed when his expression suggested he was pleased to see her too. Bacon gestured to a cushioned stool beside Basiel Zaal. Pantazis greeted them and then took his seat, with another wink to Joan that made her stomach flop over.

She wished she had paid more attention to the early-evening chitchat of her previous times here. There were unspoken rules about how supper conversations began and evolved; she knew none of them. She had reviewed certain things that might be of interest to the visitors, such as examples of the work she was doing with Bacon. She decided to follow his lead; ladies were likely not expected to steer the conversation, anyhow.

Over chicken pottage they heard details of the voyage, the Channel crossing, the barge up the Thames, the Zaals' Southwark lodgings with a kinsman. The kinsman was a mercer who'd tried to take a house on London Bridge but was denied because he was a Stranger, not an Englishman. A few desultory exchanges with Pantazis about his own journey, and his property in France. "We must talk later, Joan, about the lavender," he said.

The Zaal cousins exchanged intrigued looks when he addressed her in familiar fashion.

"What is your interest in lavender?" asked Basiel in a friendly voice.

"I've introduced him to some herbalists I know," she said.

"Joan is a young woman of many talents and interests," Bacon announced. "I've already told you she is doing valuable research for me, but she has her own felicitous enterprise as well." Joan gave him a wary look—*let's don't discuss abortifacients with the Strangers*—and he added, "However, the bulk of her time is spent as my assistant and secretary."

Pantazis smiled. "So her duties have increased since I last saw her in the bankside shed?"

"Oh yes, Master Pantazis, you should see the greenhouse," said Joan. "It is the most exquisite thing: a wooden frame full of windows with double layers of glass, large enough for me to stand up in it, and filled with plants, even this time of year."

"Interesting. What is the purpose?" Jakob asked, reaching for a piece of bread.

"I am doing some experiments on the nature of heat," said Bacon. "Or I should say I am designing them, but Joan is executing them. The greenhouse is to assess the ambient heat gain of vegetation forcibly enclosed together. We are measuring heat change with a thermoscope, which Joan attends to. As well as tending to the plants. She has been an experimental botanist since early childhood."

"Interesting. Was your family's estate near London?" Jakob asked.

Joan glanced at Bacon.

"Hugh Morgan is practically an uncle to her," Bacon said. "Her Majesty's Apothecary, retired now. She was creating hybrids before most of her friends learned how to read. I am fortunate to be her mentor and employer."

"And yet you think she should leave England for the Continent," said Jakob, studying Bacon. Pantazis shifted abruptly; Joan guessed he had not known the real purpose of this supper.

"Gentlemen, I tell you plainly," said Bacon, "the opportunity for women in natural philosophy in London is execrable. Nobody here but myself will take her seriously. My court duties grow heavier each month and I am not able to give her the instruction or opportunities she deserves. So I had the thought that if either of you had a need for her talents, it might be a happy solution for all parties, that she had opportunities to be useful elsewhere without severing her ties with me. In fact, I cherish the opportunity for her to share my ideas with you and facilitate a discussion across the Channel."

Joan felt like a cow on display at Smithfield on market day. The cousins were eyeing her, as if her appearance was somehow relevant to her ability to do good work. Having never in her life been looked at this way, she had no idea how to respond, and stared back at them.

"You do not powder your face, I see," said Basiel.

"She has not the leisure," said Bacon. "I have never met a more industrious and dedicated worker in my life."

"I was not criticizing," said Basiel. "I am indifferent to such things, but whenever I am over here, I notice this."

"Nothing about Joan is ordinary," said Bacon. "That is why she is so valuable."

Basiel and Jakob continued to study her as roast duck was brought to the table. She tried to pretend not to notice, and she averted her gaze at Pantazis, who was watching the two visitors watch her. His expression was guarded and proprietary, as John Heminges's sometimes was toward Sander.

"I would be happy to answer any questions you might have about my skills or capabilities," she said, using her shopkeeper's-daughter tone.

"Do you keep accounts?" asked Jakob.

"Not for Master Bacon, no," said Joan, thrown. "I help sometimes with my father's bookkeeping, but I have no aptitude for complex mathematical equations—"

"Oh, there would be no need of that, I am just wondering about basic skills," said Jakob.

"Joan's skills are an admirable balance of mental acuity and physical competency," said Bacon. "She is modest, so I cannot trust her to trumpet her value to you." He gave her a quick smile. "Joan? Shall I tell them all you're capable of or will you speak of it directly?"

Joan blushed, and hesitated.

"She is too modest," said Basiel, in an approving tone. "Please, sir, we would be delighted to hear more."

"Perhaps not the Women's Pocket Project," Joan murmured, and was relieved by Bacon's conspiring nod.

"In the laboratory I have had fashioned for her," he said instead, "she is carrying out a series of experiments under my direction. Besides the sun, or an open flame, there are other sources of heat, and she is helping me to measure and examine those. For example, as she mentioned to Master Pantazis, there is the small greenhouse that is being used to grow plants and measure how much heat they generate collectively. On clear nights she attempts to collect heat from lunar rays. She is measuring the heating effect of spirits of wine on different substances such as leather, wax, and wood. And we shall soon be attempting to see if it is possible to smoke fish and beef without fire but using only spices such as pepper that create heat within the human body."

"Interesting," said Jakob, and turned to Joan "It reminds me of the work of Hugh Platt." She heard Bacon make a disapproving sound. "I would imagine the trials with spices would have practical domestic applications, yes?"

She hoped he did not intend this to mean what it sounded like it meant. "We are still experimenting in the laboratory, sir," she clarified. "If the experiments bear fruit, so to speak, then Master Bacon shall write about them, and that information will become commonplace enough that housewives and chefs may employ it."

"So you're not applying it to your own cookery yet?" asked Jakob.

"As I am neither a housewife nor a chef, sir, that is correct."

"But you do cook?" asked Jakob.

Joan looked at Bacon.

"That's not a talent I have required of her," Bacon said promptly. "Cookery is a skill, and while I'm sure Joan would make an admirable cook, we are gathered tonight because of other skills she has already developed."

"So you have a cook," said Jakob. "How many of your servants are you looking to bring to the Continent with you?"

"If I may presume to speak on her behalf, she won't bring any," said Master Pantazis. "Joan is remarkably adaptable to circumstances, but she is too considerate to presume that others are as well. I predict she will be happy to work with the servants of whatever household she finds herself in, and they will find her to be an indulgent and appreciative addition to that household."

"Thank you, Master Pantazis, you have admirably summed up my position," said Joan with relief, wishing she could disappear through the floor.

"But you can oversee a staff," said Jakob. "You are equipped to function as the mistress of a household."

She would not scream, she would not scream, she would not scream. "I am unmarried and still live at home, sir, and thus have no such experience."

"But your mother is preparing you."

Joan shot Bacon another look.

"Joan's family is insufficient to her value," said Bacon. "If they were raising her in the manner you seem to wish they were, she would not have matured to be the woman sitting with us tonight."

"But there is a dowry, were she to marry, of course," said Jakob. It was a statement, not a question.

"Her dowry will come from admiring benefactors," Bacon improvised. "She has a great circle of them."

"Excuse me a moment," Joan said, keeping her face neutral. "My servant is waiting for word of how late I shall be tonight."

"I'll accompany you home, if you'd like to release him," said Pantazis, straight-faced. "We need to talk about the lavender anyhow."

"Thank you, sir, I would appreciate that. I'll just go tell him."

"I'm curious about this lavender of yours," said Basiel as Joan rose. She tried to remember what Sander did when he took leave of people as a girl. Some kind of small courtesy, a dip of the head with a coquettish expression, which she could not force herself to make.

Pantazis began a vague response to Basiel Zaal as Joan closed the door behind her. She paused on the landing, took a deep breath and slowly exhaled. Then she went down the stairs, outside, and leaned against the wall.

For several moments she stared into the dark street, shivering in the chill, listening to people pass, mostly men who smelled of beer and carried lanterns.

"You navigated those peculiar waters well, I think," said a by-now familiar accented voice.

She stiffened for a moment, then made herself relax. "Thank you, Master Pantazis. I had not expected him to try quite so hard to auction me off."

"Oh, now, be charitable. Francis is trying to give you an opportunity. He has simply been clumsy in his management of it, as he has never had a daughter." She glanced at him, wryly, and he smiled. His breath was a soft cloud in the lamplight. "And perhaps he is being selfish, in that you are a valuable commodity and he wants to benefit from his ability to have recognized you as such. He has some strange animus toward Hugh Platt—"

"Yes," said Joan. "Why is that?"

Pantazis gave her a knowing look. "Platt's father made financial provisions for his son. Bacon's failed to. So here are two intelligent men, with similar interests and similar skills. Platt has the fortune to spend his time pursuing his passions. Francis, although higher-born, is poor, and so he must strive to advance at court, in hopes it will lead to income, which in turn will allow him to do that which Platt has done for years, being happy in his birth. I think Francis relishes that he has a Joan Butler and Platt does not. He is oddly petty in wanting to diminish Platt. But also, to return to our point: I believe he wishes you to be content."

"He knows what I need to be content, and he's made it impossible."

"Forgive the presumption, Joan, but if I understand the situation, your young man is contributing to the problem himself."

"Sander isn't demanding that I choose between them."

"And yet," said Pantazis, "having been told to choose, you chose Francis Bacon."

It was such a simple truth, and had been so easy not to notice. "I did," she said, deflating.

"Do you regret it?"

Joan shrugged. "I don't know. Sander is out of his mind a bit, regarding Essex."

"I have not encountered the earl, but he is wildly popular among all the people I have met, the artists and poets and architects and craftsman. He must have some charm that wins people to him. Perhaps Sander is susceptible to it."

"But for the consequence of that to be, that all the men involved continue on as before and I, alone, must re-align my life—"

"I noticed that as well. Francis is both an optimist and an opportunist, so he does not notice it. I believe he sees tonight as nothing but a chance for you to better your circumstances."

Joan opened her mouth to retort, then paused. Then thought. Then steeled herself against humiliation and began to speak again: "If I am to be married off to somebody on account of my intelligence and curiosity, I'd rather it were—"

"Do not finish that sentence, please," said Pantazis, staring at the tavern across the way. "Do not think I have not considered it."

Joan smiled despite herself. "Then why—"

"I must tell you my heart would not be in it."

Ashamed, and defensive, Joan said quickly, "Well that's that, then. I wouldn't want someone to marry me for pity."

"Pity?" his voice rose and sounded strained. "No, no, quite the opposite. My heart would not be in it because your heart would not be in it."

"Oh." She didn't know what else to say; there was no sense claiming otherwise. "But . . ." she tried. "You and I respect each other, and I perceive a friendly spirit betwixt us." She did not want to say, *And I find you more than passing handsome*, for she doubted he could say the same of her.

He'd already said he did not fancy English women. And even if he did, she knew there were much finer specimens than her.

"I agree," he said. "Respect and friendliness, and I do not doubt an affection that could grow over time."

She gave him a look: *Well, then, why not?*

He shook his head.

"Both of us would always wonder what you lost. And that would come between us. Those gentlemen in there, they know nothing of your life. You could be sad without them knowing why, and they would never resent your grieving a lost love."

"You don't want to marry me because you would resent my missing Sander."

"Oh, no, you mistake my meaning again." He sounded amused. "I would never resent you for loving somebody you can't have. I have my own history, you know, and I understand that pain. But I somewhat resent Francis and Sander for putting you in this position, of having to consider marriage to someone you don't love or maybe don't even know. You are a remarkable, smart, interesting, enterprising young woman, and if I'd had the fortune to meet you knowing nothing of Sander Cooke, I would be first in line to court you."

Joan barked a laugh. "Court me! Ha."

"Do you remember the last time we were both here at the Hawthorn? When he gave that performance about beauty and pale complexions and all that?" She nodded. "That was for you, I thought at the time. And that endeared him to me. I wish to see you marry Sander." He paused. "But if you cannot marry Sander, marry someone who doesn't know about him. I wish I were that man, but I am not."

He bent toward her to kiss her forehead. The warmth of his lips made her shiver. He cupped his hands around her cheeks, cradling her face, and looked at her with a fond and sad expression.

February 6

"You're always fun to woo, lad," said Richard Burbage. Sander, toweling the paint off his face, made himself smile to accept the compliment. "My Henry shall never have a better Princess Katherine."

"You honor me." Sander used the removal of his wig as an excuse to turn away.

Heminges urged them outside for a free round at the Sow. The men sang out his praises and hustled from the stuffy tiring house.

The last of them to leave was Heminges himself. He squeezed Sander's shoulder: he knew how the intended praise had landed, that it had not felt like praise at all, but rather a reminder that Burbage could keep playing King Henry V for years, while Sander was soon to lose Princess Katherine forever.

There might be other roles he'd already performed for the last time without realizing it.

He had six weeks left to his apprenticeship.

Alone with the other boys, Sander oversaw their wigs, checked they'd hung up their skirts and put their props away, then released them. The younger two dashed out at once, but Kit hung back a moment. "Thank you," he said.

". . . For what?" asked Sander, wanting him to leave too.

"For being good to us," said Kit.

Sander shrugged. "I don't know what you mean."

"I was listening to some of the shareholders talking about their own early years and . . ." He shrugged. "I feel fortunate to be coming of age, in this company, at this time."

Sander was miserable but determined not to show it. "The company is fortunate as well," he said, in the warmest voice he could muster. Kit's face glowed with pleasure, and Sander took some consolation in knowing he'd been kind. "Run along and enjoy your pint, lad," he said, and began to gather his own skirts. He hung his lavender kirtle on its hook, just above the spot where he'd first kissed Joan.

He yearned to see her so badly it nauseated him. Everything was ugly without her. He glanced a final time around the room, then stepped out and closed the door behind him. He wanted to get home and sulk in a dark corner.

On the canted paving stones, a small cohort of men was milling about. Five of them, in clothes meant to resemble those of prosperous merchants: blended fabrics, elaborate linen collars, decorated cloaks and jerkins. But the hats were too plain and the gloves too fancy for real merchants. He knew them at once for what they were: noblemen out on a romp, play-acting at being of common stock. As mystifying as all the players found it, this was not rare. Grudgingly, he played along.

"Good day," he said, mustering his conditioned smile. The crisp February breeze flushed his lungs clean. "Are you in search of someone?"

As always, there was a brief hesitation as eyes and brains made sense of his unfamiliar familiarity. He considered them as they considered him. Two were certainly brothers: faces long but handsome with skin a sallow ivory; lush auburn hair and tawny eyes; both emanating a calm air of casual beneficence. Their three comrades were shorter, and slightly more believable in merchants' dress.

"You!" said the taller brother, pointing at him.

Sander immediately glanced back over his own shoulder, as if the man was pointing to someone behind him. The strangers chuckled. He looked back toward them and gestured to himself. "Me?" he cried with feigned surprise, and offered them the gracious Sander Cooke smile. It had never felt so forced. He just wanted to go home.

"Keep your head about you, Charles," teased his brother.

"I must tell you," said Charles, eagerly, "I am your greatest admirer, but in particular I must tell you that my favorite of Master Shakespeare's excellent plays is the second part of *Henry IV*, and your Mistress Quickly . . ." He brought his fist to his chest, with a grand intake of breath, looked heavenward, and shook his head. "That such an ethereal performer as yourself could be so bawdy, so *earthy*—"

"The bum-padding gets most credit for that, but I thank you for the commendation," Sander said, with a flourish of his hand, and a nod. As he raised his head, he saw there was a boy with them: the Earl of Essex's silk-clad messenger. He scanned the other faces but recognized none of them. "May I help you?"

"Who runs your company?" asked Charles. His tone confirmed what Sander had suspected: they wished to hire the Chamberlain's Men for a command performance. Why did such people feel the need to dress up like merchants or artisans? Who did they think they were fooling? They still carried themselves like gentility and always had hands too soft to have done a day's labor.

"You want John Heminges. He runs not only the company but the alehouse, just there. I'll take you." He stared hard at the Essex boy, who pretended not to notice.

The men walked close together and looked around as if they had just landed in the Indies. None commented on the day's performance, and he suspected they had not attended, had quite possibly never been to the Globe before, or even to Southwark. They had made this trip, in disguise, for the sole purpose of requesting a private performance.

And Essex was involved somehow, else his boy would not be here.

At the alehouse door, Sander heard a lively buzz within. He reached for the latch, but his admirer Charles held up a hand. "In truth, we've no time for refreshment, and we would be grateful if you might send John Heminges out to speak with us."

"He is the proprietor, and this is his busiest hour, so his availability will depend upon how much assistance there's within." All five responded with the same expression, something between puzzled and annoyed, confused not to be given what they had requested. "If you'll excuse me, I'll slip in and ask him."

The tavern was abuzz with distracted laughing, flirting, drinking customers; nobody noticed him enter. Molly was absent, perhaps upstairs with the baby. Even with Hal's assistance, John Heminges was barely managing the crowd's demand for ale; he would not feel he could leave, Sander knew this. Augie Phillips handled money matters, and Sander saw him in the corner, but he was having a raucous debate with Shakespeare and Armin, and looked already tipsy. Not the best man to send out to speak with disguised nobility. Other sharers were moving toward them, and Armin tossed dice onto the table.

"There are some gentlemen outside," said Sander into Heminges's ear, over the raucous hum. "They're pretending they're not gentlemen."

Heminges rolled his eyes. "Which play do they want?"

"They didn't say."

Heminges glanced around the busy room.

"Go on," said Sander with a forced smile. "I'll distract them." He still wanted desperately to go home, but knew he must stay abreast of All Things Essex.

A pleased nod from Heminges. "Thanks, lad."

Sander stepped gracefully up onto the low table he used as a stage. The ambient noise shifted timbre as customers noticed him. He took a breath and set his mind to performing, then held out both arms in a welcoming gesture. "Good afternoon!" he called out. A clutch of women in modest silk corsets and simple caps, all of an age and likely friends from childhood, emitted brief arpeggios of delighted cries. He batted his lashes in their direction; painfully to him, one of them was Joan's exact coloring and height. "Would anyone mind a song?" he asked.

"Sing!" shouted most of the tavern. "Sing!"

"I haven't a lute or a viol, I fear," said Sander. "But I hope my voice will please." He forced himself to give them all a dopy little grin and giggle. "It's Master Dowland's latest, if you don't mind."

"Sing! Sing!" cried the entire tavern. He saw Heminges slip outside.

"If you *insist*," said Sander, with a head toss and sly smile. He felt leaden; merely staying upright was exhausting. He needed reinforcement. "You there"—he pointed to Jonathan, the company's lute player, who was seated with the trumpeter. "You look like you can keep a girl happy beating a nice steady rhythm—" He waggled his eyebrows, and the room roared.

Jonathan stood up, grinning. "How may I satisfy you, darling?" he asked in a lewd tone. More crowd approval.

Sander blew him a kiss. "Oh, I *like* you! Are you free later, handsome?" As the crowd roared again, Sander clapped a few times at a lively, but not racing, pace.

Jonathan began to drum on the table to match Sander's beat; after an attentive moment, the crowd began to clap along raggedly. Sander hoped they were all tipsy enough not to notice his half-heartedness. He assumed a formal pose, palms pressed together before his midriff, and with over-articulated diction, began to sing:

Fine knacks for ladies,
Cheap, choice, brave and new,
Good pennyworths, but money cannot move.
I keep a fair but for the fair to view,
A beggar may be liberal of love.

It was a madrigal, not written for a solo voice, but everyone was so thrilled to hear him that he might have intoned Gregorian chant and been lauded. He wiggled his backside as he sang the first refrain—"*Though all my wares be trash, the heart is true, the heart is true, the heart is true*"—and was rewarded with raucous applause.

Heminges came back inside and headed straight for the corner where the shareholders were well into their dice game. He waved at them: Burbage, Shakespeare, Armin, Phillips, Condell, Pope, indifferent to the crowd's hubbub and inured to the charms of Sander Cooke.

Sander, repeating the chorus several times so that he could perform without having to think, watched Heminges make the company's shorthand gesture for *money*. The others left the dice on the table, crossed past two blue-ruffed prostitutes, and followed Heminges out the door. Sander moved on to the second verse.

Great gifts are guiles and look for gifts again;
My trifles come as treasures from my mind.
It is a precious jewel to be plain.
Sometimes in shell, the Orient's pearls we find.

From his raised vantage point, he could see straight out of the window to the peculiar conversation: the pseudo-merchants clustered together, and the shareholders likewise, the two groups disagreeing about something with a veneer of courtesy. Essex's messenger hung back away from the discussion, and the company's messenger, Pen, stood beside him.

Sander continued with the second verse refrain, then all of the third verse, continuing his suggestive dance steps, which probably delighted more of the crowd than Dowland's lyrics anyhow. He finished with waves, blown kisses, and a cascade of his curtsy-bows. "Hal will serve you now!" he declared, gesturing toward the young man. Hal gestured *thank you*—not so much for the business he was about to get, but for having had a respite during the entertainment. "Thank you for letting me distract you from your important conversations," Sander called to the crowd. "You are all darlings. Especially you." Here, a gesture to the drummer, who grinned and waved, taking attention from Sander. He jumped off the table, relieved to be off-duty, and slipped toward the door. He closed it behind himself to discourage admirers from following.

The close, smoky warmth of the alehouse in which he was the sun gave way to a breezy expanse where he was no more than a mote. He watched the two clutches in their courteous disagreement, and slunk around them toward the boys. The gentlemen had positioned themselves so that the players had to squint into the sun and face the breeze head-on; he wondered if they had done this deliberately.

He could read the mood by body language and expressions; it took no great insight to assess that the visitors wanted to hire the troupe to perform, and Dick Burbage was the holdout. The gentlemen were pleading with the troupe; the troupe was coaxing Burbage.

"We've not done that play in years," Heminges was explaining to Charles. "It has fallen out of fashion."

"We do not require it to be fashionable," said Charles, in a tone of forced agreeability. "We only wish it to be performed."

"Which play?" Sander asked Pen. They were downwind of the group, and the breeze was brisk, so they could speak unheard.

"King Richard," said Pen. "But Master Burbage doesn't want to learn the lines all over again."

"*Richard III*? We stage that all the time, it's our most—"

"T'other one," Pen whispered back. "The one that's all in verse and mostly just lords arguing."

"*Richard II*," muttered Sander. Burbage's reluctance made sense, then. *Richard II* was a lot of dense language, with little action. Burbage liked to talk, but he also liked activity on the stage. He had been compelling in the role, Sander recalled, but he'd never enjoyed playing it. "What else?"

"These gentlemen are willing to pay forty shillings more than usual for a command performance," Pen said, "but they want us to stage it here at the Globe, and open to the public."

Sander frowned in confusion. "The whole point of charging high fees for privacy is so rich folk may see us in their own home."

"But the gentlemen say we may also charge admission, so we would be making lots of money. It seems like they are all agreed to do it, save Master Burbage. He doesn't wish to re-learn it overnight."

"Overnight?"

"They want it played tomorrow afternoon. We haven't advertised tomorrow's show yet, and so Master Phillips is making the argument to do it."

The idea came upon Sander so suddenly it didn't feel like his own.

Before he lost his nerve, he strode into the no-mans-land between the two groups, held out his arms, and declaimed, "*Wrath-kindled gentlemen, be ruled by me!*" A knowing smile. "*Let's purge this choler without letting blood.*"

Blank stares from the noble visitors; surprised blinks from Shakespeare and Burbage. Sander wiped the smile from his face, hugged himself, made an anguished face. "*For God's sake, let us sit upon the ground*," he recited, "*and tell sad stories of the death of kings*."

"You're mad," said Burbage. He grinned with grudging admiration. "They want it tomorrow, you'd need more time."

"*I wasted time*," said Sander, tragic. "*And now doth time waste me.*" Back to his own affect: "As the Queen, I spent so many hours backstage listening to your excellent recitations, sir, I am confident I myself could personate King Richard by tomorrow, if it please you."

Charles and his well-coiffed brother looked delighted.

"*Thus play I in one person many people*," he quoted next, still to Burbage "*and none contented*." Making a deferential gesture toward Augustine Phillips: "If Master Phillips is prepared to personate Henry Bolingbroke again, of course. The Queen is a tiny role, Kit could learn it overnight, he's quick with lines. It would be a good opportunity for him." He did not say, *And also for me*, and hoped he did not seem too obviously grasping.

Burbage began to take him seriously. "But you're much too young," he said. "He should be the same age as the Bolingbroke character."

"I wrote Romeo to be sixteen, Dick, and you were . . . not sixteen," said Shakespeare drily.

"Would you excuse us a moment?" Heminges asked the visitors.

Sir Charles made a conceding gesture. The shareholders stepped into a huddle several paces distance. To avoid seeming too eager, Sander turned his back on them with all apparent offhandedness, and smiled at Charles.

"How ironic it will be," said Charles's brother, "if Richard Burbage is usurped from playing the usurped King Richard."

"Joscelyn," said Charles, in a warning tone. "Nobody is talking about usurpation."

There were far too many noblemen named Charles for Sander to keep track of, but Joscelyns were few enough to index: one Sir Joscelyn Percy had a brother, Charles.

The Percys were related by marriage to the Earl of Essex.

So: Essex was secretly requesting a play about a monarch who had been forced off the throne by a popular but exiled nobleman.

No, he thought, that's not the only way to interpret *Richard II*. When the real-life Henry Bolingbroke knocked Richard from the throne, it had kicked off two generations of horrific civil war. William Shakespeare had written many plays about it all, but two hundred years on, not everyone thought Bolingbroke a hero. Sander didn't know why Essex wanted *Richard II* staged, but it could not be to send a message to anyone, for the message would be muddled.

Pen, responding to a whistled summons, trotted quick to Heminges. Sander heard Heminges ask him to fetch Josias Brown, the tailor, from the alehouse.

The only reason to call Josias at this particular moment would be to alter the King Richard costume. It was happening. He would be Richard.

He beamed at the Percy brothers and their friends; Charles Percy beamed back at him. Charles was a handsome man, and Sander craved distraction because everywhere he looked he saw Joan's absence. He let his eyes linger on the pale bearded face, until he saw the subtle shift of expression from pleasure to appetite. He curved his lips almost imperceptibly into a knowing smile, then began a choreography of surgical precision: flicked his gaze down along the sturdy, firm limbs; back up to the face; and then he broke the gaze, lest he seem too easy. He turned his head to look away into the middle distance.

A boy was approaching the property from beyond the tavern, and he focused on this boy to show Sir Charles that his attention must be earned. The boy was pleasing to his eye, but he realized with annoyance this was because he somewhat resembled Joan.

No, not somewhat resembled. Entirely resembled. There she was, in

Bacon's livery, a stone's throw from him, easy calling distance even in the breeze. Right there. He could have walked across the yard and put his arms around her. Why the devil was she here now? This was the time of day she made sure never to be here anymore.

She was walking from the street to an outbuilding beyond the tavern, but her attention was drawn by the cluster of men, and without slowing her stride, she turned her head to look at them. Her eyes met Sander's. He saw her tense but continue walking, her gaze on him until she disappeared out of sight around the corner. The rest of the group—even Charles—was distracted with bows and handshakes and acknowledgments; nobody else had noticed Joan. How extraordinary that she should walk back into his life at just this moment: the moment he'd secured his future. A glorious omen.

Pen and Josias Brown exited the tavern. As Josias crossed toward Heminges and the other actors, Sander stepped away and gestured Pen to him. "Take a message for me," he said. "It's confidential."

"HE'S *what?*" SAID Joan again, clutching at her cap as if she were afraid her head was coming lose.

Pen repeated with careful correctness: "He is playing the role of Richard II, tomorrow afternoon, here at the Globe. He cannot see you tonight because he must study his lines, but he hopes you might be free tomorrow, after, to meet with him."

"Truly?"

"I was there for the whole of the conversation."

She dropped the quills she'd come into the office for without noticing. "Why Sander, and not Richard Burbage?"

"Sander said he wanted to play it, and Master Burbage did not care to."

She blinked, rested a hand on the table to steady herself. "That is not how the Chamberlain's Men functions."

Pen nodded. "It was unusual, and therefore noteworthy, and so he wanted me to tell you."

"Goodness," said Joan, considering. "Not just playing the lead but doing it at his own request." She smiled, giddy. "All this time, he had so much more pull than he knew. Thank God he sees that now." She smiled at Pen. "I'm grateful to receive this news, Pen."

"I'll tell him you're pleased and will meet him tomorrow evening?"

"I'm more than pleased," she said. "You may express my enthusiasm in whatever words appeal to you. Take this." She reached into her drawstring purse and handed him a penny.

The boy nodded and went out.

Alone, she sat for a long moment in the darkening office. She was giddy. Of course he would be triumphant in the role; he always was, in every role. And then he would stay, here, with the men who knew and loved him. This Essex fascination would finally fade to nothing.

And then they could be together.

Last night, when she'd gone back into the Hawthorn, she'd made it clear that the Zaal cousins needed to impress her, and not the other way around. To her amazement, they'd adjusted to this and began vying with each other to engage her. She had even considered Jakob as a decent partner, especially because he spoke so glowingly of Hugh Platt that Bacon began to simmer . . . but Antwerp had crumbled to clay in her mind the moment she had seen Sander just now. It was a miracle she hadn't walked into a wall; once their eyes had locked, she could not look away, and it hadn't been the glamour of Alexander Cooke. Almost the opposite. Scores of ordinary moments between them flashed through her mind—averting a puddle in the street as they walked together, blessing each other when they sneezed, wiping crumbs off the other's jerkin, sharing a bun in the morning, a bowl of ale in the evening. Realizing life was made of such moments, she did not want to have them with anyone but Sander.

They would never be wealthy. They might, in truth, struggle to make ends meet. But they would struggle together, and each would have what they needed most in their life, including the other one's arms to sleep and wake in.

And it had dropped out of heaven, this opportunity, this change of fortune. Her prayers were more than answered.

In a happy, grateful daze, she opened the door to return to the laboratory.

She walked directly into Sander.

"Oh!" she exclaimed, and jumped back as he said, "Oh!" and jumped back too. A beat. They both laughed tentatively.

"I ran out of quills and had just come in to pinch one when Pen found me," she said, almost sheepish.

"I need to get the roll for Richard out of the chest," he said, in the same tone.

"Because you're playing him. Sander! You're playing a male lead!"

He nodded, smiling, anxious. "That's the agreement," he said. "I told them I could learn it, so I'll be up all night making sure of that."

"It's not night yet," she said, and grabbed him. She felt him sag against her for a moment, then straighten, and then, instantly aroused, he pushed into the room and pressed her up against the wall, grabbing the back of her head and kissing her greedily.

"Oh God, I've missed you," he said in a pained voice.

"I've missed you too," she said, kissing him back. "Pity the bed isn't in here."

"I think it's back in the tiring house under the props. But I do have to stay up and run these lines tonight." But then he brought his mouth to hers again.

She pushed him away enough to ask: "Do you not need help with that?"

He blinked at her in the dim light, as if he couldn't understand the question.

"I used to help you run lines," she prompted. "*As You Like It*, and *Merchant*, and *Much Ado*, and *Shrew*. I'll tell my mother that Dorothy needs me, and then I'll come back here and help you with the rote. I can stay all night."

"You're not worried about Bacon?"

"Sander," she said, smiling. "Bacon warned me away from you only because of Essex. This is a promotion within the company, so you don't need Essex now." *Nor do I need Antwerp*, she added to herself, glad that was a chance he'd never need to hear of it.

". . . Of course," said Sander, looking flustered. He nodded. "Right. Of course."

"I think Bacon would encourage this. In fact, I'll tell him about it after tomorrow."

"If tomorrow goes well," said Sander.

She laughed lovingly. "You might as well say 'if the sun rises.' You will be glorious in the role." She kissed his cheek. "I'm already proud of how you'll do. And I'm proud of helping you to get there."

He clutched her to him. She could feel his pulse. "Before we start running my lines," he said in a throaty voice, "there's another kind of roll I'd have you help me with."

She ran her palm down the front of him, then reached across to pull closed the door.

February 7

There was no breeze the next day, but the sky was leaden and the air was just a different kind of cold. It was still enough to hear the buzzing of the audience as they assembled. The house was not a quarter full, which was a disappointment but unsurprising: a cold day in February with very little notice, for a play long out of favor, was not apt to draw crowds. Sander reminded himself that today it was the identity, and not the size, of his audience that mattered.

In an embroidered, pearl-encrusted purple gown flowing loose over his breeches and hose, he tried to pace around the tiring house, but there were too many men, and all of them were eyeing him, which made his agitation more acute. At least Burbage wasn't one of them. That would have been fatally awkward. Burbage had declared today a holiday exclusively for Richard Burbage, and, with many thanks to Sander, he intended to lie abed until suppertime.

Sander took some deep breaths and let them out slowly as he fidgeted with the crown, unused to feeling something resting directly on his own hair. Too anxious to sneak glances up to the lords' boxes, he'd been asking Pen who was there. The lad had earlier reported that a party of nine had arrived, led by Charles Percy, who'd placed a purse into Phillips's hand. Today they dressed to show off their status, rather than to hide it: the lords' box was full of plumes and velvet frills. Now Sander brought his mouth close to the boy's ear and whispered, "Do you know the Earl of Essex by sight?"

"No," Pen whispered back. "But his boy's not here. If his lordship's arrived, then he's in disguise as someone else's minion."

He could not imagine Robert Devereux doing such a thing. "Thanks," he whispered. "Alert me if that changes, but don't tell anyone I asked."

Pen winked, pleased to have a secret.

He shouldn't have let Joan stay the night with him. She was a diligent prompter, but he'd been so diverted by her scent, by the hollow of her collarbone, by the shape of her thumbs, by the smear of dirt near her ear from whatever she'd been doing in Bacon's greenhouse the day before. Twice, in less than an hour, he'd grabbed the vellum roll from her grasp, tossed it away, and climbed on top of her. Then a third time, then a fourth, and then he'd sent her home. With her amused goodbye kiss she declared that she knew all his speeches better than he did, and he worried she was right. He'd sat up with a candle and the vellum roll, running lines over and over and over until well after midnight, when the candle burned out and he'd drifted into sleep.

Selfishly he wished she could have arranged her day to see his performance; just as selfishly, he knew it was better she would not attend, because he'd be distracted by her presence, even more than Essex's.

If Essex arrived.

He didn't need Essex to arrive, he chided himself. The Chamberlain's Men would see his capabilities today, and then after his apprenticeship, they'd hire him as a leading man.

Maybe.

Essex was offering him something more certain of rewards than he would ever have here at the Globe. But until Essex and Her Majesty resolved their differences, the Essex banner complicated things for Joan.

Well, never mind then, the Chamberlain's Men was good enough.

For now.

Knight, the prompter, tapped his shoulder. "Places, Master Cooke."

The actors in hearing distance—Condell, Phillips, Armin, in their costumes of uneven provenance (Armin, as a gardener, wore a turban)—clapped him on the shoulder, cheering, "Master Cooke! Master Cooke!"

"Thank you, Master Knight," said Master Cooke, grinning.

"I'm heading up to cue the musicians now."

"But have all the lords arrived?" asked Sander.

Knight gave him a curious look. "Are you expecting someone?"

"No," said Sander, trying to sound offhand. "But whoever requested this—"

"The one who paid for it did not request we delay for a later arrival." He gave Sander a kindly smile. "We can start. You must be eager."

A moment later, music filled the cold, still space, and the audience's hum fell silent. The piece was regal but melancholy, which seemed apt. A piercing, foreboding melody on the shawm was followed by a lyrical variation of the same tune on the lute; the music, like the monarch it introduced, had a changeable identity.

AS THE LUTE sounded the second verse, Joan glanced around the box, wondering where to toss her filbert shells. She had never sat in an upper gallery before; had never watched a play while seated on a cushion, or while eating pears and hazelnuts. For all of this, she had John Heminges to thank. He had arranged for her to be here, in the box with the most oblique angle to the stage, reserved for gentlemen. Sander was unlikely to notice her here. She had it all to herself, unlike the lords' box hovering over the stage, which was stuffed with ornately dressed men. She had never seen *Richard II*. But now she knew the lines of every scene the title character appeared in, from reviewing it (deliciously interrupted) four times last night. The role had been written for Richard Burbage, who weighed half as much again as Sander. Yet she could not imagine anyone but Sander doing it. Burbage had the majesty, but Sander had the grace.

IT WAS SO peculiar to stand upon this stage—where Sander felt more at home than almost anywhere on earth—without a bodice. His chest felt vulnerable as it never did when snugged behind false breasts. He had done this before, but rarely. In a way that was no longer true when he was personating women, he felt counterfeit; he was fraudulent, somehow; he would have to try harder than he was used to, to convince people to see him as a man. His self-awareness split in two: he was King Richard and yet he was also somehow a member of the audience, looking up as the groundlings did, or seated in the galleries, watching Sander Cooke play King Richard. Shakespeare had written the role for Burbage: the king was a lion, the king was the sun, and these images suited Burbage well. In comparison, Sander Cooke was a slender, effeminate thing, but somehow (mused that part of him watching Sander Cooke perform) this almost made the words more powerful. Someone not at all lionlike being called a lion, simply for wearing the crown . . . what better way to emphasize the power and meaning of the crown itself, regardless of who wore it?

As two quarrelling lords recited their grievances to His Majesty, Sander's mind chewed on this insight. *The crown's meaning is independent of the wearer. It's like a costume, like a wig.* Of course the stakes were infinitely higher with a real crown, but the parallel, he thought, was valid. Later in this play, Henry Bolingbroke would wear that same crown, and therefore be the king . . . and later this same year, young Kit or someone else would wear all Sander's wigs and gowns, and therefore be the darling of the crowds. And then Sander would be bereft, watching someone else be adored by the world, just because they carried on their heads something that had once been his.

He'd never realized, he thought, watching himself with wry self-deprecation, that he had anything in common with a king.

IN HER PRIVATE box, Joan could almost see Sander connect with the soul of the character, in a way he hadn't when just running lines: she could feel him feeling the crisis of the moment. Augustine Phillips was a charismatic actor; he was playing Henry Bolingbroke, whom all the audience knew would end up taking the crown from Richard. But as the performance went on, not even Augie Phillips could wrest sympathy away from Sander's delicate, self-pitying, bewildered child-king.

She'd known what happened before she'd ever seen the script; to be English was to know some version of this story. King Richard had impulsively banished his cousin, Henry Bolingbroke, from England. When Bolingbroke's father died, Richard laid claim to Henry's inheritance. Bolingbroke returned illegally from exile, and gathered to him other disaffected nobles; Richard, learning of this, sank to his knees and lamented: "*For God's sake, let us sit upon the ground, and tell sad stories of the death of kings*."

Henry Bolingbroke, in contrast, never sat once during the entire play but was always active, moving, on his feet, traveling, planning—and cornering Richard at Flint Castle, demanding the return of his inheritance, and then, shockingly, demanding that Richard give up his crown. More shockingly, he demanded Richard publicly declare he'd ceded it so by choice. The angling between the two noblemen was a complex verbal dance, Shakespeare's language at once precise and yet abstract, poetic, obtuse. Bolingbroke was careful to insist he wanted only what was due to him, and not the crown. Yet somehow, Richard's agreeing to this was the beginning of the end of Richard's kingship.

Sander was so vulnerable and genuine that Joan could sense nobody in the audience much liked Phillip's Bolingbroke. Richard may have been a self-pitying egoist, and a terrible ruler, but his humanity was so heart-wrenching, little else mattered. For Joan it was even more poignant, because she recognized it. King Richard had been crowned at ten years old; his identity was defined by his public office . . . so who was he now, without his destined and long-accustomed role in the world? The floundering to answer that was Sander's own floundering, the rage and confusion and resentment and fear—all of it was Sander's own, pouring out through Richard's words in iambic pentameter.

Finally they reached the deposition scene, in which Richard was coerced to tell the populace that he was not being coerced, so that Henry Bolingbroke would not be called usurper. Sander's casual gracefulness disappeared; he moved about the stage in sharp, clipped, agitated movements; sometimes breathless, sometimes gasping. And here too Joan saw how much of this came right from Sander's soul: after more word-wrangling, in which Richard spoke only of Bolingbroke *seizing* the crown and Bolingbroke spoke only of Richard *resigning* it, Bolingbroke demanded, one final time: "Are you contented to resign the crown?"

Joan watched Sander gazing at the costume piece in his hands, as if it held his future.

"Ay," he said, sounding reconciled. He began to hand it over, but as Bolingbroke's fingers touched it, he hastily pulled it back, declaring, "No," then pulled farther away, his robed body hunched around it, sobbing: "No!" . . . then realized he was surrounded by figures who were of lower status than a king and yet outpowered him. With a nauseated expression, he crossed back to Bolingbroke, sobbed, "Ay," and reaching up, placed it onto the other man's head.

It was, she thought, a little like his wigs that way: someday those wigs would rest on others' heads, and who would Sander be then? She wagered he was thinking something similar.

The rest of the scene was an excruciating recitation of all that Richard was "willing" to give up. Sander rattled off the list with mechanical slickness, as if he could not bear to consider the import of the words. He concluded, his voice breaking: "All pomp and majesty I do forswear."

She wished she could embrace him, now, right now—run down through the yard, pushing the groundlings out of the way, and leap up onto the stage, and comfort him. How bewildered his King Richard was, wild-eyed and disbelieving, that now he must be held accountable for behavior that had always been intrinsically acceptable, just because of who he was to others. Giving up the crown and scepter meant he was a mere mortal, and he had no experience of being such a thing.

It was so Sander, so very Sander. She felt herself choke up, felt her arms tighten in a protective need to comfort him. In a few more scenes, Richard would be murdered by an agent of the newly crowned King Henry; she almost couldn't bear to stay to watch it.

HE LOVED HIS final scene. Rarely did he die on the stage, and never had he killed someone. But the imprisoned Richard—although as delicate as Sander Cooke—expertly and believably felled two would-be assassins before the third stabbed him to death. He died upstage center; a curtain was drawn before him, to mask him for the final scene, in which the new-crowned King Henry lamented his murder.

From where he lay, Sander could just make out the nobles in the lords' box. Essex had never arrived to enjoy what he was paying for. He had not seen Sander deliver what Sander knew was the best performance of his life. The character was self-absorbed, moody, vain—and somehow Sander had made him sympathetic and forgivable. He had performed an act of alchemy, and the man he'd most wanted to impress had passed him over.

Never mind, he reminded himself. *Now the Chamberlain's Men know what I can do.*

When they were finished—after Armin's final jig, after the bows, after the careful shedding of costumes—the company surrounded him in the cramped tiring house and clobbered him with raucous hugs and shoulder-claps.

The back door flew opened without warning and there stood Richard Burbage. He was in his nightdress, affecting an exaggerated yawn. "I had a lovely dawdle. What did I miss?"

They all erupted into laughter. "We saw you in the audience," retorted Augie Phillips, shrugging out of his Bolingbroke doublet.

Plucking at Burbage's nightshirt, lumpy over street clothes, Sander said, "I'm flattered you made the effort to dress up for me."

Burbage winked. "Well done, lad. You should take those extra forty shillings."

"Hey, now," said Phillips, "he's not the only one who had to stay up all night studying his lines."

"Well, give him *something*," said Burbage. "That was a triumph. If I didn't own the building, I'd be quaking in my boots—this lad could replace me."

Sander somehow contained his thrill at this declaration. He was a made man. "Thank you, sir. It would be my honor to do it again upon any necessity."

"Come to the Sow and I'll treat you to as many ales as you've the stomach for. Just mind you get the costume back to Josias so he can let it out for me, good lad." And he was gone.

Sander, not a made man after all, steadied himself against a post and made sure to keep a smile on his face.

"Sander!" Heminges clutched him with fatherly pride. "That was astonishing." He gave him a private smile. "I expected much, and you exceeded even my expectations. Will is more impressed than he dare admit, in Dick's hearing. But don't let that stop you from drinking at Dick's expense. Ha!"

"Thank you, sir," said Sander. "May I speak alone with you?" Essex hadn't seen him; Burbage had disregarded his offer to perform again. It would be appalling if this led to nothing. He would have to do the thing he loathed: ask for something he had no surety of receiving.

Heminges looked around for his hat. "Of course. I'll meet you outside."

Sander stepped out onto the paving stones, into the chilly afternoon—and Joan's embrace. She covered his face with kisses.

He drew breath and whispered, pleased, in her ear, "But now I can't describe it to you!"

Joan held his head between her hands, and gazed into his eyes. Finally she said, "You're my favorite."

He turned pink with pleasure. "Now all other compliments will fade in significance."

"Oh, that's wasn't a compliment. Your acting was dreadful, but you're my favorite anyhow." She released him, laughing, with a delight like a child in summer sunshine.

"Come to the Sow?" he said. "I just need a word with Heminges."

"Of course you do," she said, with a significant tone. "Of course you do! Good luck." They kissed, and then he turned to greet Heminges as he exited the tiring house.

"Master Cooke!" said Heminges. "What would you?"

"I did well today," said Sander. Heminges nodded. "Did I do well enough?"

". . . Well enough for what?"

"For my future employment here?"

Heminges blinked. "You've always had a future here, lad."

Sander gave him a knowing look. "I mean a future where I play roles like this one."

Heminges sobered. "Sander. This was not an audition."

"I know, but—"

"I don't think you do. You did a tremendous bit of work, we are all impressed and grateful—in fact I agree with Dick that you deserve the forty shillings. But you know one performance does not make a shareholder."

"Very well, then, what would?" Sander asked, without peevishness. "You know I have the talent, so if I would put myself up for consideration, what else must I demonstrate?"

Heminges looked pleased with the question; Sander noticed, and this in turn pleased Sander. "For one thing, attend to the boring business side of things. The adult equivalent of all those apprentice chores you're slack at. Paying bills, hiring stagehands, haggling with Tilney at the Revels Office, all of that. We each contribute to the work."

"Of course I'll do that," said Sander. "The next time there is boring business to attend to, bring me with you."

Heminges laughed. "I'll try. Especially if it's to do with the Revels Office."

"I'm serious," said Sander.

"I warrant that," said Heminges. "I find these developments agreeable in you. In the past you made it an art to avoid dull responsibilities."

"I swear I am reformed." Sander put his hand out.

Heminges clasped his hand, shook once, and then gently tugged Sander closer to him. "While we're speaking, I've a question you might know the answer to."

"Ask me."

Heminges released him but remained leaning in close. "Who did we just perform for?"

Sander shrugged. "You count heads as well as I, it was a small house, but I'd say a few hundred?"

"That's not what I meant. The gentlemen who paid us, who were they? We've never been hired to do a command performance in our own Playhouse before. It's odd. They seemed to know you. Did you know them?"

"Everyone always thinks they know me," said Sander with the long-suffering patience of celebrity.

"And that is the sort of answer you give when you don't want to answer straight. Do you know them?"

"No," Sander said in a breezy tone. "But the one whom you spoke with, I believe that may have been Sir . . . Sir Charles Somebody."

"I saw Sir Charles Blount upstairs just now. That wasn't him."

"Some other Sir Charles, then," said Sander with a shrug. "There is a legion of Sir Charleses about."

"The presence of Sir Charles Blount makes me wonder who our patron was today."

A wave of unease buffeted Sander. Everyone knew Charles Blount was close to Essex. Too late now to feign ignorance. "I believe it was someone named Charles . . . Percy?"

He could see by Heminges' expression that Heminges understood, but was going to make him walk through it anyhow.

"Sander," he said. "Who paid us to perform this?"

"Didn't Sir Charles give you—"

"Charles Percy does not own a wallet out of which he can casually extrude ten pounds for a two-hour entertainment," said Heminges.

Sander tried to look at nothing.

"Alexander Cooke," said Heminges, growing sterner. "We just performed a play about a vain monarch being deposed by an earl who's beloved by the masses. Who paid us to do that?"

"We've performed it before, and it never was a problem," said Sander.

"It is one thing to have performed it. It is another thing to have performed it at the direct request of the Earl of Essex, at this moment in time. And you know that. I, at least, have the excuse of not suspecting it was Essex until this afternoon. But I wager you knew when you offered to take on the Herculean task of learning the roll overnight."

It seemed unfair to be scolded for something he was benefitting not one whit from.

"Essex didn't come," he said, as if that resolved the matter.

Heminges frowned with annoyance. "But you wanted us to do it because you believed he would."

"Who doesn't want to perform for an earl?" said Sander, regretting the words even as he heard them come out of his mouth.

"If you're determined to tie your fate to *that* earl, you're free to do that in a month, once your apprenticeship is over," said Heminges, the warmth continuing to drain out of his voice and face. "But you have no right to tie the Chamberlain's Men to him."

"I didn't!" said Sander. "I volunteered to do the part before I knew. If I hadn't realized who Charles Percy was, I would not know, even now, that Essex was involved—but still I would have volunteered. I swear to all that's holy. As you said, I'm a company man."

Heminges' tone shifted, to something much harder for Sander to hear: disappointment. "A company man would have said, *You should know that the Earl of Essex, who has been disrespecting his sovereign, is the one who wants us to stage our play about an out-of-favor nobleman disrespecting his sovereign. You should have that information before deciding.*" He shook his head. "I wish you had said that. We might well have done it anyhow, but we would have known the potential repercussions. And I would have known I could trust you to be forthcoming with me. Now I know I can't. That saddens me."

So the day's triumph would yield him no benefit, and instead all that effort was dragging him into trouble. "I apologize," he said, and made himself meet Heminges's gaze. The older man looked heartbroken. He was the only father or mentor Sander had ever known. Sander silently cursed himself. "You're right, sir, and I am ashamed. It was ill conceived of me, to believe it did not require mentioning. I grieve to have disappointed you." He tried to relax the choked feeling in his throat. "But on a practical level, sir, I assure you, nothing ill shall come of this. He wasn't even here, and there is nothing to trace the request to him."

Heminges, after a pause, softened, and rested a hand on Sander's shoulder. The touch, the moment of connection, reassured Sander. "Very well. I believe your remorse, and I accept the apology."

"Thank you, sir."

"And," continued Heminges, "I suspect you're right about the outcome. Therefore this conversation may remain between the two of us."

"The three of us," said Joan.

When Sander had turned back toward the door, she'd waited to walk together to the tavern. She'd heard the whole exchange.

Sander cursed.

"I'll leave you to it," said Heminges, and made haste for the alehouse door.

They were left staring at each other.

"Joan—"

"Which is worse, do you think?" she said, jaw twitching, eyes boring into his. "That you are still in thrall to the only man in England who complicates our future? Or that you are not honest with me about it?"

"Joan—"

"Which is worse?" she demanded.

He could barely make himself form the words. "The dishonesty," he whispered.

"Why?" she pressed, eyes wet.

"Why is it worse, or why did I do it?" He thought he might be sick.

"I know why it's worse!" she snapped. "Why did you do it?"

"You seemed so happy and I didn't want to ruin the moment," he said.

"Well," she said bitterly. "Now you've ruined all the moments."

"Joan—"

"*Don't*," she said. "Don't address me as if I require correcting, when the opposite is true." She turned away. "I'm leaving now. So sorry your favorite person wasn't here to lift your spirits."

He grabbed her arm. "Joan, stop that, you know my—"

"Your hunger for that man's regard confounds me. What good has he ever brought you?"

"It's not as simple as—"

"This *Essex*"—she wrested her arm from his grasp—"has turned you into a stranger, into someone who behaves without honor toward everyone who loves you. Everyone calls him dangerous or mad. What charm has he put on you?"

"No charm," said Sander, quite humiliated.

"Then you are choosing to behave this way," she said. "And you imagine I should continue to esteem you? Even if he were the flower of virtue, he's made you dishonest, and you have not even reaped a benefit from your dishonesty!"

He shouted with frustration, raised one arm and smashed the flat of his hand against the limed plaster of the Playhouse as hard as he could—then a second time, but not just his hand, his entire arm this time, flailing it against the wall. He yowled with pain, although it was gratifying in some primal way; he walloped the wall, again and then again and then again, shouting with rage and pain and frustration and confusion. He raised his other arm. But something hindered his movement.

"Stop that!" Joan nearly screamed, and smacked his perfect cheek.

He blinked, disoriented.

She was holding his right hand in her left one, her free hand high, prepared to strike again. "What are you doing?" she demanded.

A sob burst out of him and he leaned forward, nearing retching. He expected her to mock him for being weak, or feeble, or manipulative.

Instead, she let go his hand and pushed him upright. He sobbed, heaving in her grasp. She was unmoving, taking his weight.

When he had calmed, she said, "Sit with me."

She sank down onto the green-mossed paving stones that edged the Globe, and leaned back against its wall. She patted the space beside her. Uncertainly, ashamed of his outburst, he joined her.

For several silent minutes the two of them sat, staring across the winter grass, the daffodil buds, their own shoes. Once he made a feint of trying to say something, but was relieved she shushed him. The point, he realized, was to sit in silence alone together. This was how Joan was trying to repair things.

The clouds began to lift. The wind picked up a little.

"I disagree with what you're doing, regarding Essex," she said. "But I also recognize you're trying to do something for the two of us."

"I am."

"You're failing at it. I must tell you something that will be difficult to hear."

That she was even talking to him was magnificent. "I deserve whatever difficulties you throw at me," he said.

"Two nights ago, I was offered the opportunity to make a new life for myself on the Continent."

A pause as Sander tried to understand how this could be possible. "What manner of opportunity?"

"There are men with means, and education. Landowners and philosophers, who would vie to show me they are worthy of me—"

"What?" He pressed the heels of his hands against his temples. The world swayed and he needed it to stop.

"You assume you have me, no matter what. *I can disrespect her, it's not like she'd abandon me for someone else, for who else would have her?*"

"What are you talking about?" Sander demanded, almost collecting his wits again. "I think everyone should want you, Joan. It's a mystery to me that I've no competition."

"I'm telling you that now you do," she said, looking straight ahead and not at him. "There are men who would offer me either paid employment or matrimony if I leave England with them."

"Oh God," said Sander in a small voice.

"It is an extraordinary opportunity."

"Oh, God," he said in an even smaller voice.

"But when I saw you yesterday. I realized. I won't marry someone I don't love."

He sagged against her. "Thank you," he whispered.

"Don't thank me, just listen. I might still go, without marrying. They would employ me. There's still a choice to make. What common-born woman gets such a choice? But since it *is* a choice, I've no right to say: *I've chosen to stay in England for you, so now you're obligated to behave the way I wish you to.* I must either accept you as you are, or go to Antwerp. It astounds me not to understand you anymore, but I don't. So I require your assistance. If I stayed here, who is this Sander Cooke that I'd be staying for?"

Sander stared into his hands. "I don't know who I am now, Joan," he said at last, "so I don't know who you'd end up tethered to."

"Can you promise me I would not be tethered to a liar?"

"If I make that promise, will you believe me?"

She blinked. Frowned. "I don't know."

"That's fitting. I don't deserve you to have faith in me. I don't deserve you at all."

She gave him a cross look from the corner of her eye. "Are you trying to make me choose you out of pity?"

He buried his face in his hands. "It's awful that you'd think me capable of such a thing, but understandable. When must you make this choice?" He raised his face, looked at her.

She shrugged unhappily. "Soon. I'd have said yes already, except I thought you and I might have a chance."

"We have a chance," he said quickly, urgently, and took her hands. "We do, Joan. I'll prove it to you."

She looked down at her hands in his. She did not clasp back. "How?" she asked, in a tone that sounded more indulgent than believing.

"I don't know, but I will. Give me one week. Will you do that? Don't answer them for this week and I swear to you—" She glanced away, which worried him. "Three days, then. Not even a week. Please, Joan. Give me three days to reform my life, and I will show you that staying with me is your best choice. I'll make it effortless for you to turn your back on Antwerp."

After a moment, Joan circled her wrists to break Sander's hold on her. He reached for her again; she pulled her hands away. "Very well," she said, face and voice neutral. "The visitors from Antwerp are here for a month. They can wait a few days." She got to her feet, kissing the top of his head as she rose. Feeling the kiss he reached for her again, but she stepped away. "I'll see you in one week," she said.

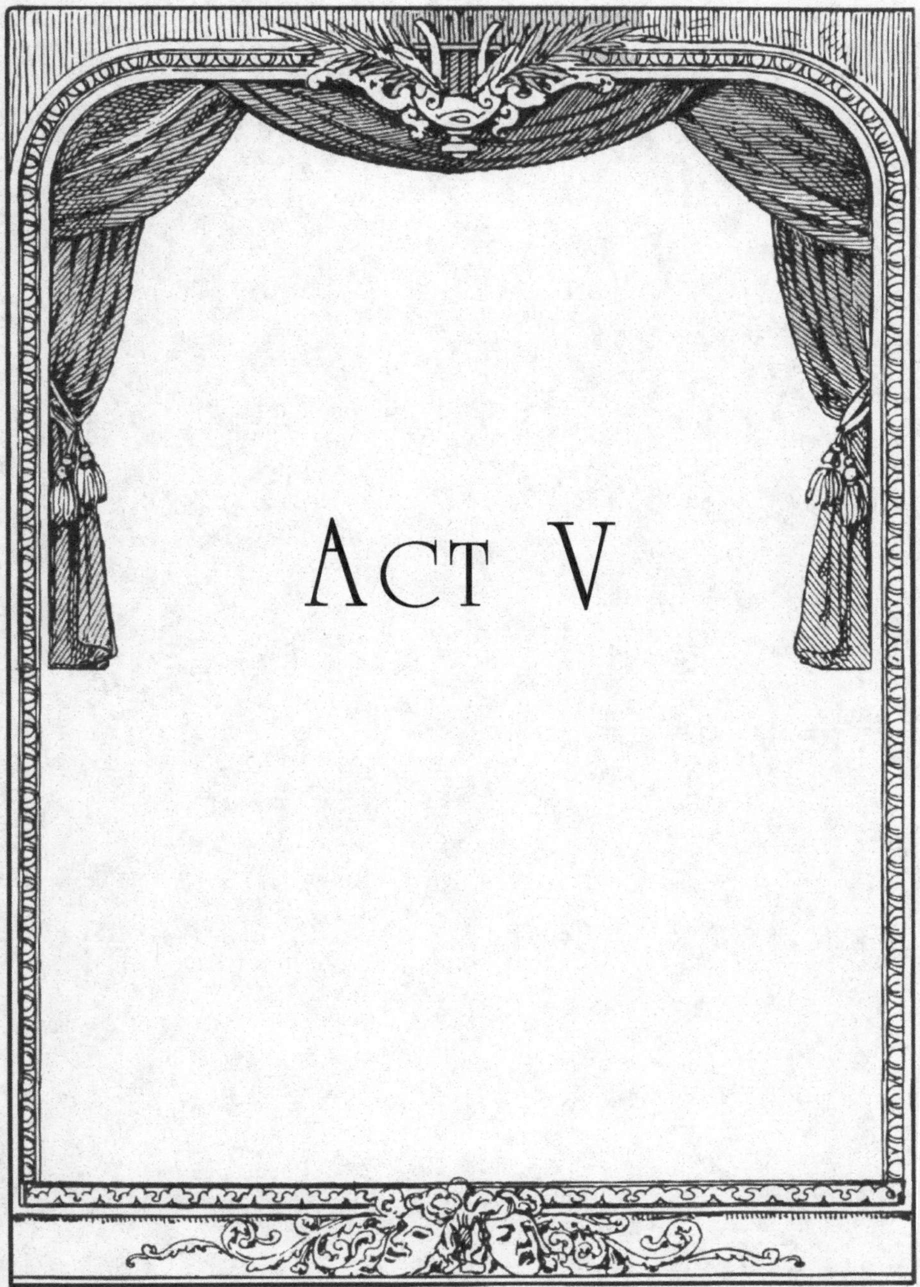

Act V

February 8

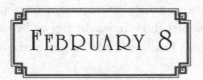

THE NEXT MORNING FELT CRUEL to Sander. As Rebecca Heminges prepared the morning pottage, he halfheartedly corralled the children to the table, oversaw their handwashing, prompted them through saying grace. With so many little ones underfoot, there was always something innocent to talk about, which spared him from acknowledging John Heminges's inquisitive looks. The man wanted to know how things had gone with Joan. Sander appreciated his concern, and also resented it. He had mucked his life up on his own and wanted to be left alone to sort it out.

After breakfast and an early service at St. Mary's, he excused himself from the Heminges household and set off alone down Milk Street toward the city center, past mounds of bricks awaiting to be set and cemented for half a dozen building projects along the way. He was heading toward Essex House.

He didn't know why he was going.

That wasn't true. He knew several reasons but did not know which was most sincere.

No, that wasn't true either. His vanity wanted to know if Charles Percy had reported well of him, and if Essex regretted missing the performance. But he knew that he would in fact tell his lordship bluntly and directly that he, Alexander Cooke, could truck with him no further; he would give up a glittering future for the woman he loved.

He would do this. He would tell Joan he had. Everything would begin to improve.

He reached Cheapside: more bricks, awaiting larger remodels of more expensive homes, in London's constant buzz of re-building and re-creating. He wondered how it would feel to be in Essex's presence. The idea of something, Heminges had taught him, was not the same as the thing itself.

Not that it mattered. No matter what his pride yearned for, he would disavow the earl.

As he neared Christ Church and St. Paul's, he passed clusters of families, well-dressed, walking to Sunday mass. Passing between the two huge churches along Paternoster Row, he dodged fine carriages with servants trotting alongside. Most of the carriage owners had their own home chapels, but St. Paul's was the best place to gossip and show off wardrobes. He'd attended Sunday mass at St. Paul's a few times when he was younger. A year ago, the priests had asked Heminges to keep him home, because his presence was distracting.

Once he'd passed the looming hulk of the cathedral, the current of traffic shifted so that now he walked against the flow of carriages. He crossed Ludgate Hill, and then the length of Fleet Street, with its shops and comfortable brick homes. Crossing through the wooden portal of the Temple Bar, he heard noises ahead, in excess of Sunday carriages: voices calling in greeting; rough mirth; hooves stomping; snorts and whinnies.

He approached the gates of Essex House. The sounds were coming from the courtyard, and some dozen passers-by in Sunday dress had paused to look within, with perhaps another score moving toward the sounds, distracted from wherever they'd been heading. It was usual to have commoners peering through the bars of the Essex House gate, but it never stood ajar like this.

He was astonished by the size of the gathering in the courtyard. More than a hundred riders, from noblemen to servants, and at least another hundred on foot. They were in chased leather much too fine for soldiering. They must be heading out to St. Martin's or Soho for an afternoon of hunting. He was glad not to have missed them, and began to slip past the gawkers.

But he paused just at the open gate, reconsidering. The men within were grim and watchful, and their looks toward him cold. Calls of "Name yourself!" began to overlap around the large courtyard. The horses backed away from the gate, as a dozen young men in Essex's green and black marched toward him in formation. Sander felt the small crowd of commoners fade back into the street.

He struck a graceful pose and waited for somebody to recognize him. Somebody always recognized him. He'd have no idea what to do if he wasn't recognized; since he'd first stepped foot on the Globe's stage, that had never happened.

Reliably, he heard the whispered syllables of his name echo around the yard and bounce out into the street; he saw the confused faces of the men as they came to an awkward halt.

He took one step through the gateway. A woman in the crowd *oohed*, as if he'd just stepped onto a stage.

"God ye good day," he said, charmingly polite. An unsure chorus of grunted responses from around the courtyard. He smiled and some of them returned small grins; a few waved.

There were too many horsemen for a hunt. The household must be about to embark on a journey somewhere. Not a good time to ask his lordship for an audience.

But it would look odd if, having publicly presented himself, he turned and walked away now. Feeling unwonted awkwardness he hesitated, glancing between the street and the courtyard.

"Hallo there!" came a voice from farther within.

Sir Charles Percy, handsome and well-dressed in an embroidered scarlet cloak and matching breeches, collar, and hat, came striding toward him, arms akimbo, rapier at his side. This was not dress for a hunting party—nor for travel. "What a pleasant surprise!" he exclaimed, as if he wasn't shouting to be heard over whinnies and the creaking of saddle leather. "Do come in, Master Cooke, we would be honored by your company. My friends and I had no chance to commend you yestereve for your remarkable performance."

Sander smiled and considered how to excuse himself.

"Come in, come in," insisted Sir Charles, beckoning. "Robert will be pleased to see you. He was sorry to have missed you yesterday, once we all described it to him."

He felt more flattered than he wanted to. "I'm honored."

"Come in to tell his lordship so," said Sir Charles, passing by men and horses as if he didn't see them, coming to the gate and taking Sander by the arm. "It has been a troubled morning and your presence will cheer him."

"What is all this?" Sander asked.

Sir Charles made a brushing-off gesture. "A tedious business," he said. "No concern of yours."

"All these men—"

"They're here to defend Robert. There was an attempt on his life."

Sander doubted this. "Why would somebody hurt his lordship now, when he's out of favor and a threat to no one?"

Sir Charles shrugged. "We've a man of our own inside the court. He warned us that Walter Raleigh intends assassination."

"And you expect him to attack openly?" asked Sander, shocked. Dammit, he should never have set foot through the gateway.

"We don't know, so we wait and watch. It's tedious, above all for those hoping to go for an afternoon in Soho. Please come in. It would do him a world of good to hear a song or have his attention distracted."

Sir Charles looped his arm across Sander's upper back and squeezed his shoulder, snugging him up against himself. The absolute confidence of this behavior, coupled with his affectionate tone, was disorienting. There was some reason to be cautious before entering, but the reason could not be half as vital as whatever opportunity this beautiful and considerate man was ushering him toward.

BACON HAD SENT word to meet at the Temple Bar, and included coins to pay Joan's passage across the river. She was to wear his livery and make sure her boots were clean.

After the Antwerp supper—perhaps to mollify her—he'd told her of a premise forming in his mind that he wanted her assistance to examine. An idea had come to him while he was visiting his estate at Gorhambury, where one could see the stars at night. If starlight began someplace very far away, and eventually reached Earth, then the light had to travel through the ether to reach them. That must take time, he reasoned. Which meant the light that reached them must somehow age—by moments, or by hours—from the moment the star emitted it.

His thoughts were abstract and confused, he had told Joan. He was so uncertain how to pursue this notion, he had yet to mention it even to his close associates. Nobody thought about starlight in smoky London, where it was rarely seen. Those who regularly saw the stars, he had explained to her, were of two sorts: rustics, whose work left them no leisure to consider matters philosophical; and landed gentry, who rarely glanced up from their immediate glorious environs and the headaches involved in maintaining them.

But he, Francis Bacon, had had this thought. Only he did not know what to do with it. He wondered how he could measure the age of the light that reached his own eyes, and had invited Joan to help him dream up some way to do so.

It was Joan who'd suggested visiting the shops. The instrument makers she knew, most of them Flemish or French, were more than craftsmen; they were natural philosophers too, contemplating how best to measure things, and what to measure, and how, and why. They made astronomers' staffs, astrolabes, quadrants, cross-staffs, compasses. Bacon, intrigued, determined they'd peruse the shops on Monday afternoon.

But then, he'd sent word to meet this morning—Sunday morning. That was odd. He had little to do with city life, but surely he must know shops were closed on Sundays?

Disembarking from the wherry, she headed up the stairs through the water gate, and trudged the steep slope up Middle Temple Lane. At

Temple Bar, she saw Bacon waiting for her, his cheeks flushed from the cold, his silver-edged compass cloak wrapped tight around him.

"Sorry to keep you waiting, sir," she said, approaching.

"I just arrived myself," he said. He gave her an almost fatherly smile. "The Antwerp philosophers came to see me yesterday. They are eager to hear news of you."

"I need one week," she said. "Surely they can grant me seven days to determine the rest of my life, sir. Are you so eager to ship me off?"

His smile remained steady, and affectionate. "Of course not, Jack. I'm just reminding you, you have admirers who'd bring you opportunity."

"Thank you, sir. Why are we here?"

"I require calm and quiet to think," he said. "I wish to determine which shops are of interest, on a day when the streets are quiet, so as not to be jostled by throngs. I wish to establish today, in the calm, where we should return tomorrow, so that tomorrow's endeavors will be more efficient."

"You do realize, sir, the shops are closed up tight, even the windows covered, and so we can see nothing of them now?"

"But you know what and who are in each one, do you not, Jack?"

"I do. The Flemish and the French as well as the locals."

"Then we'll walk up the Strand, and you shall tell me the best features of each." He gestured her forward toward the bar.

The bar was raised in daytime, and the keeper was away from the gatehouse, so they walked through, toward the hubbub. A confused, and then concerned, look troubled Bacon's face.

"The shops are just beyond the noise, sir."

"That noise," said Bacon. "It is coming from Essex House."

Joan had walked the Strand a thousand times, and on occasion admired Somerset or Arundel or other grand homes, their decorated gables or towers—but the plot of land the noise seemed to be coming from had never caught her attention. The buildings whose tops she could see were imposing in their height, but uninteresting. No trim, no stained glass, no fanciful folly. How ironic that a man who'd captured the imagination of all London would live in such dull architecture.

"Are you not wanting to cross past the gate?" she asked. "We might skirt it if we went up Shire Lane, but the footing there is always muddy."

"Never mind. It's just a hunting party preparing to head out, I'm sure. He's had few opportunities for such outings over the past year, heavens knows. Perhaps this will clear his head a bit."

A small crowd in elegant cloaks and fine galoshes, all heading to or from a church service somewhere, was paused at the open gateway to watch whatever was within. Down the road from either direction, Joan saw figures moving nearer. At the Essex gate, Bacon stared straight ahead and walked faster. Joan, curious, turned to gaze inside.

There were scores and scores of horsemen and at least a hundred men on foot milling around, and nothing festive about any of them. As her eyes glanced around the open yard, she saw it almost a village writ small: the main house, of brick, with a dozen chimneys, and to either side a wing of outbuildings: carriage house, stable, kitchens, and weaving through Essex's armed retainers, a stout well-dressed gentleman retreating toward the house, with his arm around somebody who looked like Sander.

"Oh!" she cried.

Bacon glanced, cursed quietly, then grabbed her elbow and pulled her so hard she stumbled off balance. "Don't," he whispered urgently. He pointed with his chin to a party of four men who had just approached the gate from the west. They wore dark robes with sable collars and cuffs; Joan was unschooled in decoding colors and insignias, but these were clearly men of status.

The leader of the quartet was an aging gentleman with a long beard and gilt decorative stripes running down his long full sleeves. He called to the guard at the gate, who in turn called to the stout scarlet-clad nobleman. The nobleman paused, released his grip on Sander's shoulders, and with a gesture for Sander to wait, he came back toward the gate to meet the new arrivals.

"Who are these people?" asked Joan.

"The man who just spoke is Tom Egerton, Lord Keeper of the Seal.

The others are court officers—Chief Justice Popham is the short one. The young man in red welcoming them into the yard is Sir Charles Percy."

As soon as the foursome were inside the gate, the mood in the courtyard shifted. Dozens of the riders surrounded the newcomers and drew swords or shifted lances and muttered with loud gruffness, but Joan could not make out the words. The horses began to fidget.

Egerton held up his hand and shouted once into the damp morning, to silence them. The courtyard din softened to a hum.

"We have come to fetch his lordship to the Privy Council," he called out in a long-suffering voice. "Regarding intelligence of a new Spanish Armada. It is an area of his expertise and Her Majesty desires his counsel. He was twice summoned yesterday and twice failed to appear. That is an offense to the Crown, and we have come to help him undo the offense."

"He didn't go to Westminster because he was ill." This came from another well-dressed gentleman who'd just exited the main house. He was crossing briskly toward them, trusting the armed men to give him room. Which they did.

"Gelly Merrick, you are a liar," retorted Egerton. "I have heard of his perfect health from guests he entertained last night at supper." The riders surrounding him raised swords, urged horses closer.

"Stand back now, men," said Gelly Merrick, whose accent was Welsh. "He's right, I am a liar, but only because the truth sounds too outrageous to believe. His lordship did not obey the summons only because he was warned that Cecil and Raleigh had agents lying in wait to ambush and assassinate him."

The armed riders around the quartet shook their weapons and made threatening sounds. Gelly gestured them to quiet.

"God's light, that is tilly-fally," said Tom Egerton. "Ask yourselves who convinced you of such a mad falsehood, for that man is not your friend. That man is sowing unnecessary discord and making things worse for your master."

Joan glanced at Bacon, who was horrified.

"Please sir, shall we collect Sander and leave," she whispered. Sander was watching these developments from the side of the courtyard, wide-eyed, unmoving.

"He is in the thick of it," said Bacon.

"He isn't, sir," countered Joan. "Last night he said he's breaking from Essex. I'll wager that's what he's come to do."

"He has feet," Bacon retorted. "He isn't using them."

Joan opened her mouth to argue but their attention was drawn toward a new person exiting the house.

He was wearing silk and velvets, even grander than Edgerton's ceremonial robe. Almost all of it was cream-colored, which set off his pale but rosy skin. On his head was a tall, fantastically decorated hat. He was handsome and graceful and had a spirited, arrogant gleam in his eye. The footmen and the horsemen not directly around Egerton turned to acknowledge him, bowing and *huzzahing*. So did all the watchers at the gate.

Bacon shifted closer to the wall of Essex House, to be less conspicuous. Joan stayed put, studying the nobleman who held Sander in such sway. She hated him.

"Stand down!" The Earl of Essex commanded the courtyard as he crossed toward the gate. Immediately the men surrounding the Westminster four backed away, allowing room for Essex to approach. But nobody lowered a sword or a lance, and his lordship did not ask them to. All around Joan, people were gaping wide-eyed at Robert Devereux, 2nd Earl of Essex, the way they gaped at Sander Cooke on the stage.

"My Lord Keeper," said Essex, with a slight nod of his head, without removing his remarkable hat. "Chief Justice Popham."

"Your lordship must come with us," Egerton said, terse.

"My men won't let me leave here unaccompanied," said Essex with a complacent smile. Joan recognized that they were performing their roles; if they had been having an actual conversation, their voices would not have carried out to the street.

"Why not, Robert?" said Egerton in a long-suffering voice.

"Because, Thomas," replied Essex, "Sir Walter Raleigh would assassinate me. My men have mustered for my safety and they take their charge seriously. That is the only reason we are gathered here."

Egerton glanced around, at both the gathering crowd without and the armed men within the gate. "I see noblemen among this gathering who are neither servants nor sycophants, but conspirators."

Joan glanced at Sander, half-visible now behind the press of men. He was watching Essex and Egerton with a stupefied expression. She wished she had a pebble she could hurl at him to knock purpose into him. "This," continued Egerton, "has all the marks of *your* planning to attack something. Or someone."

The armed men muttered and made ugly faces; their swords twitched. The horsemen's lances lowered, pointing.

But Essex raised his face toward the cloudy heavens and laughed scornfully. He waved at his men. The growling subsided, but not a man put up his weapon. "Why would I attempt such a thing?" he demanded of Egerton. "It would displease Her Majesty and my sole *raison d'être* is to improve my standing in Her Majesty's sainted eyes."

"Refusing two summonses in one day will improve nothing for you," argued Egerton.

Essex spoke now in a normal voice, and Joan could no longer hear him. He scowled at the assembly, but they all seemed to think it was their job to intimidate the visitors no matter what their lord requested. Essex gestured toward the main house. Egerton and Opham turned to discuss something, then turned back to Essex, nodding.

"I'm taking them inside!" Essex roared at the armed men. "Quiet yourselves now!"

"Take them captive!" shouted somebody, and half the yard cheered in an ugly tone. Essex shook his head and gestured for the royal party to go ahead.

In the confusion, Joan saw Essex turn to Sander, who bowed.

Essex gestured Sander to follow the other visitors inside.

Sander bowed again, but as he straightened, he made an apologetic gesture, and pivoted toward the gate.

Relieved, she turned to Bacon. "You see? He's taking no part. He's leaving. Let's wait for him so you can let him know he's done the right thing."

Bacon gave her an exasperated look. "Absolutely not. The best I can do for him is to never let on that I've seen him here. This is more serious than you can imagine, Jack."

"Wh—"

"Come with me to the Inn and I'll explain. I feared a day like this would come."

"What's happening?"

He circled his finger to point out the growing crowd at the gates. "Gray's Inn. Now."

They turned back toward the Temple Bar, an arrowshot distant. But the bustle of fascinated onlookers had fast increased as church services let out throughout the parish, and the street had grown congested with onlookers, in all manner of dress—taffeta to fustian, woolen caps to gold cauls, civet-scented, reeking, a mix as lively as an afternoon at the Globe—all stretching their necks to glance inside the gate. Joan pitched forward to hurry through the crowd. A large man in her way began to step aside for her but then froze, his attention arrested by something behind her. He waved and shouted to his mates. Tripping forward almost into his armpit, Joan pivoted to see what he was pointing out.

A carriage was approaching the front of the Essex Gate, coming from the direction of Westminster. It was grander than the one Joan had ridden in as a child, when Morgan and Cole had taken her out to plant her hybrid plum tree. This was a roofed box covered with velvet hangings, and what was visible was gilded, even the muddied wheel-rims. An open window allowed the passengers to see and be seen, but the angle of approach blocked them from Joan. Bacon frowned as if he knew the carriage.

The driver turned the horses into the gate, but now there were too many onlookers, too many footmen, too many horses, too much confusion, and too much wariness to allow entry. Once it turned, Joan could see two figures within it but their faces were in shadow; she could make out only ruffs, lace, feathers, plumes, frills.

Finally the driver yielded. With exaggerated expressions of frustration, he set the brake and relaxed the reins. The horses snorted, their ears twitching around to make sense of the confusion.

Some Essex men spilled out of the gate and surrounded the carriage, snapping at the onlookers to make room for the passengers to alight. One liveried man reached up, opened the door, and unfolded a set of steps. He offered his raised hand to the passengers.

A woman of middle years exited first. She was calm, fair, and elegant in both comportment and dress. In fact, despite her age, she was the most beautiful woman Joan had ever seen. She was more beautiful than Sander. Everyone within the yard quietened and bowed; the onlookers on the street began to murmur with excitement, the way crowds at the alehouse did for Sander. The lady somehow seemed to both acknowledge and yet disregard them. Every gesture, every expression, eye movement, step, turn, everything, was perfect; she was delectably watchable.

"So," said Joan, realizing. "Here is Penelope Rich."

Behind her, almost unnoticed, a velvet-clad younger man came down the steps.

"This is appalling," said Bacon, sounding nauseated. He was behind Joan and directed this into the top of her head, but he was speaking to himself.

"Who is he?" she asked.

"Edward Russell. The Earl of Bedford. He's an Essex man, but he's sensible. I cannot believe he would join this travesty."

Bedford regarded the growing crowd around him. He glanced into the courtyard as Egerton and the others disappeared into the house; Essex give a final flourish to his men demanding quiet, which none of them heeded.

Bedford shook his head, appalled, and turned to Lady Rich. He said something to her low and fast; she answered, taking his arm, pulling his closed fist to her own heart in intimate entreaty. Bedford retrieved his hand from her grasp, turned on his heels, and marched back up the Strand from the direction the carriage had come.

"Thank God," said Bacon. "And we are likewise leaving, Jack. This is going to get worse."

The armed men near enough the gate to see Bedford leave hollered shocking slurs at him, until Lady Rich raised her hand. They stopped, bowing and begging her forgiveness, more attentive to her than they had been to Essex. The watchers in the street, however, shouted angrily at the retreating Bedford, variations of "Don't be a coward, go within and help his lordship! The earl needs everyone's support now!"

Sander was slipping his way through the armed men in the yard, trying to leave. He neared the gate just as Penelope Rich entered through it. Her progress was easy and swift because everyone fell back to make room for her. She was heading for the main door of the house but with an excited exclamation, she veered to intercept Sander. He bowed, but she took his arm, raised him up, and embraced him. He seemed to melt at her touch. She touched his cheek, took his arm, and turned him back toward the house. He went along with her, as if sleepwalking, staring adoringly. Joan lost sight of them in the crowd.

"Oh God," she said.

"We're leaving," repeated Bacon, pulling at her elbow.

As she turned from the gate, the man who'd helped Lady Rich out of the carriage gestured at Bacon, eyes wide with recognition. "Hey now, there's one we know, Sir Gelly!" he hollered over his shoulder. "Let's pull him in to be with us all today!"

"Damn you, Salisbury," Bacon muttered. He grabbed Joan's hand hard and dragged her down the road at a run.

THE PLEASANT PRESSURE of an arm around his shoulders eased just as the jasmine faded, and Lady Rich stepped away from him. They were in dim light, surrounded by dark paneled walls.

"I'm so glad you've joined us, it will gladden my brother's heart," she said.

They emerged into a small atrium-like room three stories high, with balconies around the upper floors, and clerestory windows at the top allowing pale light to filter down. There were small service corridors leading off at random angles, and two large doors faced each other to either side. Sander remembered from earlier visits that one of these opened to a leather-paneled dining room, and the other, to a library. Somehow, this house was never cold or drafty.

"Won't you go in and settle yourself until Robert is free," said Penelope, gesturing toward the library. "I'll have my girl bring you wine and pears."

"What is happening, m'lady?" Sander managed to say. "I cannot conceive your brother will have time to receive a visitor."

She took both his hands in both of hers and smiled comfortingly. "Alexander," she said, "You are always welcome here."

The sounds of an argument burst from the dining room; the doors flew open and the four Westminster officers were shepherded at sword point by six Essex men; the earl himself followed on their heels, arguing with one of them.

". . . but *very* unwise all the same, Gelly," Essex was saying with the precise diction of the irritated as they spilled out of the dining room. He had removed his hat and handed it off to a page boy, who disappeared down a corridor with it.

"And what would you call wise in this situation, your lordship?" Gelly retorted with his Welsh lilt. But: "Hold," he ordered the guards.

For a moment there was tense silence, everyone eyeing everyone else across the atrium. Then:

". . . Is that Sander Cooke?" murmured one of the Westminster men.

It was such an ordinary comment, Sander nearly giggled. He funneled his nervous energy into a polite smile, feeling like an idiot and wishing he were invisible.

"It is indeed him," declared Penelope, as if she were revealing a surprise dish at a feast. "Robert, put your guests in the library," she continued, without losing her preternatural calm, and beamed at Sander. "Would you like to join them, Alexander, or would you prefer to take refreshment in the dining room with us?"

Sander stared at her, stupefied.

"The library is the only room with no connecting doors," Penelope explained, to her brother's questioning look. "Lock this one door, put one guard outside it. They can't hurt you, your men can't hurt them. Everyone stays safe."

Essex considered the naked blades, and then the library doorway. He nodded. "Gelly, do it."

After an angry pause, Gelly—not pleased with the decision—gestured for the guards to sheathe their weapons.

"Get in there," he ordered the four gentlemen.

"Gelly Merrick," said Penelope Rich in the voice of a stern older sibling. "Address them as is worthy of their status." She smiled apologetically at the quartet. "Dearest Tom," she said to the man with the most decorated sleeves. "Please forgive my brother's steward. I'm sure there's been a terrible misunderstanding, and—"

"Dearest Penelope," the gentleman interrupted icily, "The misunderstanding is your brother's. He misunderstands his status relative to Her Majesty. He seems to think he can do as he pleases regardless of her wishes."

"As I *please?*" retorted Essex in a mocking voice. "I do nothing that I *please*, I do only what I *must*."

"Robert," began Penelope, but he turned his back on her.

"Gelly," he said. "Put them in the library, bring them wine and bread and lock them in. Immediate death for anyone who harms them." He stalked across the space out toward the courtyard. As he strode he shrugged himself out of the pale embroidered mantle, let it drop to the floor, and hollered for a riding coat.

Remaining by Penelope's side, Sander watched Essex's departing form, heard the celebratory huzzah erupt in the courtyard.

The slamming boom of the library door made him jump. The four men from Westminster were protesting from the other side of the door; Gelly Merrick was shouting at the servants and the guards; Penelope's eyes were darting about, tracking everything in the dark contained space.

"I think the dining room, for a libation," she said to Sander, as if this were one of many excellent options. Seeing the confounded look on his face, she added, almost apologetically, "Robert prefers guests not congregate in his receiving chamber when he's out. His wife is upstairs, but she isn't seeing visitors this morning. So 'tis only you and me for now. Shall we?"

She was convincing, but he knew performance when he saw it. And he had no reason to be here but to speak to Essex, which couldn't happen now. "My lady," he managed to say. "I should not stay while your esteemed brother prepares to ride out with dozens of furious armed horsemen."

"Oh, that," she said, with a dismissive gesture. "Yes, of course, if you don't know what's going on I can imagine we seem like terrible hosts. Allow me to make up for that now. Come into the dining room and tell me what's brought you here today."

He knew if he confessed his reason for coming, she would try to talk him out of it. He was not certain, in this disorienting situation, if he would manage to resist her arguments. "My amazement at what I've been witnessing has driven my intentions from my head, milady."

"Well, that's a bit dramatic, surely," she declared, and began to saunter into the dining hall, gesturing for him to join her. Almost against his will, his feet followed hers. *For one cup*, he thought, *so as not to offend her*. Then he would leave, on friendly terms with her at least, and she might still help him to a patron.

The paneled walls spangled with gold leaf painted onto the leather in an intaglio pattern. On a dais waited a bare table, toward which Penelope led him. Along one wall ran a cupboard, colorful with Murano glass goblets—Sander had never seen so many together, twenty at least, more valued than their equivalent in gold. Beneath this was a copper tub of water in which rested several bottles. Past this, the ewery board, with jugs of water, washing basins and small towels, awaiting dinner service. "True, there's quite a bustle here today, but it's not as if you've watched us summoning demons or disemboweling Tom Egerton. Will you drink? We've malmsey, aligaunte, and secke at hand, but there's a cask of Corsican in the cellar if you'd prefer."

Sander knew the name. The Keeper of the Great Seal had just been locked in the Essex House library and Penelope Rich was believably blasé about it. What a wretched time to have arrived, just as the Devereux siblings were descending into madness.

"Thank you for the invitation, but I must leave, milady."

Penelope Rich looked displeased. She had never been displeased with him before; her pretty face, scowling, unnerved him. "Sander, the gentlemen in the library have recognized you. Now they assume that you are allied with my brother and they will report that to the Privy Council, who will report it to Her Majesty."

"I am an apprentice whose master may be held accountable for my actions, so I do not wish to be allied with anyone, milady. That is why I must leave here. I must make obvious my lack of allegiance to anyone but John Heminges." She pouted. Enough of this, he thought, and steeled himself. "To speak true, the purpose of my visit here was to inform his lordship that I must decline his generous offer to lead his acting troupe."

A pause. Something hardened in her expression. He had never seen that before. "The gentlemen in the library are not aware of your reformation. You have been indelibly associated, by inner members of the court, with my brother and his actions today."

"I do not judge his lordship for his undertaking, milady, but I am not a part of it, and I must correct any impression that I am."

She gave him a measured smile, but the hardened quality did not leave. "Dearest Sander. Because I wish to see you thrive, allow me to help you assess your situation. There are four potential outcomes to this day for you. One, you abandon us, and my brother is defeated by his enemies. In such a case, you will be seen as innocent. Two, you *remain* with us, and my brother is defeated by his enemies. In such a case, Shakespeare and Heminges and the rest will defend you to the Privy Council, and you shall be exonerated. Three, you remain with us and my brother prevails, which is likely to happen once he has the queen's ear. In such a case, you will benefit mightily as an Essex insider. So. There is no harm to you in any of those three scenarios." A brief smile, and then her expression sobered and her voice flattened from its usual mellifluousness. "Four, you abandon us, and my brother prevails. In such a case, he will be the most powerful man in England and he will resent you for losing faith in him. Things will not go well for you." She sat upright again; the smile returned to her lips and the lilt to her voice. "So. You'll stay for dinner."

"NOW THEN," SAID Bacon, still breathless, and gesturing to the bench across the desk from him. Joan sat. She was fitter than he by far but she could feel her heart still pounding from their urgent jog up from Chancery Lane.

At the entrance to Gray's Inn, Bacon had sent messengers running to both Westminster and Whitehall Palace. Then still rushed, he'd gestured Joan to follow him up to his rooms, and poured them each a cup of wine. It was a Sunday and Pierre was off work, so the wine was whatever dregs he'd had lying about. They'd sat in silence recovering their breath.

Once he could speak again, Bacon asked, "What do you understand of what we've witnessed?"

"Only that Sander intended to leave, until that woman arrived."

"You will not refer to Lady Rich that way."

"Pardon, sir."

"And you will not make excuses for Sander." A brief, grim pause. "She did not take him captive. He made a choice."

"But sir, please, you saw—"

"I saw what you saw," said Bacon. "And as I said, the best thing either of us can do for him is to pretend we did not see it."

She took a moment to calm herself, staring out into the courtyard. She wished the hearth was lit.

"You saw that the earl refused to come, then took the queen's officers hostage, in a courtyard full of armed men. He will survive this mad episode with his life—Egerton, the Keeper, will talk sense into him, I warrant—but he will lose everything. His supporters will be brought to heel as well. Since Sander Cooke was standing about in his courtyard, there is a good chance that Sander is about to be dragged before the Privy Council for an interrogation. Do you ken how serious this is?"

Joan felt all the blood in her body sink into her feet "Yes, sir," she said. "That is, I do not understand what it means exactly, but I know it's fearful. I beg you please to use your influence to protect him if that happens. Surely you acknowledge that he did not understand what was going on around him."

Bacon looked almost annoyed. "I have already stated my intention to protect him. Even though it will be at a cost to myself. I have resisted the queen's intentions in the past, as a member of Parliament and as her Counsel, and I always pay a price. And yet . . ." He sighed. "I'll do it. We are all victims to that boy's charm. And I gave you my word."

"Thank you, sir—"

There was a rap on the door. Bacon glanced toward it as a boy's voice on the other side said, "The Privy Council's sent for you, sir."

He looked back at Joan and pointed toward the smaller door, where she and Sander had exited before. "I'll keep you out of this," he said.

"Thank you, of course, sir," she said, shakily downing what remained of her wine. She rose and rushed for the smaller door, opened it, stepped through into the shadowy back landing, closed it behind her. She began to trot down the stairs, letting her feet land heavily on each tread to ensure he heard her leaving.

Halfway down, she stopped. Listened to voices in urgent discussion above. Silently, she came back up the steps, and sat beside the door with her ear to the keyhole.

"Temple Bar is there to bar invaders from the city," Bacon was saying with irritation. "Why didn't the porter lower—"

"There were hundreds of them, all armed and half on horseback," interrupted another voice, deep and confident and just as irritated. Whoever it was spoke to Bacon without deference; the tone was impatient and familiar.

"It's precisely against such raiding parties that the damn things were built," said Bacon. "So where are they now?"

"Headed toward St. Paul's, where the mayor and the aldermen are attending mass. We assume he intends to take hostages."

Bacon made a derisive noise. "Not in his maddest moments would Robert do that."

"Francis, do not call him Robert to another member of the court, not even to me. This is an ill day to remind anyone you're intimate." A pause. "We've a man in Essex House who sent word the earl has locked the Lord Keeper and the others in the library as hostages."

"What others?"

"The four who arrived there together. Who else would there be?"

"Nobody," said Bacon. "Do you know where Penel—where his lordship's sister is?"

"She's in the house as well. Our man reports there are other notables attending her, but did not say who. The Council will investigate that."

Joan bit her lip so hard she almost yelped aloud.

"I don't see why the Council would waste their time with people who did not march out with Essex," said Bacon, sounding dismissive. "Speaking as Her Majesty's Counsel, I would interrogate those who *are* marching with him."

"Gelly Merrick is still at the house, and he's instrumental to the scheme," argued the other. "Remaining at the house is no evidence of innocence. But Her Majesty needs you, we must speak on the way."

"Of course," said Bacon, and Joan heard his chair creak as he rose. She waited until she reckoned he had exited the building, then headed back down the stairs.

At the bottom of the staircase was the robing closet, unlocked but unused on a Sunday. She sank down to the floor with the dusty hems of garments brushing against her shoulders. She was trembling. Why did she down that wine? She should have kept her head clear.

She tried to think what best to do. She could not go back for Sander and she mustn't tell Heminges where Sander was. So she should get home to Southwark. But she could not think how to make that trip without risking an encounter with Essex's armed mob. She tried to remember the map of the wider region a cartographer friend had shown her.

Any direct route from here to home risked intersecting Essex's march. She would have to skirt the city widdershins, reversely: go west out to the hunting fields of Soho, then down around through Westminster and Whitehall, where the Thames bent a full cardinal direction of the compass. From Whitehall, she could cross over the river to the mucky western fringe of Southwark and then trudge east back toward home.

All she wanted was to know that Sander was safe. To move away from him made her stomach hurt. But she pushed herself to standing, breathed in the perfumed-musky scent of the robes, and exited.

She hurried down Gray's Inn Road to Holborn, along a line of bare-branched elms. She knew every stone and ditch to the left of here, but she turned her back on that, and headed west out of the city for the first time in her life.

She walked fast. Holborn was broad by London standards. The way was quiet of travelers, although a few creaking carts with barrels and crates crept in either direction far up ahead of her. Most people were in church. Why hadn't Francis Bacon gone to church? What chaos-loving demon had made him tell Joan to meet him on the Strand? If he'd been a good Christian he'd be on his knees in a pew somewhere, and Joan would be in Southwark, and even if Sander were at Essex House, she would never need to know.

She rushed along under pewter clouds. Fine private homes gave way to broad fields, with occasional huge old trees along the roadside; this landscape was foreign to her. Sheep in heavy winter fleece grazed winter stubble; two boys sat on a large stone, pretending to watch the sheep but really playing dice. It was quiet and peaceful; the sounds and smells of the city faded quickly, since she was walking into the February breeze. The damp snuck through the folds of her wool and chilled the linen against her skin. She walked faster to warm up, and tried not to think of Sander. She was heartbroken and furious and worried and confused. Over and over her mind grasped at the image of his melting into Lady Rich's pearl-covered arms. She hated Lady Rich. Joan could not think of a single instance of Sander changing course at her own insistence. Penelope Rich had simply put her arms out, and Sander tossed the future into them.

Ahead, the road widened and curved through open fields that continued out of sight, with distant settlements and manors looking like children's toys. She was unused to broad open space and could not guess the distance, but after what felt to her legs about a mile, she drew near enough to a settlement to see it was, in fact, a church. Three unattended horses were tied at posts near the door. That meant in this part of the parish, there were a few men with money enough for a horse but not for a servant to guard it. Or perhaps they trusted their safety as nobody in Southwark did. She wished she knew how to ride. Another way in which Sander's world was larger than hers. It was so easy, in his company, to forget how many elements of their experience did not match up. But there were many misalignments, and in all of them, his life was richer and more complex than hers, and even if they somehow survived today, the imbalance would always plague them. She should marry one of the Flemish philosophers and move to Antwerp right away.

SHAFTESBURY AVENUE read a painted wooden sign by the church. From within came voices singing in somber Latin. Beyond the church was another signpost pointing through the fields: ST. MARTIN'S LANE. The way was unpaved but broader than any city street she knew, and in good repair, because Westminster was full of gentry who wanted comfortable rides. The lane was empty now, but on the far side of the church was a courtyard full of waiting carriages.

She rushed down the lane, rubbing her arms for warmth, trying to remember what it felt like to be content with Sander in her life, trying to erase all these mad embellishments of fate and intrigue and irony.

Suddenly there were buildings to either side: a dispensary for medical supplies, a tavern above, houses, a half-built bakery, a tin smithy being renovated; everywhere was brick dust. The road narrowed to a street, with closed shops and quiet houses on both sides. She'd swung back around into the city's western outskirts. More houses as she continued south, and then along the street began a long wall, taller than herself. The warm, musky scent of horses and horse manure and the acrid smell of horse piss hit her nostrils. THE ROYAL MEWS proclaimed a sign. But the gate was closed and she could not see inside.

Past the mews was a three-way intersection, speared in the middle by a tall, ornate wooden cross. This she knew from reading maps: to have arrived at Charing Cross meant her trek in unfamiliar hinterlands was over. Now there was only to go downhill to the river bend, and hale a wherry home to Southwark.

"WHAT IS IGNORED in all this are my brother's political concerns regarding Spain," Penelope was saying. They were still in the dining room, seated across from each other on benches near the earl's chair.

As if it were an ordinary Sunday, all around them the domestic staff bustled at dinner preparations. The white cloth had already been unfolded with rods, to prevent hands from soiling it. The saltcellar had been set upon it beside a loaf of manchete bread, the ashy bottom crust cut off. It smelled heavenly. The men had washed their hands and donned their Essex livery coats—green on the right, black on the left—and now swarmed around the room with efficient but calm familiarity: waiters and ushers, serving towels draped over their shoulders, and ewery-men who filled the ewers for hand-washing. The yeoman of the cellar took his place beside the cupboard. Sander had nursed his one glass of secke slowly, but it was empty now, and Penelope signaled for a fresh one. The cellarer snatched away Sander's empty goblet, rinsed it in the copper tub, took another—also ornate and cheerful—poured more secke, brought it back to him, and bowed.

Penelope returned to her point. "When it is cast as a story of feuding courtiers, he will come out the worst for it. He is a gallant figure, and the queen loves him more than any man alive, but he isn't easy. His rivals work against him, and they themselves are sycophants. So when gossip and intrigue make this a story about personalities, Robert looks bad. And yet, he is beloved by the people. Plenty of the men out in the yard are not his men. They came in from the countryside to defend him, because he is a hero to many."

Sander wanted to ask what had made him a hero but worried that even the question would sound disbelieving.

"However," Penelope continued, "his only concern is the safety of the state. Cecil and Raleigh would sell England to Spain for their own profit, and they advise Her Majesty accordingly. Spain is Catholic. Do you know history? Do you know of Bloody Mary?"

"Well enough to appreciate Her Majesty's religious tolerance."

"That tolerance was originally championed by Francis, but of course Her Majesty does not like to credit him for it. And there shall be no such tolerance if she bequeaths England to the Spanish crown. We shall all be burned or forced to convert to Papist beliefs. Robert is the only courtier counseling Her Majesty against such developments, and he is frantic to regain her ear. But I'll wager this is the first you've heard of that."

Sander nodded.

"That's because it is more titillating to talk about his breaking into the queen's bedchamber. Which he only did because there was no other way he could gain direct access to her, due to his enemies' meddling."

"Even with you at Her Majesty's side many hours a week, my lady?"

"I am not allowed to speak on his behalf to Her Majesty. That is the sole condition of my remaining at court." Penelope signaled the cellarer for a fresh glass. He whisked hers away, put it into the rinsing tub, and brought her a fresh one of malmsey. As she spoke, her fingers fidgeted gracefully with the curves of the glass. "Raleigh and Cecil are not boorish enough to slander my brother in front of me, but they slant discussions of him unfavorably, knowing that I may not correct them. They speak of Robert's failure to subdue Ireland, and I may not point out that this is because they themselves convinced the queen not to send the troops or supplies he begged for. Look at what he accomplished at Cadiz! He's a military genius, but he requires manpower and weapons. They undermined him in Ireland. So now the Irish have self-rule, and being Catholic, they are in league with Spain. Cecil and Raleigh are playing the long game, for now they can claim that my brother signed a treaty with the Earl of Tyrone by choice, which makes him appear as a Catholic sympathizer, when in fact *they* are the ones who caused all this."

Sander had not expected to hear anything this sensible. He wondered if it would hold up to scrutiny. "Why did they do it, my lady?"

"They seek power, and Robert always had more than they did because the queen loves him more. They seek it not just for the immediate satisfaction of power, but because it allows them to control the stories being told, which then guarantees them and their offspring continued power into the future. Won't you dress for dinner?" she said, as if not changing the subject. "Those apprentice weeds of yours do not display you to your best advantage. I'm not sure when Robert and his men will be home but I'm sure none would begrudge you the loan of a doublet and jerkin."

"Thank you but no, milady," Sander said, fighting alarm. "I am still John Heminges's man and I am loyal to him."

She smiled at him. It was hard to believe those earlier veiled threats had ever been uttered from such a sweet and doting face. "I am delighted to see evidence of your loyalty. As it is a quality my brother cherishes, I'll be sure to praise you to him."

RISING UP AHEAD of Joan, an arrowshot away, was the most ornate gatehouse in the city, leading to the largest courtyard. It was so enormous she knew what it was with no sign telling her, and its existence angered her. Her ending up here angered her. This was Whitehall Palace, and somewhere beyond that gatehouse was Her Majesty, Elizabeth Tudor, the source of Essex's madness and thus the source of all Joan's woes as well. She would not allow herself to hate her queen, but neither could she cherish her today.

A tall wooden barricade had been erected between where Joan was and the actual gatehouse, with an opening just large enough to drive a wagon through. It looked improvised, and she supposed it had been thrown up overnight, as anxiety about Essex had escalated. It could offer at best a brief defense, were there an attack. It looked as if it would fall over if a dozen men threw themselves at it in concert.

She resented that she knew to even think about these things. Sander had no right to pull her into such orbits. She benefited nothing from it. If he survived the day, she should foreswear him. They did not fit together, even if they wished to.

The only access to the river was through that gate. Joan took a breath and stepped through the opening in the barricade.

To find herself facing a phalanx of armed guards.

She jerked back so quickly she nearly fell; gaping, she swore aloud before she could stop herself. Then uttered a silent prayer of gratitude for being in boy's clothes, at least.

"Passage not allowed!" The yeoman guard who barked this had a silver-white beard. Like the other guards, he held a pike. He pointed this at her with irritation but no malice, and she guessed he was relieved it was just a youth who'd entered. "No entrance to the palace grounds today, boy."

"I just need access to the river. Isn't the Whitehall Stairs—?"

The silver-bearded guard held up a hand to silence her, turned to the flaxen-haired yeoman behind him, and began a fierce exchange of whispers.

"Where've you just come from, lad?" asked Silver.

She panicked. She couldn't think what to say. If she knew too much, they might call her in to be questioned—possibly by Francis Bacon. But playing the ignorant was unwise, for she did not dissemble well. She had to be both coming from somewhere and going to somewhere that would justify her arriving here, as Whitehall was bracing itself against a possible invasion.

"Look, he's Bacon's boy," said Flaxen-head, pointing to the blazon on Joan's jerkin. "Go on in, lad," he said, and gestured for Joan to go forward through the towering gatehouse.

"Oh, oh, thank you, sir, but I'm not here for my master," Joan stammered. "I'm trying to get home to Southwark. Master Bacon recommended the Whitehall Stairs as quickest."

"So you haven't just come from the city?" asked Silver.

"No," Joan said, quicker than she should have.

They exchanged looks then nodded. They knew she was lying.

"News?" muttered Silver conspiringly.

This could not be happening. She wanted none of it to be happening.

"You first," she answered. The man scowled, in a way that suggested a buzzing fear beneath his gruffness.

She and the man exchanged sizing-up looks. He grimaced; she aped him. He nodded; she aped him again. Now he thought they were speaking the same silent insider's language, which wasn't true, but it suited her for him to think so.

"Look," she said, "I've no official business here, I'm trying to get home to my parents for Sunday supper."

"You've seen things," said Flaxen.

"I want to be home before they worry," she said.

"What have you seen?" demanded Silver. "What do you know?"

She glared at him. "You must think me a poor servant of Francis Bacon, to say things I mustn't. Had I news, I'd deliver it only to the ears it's meant for. But I haven't even that. Truly, I am only trying to get across the river. May I do that here or must I turn around and leave?"

Flaxen tapped Silver's arm and stepped ahead of him. Both of them looked anxious in a way she did not associate with yeoman guards, not that she'd seen many. "We're not refusing you, lad. Just asking for an exchange. Information for us, access for you. We've been here since sunup. They doubled our numbers some hour back, around when your master was summoned."

"If he had nothing to say to you, neither do I," said Joan. She crossed her arms and spoke in a low growl, her feet planted farther apart than felt natural, even in her boy's clothes. "So you've two choices now. Either let me access the river, or take me to see my master so I can tell him you won't let me access the river. Or send me away and I'll tell him later. I'll remember your faces for when he lines up the guard to complain to Her Majesty."

Flaxen made a disgusted sound. "I'll take him to the river stairs," he muttered.

Because of the flood tide, the wherry man dropped her at the far western extreme of Southwark, by Lambeth Palace. There was little out this way but the palace and its enormous marsh. As the crow flies, it was just a mile to the Globe, but she had to skirt the marsh, which meant a hurried damp trek of another hour, following the road that hugged the curving riverbank. Winter was already being shrugged aside by hints of spring. Hundreds of willow trees dipped their greening fingers toward the Thames. On any other day she'd stop to admire them, to pluck some buds; today all she cared about was getting home and getting news.

The marsh finally behind her, she neared the Paris Gardens, straining to listen to sounds from the city, stopping every few dozen strides to stare across the river. The Thames was never quiet, but this was a Sunday and there was less traffic on it. Nobody on the river seemed perturbed; nobody was staring or pointing.

Unless . . . were those explosions on the northern shore? Was that screaming? Or did her distraught imagination invent those sounds?

She could see nothing but the opposite bank and the gated wall that edged it. Some bare treetops and smoking chimneys of the grand river houses were visible up the slope. The only humans in view were down on river stairs, hailing boats and looking unremarkable. She could hardly make them out; most were well-dressed in church clothes.

Perhaps that was a skirmish there, at the Blackfriars Stairs?

Or perhaps just people returning from family visits, competing for river transport home. Perhaps all bad things were in her imagination.

As she continued hustling eastward, she saw on the broad Winchester Stairs a dozen men of different classes—merchants, laborers, artisans—staring across the Thames toward St. Paul's huge steeple. They were muttering together. She rushed in their direction, but three boats pulled up and the group disbursed to travel before she reached them, leaving one man on the stairs, awaiting another boat with a harsh expression on his face. She felt bold in her boy's clothes, but she was leery of begging for news. She didn't care about Essex anyhow; all she cared about was Sander, and Essex being someplace did not mean Sander was with him. He might be playing the lute for her ladyship, or singing "Fair Phyllis" with the servants in the kitchens.

Or brandishing a borrowed sword and storming St. Paul's.

Or bleeding to death in the Essex House courtyard, his throat slashed by the earl's overzealous guards.

At Maiden Lane she turned from the riverbank and dodged past the locked-up Rose Theatre, a stone's throw from the Globe; hurried past the Globe as well, and finally reached the Sow.

Banging on the door, she pushed it open to hear an infant bawling upstairs. Molly and Hal were making shushing sounds together; there was an amused tone to their voices, as if the babe's tantrum was somehow adorable.

"Hello?" she called out, just as the wailing stopped. "It's Joan, may I enter?"

"Joan!" came Moll's voice from above. "Hal will be right down, I'm nursing." There was hushed murmuring between the two of them—again with an amused tone, a relaxed attitude she'd never witnessed when the alehouse was open. She paced anxiously between the tables, relishing the quiet, the way that the smell of hops and barley was more acute when not adulterated by the whiff of sweaty bodies. Hal came down the ladder.

"God ye good Sabbath, Joan," he said pleasantly. He looked happy. She was fleetingly, bitterly jealous of their domestic simplicity. "What do you of a Sunday?"

"Have you any news from the city today?" she asked. "About armed men near St. Paul's?"

He blinked in astonishment. "What? No. Not that we are positioned to hear such rumors."

"Not rumors," said Joan. "I was there, I saw it myself. But it's been two hours since I left and I would have news."

"An invasion?" asked Hal incredulously, and moved almost by instinct toward the bar. He drew out a dagger from behind one of the casks.

"I think on this side of the river we're safe, but I must know the outcome."

He gave her a curious look. "How came you to see it?"

"Master Bacon and I were walking near to Essex House and saw a mustering, and later heard the earl had ridden into the city. I came home around through Soho and Charing Cross to avoid it."

Hal considered this. "The criers will have news at dusk," he said, putting the dagger back.

"I can't wait for dusk," said Joan. She was almost bursting with the need to say why but remembered Bacon's declaration: the best thing she could do for Sander was to pretend she had not seen him. "I'm cursed with curiosity," she said instead.

Hal chuckled. "One of your several charms," he said. "If we learn anything we'll send to your folks'. Tomorrow morning the players will be coming over from the city. One of them will have some news."

"I must learn patience, then," she said with a forced smile, and excused herself.

HER PARENTS WERE out when she arrived; she hurried to change back into her women's garments, and had shoved her boy's clothes between her rolled-up bed and her pillow when the door opened downstairs.

Joan rushed down to greet her parents. As they hung their winter coats on pegs, they greeted her casually, as if she'd just stepped out to collect the milk.

"You missed mass," said her mother, without rancor. "There was a smart sermon at St. Saviour."

"Pardon," said Joan. "Have you heard rumor of anything strange happening over in the city?" asked Joan.

"What manner of strange?" asked her father.

"Violence? Fighting?"

Her parents exchanged indifferent glances. Both shook their heads. Neither asked her why she thought there might be. This did not surprise her.

Agitated, she went out into the yard, hoping the chickens might distract her by being more fidgety than she herself was. All but one were in the coop, and the one in the yard was staring at the ground as if waiting for a bug to present itself as dinner.

Her stomach growled, although she had no appetite. Excusing herself from dinner, she left the house, pacing through the streets near London Bridge—which was eerily quiet—and went into every tavern that was open for travelers, but nobody knew anything.

She began to doubt her sanity. Had she imagined the entire morning's madness?

The day had been dreary and overcast, but now the clouds pulled apart enough for a late-afternoon golden glare upon the river. The sun was never high this time of year, even at noon; as it slunk to the west and shadows lengthened, the temperature dropped, the breeze picked up, and voices carried over the Thames.

But not clear enough to bring her any news.

She wrapped her mantle tighter around herself and considered crossing the bridge herself, to seek out Heminges, only she knew it wasn't safe if Essex and his men were still at large. But who could she talk to on this side of the river? Who might know anything?

With a quiet yelp of relief, she raised her skirts enough to run, and rushed east along Tooley Street, past the bridge, toward Morgan's Lane.

The shop was closed, but the women, she knew, would welcome her inside. She rapped once and pushed the door open, calling out.

Dorothy and Eleanor were reclining in their matching cushion-crammed chairs, feet up on footstools, staring into the embers of a fire that the small, tight room barely required for warmth. Dorothy was smoking, and both were drinking ale. The rush mats on the floor were fresh and smelled of hay, but could not mask the pungent odor of tobacco smoke.

As Joan entered, she heard Dorothy say ". . . St. Paul's Cathedral, to take the Lord Mayor hostage," and she almost yelped.

"What happened then?" she demanded, stepping in.

The two of them started, and then Dorothy pointed to a stool beside her. "Joan! Sit. Have you heard about the excitement?"

"I saw the beginning of it," Joan said.

They were delighted. "Ooooo," said Dorothy, "Tell us."

"I'll tell you after, first tell me what you know."

Dorothy leaned back in her chair, and took a long pull on her ale. "Well. You know that Essex entered the city with armed men?" Joan nodded. "And of course he thought thousands would flock to his banner, because he's adored throughout England, and perhaps he'd have been right. But Robert Cecil somehow heard at once what the earl was planning, and he was too clever to send out troops to meet and fight Essex; instead, he sent out heralds to follow along *just behind* him, proclaiming to the populace he was a traitor. That sent the citizens home right quick. And more, Essex's own sycophants and hangers-on began to fall away. By the time he got to St. Paul's, his party had shrunk by half at least, and poor fellow, to make it worse: the mayor and alderman he intended to take hostage had all been warned by Cecil, and they'd gone home."

"How do you know all this?" asked Joan. "I have been asking and eavesdropping for hours now and I've heard nothing."

"She has eyes everywhere," said Eleanor with droll approval. "She'd have heard it from a street cleaner, or a barge captain, or a ragman."

Dorothy winked at Joan. "Or all three. Anyhow, there's more."

"Tell me," Joan said.

"Cecil and Sir Walter Raleigh sent their men to chase Essex along the river back to Essex House. At this moment, Essex House is under siege, but Essex, last I heard, had not surrendered. His steward was last seen on the roof of the house, hurling invectives at Raleigh's men." She grinned, her eyes sparkling. "In *Welsh*!"

"She loves the Welsh," muttered Eleanor, in a tragic voice, to Joan.

Joan was fighting off a wave of nausea. "Whoever told you this, can he tell us what is happening right now?"

Dorothy shrugged. "The last report was half an hour past, from someone watching the attack from the river."

"I was on the river, watching," said Joan. "I saw nothing."

"He's a boatman, and went ashore at the Temple Stairs to watch. Now he's gone back over to keep watching. I expect no more news until the matter is resolved. Might take until morning."

"It can't take until morning," Joan said, trying to keep her head. "I need to know before I can sleep tonight."

Dorothy gave her a sidelong glance. "What matter is it to you, what's going on in the home of some idiot noblemen with too much ambition?"

Finally she could tell someone. "Sander is in Essex House."

They gaped.

"When I last saw him, I mean. Hours ago it was now. I don't know where he is, I don't know how to reach him. I can't ask John Heminges because I don't want anyone to know he was there."

"Oh my dear girl," said Dorothy. "But there's nothing to be done tonight unless he shows himself. Let me give you something to help you rest at least."

"I can't rest," said Joan. "I need to know he's safe."

"Well, you can't," said Eleanor. "Not this moment. Dorothy has made an offer and you need it. Say yes."

Joan crossed her arms, shoving her fists into her armpits, and finally allowed herself to sob.

February 9

SANDER SAW JOAN BEFORE SHE saw him. It was a coal-smoke hazy morning and she was carrying a pin cask of ale into the tavern from a donkey cart. Her arms had grown strong from lugging river water all winter; his palms tingled remembering the feel of those muscles rippling under his touch. Her stride was balanced and sturdy, the sway of her skirts so unlike the well-born ladies who preened for his attention. Her face without decoration, her manner without affect, her expression without a simper. All this made her so real, so grounded, so blessedly different from most of the rest of his life.

She came out of the alehouse, and he sashayed toward the cart to get her attention, pretending to be buffeted by imaginary wind. Her reaction surprised him: relief softened her sober expression, then she burst into tears and sprinted to him.

"There you are!" She grabbed his shoulders, embraced him, pulled away, shook him, embraced him again.

"Joan! What?" he said, grabbing her hands in each of his.

"Where did you go yesterday?" she demanded, teeth gritted. She tried to pull her hands free but he kept his grip.

"Had we plans to meet?"

"I thought of going up to Master Heminges's to seek you, but there was madness in the city and I feared it wasn't safe."

His stomach clenched. He studied her face to see if she suspected anything. Usually he could read her mood, but now he wasn't sure. "After Saturday's performance, and our talk, I thought the understanding between us was that I must be clear with myself, and therefore with you, about my intentions for my future. You would give up a life across the sea to be with me, so it falls to me to tell you if I am worthy of that sacrifice. I thought to spend the day alone with my conscience."

Something in that haphazard stew of phrases ruined him: he watched her expression harden, her eyes blink away sudden, angry tears. She stepped back and broke his grasp on her wrists.

"And you reckoned," she said stonily, "that the best place to be alone with your conscience was the courtyard of Essex House, surrounded by soldiers?"

The clench in his stomach worsened. "What?" He attempted innocent confusion.

"I saw you." She said it in a tired, resigned voice. "I was walking up Fleet Street with Bacon."

Sander heard himself groan before he even realized he had the impulse to groan. "So Francis Bacon thinks I am in league with the earl."

Joan's eyes bore into his. She frowned. "Well, so does the Keeper of the Seal. And the Lord Chief Justice. You'd be known by them, even if we hadn't seen you."

Sander shook his head. "They know nothing of my prior dealings with Essex. I was counting on them to know that I arrived by chance, and was indifferent to the day's events. Bacon is a different matter."

"But what were you doing there at all? And why did you just lie to me about it? Why do you *always* lie to me about that man?"

"I doubted you'd believe the truth, but the truth is this: I went to tell him that I decline his offer of employment, and that I will have nothing more to do with him." He gave her a triumphant look, as if this answer alone exonerated him. She looked pleased, but then immediately sceptical. He rushed on: "I thought they were heading out to Soho for a hunt, and once I realized I had misjudged, I tried to find some gracious way to excuse myself, but I failed. What did you see?"

"Penelope Rich," she said.

He winced. "If Bacon saw that, I'm finished."

Almost grudgingly, she said, "Actually, he promised me he'd shield you from harm."

Sander raised his eyes to meet hers. "Truly?"

"His only argument with you, ever, has been Essex. Molly told me this morning that Essex is in custody and will be tried for treason. So that's the end of Essex."

That same rumor had filled the streets of London on his trek here from home this morning. He was sickened to hear it, but not surprised. "I could be accused of collaboration."

"Bacon said he would protect you. Keep your head down, and the tempest that's about to hit will pass over you. Then all this will be behind us."

He clutched her to him. "Thank you," he whispered into the top of her head. "Thank you for forgiving me."

"I don't recall forgiving you."

"But you're about to." He nuzzled her ear. She shivered. He held her more tightly to keep her from pulling away. After a moment, she pressed herself against him.

"Why should I forgive you?" she growled into his shoulder.

"Because I am a tortured lad who finally did right by his lady, and you have a weakness for that kind of thing."

"I don't. You're confusing me with one of your other ladies."

"Yes, the one I'm about to take inside and kiss all over."

She raised her hands and hooped her arms around him. "Kissing is insufficient," she said.

He was alarmed at first. But there was a twitch in the corner of her mouth that reassured him.

"I am capable of more than kissing," he said.

"Prove it," she said, and reached for the door of the tiring house.

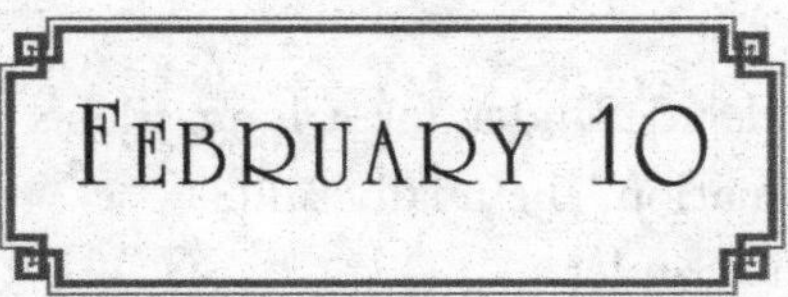

February 10

THE PERFORMANCE OF *The Merry Wives of Windsor* the next afternoon was at Arundel House, on the north bank of the Thames.

It was raining and the damp drifted everywhere. They had piled on woolen layers in the morning, to review their lines on the canopied Globe stage. Afterward, Heminges opened the Sow and the company gathered inside over a trough of hot stew, to fortify themselves before the river crossing.

Sander was draped in an old sheet, so he could eat without worry of staining his Mistress Page gown. He was plucking a piece of oat bread that had fallen to his lap when he heard Heminges's voice low in his ear, "You wish to learn the dull business of the shareholders?"

Heaven was rewarding him for making correct choices. "Indeed, sir," he said, glancing up.

"The Master of the Revels thinks we owe him money. We shall head there straight after the play comes down at Arundel House. Come along to his offices with Phillips and myself while we sort it out."

"I will!" said Sander. To justify his enthusiasm he said, "I enjoy visiting the Revels Office."

"We are not reciting a new script for him," Heminges clarified. "Nor finding costumes for a court performance, or any other amusing task that has brought you to the Revels Office in the past. This is a misunderstanding about money, that's all. It is the epitome of tedium."

Sander smiled at him. "I will enjoy even the tedium," he declared. "To be of service to the Chamberlain's Men is the greatest privilege of my life and I would make amends for recent months during which I forgot that."

Heminges considered Sander for a long silent moment. "I credit Joan with your reformation," he finally said.

"She helped," said Sander.

HE WAS SO pleased to be going to the Revels Office in the capacity of shareholder-in-training, that he flew through the performance at Arundel House almost in a reverie. *The Merry Wives of Windsor* was a ridiculous play, but Mistress Page was fun to personate, especially opposite Heminges, who'd taken over playing Falstaff from the aging Thomas Pope.

Once they'd changed back into their street clothes, most of the company left the manor the way they'd come: out the back and down the slope to the Thames. But Sander followed Heminges and Phillips out the ornate front gate so they could travel north to the Revels Office.

The moment they were on the Strand, he cringed: he'd forgotten Arundel was directly beside Essex House. He walked fast, looking straight ahead in the rain. The two older men were discussing how to fix a hole in the buck basket before the next *Merry Wives* performance; they did not even notice the Essex gate, despite a small gaggle of soggy onlookers peering through and listening with rapt expressions to a minstrel describing what he'd seen the day before.

Sander relaxed once they were past it. No matter the fate of Robert Devereux, he himself would never enter there again.

Up ahead, a thick queue of foot traffic in sodden gabardine, and carts of sundry sizes, had built up at the Temple Bar. He saw two pike-bearing yeoman guards there in the covered archway, stopping to question and sometimes search those entering the city. He made himself breathe slow and calm, and wondered how ignorant he should pretend to be.

Phillips pointed to the queue. "The damn guards are everywhere today. Let's go the back way—skirt Lincoln's Inn up to Holborn."

"That'll be dreadful muddy," said Heminges.

"Well, but we also miss Smithfield Market, which'll be rivers of cow dung in this rain."

Heminges grimaced in acknowledgment.

They turned up a narrow unpaved lane, full of deep puddles. Sander knew this part of the route well enough: right on Holborn—more guards—left on Gray's Inn Road. As they slogged past the gated entrance to the Inn, he thought of Francis Bacon just inside, in his upstairs chambers in Coney Court with the beautiful large wooden desk. Bacon had promised Joan to keep Sander Cooke from trouble. Sander sent a silent prayer of gratitude toward him.

They continued up Gray's Inn Road—mostly gardens and meadows—to where it ended at Clerkenwell Road. More guards.

"A lot of them out today," said Sander, hoping he sounded casual.

"Yes," said Heminges blandly. "Perhaps that's because yesterday the Earl of Essex attempted an armed uprising against his sovereign." Sander made a noncommittal noise. Heminges added, "Yesterday being, in case you have forgotten, the day after his men paid us to stage a play on that very theme."

"Is that the play we owe money for? Are you in truth bringing me along to punish me for not telling you of Essex?"

"What about Essex?" asked Phillips.

Heminges said, "We're bringing you along to show you how to be an adult troupe member."

"In truth, your presence almost makes things pleasant," added Phillips. "Edmund Tilney and I always argue about money, and Tilney's always got some argument with John."

"True," said Heminges ruefully.

"Nobody ever argues with you, Sander."

"I wish that were true—" Sander began, but Phillips talked over him: "He will be friendlier to us if you're with us. Put on your girlish smile and he'll be agreeable like they all are. I'll need a drink once he's done with us, but at least if you temper him, I'll only need a small one."

They nodded to the drenched yeoman guards who pretended not to be drenched. A plodding right onto Clerkenwell Road; after crossing the Fleet, they wended their way along short intersecting lanes to the huge St. John's of Jerusalem, now the Revels Office. In this case, Office meant something closer to estate: here were workshops and storage for the props and sets that all the playing companies used when performing for Her Majesty. Sander knew the compound well; each time the company had a new play, they were required to recite it for the Master, Edmund Tilney, before he licensed it (at some expense to them) for performance. The recitations took place in the expansive well-lit great hall on the ground floor. For other visitations, to do with business and most especially with money, they were escorted upstairs to the Master's office, as happened now.

This room too was large, but undecorated; there was a large worktable in the center, and deep shelves all around the perimeter stuffed with scripts, inventories, and designs for stage sets.

Usually the door to Tilney's office was opened from within by a page, who would invite them to enter, but today the Master of the Revels himself stood at the threshold. Tall, patrician, and severe, he regarded the rain-soaked shareholders with a tight smile. Staring straight at Heminges, he said, "I hope the questioning goes well for you."

"Questioning?" said Phillips. "You want a fee from us for staging *Richard II*. We don't understand why you feel entitled to that, and assumed you were calling us here to explain yourself to us. Not question us."

Tilney considered this. "An interesting interpretation of the summons you received, but incorrect. I know I'm not entitled to a fee, and even if I were, that's of no interest to the court."

"The court?" echoed Heminges. "Her Majesty has sent someone to question us?"

"About *Richard II*. Yes."

Heminges and Phillips exchanged looks.

"Why were we summoned to *here* for that?" Heminges asked.

With a patient sigh, Tilney said, "If the Chamberlain's Men come to the Revels Office, it appears to be ordinary business."

"Yes, that's what we thought," said Phillips.

"If the Chamberlain's Men are summoned to court, two days after staging *Richard II* under the circumstances that you staged it, that will set tongues wagging. Her Majesty does not wish any more tongues to wag. Do you understand?"

Heminges and Phillips nodded, looking uncomfortable. Sander felt dizzy.

Tilney stepped out of the way. The three of them filed in, Sander last. He bowed to Tilney; Tilney returned the bow; Tilney closed the door with fastidious gentleness, and then positioned himself near it.

Sander turned his attention toward the large table in the center of the room. It was high enough to write on while standing up, which allowed Tilney and his clerks to attend to multiple projects at once. Now it was deserted, save for two men on the far side facing them. One was a black-robed youth bent over a large leaf of paper, taking notes. The other—their black-robed interrogator—went pale when he saw Sander.

Sander closed his eyes in resignation. Of course it would play out this way, he thought. How foolish to think otherwise.

"Alexander," said Francis Bacon, sounding unhappy. "How regrettable to see you here."

"Pardon?" said Phillips.

"There are conversations I would prefer not to have with you," said Bacon, ignoring Phillips. "But as we are in the same room, in the presence of the Privy Council's secretary, I'm obliged to ask."

"I'll leave," offered Sander too quickly.

"What's going on?" asked Phillips.

"Too late," said Bacon, grim. He glanced in Tilney's direction, and then the scribe's, and then around the room: a cluster of Revels clerks in one corner, and two armed guards near Tilney. "I cannot have witnesses reporting that someone was here, and I sent that someone away without questioning him," he continued, sounding very pained. "So I must question you."

"Why?" demanded Heminges. "About what?"

"First I must question *you*, sir," said Bacon. He cleared his throat. "Why did you accept a commission from the Earl of Essex to revive a play that he wished staged for seditious purposes?"

"We did not know the Earl of Essex had commissioned the staging," said Heminges.

Bacon's eyes darted to Sander and then back to Heminges. "None of you knew?"

"None of the shareholders knew," said Heminges. "The shareholders made the decision as a company, without knowing the Earl of Essex had anything to do with it."

"And you were not influenced by any other members of the company?" Bacon pressed, with another glance at Sander.

"Give us credit, Master Bacon. Eight shareholders could not be overruled by an apprentice."

"He's not just any apprentice, though, is he?"

Heminges remained calm but Sander could feel the effort it cost him. "The shareholders made the decision," he said.

"Were you paid at the time?" asked Bacon. He glanced at the secretary's scribbling.

Heminges looked to Phillips, who managed the company coffers.

"We were paid on performance day, not prior," said Phillips. "The money came from a nobleman who did not identify himself as an Essex man. We were ignorant of the connection until John recognized one of the attendees, Sir Charles Blount, as being an intimate of the earl's. By then, we had been paid and the play had been performed. There was never any direct contact between the earl and the Chamberlain's Men. If you've summoned us to root out collusion, you may put your mind at ease. There was none."

Bacon gave Sander a searching look. Sander steeled himself. "Alexander, I must ask you this because there were other witnesses: did you go to Essex House yesterday morning on your own volition, or as an agent for the Chamberlain's Men?"

Heminges drew a sharp breath and Phillips muttered, "What?"

Sander glanced at Heminges. Heminges stared at him a moment, appalled, then turned his head away.

"Why does that matter, sir?" Sander asked Bacon.

Bacon gave him a warning look. "Apprentices are accountable to their masters. The legal presumption is that you were acting on John Heminges's behalf. Is that correct?"

Sander looked at Heminges. Heminges studied the unlit empty air above Bacon's head. His jaw was clenched.

"Alexander," said Bacon, sternly. "Look at me." Sander dragged his gaze back to Bacon's face. "Answer me. If John Heminges sent you, then I will interview him in greater detail to learn why he sent you. If his reason does not offend the Crown, that will be the end of this."

"He will have nothing offensive to say, I assure you, sir. Please may we leave it at that?"

"You must answer my question because this is on the record," said Bacon, with a nod toward the secretary. "Did John Heminges send you to Essex House the morning the Earl of Essex was gathering supporters to seize the throne?"

"That's not what—"

"Sander, listen to me," said Bacon. The tone was intimate, imploring, urgent. "If John Heminges sent you there, for whatever reason, then you are not responsible. Suspicion shifts to Heminges. If Heminges can demonstrate that he was innocent of what was brewing at Essex House, that is the end of this interview. For all of us."

Sander glanced nervously at Heminges, who continued to ignore him.

"Sir, how might he prove his innocence?"

"As an apprentice, that is not your concern."

"I do not want to cause trouble for Master Heminges," Sander said.

Francis Bacon crossed his arms and rested them on the table. "Your concern for your master is commendable, and understandable, but also out of place."

Sander looked at Heminges again. Heminges finally glanced at him, but his face was unreadable.

Francis Bacon was a strategist, and he was nudging Sander to blame Heminges. This must be the best way to keep Sander himself out of trouble. Surely Bacon's strategy included protecting Heminges; surely even Heminges knew this, else he would have objected, and spoken in his own defense.

Sander opened his mouth to play along.

The image of Joan arose so clear in his mind that he almost believed she was in the room with them, and he glanced around in search of her. Once he felt her presence, he couldn't shake it, and then he couldn't speak. He could not say the words that Bacon was guiding him to say. The strategic insincerity would be an affront to Joan's notions of right action.

"I went to Essex House without Master Heminges's knowledge, for reasons of my own," he blurted. "But it had nothing to do with the assault on the city."

John Heminges exhaled.

"This is all very strange," muttered Phillips.

"Master Heminges," said Bacon, grim. "Is your apprentice speaking the truth?"

"My apprentice is an honest young man," Heminges said, still staring just above Bacon's head.

Bacon, agitated, looked down at the table. He fidgeted with a spot on the surface, as if there was a stain and he wished to rub it off. After a moment, he looked back up at Sander. "Do you understand the consequence of your answer?" he asked.

"Yes, it means you will now continue to question me, rather than Master Heminges. I am prepared to answer your questions."

"No," said Bacon, grimacing. "It means I must arrest you on suspicion of treason."

"What?" said Heminges and Phillips.

Sander gaped. "But, sir, I have a defensible explanation—"

"I'm glad to hear that, Alexander. There will be a hearing at which you may defend yourself."

"Why can't I just tell you now?" Sander asked. "You'd have let Heminges tell you now."

Bacon shot his hand out to rest on the secretary's, to stop his writing. "We both know Heminges is innocent, you fool," Bacon spat. "And we both know you are not."

"Why are you harassing my apprentice?" Heminges demanded.

"I am innocent," Sander said. "I went to Essex House solely to *break from him*. I was the victim of terrible timing."

Bacon released the scribe's hand. "All hearings for this matter require at least one member of the Privy Council," he declared to the room at large.

"I can clear my name in under a minute, so let's have this hearing over with as soon as possible," Sander said, displaying a calm and confidence he did not have. "May it be this afternoon?"

"The Privy Council have their hands full this week, thanks to the fatal impatience of your friend Essex."

"He's your friend too," snapped Sander. "For God's sake, you've done more for him and he for you, than he has ever done for me." He turned to the scribe. "Add to your notes that Francis Bacon knew I was at Essex House because Francis Bacon himself also was at Essex House. And does the Privy Council know that just a few months ago, Master Bacon forged letters on the Earl's behalf in a scheme to fool Her Majesty—"

"Alexander, stop," said Bacon, with a quiet fury that brought Sander up short. Heminges and Phillips where staring between the two of them, agog. Bacon collected himself. "It will be several days before the Privy Council can arrange a hearing for you."

Heminges contributed a tentative cough, which echoed in the empty space above them. "Clearly there has been more going on than I understood. Since my apprentice must have a hearing, I will be his surety until then. Speaking as the company manager, however, I must ask if he is allowed to perform in the meantime. I'm sure Master Tilney requires that knowledge as well, as he will be arranging our court appearances, which are frequent this time of year."

Bacon frowned at Heminges. "You fail to grasp the severity of this situation, John. Sander's not going home with you. He's going to the Tower."

Sander somehow managed not to faint.

"He is not," Heminges declared.

"He is," Bacon corrected, in a regretful voice. "It is the protocol for suspected traitors, and I have not the agency to stray from it." He signaled, and the two guards moved toward Sander. The one in front had rope cuffs which he began to unwind.

"This is madness," Heminges said softly to the heavens.

"What the devil's going on?" asked Phillips as the guard grabbed one of Sander's wrists.

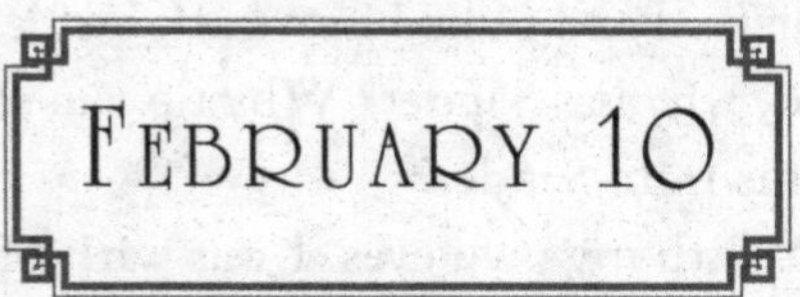

February 10

THE RAIN HAD LIGHTENED OVERNIGHT but never stopped, and now Joan was accosting Heminges on planks laid down between the alehouse and the Globe.

"Where is he?" she demanded. "Molly said he's been arrested."

Heminges pursed his lips and stared over her head.

"That expression does not inspire trust, sir," she said. "Please give me the truth."

A beat, and then he met her look. "Her Majesty required the Chamberlain's Men to be interviewed about our relationship to the Earl of Essex."

"Because of the Richard play?"

"Yes. It is now clear, with the dust settled, that he paid us to perform it expressly to roil the London citizenry, putting into their heads the notion that a weak monarch should be taken in hand and overpowered. The Council needed to ascertain how aware we were of Essex's plans."

"And?"

"And we convinced—" He stopped himself. "We were able to convince the Council's agent that most of us knew nothing."

Joan grimaced. "So Sander's in custody because he knew more

than the rest of you."

"Not quite. Francis Bacon saw him enter Essex House as they were preparing to act treasonously."

Joan glared. "Sander went to Essex House to tell Essex he would have nothing more to do with him. He was about to walk out of the gate when Essex's sister arrived and pulled him back inside. If Penelope Rich has not been arrested, why has Sander? Why do you stare at me, sir?"

"Did you hear this from Sander?"

"No, sir, I saw it with my own eyes. I was with Master Bacon."

Heminges shook his head and pressed a finger against the bridge of his nose. "I . . . what?"

"We were working on a project of his. He saw, with his own eyes, Sander trying to distance himself. And yet he's interpreting all the evidence as if it means something else, because . . ." She tried to think how best to explain it. "He has pre-existing beliefs about Sander which bias how he interprets the evidence." With gleeful disgust, she held out her hands and declared, "That damnable hypocrite, he's failing at his own philosophy!"

"Come again?"

Considering it, Joan nodded and muttered almost to herself, "His old beliefs are unduly influencing how he interprets new data."

Heminges shook his head. "Again, please answer as if I were an ordinary sort and not a philosopher."

Joan clapped her hands together, nodded, and looked up. "Pardon, I will explain later why he is such a monstrous ass. Now I must change." She curtseyed, then rushed off along the planks into the alehouse, leaving John Heminges in the drizzle.

Her boy's garb lay on its usual stool by the hearth. Molly, brushing off the tables from yesterday's carousals, gestured with her head toward the stairway. "Hal's in the back, so go on upstairs to change."

"Thanks," said Joan hurriedly, grabbing the clothes and rushing for the steps. "Lend me a penny to cross the river?"

SHE KNEW THE route well now. Across the Thames upriver to Blackfriar Stairs. The Flemish instrument shop; the German pie shop; her favorite baker. Up the slope of Water Lane to Ludgate to Fleet, north on Shoe Lane, rank with leather and glue. Holborn taking her west up a mild hill, the houses growing larger and beginning to thin out. As she strode, this final time, she thought of that first journey to Gray's Inn, with Sander, before they had ever kissed. When she had considered Francis Bacon a demigod. *Oh, how are the mighty fallen*, she thought furiously.

She had reached Gray's Inn Road, the strange amalgam of long houses and open fields. Every inch of ground was sodden, but as a major thoroughfare, it was well-treated and not too muddy. She pulled the hood of her cloak snug around her face and hunched against the chill.

At the gate to the Inn, she straightened, and without removing the hood, pushed back the left side of the cloak to reveal the emblazoned star. "I'm here for Master Bacon. I'll see myself there." Although Bacon had had the insignias embroidered into her jerkin, she'd never been brazen enough to saunter in without an escort.

Now she felt brazen enough to do anything.

The porter nodded her in. She began to stride past the chapel, and toward the door that led up to Bacon's rooms.

At the last moment, she diverted around a corner and made for the door she had last exited.

The robing room.

February 15

It was maddening to be so ignorant. If this was a holding pen for those whom Francis Bacon had espied at Essex House, there should have been at least a hundred men in here occupying the other cells he could see across the corridor, but all those were empty. Several times a day he shouted for compatriots, but there was always silence.

Rumors about the Tower of London were exaggerations, both good and bad. It had once been the home of English rulers, and many of its captives were highborn nobles; it was known to be a comfortable place to be retained. His small stone cell belied that: a straw bed on the floor was adequate enough, but the only other objects in here were a bucket for a toilet, and a wooden stool. The Tower was also notoriously horrific—he'd heard stories of the Pit, the Rack, the Little Ease—and he was spared such torments. So far. But no amount of charming or pleading could coax any information from his silent captors.

He'd been here between three days and five; he could not keep track. Except for the attendants who emptied the bucket and brought him food (which was, admittedly, not abhorrent: pigeons in nutmeg and cinnamon; roast mutton), he saw nobody. After his first miserable night, he'd begged for a lute, and was offered a mediocre one.

After tuning it as well he could—the fourth string flatted within minutes—he played every John Dowland tune he could think of, then all pieces attributed to the queen's father, King Henry. He ran through what he remembered of Byrd, Tallis, Campion, and Gibbons, stopping only when his fingers ached. He decided he'd sing every song he knew. But moments into "Flow My Tears," he stopped: the cavernous cold stone echoed his voice more than it had the lute, in a way that emphasized the absoluteness of his solitude. There was nothing to absorb the sound, not even another human body.

At supper he asked for a recorder, but was told there were none available. It was the only time anyone spoke to him in the three or four or five days he had been in isolation.

He had never, since the age of twelve, gone so long without some stranger marveling at his existence. He could not even marvel at himself. There were no mirrors; the small window had no glass, only oiled canvas. Sometimes he slapped himself or twisted his own wrists—still raw from rope burns—to prove to himself that he existed.

He slept as much as possible because consciousness was increasingly unbearable.

One nap was troubled by a dream. In the dream, Richard Burbage was singing dolefully, "*In darkness let me dwell; the ground shall sorrow be, the roof despair, to bar all cheerful light from me.*"

He was lucid enough to know it was a dream. *I was playing that tune before I fell asleep*, he reminded himself. *That's why I dream it now.*

"A bit on the nose, don't you think, Dick?" William Shakespeare's voice asked placidly. The resonance was perfect for a large, enclosed stone stairwell, and Sander was pleased with his dreaming mind for summoning such exact sounds, when he realized his eyes were open and he was looking at three familiar figures on the other side of the bars.

Burbage, Shakespeare, Heminges.

He was on his feet instantly, grabbing through the bars for their hands, their arms, anything close enough for human touch. "Oh, thank God. Take me home!" he begged.

A fourth figure—the unspeaking man who brought his meals—

stepped into view. Heminges turned to him; the man, looking bored and in no hurry, took out a key and unlocked a padlock that held an iron bar across the iron door. With effort and loud clanging, the bar was moved out of place enough for Heminges to slip inside.

Sander threw his arms around him and squeezed him hard, with a high-pitched sigh of relief. Heminges laughed uncomfortably. "Lad, there, there," he said, gently embracing Sander in response.

An awful realization struck and Sander pulled away from him. "Why are you in here instead of my being let out?"

Heminges clapped his large hands around Sander's finer ones and held them hard enough to give Sander a sick feeling. "There will be a hearing. Soon."

"Excellent! 'Twill take but a moment for me to clear my name."

Heminges slowly shook his head. "Circumstances have shifted. As they have rounded up more Essex allies, a picture is becoming clear."

"But I'm not part of that picture, I must needs tell them that. It's outrageous that they've locked me here for days when all I need do is deliver one statement to redeem my reputation. Bacon sent me here for spite. He wants to marry Joan off to some philosopher in Antwerp."

Heminges looked tired. He sighed. Even the sigh was tired. "This has naught to do with Joan, Sander. We have been doing all we can to get you released. We've sent petitions to Her Majesty, to the Privy Council, to Bacon himself."

"Will wrote a sonnet on your behalf," Burbage chimed in from the other side of the bars.

"We sent complaints about Francis Bacon's bias to Her Majesty, but Bacon is Queen's Counsel, so everything we say is dismissed."

Sander pulled out of Heminges's grasp and slammed the flat of his hand against the stone wall. "So now what?" he demanded.

Heminges pursed his lips, considered, and then continued. "It is not enough for you to claim that there is an innocent reason for your visiting Essex House that morning. Now the demand is, you must somehow prove that you were not colluding with Essex."

"How can I prove the absence of something? That's absurd!" He slapped the wall again. "Why are they making that demand? Bacon required me to give a reason for being there. That reason is *to break from Essex*."

"As I said, they've a clearer sense now of what happened, and who was involved. There are many collaborators, there are threads of evidence being woven together. Bacon saw you go into the house with Penelope Rich."

"Is she in custody too?"

"Not yet."

"Then why am I?" demanded Sander. He paced furiously around the enclosed space, circling Heminges. He could feel the tendons in his neck stiffening with panicked rage. "If my guilt is that I clung to Penelope Rich, but Penelope Rich is innocent, then how am I guilty? That is madness."

"She probably is headed for the Tower," said Heminges. "Essex has blamed her for pushing him to rebel, and has even claimed that he would never have attempted his uprising were it not for her insistence."

Sander stopped abruptly and gaped at Heminges. "I cannot believe he would say that."

"Is it a lie, then?"

Sander brooded. "She despised his enemies at court, but she'd never propose anything that might endanger the queen."

"Did she exhort him to attack the city?"

"She justified it to me, but I never heard her *exhort* him—but never mind her, *I'm* the one in trouble!"

"She is a bellwether. Her fate might indicate what we can expect for you."

Sander bit his lip, ran his hair through his matted hair. "Will she survive this, think you?"

"Will anyone?" asked Heminges. "We have an ancient, heirless queen whose court is tearing itself apart. Her Majesty is less interested in justice than in staving off calamity. If somebody's death, justified or not, puts out a fire, she will do it."

"I'm not a fire! How am I a fire?"

"Charles Percy says you're the reason we staged Richard—"

"We staged Richard because the shareholders decided to, as you told Bacon!"

"Let me finish. Percy testified that you alone knew why we were asked to stage it, that you convinced us when we'd have said no, and that you rushed to Essex House next morning to be rewarded by the earl."

"That's a lie!" Sander shouted. "To hell with Charles Percy! Is *he* imprisoned?"

"Of course."

Sander rubbed his hands over his face. He wanted in the same moment to fall into a stupor and to shriek. "Is it a hearing or a trial?" he asked.

"Does it matter? To be accused of treason is to be condemned for treason."

He sat down hard on the floor. Shivers ran up and down his arms, then his spine, then the outside of his legs, then the inside of his legs. "You're saying I'm a dead man."

"I'm saying we don't know how to save you. It doesn't mean there's no hope. Francis Bacon could redeem you in a moment. I don't know why he won't."

In a small voice, Sander asked, "Where's Joan?"

The pause before Heminges replied was too long. He could sense all of them exchanging glances.

"Just tell me," he implored.

"I wish I could have, lad. She disappeared a couple of days ago. She's been absent so long, even her parents noticed."

"Ha," said Sander bitterly. "She's probably gone off to marry Bacon's friend in Antwerp. Is she still working for him?"

"Bacon? If she is, it's only to have the chance to poison him. Last I saw her she was furious."

"Well, that's gratifying, anyhow. You should ask the midwife—"

"Dorothy? She came to us, looking for Joan. So did those botanists from Lime Street. Joan has vanished."

February 20

He had feared they would use his celebrity against him, that they would parade him through the city, denouncing not only Sander Cooke, but also the Chamberlain's Men. Instead, he was bundled into a hooded woolen gaberdine and hustled into a barge that shipped out of the Tower of London through Traitor's Gate, slipping past salmon weirs into a heavy river fog.

He'd worn the same clothes for a week. His hair was matted. In seven years, he'd never gone so many days without rubbing paint off his face; now his face was grimy. Worse, he could feel a week's worth of scraggle on it. His joints were stiff and his muscles clenched in a way he'd thought afflicted only old men. He was so exhausted that despite his dread of what was coming, his eyes slid closed and he slumped against his silent guard. The yeoman, in his crisp scarlet tunic, did not object. He was probably delighted that he could go home to his family and boast that Sander Cooke had leaned against him.

No. Of course the guard wasn't thinking that. Nobody would ever think such a thing again.

Sander kept his eyes lowered to the open deck, sliding in and out of wakefulness with the rocking of the boat. He thought he heard men's voices muttering that the Earl of Essex was tried the day before and been found guilty, and that Francis Bacon was the prosecutor. In the more wakeful moments he hoped that was a dream. He thought of asking the guard beside him but was afraid to hear the answer. There was an ebb tide and they were going upstream against it. A slower journey, which suited him.

He was nudged awake. With some help he disembarked, found himself on familiar stone stairs. How often had he come to Whitehall Palace in the past—and always so adored. Eyes averted, he began to mount the steps. At the top, the gravel path continued, too steep to be leading to Whitehall. Had they come directly to Westminster? But the Westminster Stairs led to nothing so steep as this either. He wondered where he was, but did not want to expose his face to any passers-by, and so he kept his head bowed and walked straight, trusting the guard to prevent his stumbling. Another staircase went up thirty steps and then kept going, but his anxious thoughts made him lose count. The only path above river-stairs he knew so steep were at the Middle Temple. But that was by Essex House, and that made no sense.

Numb now, he played a game of guessing where they were and thus anticipating what would happen next, but he was wrong each time. They would turn left to enter Essex House for some reason; but no, they veered right, jogged through a wide empty space, so they were somewhere else. Charing Cross? Charing Cross should mean a left turn to Westminster, but no, they kept straight, the slope leveling, and after some quarter mile (or so he guessed) a right turn, and then after forty paces or so, a left turn. The noise of the city dimmed behind them. They paused and there was muttered conversation with a porter.

They crossed a cobbled courtyard that felt familiar. Up broad stone steps—wide enough for himself and a guard to either side of him—and then through a door. The floor within was polished stone, but the room itself smelled of wood and wool, and his guards' voices softened in a way that suggested heavy tapestries.

"Off with the robe, now," said one guard, tugging at Sander's sleeve.

Finally he raised his head and looked around.

They were in a large room, unfamiliar to him. A council room he reckoned, council table removed. The wood was dark, as were two tapestries, but there were wall sconces, a candlebranch, and windows all along one wall. The day was gloomy but the room was lighted well enough for Sander to see that the design above the unlit fireplace was a golden gryphon. They were somewhere inside Gray's Inn.

He had assumed they'd be going to the Star Chamber, that infamous room where the rule of law was sometimes forgot. Of course, he reminded himself, the Star Chamber itself was merely a room, but the processes it hosted could be conducted anywhere. He closed his eyes a moment to steady himself, then looked around for Francis Bacon.

But he, his guards, and a silver-haired man in Gray's Inn livery were the only ones here. The Gray's Inn man pointed toward the hearth, and Sander's guards walked there, hands behind his shoulders to bring him along. At the fire, they positioned themselves one pace away from him to either side. At least it was a warm spot to face perdition from. The Gray's Inn man nodded in approval.

"I'll call them now," he said, and left through a side door.

For what felt like an excruciating quarter-hour, Sander stood and waited for his future to walk into the room. Finally a parade of some half-dozen men entered, in black robes. From the hems and cuffs poked out evidence of colorful and jewel-emblazoned doublets and jerkins. They seated themselves at benches placed around the room. They were expressionless, and mostly older, with powdered faces and expensive-looking wigs.

A pause.

The door opened again. Francis Bacon walked in.

Over his usual excellent haberdashery, he wore an open robe that fell to his knees, with long pendulous sleeves. His face was grim; he looked so spent and exhausted that his skin was pallid. Sander took some cold relief from that. In his imagination, Bacon had been rubbing his hands in eager anticipation of this hour.

Bacon looked toward Sander; Sander dropped his head and studied the grain of the wood in the floorboards. There was a recitation of introductions; some of the men were from the Privy Council; some were common-law judges. Sander finally looked up again and surveyed the assembly. Himself, Bacon, the guards, the Councilors, a page at either door.

There were also two scriveners, seated in each corner behind Bacon, portable desks balanced on their laps with inkwells sunk into them; quills hovered over paper, or perhaps it was parchment. Parchment cost more and lasted longer, and these days was used only for weighty matters, so he hoped that it was paper. He remembered watching Master Shakespeare scribbling by lamplight in the corner of the tavern on autumn evenings; remembered how, when first Sander was apprenticed, the playwright wrote on parchment, saving paper for the final draft once he was confident of it; the parchment could be scraped clean and then re-used. Over the years of his apprenticeship, cheap paper had become available in London; he could not remember the last time he'd seen parchment. But he remembered the feel of it, something close to dried-out leather—

". . . Alexander Cooke." He started out of his feverish, rambling reverie. Bacon had been reading the formal charge against him.

"Sorry, sir, how shall I answer?" he said.

Bacon raised his brows at him expectantly. Sander's mind flashed back to the previous summer, saw Bacon sitting in the Happy Sow, raising his brows in an almost identical gesture, but the purpose then had been to summon him closer for a supper invitation. He had asked Joan's question about Mount Olympus that evening. Francis Bacon had been pleased.

He was not pleased now. "You've heard the charges, Alexander."

"I refute them. I went to Essex House to forswear him, and was caught up in the confusion of the day. I did not then, nor do not now, approve of rebellions against Her Majesty."

"You need not be an active agitator, to be guilty of collusion," said Bacon. He looked weary. "Any Essex toadeater is under suspicion now of aiding and abetting him."

"I was not his toadeater," said Sander. "Any more than you have ever been, Master Bacon."

"Careful, boy," said Bacon sharply.

"I never was his man, sir. He offered me a position that would have made me so. But I approached his home that morning expressly to break off from him."

"Very well. Name a witness to the conversation in which you broke from him."

"I was not able to have the conversation."

"So you did not break from him. Instead Lady Rich brought you inside, where you remained even after the earl had left the courtyard surrounded by armed men on horseback."

"I left as soon as I could."

"When Thomas Egerton and his companions were released from the library that afternoon, hours later, you were still in the house. They report they heard you singing in the dining room with Lady Rich, and one of you was on a lute. While his lordship was *attacking London*."

"Appeasing Lady Rich was the quickest way to excuse myself. She—" He wanted to explain her manipulations, but his mind was so uncertain that he didn't trust himself to make the case well. "It is difficult to safely excuse oneself from such a setting. If you have not been in it yourself, it is hard to imagine the difficulty."

"You left when it became clear that the earl would fail. You were as faithless to him as you had just been to England herself."

"That is not true, sir. I had no idea what was happening in the city. I left when I could, not because the earl was failing to achieve his goal, but because he was *trying* to achieve it."

"As you cannot prove that, why should we believe you?"

There was a noise from outside the smaller door, to Sander's right. Bacon's eyes glanced that way, then back to Sander. "If Essex had succeeded at his nefarious goals, your proximity to him would have benefited you. Regardless of when you left the house, you went to the house, and tarried there, to align yourself with him."

"That's not true, and you can't prove it," said Sander angrily.

"Common sense is evidence enough," said Bacon. "You remained there."

"You know as well as I the sway of Penelope Rich."

Bacon shrugged and shook his head. "You are confessing attachment to the earl's family. You broke bread with his sister while he stormed the city. Had he been successful, and taken the day, you would now be at his elbow. Or at the farthest remove, his sister's elbow. You have said nothing that mitigates your guilt, and your supposed defense—the allure of Lady Rich—is only further evidence of your attachment."

"I was never near as attached to the earl as Lady Rich is. If her attachment isn't reckoned treasonous, then why is mine?"

"Hers is familial affection. Yours is a calculated attempt to mingle with your superiors in seeking patronage. Your apprentice term is ending soon, and you've no guarantee of work."

"That isn't true," said Sander. "The Chamberlain's Men will keep me."

"But not in the manner you wish to be kept," Bacon shot back. "You have told me frankly of rejecting the paltry security they offer you. Do not waste your breath claiming otherwise. You have been desperate for a patron, and you set your sights on Essex. Despite my warning you against it!" He looked around at the robed men. "Lords and honored gentlemen, surely you recognize the truth of what I'm saying."

The sound outside the door again: voices in dispute.

"What *is* that?" demanded Bacon to the guard on Sander's right. "Attend to it." The guard stepped away. Sander lowered his eyes and studied the floor again. That impossible combination of urges—to sleep and to shriek, at once—plagued him again. He took a deep breath and made himself let it out between clenched teeth, feeling the air move around his teeth and lips. He inhaled and exhaled this way a second time, and then a third, until the guard stuck his head back into the room.

"Pardon sir, it seems the Chamberlain's Men have sent a lawyer to defend their boy," said the guard, from the threshold.

Bacon startled and, looking through the doorway, scolded, "*No*," as if telling off a dog, then glanced around the room. "Excuse me, this will only take a moment." Without waiting for responses, he strode toward the door with furious intensity. "Close it behind me," he ordered the guard, and a second "*No*" was truncated by the door swinging shut.

"*No*," SAID BACON, eyes blazing, flinging himself down the wainscoted corridor. He lowered his voice to a hiss. "Have you fingers enough to count the ways you are causing trouble for yourself?"

Joan held her arms out triumphantly, showing off the short sleeves of a law student. "Prevent me," she said.

"Remove that robe and leave."

"I won't," said Joan.

Bacon stopped, half a pace away from her. He held up a fist, extending fingers as he spoke. "Count one: stealing Gray's Inn property. Count two: trespassing. Count three: counterfeiting to be a man. Count four: counterfeiting to be a law student. Count five: interfering with legal proceedings." He held his taut outstretched hand half an inch from Joan's face; she did not let herself flinch. "I have not even stopped to think and already it's enough to imprison you." He lowered his hand. "This is not one of Shakespeare's comedies. Disrobe and leave at once or I'll summon the guards."

"And what will you tell them? Jack Buckler's face is familiar here, and under this robe I wear clothes you had fashioned for me, with your own badge. You're the one responsible for my being here, and in disguise."

"I require you to leave at once."

"Are you afraid I'll undermine your case?" asked Joan.

"Of course not," Bacon snapped.

"Then what's the harm in Sander having counsel?" she asked. "If he is defended and defeated, that validates your judgment of him to the public, and to the Chamberlain's Men."

"If he is to be defended, it must be an actual lawyer."

"But who would be willing to defend an apprentice charged with treason, before the brilliant legal mind of Francis Bacon?"

"None would, because they'd know they'd lose. Do you know what happened yesterday?"

She pursed her lips. Having to say it aloud made it real in a way she didn't want to think about. "I heard the Earl of Essex was put on trial, and the queen forced you to be the prosecutor, to prove your loyalty was to her, not him."

"Yes. And what else?"

"You convicted him."

"And do you know what happened just an hour past?" She shook her head. "I stood beside Her Majesty as she signed his death warrant." He hesitated; his eyes, she noticed, were bloodshot. "Whatever you think of me, you cannot fathom the upheaval in my soul today. Do not cross me. You'll validate Sander's guilt by presenting an ineffectual defense. Why would you do that? He's already doing it himself."

"Let's consider it an intellectual exercise," said Joan. "If he's already lost the case, then it doesn't matter if I'm apt or not."

"You're appalling. Disrobe and leave."

"If you deny Alexander Cooke a lawyer, John Heminges will take action against you."

"Heminges sent you?" Bacon asked, disgusted.

"He has no idea I'm here. Yet. As you may be aware, he is not only the company manager, but as an officer of the Grocers Guild, he's responsible for the distribution of coal around the city. Does Gray's Inn depend on coal for heat?"

He stared stonily at her. He was silent long enough for her to suspect she'd worried him. "What do you want?"

"I told you, I want to defend Sander."

"You'll only make things worse."

"At least I'll have tried." Her eyes smarted, but she forced her lips into a challenging smile. "I cannot live with myself if I don't try. And I've been tutored by the smartest man in England, so I believe I'm capable. Anyhow, I am entitled to your indulgence. You told me you'd protect him and now you're hanging him. Appease me by giving me five minutes."

"I'll summon the guard—"

"I'll summon your tailor," Joan retorted quickly, tapping the insignia on her left breast.

Bacon grimaced. "Come on, then," he said with a scowl, pivoting back toward the chamber. "Make this even more of a travesty than it already is."

A fluttery sensation rose from her gut up through her ribs and down her arms; she clasped her hands together at her breastbone, and assumed the sternest expression she could.

Bacon entered the chamber. She followed, her eyes adjusting to the light. The room was stately, but less handsomely appointed than Bacon's study. A murmur rippled through the room at the unexpected interruption by a youth. She dared not glance around, lest her eye meet Sander's.

"Gentleman," said Bacon, stepping to the center of an arc of robed figures. He was the only person she looked at; from across the room, she heard Sander make a sound of startlement. Quickly she curled her fingers into her palm, signaling to him: *Do nothing; I can manage this*. "My lords. This is Jack Buckler, a law student whom the Chamberlain's Men have seen fit to send in defense of Master Cooke."

"That is not how this works," protested one of the other robed men. She met his gaze, attempted to reflect his scorn back at him. She could feel her heart thudding so hard she was sure the pulsing of veins in her neck was visible.

"We will allow it," said Bacon, without enthusiasm, "as an indulgence to the Chamberlain's Men, for depriving them of their most valuable apprentice."

"I thank you on their behalf," said Joan, in a tone of bland complacency. She was shocked at her own ability to counterfeit confidence. She glanced toward the hearth and saw Sander staring at her with bald astonishment; he was unwashed, wan, enervated, barely able to stand upright. Strangest of all, a short down beard covered his cheeks. She looked away and knew she must not glance at him again.

SANDER HAD NOT realized one human body could contain so many emotions at once; his liver should burst open, or his heart stop. She was alive. She was here. She offered help, and hope, but surely she was imperiling herself.

His mind was buzzing so furiously he could not hear what Bacon was repeating of his sins.

"So you are saying," Joan intoned in her deepest voice, "Alexander Cooke's crime is that he acted from extreme self-interest."

"Alexander Cooke's crime is that he lingered in the home of a traitor."

"Do you consider the earl's servants traitors? Or the men he held in the library? All were lingering at Essex House that day."

"None of those parties had the agency to leave. Alexander Cooke had the agency, yet he chose to remain."

"So you acknowledge it is not the *fact* of remaining in the house, but the *reasons* for remaining."

Bacon made an exasperated gesture. "His reason indicates his crime."

"And his reason, you claim, was self-interest. Therefore his crime is self-interest."

Bacon held up one index finger, shaking his head. "All of us indulge in some self-interest. But his was so absolute, it vanquished his morality and led him to abet treasonous acts. He should have departed the place immediately and come straight to me, or to the Privy Council. He would have been granted immediate access to men who could have stopped the uprising as soon as it began. He'd have been hailed a hero."

This had never occurred to Sander; he was ashamed.

"I challenge your premise that his self-interest is morally corrupt," said Joan.

Bacon looked bemused. "To what end?"

"If I can demonstrate that his behavior was bounded by a moral code, then is it not a false premise to claim Alexander Cooke's self-interest is absolute enough to be treacherous?"

"A false premise?" echoed Bacon.

"A term from your own philosophy. I believe you refer to it as . . ."—she did a convincing job of trying to recall the phrase—"inductive logic?"

Sander could read Bacon's sardonic look well enough. "Logic and justice are not the same," he said.

"But logic must guide justice," she argued. "An illogical argument cannot condemn a man."

"Nor can it save him," said Bacon. "You suggest he has behaved without self-interest in some other circumstance, and this somehow proves he did not operate from self-interest at Essex House. How is that inductive logic?"

She tipped her head back and looked at Bacon like a nervous horse. "That is not my argument," she clarified. "But once I demonstrate that he can act, and has acted, without self-interest, then it becomes a false premise to say he *always* acts from self-interest. Meaning, you cannot charge him with treachery if your only proof of treachery is his self-interest."

Bacon gave her an arch look. "Spoken like someone who never mastered inductive logic," he said. "But you have arrived here determined to say things, so say them and be done."

"Thank you, sir. My purpose here is to demonstrate Alexander Cooke's capacity to act without self-interest."

"His occasional capacity," said Bacon.

"Occasional or otherwise, it takes but a single instance. And I have three instances," Joan said. "Here is the first one. Is it not true that he has been often at your table?"

"Not of late," Bacon said quickly, with a glance around the room. "I parted company with him once I realized his attachment to the Devereux family outweighed all other loyalties. Prior to that, admittedly, we had been social acquaintances."

"Was he not in your company with deliberate frequency last autumn, sir?"

"Yes, in hopes of finding a patron. That is self-interest."

Words of protest formed in Sander's mouth but he saw Joan close her hand into a fist, signing him to stop. He pursed his lips closed.

"But you know that was not his purpose, sir," she said. "A friend of his wished to learn from you, the great Francis Bacon, and the condition you set was that Sander was to attend you at supper with his friend disguised as a servant."

Bacon blinked and then, slowly, shook his head once. The gesture was lost on anyone but Joan and Sander, who knew it meant: *do not take this path*.

"Do you deny it, sir?" Joan asked placidly.

"It happened only once. His friend did an atrocious job of counterfeiting."

"Did he?" Joan said, mildly. Bacon's jaw twitched. "But thank you for acknowledging that it was in the friend's interest and not his own."

"It was in both their interests," Bacon corrected icily. "Beyond whatever he wished for his friend, he was seeking patronage, and my suppers are an obvious place for such activity."

"Every door in London opens to Sander Cooke," said Joan. "He did not require yours. Only his friend did. He entered into that particular understanding with you solely for his friend's sake."

"As an intimate of the situation," Bacon responded, "I reject your description of it."

Joan shrugged, as if this was of no consequence. "As you will. Dismiss my first example. I have two more. He took the role of Richard II, memorizing the role overnight."

Bacon snorted dismissively. "That was obvious self-interest, else you know nothing of how theatre works."

"He was not paid, being an apprentice. He was not lauded, as few saw the performance. He was not attempting to impress his superiors—"

"Of course he was," Bacon interrupted. "If you resort to such nonsense, you are only hastening him to the gallows."

"Bear with me, sir. A few weeks prior, he had been rewarded with the greatest role of his life, Viola in *Twelfth Night*. A character William Shakespeare wrote expressly for him, to debut before Her Majesty. Why, after such a triumph, would he feel the need to play a less endearing role, in an inferior play, in front of almost no one? He was, out of selfless decency and despite considerable toil, solving a problem for the company to which he is apprenticed. It earned them a handsome sum, of which he received no penny."

"He did it to impress the Earl of Essex," said Bacon with increasing impatience. "He is about to conclude his apprenticeship, he needs a patron, and he wished it to be Essex. How is that not self-interest? And since he cleaved to Essex, how is that not criminal?"

"The Chamberlain's Men wish to keep him. For himself, he has no need of a patron. And yet, he sought a patron—"

"For his pride. To feed his pride. He loathed the notion of playing small roles while new boys came along to eclipse his celebrity. You are dishonest if you say otherwise. If that is your second instance, I reject it too."

"All men seek to preserve their status and their pride," Joan said, "including yourself, sir. That is not singular to Alexander Cooke and cannot be held against him. What you must add to the equation is that he sought out a patron so that he could afford a wife."

Again, Bacon paused long enough to slowly, warningly, shake his head. "He doesn't have a wife."

"That is because he could not marry until he had means to support one."

Bacon huffed. "Nonsense. Supporting a wife is entirely self-interest, because man and wife are one. If that is your third instance, we are finished, he is finished, and you must leave."

"You have not yet seen my third instance," said Joan. "Indulge me a moment longer. Sander Cooke sought a patron because he wanted his wife—not himself—to have access to men of learning. He was attempting to position himself specifically so that his betrothed would obtain a status that would exceed his own. How is that self-interest?"

"To have a pleased and admired wife is self-interest," said Bacon.

"But to toil for such a thing is not. Alexander Cooke is not one who willingly toils."

"That, at least, is true," Bacon admitted wryly.

Sander saw her repeat the *do nothing, I'm in charge* sign. "If he stayed with the Chamberlain's Men, he would have easy income for doing easy work. He would never be short of lovers, that is no secret, nor would he be burdened with the expenses and efforts of matrimony. The Earl of Essex is a complicated and demanding gentleman, and Alexander Cooke would not have bothered with him, were he not trying to serve the woman he loves. There were other, easier futures available to him. It is not in his nature to make unnecessary efforts; in this case he did it for another's benefit with no benefit to himself but pleasing her."

"If that is your third instance, you have failed at your mission," said Bacon.

"How so?"

"He has no wife."

"He does. I have the proof of it, which I will now present, and which will demonstrate my third instance."

Sander understood her intention. He watched the unspoken exchange of dares between them. *You will not do this* could have been inked onto Bacon's forehead and been no clearer than his actual expression.

Joan gave Bacon a radiant, knowing smile. Slowly, as if moving through water, she reached up for the law-student cap on her head. Despite the confident affect, Sander saw her hands trembling almost too much to grasp it. But she managed, and pulled it off. She had braided her severed tresses into the short fall of her boy's coif, and now it unrolled, tumbling down her back. Bacon closed his eyes. His face went ashen.

The reaction around the room was immediate and loud. Sander was so dazzled by the risk she was taking, he did not parse what any single voice was calling out. Finally she turned her head toward him, and they made eye contact. Her eyes brimmed with nervous amusement. He found it hard to breathe. *Go ahead, you can do this*, he signed, opening his hand. She returned her attention to Bacon, who was angrily motioning for quiet.

"So you yourself are a woman," he allowed. "That means only that your presence here is unlawful and you are about to be forcibly removed, having provided no examples to save Alexander Cooke from the stain of irredeemable self-interest. Being a woman does not make you a wife.

Quiet, please, my lords!" he snapped over the hubbub.

Joan waited for silence. Then: "My father has given formal consent to our union, and Master Heminges knows of it."

Bacon shrugged. "Betrothal is not wedlock."

"The Anglican Church does not require a ceremony, sir. It accepts that a couple betrothed and copulating is the same as wedded," Joan asserted. "And that is the state of our relations." More outrage from the gentlemen. As if sensing Sander's growing agitation she once again signed to him, hand curling closed: *Do nothing, I am handling this*.

"How convenient for you, to claim something is true when there is no decent way to make you prove it," said Bacon.

For a moment, Joan looked confused. "You're claiming we have not copulated?" she said, and rested her hand on her belly. "Then can you explain how I come to be carrying his child?"

HE HAD FAINTED. He awoke on the floor, feeling as if he had no bones left but in his skull, which was throbbing.

The voices were confusing, coming from everywhere at once. Half a dozen men were staring at something near the door. He wondered where his guards were.

"This is only a distraction," Bacon's voice was braying over the noise. "It has no relevance here. She has given us no evidence. *Silence, sirs!*"

There was quiet.

"You have given us no evidence," Bacon insisted in a steadier voice.

"Summon a physician or midwife," Sander heard Joan say, defiantly. He could not see her from his collapsed position, and struggled to sit up higher. Nobody moved to helped him.

"I don't refute your condition," said Bacon. "I refute that your condition is any evidence of Sander's self-sacrifice. It means only that he convinced a penniless commoner to open her legs to him."

"You've not yet seen the evidence," said Joan. "Be patient."

"I'm also disappointed by your failed inductive logic. I took you for a better student."

Sander cleared his throat and said quietly, "Master Bacon, sir." The Privy Councilors turned their heads in astonishment between himself and Bacon. Not even the Chamberlain's Men could have staged such a moment, he thought with bitter amusement. "If you execute me, you rob her and the child of a future. As an unwed mother, she risks becoming a beggar in the street, and the mother of a future beggar."

"You should have thought of that before you sold yourself to Essex," Bacon said.

Sander closed his eyes and tried to remain upright. He was dizzy. His head was throbbing. "I never did that, and you know it, sir. For her sake and the child's, let me live."

"Even if you escape hanging," said Bacon, "you will never attract a patron now, with this stain upon you. So you would have to remain a player, and as the wife of some ordinary player, she will never have access to men like me."

"That's sophistic," argued Joan. She took a step forward into Sander's view. The guards were on either side of her now. "I already have access to you. You built me a laboratory."

"Jack's laboratory has no nursery," said Bacon. "And an ordinary actor's wife cannot afford a nursemaid."

Joan pursed her lips. "Sir, I believe you value me as your assistant."

"I *did* value you," Bacon clarified.

"What would make it possible, for me to remain in your employment?"

Bacon considered her. An expression like a nervous smile crossed his face; instantly it returned to a somber glower. "The widow of the celebrated Sander Cooke would have a certain status, no matter his cause of death. I could employ you—even pay you enough to afford a nursemaid. But I cannot extend that offer to an unwed mother of no standing."

Joan signed to Sander: *It's your turn to act*. Instantly, he knew what she wanted him to do.

"Then I pray you, Master Bacon," he said, sitting upright, "find a chaplain to marry us, and after, send me to the gallows."

Bacon laughed mirthlessly. "Nobly intoned, but this is not a game,

Alexander."

His lip hurt. He licked it and tasted blood. He was glad there was no glass in which he might see what a mess he was. "If it's best for her, marry us then hang me. Bring me paper and a quill and I'll sign my name to anything you like."

"And there you are," said Joan, triumphantly. She spread her arms wide, a theatrical invitation to the whole room of dumbstruck men. "My third instance. Alexander Cooke has offered to literally sacrifice his life for the well-being of the woman he loves and a child he will never meet. I ask your lordships all, is this self-interest? Will it not suffice to clear his character?"

February 25

The morning of the execution, dense fog smothered the river, slivers of it moving unevenly up river stairs and lanes. The sun's slanted sharp light barely brightened it. A distressed murmur, ten thousand voices strong, rippled invisibly across the Thames from the Tower of London.

In Southwark, at the end of Morgan's Lane and directly across from the Tower, Sander and Joan stared into the opaque mist, arms hooped around each other, grimly imagining the scene on Tower Green. "This would have been my fate too," he said. "Were it not for you. Damn Francis Bacon to hell."

She considered this. "Perhaps just to purgatory. And only briefly."

Sander stiffened. "Joan, he tried to murder me. How can you give him any quarter?"

"He was acting on the queen's orders. He loved Essex, and he admired you. He had to obey her instructions in front of the Privy Council, but I wager he was secretly relieved I had a plan."

"He hid it well enough," said Sander acidly.

"I suppose he did," said Joan, "since nobody realized he knew that I was lying."

Sander took her chin in his fingers and turned her face toward him. "Don't be absurd. I myself didn't know you were lying, how could he?"

She mirrored him, taking his chin in her fingers and waggling his head gently. "Consider it, Sander. He knew about the Women's Pocket Project, that it is my creation. How likely is Joan Buckler, of all the women in London, to have an unwanted pregnancy?" She released his chin and pressed her hand lightly against his chest. "You were too distressed to think clearly when I said it. But I warrant he knew I was bluffing, and he played along, so I might exonerate you."

He released her, shook his head. "He did not looked pleased when you succeeded."

"Looks can deceive. Did you not see him smile, for one blink, just before you offered to be hanged?"

"What a moment that was," said Sander, hand to forehead.

"I think he realized what I was after, and he knew you'd say what was needed." She peeled his hand off his forehead, kissed it, then wrapped his arm back around her. "It's true he's not our friend, Sander, but nor do I think he's evil."

He considered. Shrugged. "You're more generous than I."

"How fortunate for you," she said with a wink, and kissed his cheek with tenderness.

The crowd noise from across the river loudened into a despairing cry. Sander winced, and gripped her harder.

Then came silence.

A bell began to toll through the fog.

"May God save his soul," Sander said. He closed his eyes and shuddered. "It is hard to imagine London without the Earl of Essex."

Joan grimaced. The bell tolled many times. Then it stopped.

More silence.

"Well," Joan said, after a bit. "Your rehearsal must be starting soon. I'll walk you to the Globe."

He nodded, but didn't move. Joan linked her arm through his and turned them both around to put the river behind them. The fog was still thick here; she took one step forward, nudging him, and he followed slowly.

"Are you playing Burbage's sweetheart in this new one, as usual?"

"No," said Sander. "I was at first, but they've just moved me." He smiled wanly. "Now I am his mother."

She stopped abruptly. "His what?"

Sander shrugged. "Penelope Rich put the thought in my head, that Master Shakespeare has written few enough mature women. I proposed that he might amend that. So he has expanded Gertrude, Hamlet's mother, and given me the role. She's no Viola or Rosalind, but she's complicated, and I like the challenge."

Joan's eyes widened. "Might this be the beginning of a new career?"

Biting his lower lip, Sander shrugged. "Perhaps. He did say his best writing in *Julius Caesar* was Mark Antony, and that the real-life Antony fell deep in love with Cleopatra. If they keep me on, perhaps he'll write that story, too."

Joan allowed herself a brief, ecstatic squeal, and squeezed his arm. "You'd make a lovely queen of Egypt," she said, beaming. "This all sounds promising."

He nodded, almost bashfully. "Not so promising as your own fate," he said. "When is the interview?"

"Master Pantazis has arranged for me to meet Hugh Platt tomorrow," she said. "I'll spend today at the Sow writing a summary of all I did for Master Bacon. Their work is similar. Platt seeks somebody to help him, as I've helped Master Bacon, and Pantazis has sung my praises to him."

"That was good of him."

"Yes," said Joan, and her gaze grew briefly distracted. "He is a good man."

"I confess a certain satisfaction that Bacon will lose you to his rival."

"It isn't me he's losing," said Joan. "It's just Jack Buckler." They had reached Tooley Street, and turned onto it. The fog was lifting here. They could see some way ahead of them.

"But how will that work? Will you be Joan, or Jack, who might be hired?"

Joan stopped in the middle of the street. Grinned a delighted grin, like a toddler discovering how large and welcoming the world could be. "I will be a natural philosopher," she said.

Author's Note

TK

Acknowledgments

TK